FINDING OLIVIA

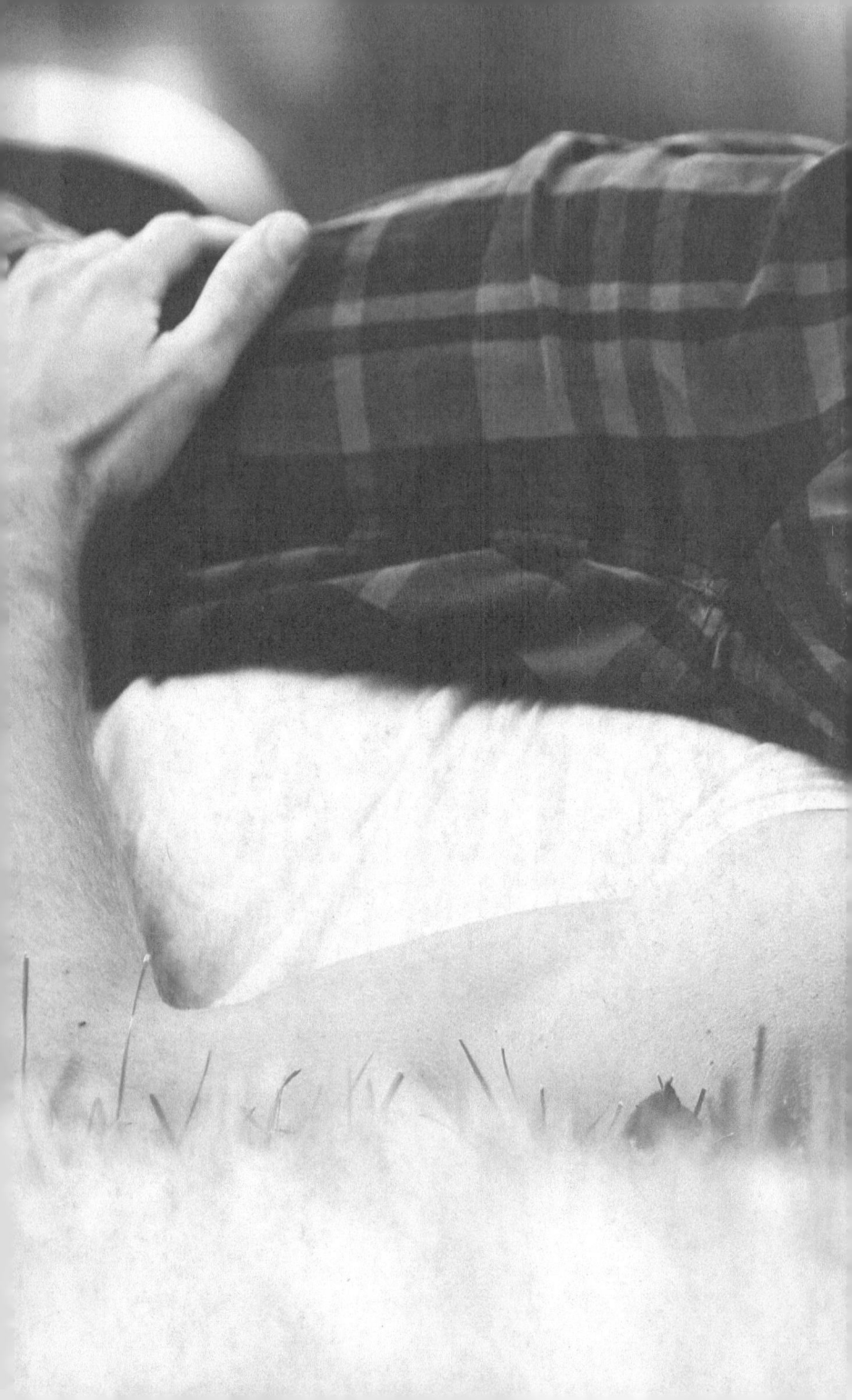

FINDING OLIVIA

THE TRACE AND OLIVIA SERIES

FINDING OLIVIA

CHASING OLIVIA

TEMPTING ROWAN

SAVING TATUM

Copyright © 2013, 2016, 2017, 2020, 2023 Micalea Smeltzer
All rights reserved.
This book or any portion thereof may not be reproduced or used in any manner whatsoever without the express written permission of the publisher.
This is a work of fiction. Names, characters, businesses, places, events and incidents are either the products of the author's imagination or used in a fictitious manner. Any resemblance to actual persons, living or dead, or actual events is purely coincidental.
Cover Design: Emily Wittig Designs
Photos: Regina Wamba
Formatting: Micalea Smeltzer

To anyone who has ever needed that extra push to spread their wings and fly.

"LIFE IS NOT MEASURED BY THE AMOUNT OF BREATHS YOU TAKE, BUT BY THE MOMENTS THAT TAKE YOUR BREATH AWAY."
–UNKNOWN

PROLOGUE

It's hard pretending you're perfect when you're anything but.

For as long as I could remember, my dad, his eyes cold and calculating, judged every move I made.

I could hear his gruff voice, clearly in my head, scolding me, "No, Olivia! You can't play outside! You'll get mud on your dress!" Or, "No, Olivia! You can't play with those children! Their parents don't go to church!" And one of my favorites was, "No, Olivia! You can't go to that school dance! You might end up pregnant!"

He kept waiting for me to mess up, to make a mistake that was unforgivable. It was like he knew that I really wasn't this perfect girl that I pretended to be.

But I refused to give him that satisfaction.

As long as I lived under his roof, I hid who I really was. I was the perfect preacher's daughter that he always wanted me to be. I wore my dresses and attended church every Sunday. I pretended that I wasn't slowly suffocating on the inside.

I wore a smile on my face to hide the pain I felt while I counted the days until I could leave.

I purposely picked a college that would put as much distance as possible between my father and me.

I wanted to live and spread my wings.

I wanted to be wild and spontaneous.

I wanted to make mistakes.

And that's why I sat down and made my list on the last night I lived under my father's oppressive roof.

That list was my way of finding myself.

I only hoped it worked.

Or had too much time gone by, and the girl I was supposed to be was lost forever?

CHAPTER ONE

"No, no, no, *no!*" I beat my steering wheel with the heel of my hand. "No! You've got to be kidding me!" I pulled off the road, my tire bumping along.

I put my car in park and climbed out to assess the damage, my feet crunching on the gravel scattered alongside the road.

Immediately, the oily burnt smell of my peeling tire met me. Calling this a flat tire didn't do it justice. This was complete and utter carnage.

I looked behind me at the trail of tire pieces leading straight to my car like a path of breadcrumbs.

It was starting to get dark, and this wasn't exactly the safest road. I was also a twenty-year-old girl, ripe for the picking.

I kicked the side of my car. "I don't have time for this!"

I stalked around the back to the trunk, lifting it and looking for the necessary tools to change a tire.

Which was pointless, because, unfortunately, I didn't know

the first thing about changing a tire. My father had made sure that I only knew how to do a *woman's work*.

I slammed the trunk closed and stalked back to the driver's side, pulling at the ends of my hair. I glared at the offending nail that had to be four inches long sticking out of the tire. How many nails did people drive over a day, and I was the one to get a flat freakin' tire?

Not cool.

Not at all.

I opened the door and reached for my phone to call my roommate to come pick me up.

The sky was darkening, and I didn't want to be stranded.

I wrapped my lightweight jacket tighter around my body as the wind gusted around me, blowing leaves off of the nearby trees. I watched the red, yellow, and orange leaves fall down and scatter over my car. One, unfortunately, got caught in my hair. I reached up and pulled it out before letting it drift to the ground.

Gravel crunched behind me. I turned quickly to see a guy getting out of a black car that looked like something old but classic.

I hadn't even heard him pull over.

I backed a step away, thinking he might be a murderer or a rapist, but when I got a look at his face, I was stunned.

He was tall with a lean but muscular body. He had short, dark brown almost black hair and the greenest eyes I had ever seen. Five o' clock shadow covered his cheeks and chin. My eyes trailed down over the white t-shirt glued to his chest and stopped there. I could see black ink underneath the white shirt and licked my lips. The fact that he had tattoos only made him hotter. To protect against the cold, he was wearing a long-sleeved plaid shirt.

"Uh, can I help you?" he asked, smiling pleasantly at me and putting my earlier fears about him being a murderer or rapist completely to rest.

Help? With what? I needed help?

"Huh?"

He grinned crookedly, tilting his head. "With your tire. Do you need some help?"

He had the deepest, huskiest voice I had ever heard. I shivered at the sound. I was pretty sure I'd be happy for him to help me with a lot of things, and none of them included my tire.

"Help would be great." I blushed, ducking my head.

He chuckled. "You do have a spare, right?"

"Yeah, it's in the trunk." I pointed, like he didn't know where the trunk was.

He grabbed the spare and all the necessary tools and sat down next to the ruined tire.

"I, uh, would've changed it myself, but, uh, my dad never taught me." I ran my fingers nervously through my wavy brown hair. "He said something about it not being appropriate for a girl to do and if I ever got a flat tire, I better hope Prince Charming came along. My dad's very, uh, old fashioned," I stammered.

He looked up at me. "Does that make me Prince Charming?" He grinned.

"Oh, uhm, Prince Charming is fictional, so I guess not, and he, uh, usually rides a white horse or something ... I think."

Somebody stamp AWKWARD across my forehead already.

The guy threw his head back and laughed. "I guess a shiny black '69 Camaro doesn't count as a white horse. You watch a lot of Disney movies or something?"

"No." I blushed tomato red. "At least, not anymore."

He squinted up at me, shielding his eyes from the orange glow of the setting sun. "You're funny."

"I hope that's a good thing," I muttered. Unfortunately, I wasn't trying to be funny.

"It's a very good thing ..." he paused, waiting for my name.

"Oh, uh, Olivia. Olivia Owens."

"I'm Trace." He reached a hand up to me, and I took it. It was warm and calloused, swallowing mine whole. He grinned when my hand jerked at his touch. "Trace Wentworth."

We were both silent after that as he changed my tire. When he was done, he packed everything away and put my ruined tire in his trunk.

I reached for his arm. "You don't need to do that." The guy had already stopped to help me; I certainly didn't expect him to haul my ruined tire away as well.

"I'm a mechanic, I'll get rid of it at work." He closed the trunk with a shrug. "You need to get a new tire on tomorrow. That spare won't last you long."

"Right." I nodded, committing that tidbit of information to memory.

"Bring it by Pete's Garage." He opened the door to his car and held onto the frame. "I'll be there and fix it up for you."

"Oh, um, okay. Thanks for fixing my tire and for, uh, stopping," I said, walking backward away from his car and toward mine.

"You say, uh, a lot," he commented, a grin tilting his lips up at the corners. He had one of those smiles that made panties around the world drop. I was tempted to check and make sure mine were still firmly in place.

"I know," I grimaced. "It's a, uh, bad habit."

Actually, I rarely ever said, uh, it was just that Trace turned me into a blubbering idiot.

He grinned, tapping his car door with his hand like he was playing a drum. "I'll see you tomorrow, right?"

"Yeah, you'll see me. Gotta get this stupid thing fixed." I smacked the hood of the car.

"Ask for me, okay, Olivia?" His eyes grew serious.

"I will." I gave him a thumbs up, hating the way my body reacted to the way he said my name.

Wait, I gave him a thumbs up? What is wrong with me? That was not cool! He probably thought I was so dumb. Heck, *I* thought I was being dumb. How was it possible for one gorgeous guy to turn me into a complete pile of mushy goo? That didn't seem fair.

Trace waited for me to get into my car and drive away before he did the same. Despite the bad boy appearance, he was obviously more of a gentleman than most of the guys I knew.

I smiled to myself as I drove down the road and toward the college campus. My roommate and best friend wasn't going to believe this. Things like hot guys pulling over to help a damsel in distress didn't happen to me. In fact, I was pretty sure it didn't happen to most people.

"WHAT? OH, MY GOD! *OLIVIA!*" Avery, my roommate shrieked, as she gripped my arm like she was afraid I was about to run away. "*Puh-lease* tell me you got his number!?"

"Uh, no," I mumbled. "I didn't even think about it."

"Olivia! If he was so hot you should have been *all* over that!" She finally let go of my arm, and I grabbed my laptop off my desk, sitting on the edge of my bed.

"He did tell me to come by Pete's Garage and he'd put a new tire on." I shrugged, turning on the laptop and entering my password. I really hoped Avery never figured out my password or she'd be itching to get her hands on my computer and dig up my deep dark secrets. Because, according to Avery, everyone had a secret.

"He's a *mechanic*?" she shrieked, clapping her hands together. "That's so hot! Just picture him shirtless, sweaty, and covered in grease." Her tongue flicked out to lick her red colored lips. "Oh, yes, I do approve."

"You haven't even seen him, I could be lying," I teased her.

She snorted. "I doubt that, I've never seen you wear such a

goofy look on your face. Plus, his name is even hot. Trace Wentworth." She fanned herself.

"It doesn't matter," I said as I scooted farther back on my bed, "I'm not going. I'll find somewhere else to take my car."

In fact, I was already doing that. It wouldn't be hard to find a mechanic in Winchester, Virginia. One that *wasn't* a particularly hot guy with emerald green eyes.

Avery gasped like I'd said the craziest thing on Earth.

Hopping onto my bed and jostling me, she brushed her red hair over one pale shoulder. "You *have* to go there!"

"And stutter like an incompetent fool again?" I glared at her. "I think not!"

She narrowed her dark green eyes at me. "You *are* going, Olivia Camille Owens, even if I have to drag you there."

Oh, no, Avery had that determined look on her face, the one she only got when she meant business.

"I'm not going, and you're not dragging me."

Her eyes narrowed further until they were slits. "Don't make me drug you, Livie; I keep Benadryl on hand for occasions just like this."

"Fine," I conceded, throwing my hands in the air then snapping the lid closed on my laptop. "But *only* if you go with me." I pointed at her. "You'll make sure I don't say something stupid." Like I had tonight. Trace probably hoped I *wouldn't* show up.

She squealed shrilly, jumping up from my bed. "Deal! I have to figure out what we're going to wear!"

"We need to get dressed up to get my tire replaced?" I asked her incredulously.

"No—" she rolled her eyes "—*you* need to get fixed up for Trace, and *I* need to get fixed up in case there are any other hot guys working there. I swear, do you not know anything?"

"Apparently not," I muttered and laid back on my twin-sized bed, covering my face with my pillow.

I knew it was going to be a long night, one filled with Avery pairing every possible clothing option in her closet and then proceeding to pick them apart.

I'd probably show up to get my car fixed, looking completely fashionable thanks to Avery, but dead on my feet from lack of sleep.

I'm sure Trace wouldn't find it attractive if I yawned in his face. I don't think *anyone* found yawning attractive.

"Avery," I huffed, throwing my pillow off my face and sitting up. She turned away from her closet and raised a brow. "If I'm going to go through with this, then I need my sleep. Don't spend all night in your closet."

"You suck." She stuck her tongue out but closed the closet doors. "This will only make it take longer in the morning, but whatever." She shrugged, climbing into her bed and adjusting the straps of her tank-top. I didn't understand how she slept in a tank and shorts, even in the winter.

I rose from my bed and changed into my pajamas, hoping that tomorrow went smoothly but knowing with my luck it would be *anything* but smooth.

CHAPTER TWO

"AVERY!" I SHRIEKED, COMING AWAKE AND SITTING straight up in bed, my hair sticking up in random places. "For the love of my sanity, *please*, go back to bed!"

She turned around, pouting her lips at me, and placed a hand on her slender hip. "You convinced me to go to bed last night without planning our outfits. I agreed. Now, you want to get huffy with me for getting up *early* to help *you*?" She eyed me.

"I *reluctantly* agreed to this, and I already regret it," I groaned, covering my face with my hands. "It's six AM, Avery. I'm pretty sure I'm not going to see Trace in the next hour."

She eyed my sleep-raddled appearance. "I would certainly hope you're not seeing him in the next hour. It will take at least two ... maybe three to have you looking decent." She turned back to *my* closet and scanned through *my* clothes.

"Avery!"

"God—" she turned around, glaring at me "—you are so

cranky in the mornings! This is the last time I try to help you! I fully expect a Starbucks Frappuccino for this."

I rolled my eyes. "Don't worry, I'll make sure you get your Frapp fix."

"That's all I ask." She grinned, climbing onto her bed and looking through one of her various fashion magazines.

"Ugh," I groaned when a few minutes passed and I hadn't fallen back asleep.

"What?" Avery asked, not bothering to glance away from the glossy pages of the magazine.

"Thanks to you, I'm wide awake," I grumbled, rolling over on my right side and facing the wall. I punched my pillow to fluff it up, but nothing was working. I was awake, and I knew there was no hope of falling back asleep. "I hate you so much," I muttered, sitting up in bed.

Avery grinned. "Does this mean I get to pick out our outfits now?"

"Ye—" The whole word hadn't even left my mouth before she was up and across the room.

I rolled my eyes and slipped from the bed.

Since I was up early, I decided I might as well shower, so I grabbed my bag of necessities and stepped into the bathroom we shared with the two girls beside us.

If there was one thing I missed about my dad's house it was having my own bathroom.

I luxuriated in the quiet space. I knew that as soon as I stepped back into our room, Avery would bombard me with five hundred different clothing options and then force me to try all of them on.

I got out of the shower and brushed through my wet hair before pulling it into a bun then dressed in a pair of sweatpants and a t-shirt, knowing I'd be changing into something else in a matter of minutes.

"That took forever," Avery complained when I opened the door.

"You're annoying," I snapped, putting my bag down and sitting on my bed.

Avery continued like I hadn't said anything. "I think I've figured out what you should wear." She motioned to an ensemble spread out on my bed. Funny, I hadn't even noticed it.

"I think you should go simple but sexy. Just give him a taste, you know? We don't want to show him all the goods up front," she rattled, grabbing her breasts for emphasis. "So, I was thinking these jeans …" She stood beside me and pointed to them. "Paired with your yellow tank top and this loose gray sweater, that's mine," she said, as if I didn't know that sweater *wasn't* mine. "And—" she backed away "—I just bought these shoes, but since you're a sister in need, I'll give them to you." She bent down, skimming through items on her closet floor and pulled out a pair of black bootie high heels. They laced up the front and had three rows of studs on the side. "Since you said Trace had that whole bad boy thing going on," she said as she shrugged, "they're perfect. What bad boy could resist these babies?" She held them up for my inspection.

"I'll die in those," I scoffed. "But they look amazing." I reached for one.

Avery shrugged and handed both to me. "If you fall, make sure Trace is there so he can help you up."

I rolled my eyes. "Woman, you are ridiculous."

"It's in the *How to Get a Guy Handbook*." She grinned.

"This handbook sounds stupid," I joked.

"Hey," Avery raised her hands in front of her chest in mock defense, "*I'm* the one actually having sex, so it must be working."

"Whatever," I laughed. "We'll do it your way."

"Good." Avery grinned maniacally. "Poor Trace Wentworth doesn't stand a chance."

I LOOKED at myself in the floor-length mirror on Avery's side of the room.

I don't know how she did it, but I actually looked *good*.

My jeans hugged my legs and hips in all the right places. The small portion of the yellow tank top that showed made me look like I still had a tan from the summer. The gray sweater looked casual, like I wasn't trying too hard. And the shoes? Oh, the shoes. They made the whole thing come together.

Avery clapped her hands together. "I told you so."

"Yeah, you did," I agreed, smoothing a hand down my leg. "But are you sure I don't look, you know, *too* fixed up?" I fingered the end of the fishtail braid Avery had done. I had insisted on doing my own makeup. If I let Avery do my makeup I'd end up looking like I had my face painted on.

I turned around just in time to catch Avery rolling her eyes. "You look hot. Stop worrying about everything. Tracey-poo won't be able to take his eyes off of you."

I made a face of disgust. "You did not just say Tracey-poo."

"I do believe that those were the words that left my mouth." She winked before looking in the mirror and swiping on *another* layer of her favorite lip-gloss. If she put on one more coat, her lips would stick together.

She had curled her red hair so that it hung down her back like a shimmering curtain. Despite the fact that it was autumn, and definitely not warm outside, she was wearing a pair of high-waisted shorts with ripped black tights underneath. The shirt she wore was red and glued to her body covered by a pale jean jacket with studs on the shoulders. Her high heels were super pointy and could double as a weapon. I definitely wouldn't want to be on the receiving end of one of those spikes.

"All right, we can go now." Avery gave her hair a final fluff and then looked me over.

"Great," I snapped. "Maybe, we'll get back in time and I won't be late for my afternoon class." It was already close to noontime.

"Oh puh-lease, Livie, it's not even lunchtime."

I pouted. "Don't remind me, I haven't even had breakfast yet."

"You're such a baby," Avery scolded. "Seriously, chillax." She rummaged through her purse and produced a Special K Bar. Holding it up proudly, she waved it through the air. "*Here* is your breakfast."

"That cardboard hardly constitutes as breakfast," I grumbled but snatched the bar from her hand anyway. I ripped open the wrapper and began nibbling on it.

"Don't be dramatic," she said, then she dragged me behind her and down the stairwell.

The glass double doors opened to the campus grounds, and I was happy to see that it was a sunny day. The past week had been full of bleak, overcast, gray skies.

I unlocked the doors to my beat-up Ford Focus and Avery eyed it like it was the grossest thing she'd ever seen. She constantly looked at my car like that, but it had always been reliable. At least, until last night, but it wasn't really the car's fault for getting a flat tire. It was mine. No, it was the nail's fault. Better yet, it was the person's fault that lost the stupid nail.

I brought up directions to Pete's Garage on my phone and pulled out of the campus parking lot into the morning traffic.

Surprisingly, it wasn't far, maybe only ten minutes from campus and in the older part of the city.

I parked the car and stepped outside, searching for dark hair, searing green eyes, and a cocky smile.

Avery slipped out of the car elegantly and looked around for her next conquest.

Licking her lips, she said, "I really hope that's not Trace over there because I'm about to be all over that guy." She swayed her hips dramatically.

"Avery!" I hissed.

"What? Look at him." She pointed.

I did, and thankfully, it wasn't Trace.

The guy was probably the same height as Trace but broader. The thick-corded muscles of his arms were on full display because he only wore a vest—one of those vests that guys usually wore with suits. His jeans were loose on his wide frame and riddled with stains, his hands shoved into the pockets. On his head he wore a fedora, the wavy ends of his shaggy golden-brown hair sticking out from underneath. Sandy brown stubble dotted his prominent jaw and his eyes were a piercing light blue. In fact, I didn't know eyes could be that light. And between his pouty lips, sitting there as if it was an afterthought, was a lit cigarette.

"Is it him?" Avery asked.

"Huh?" I shook my head, turning away from the guy and toward her.

"Is that Trace?" She pointed to the guy in the vest again.

"No," I answered, "that's not him."

"Thank God for that." She sighed in relief, making sure her clothes were in place before sauntering toward him.

Vest man looked up and smirked, taking the cigarette from between his lips and dropping it to the ground, crushing it with the toe of his boot. He looked Avery up and down, much the way she had studied him, and I hoped that she had finally met her match.

Not caring to stay around for the PDA that was bound to ensue, I walked into the garage.

No one seemed to be around but I heard the clanging of tools.

Several cars were up on lifts with various parts scattered about. The windows in the back of the garage were clouded over with age, making it even darker in the space.

"Hello?" I hesitantly called out.

"Hey," a voice answered from behind me. The sound of wheels scooting met my ears, like whoever had spoken was on a scooter.

I turned around, expecting to face a person, but found no one.

"Down here," the voice said again with a chuckle.

I glanced down and found Trace staring up at me from this plastic bed looking thing with wheels.

A scream crawled up my throat and echoed around the empty garage. In my haste to scoot away, my feet tangled together in those darn heels, and I fell across the top of his chest.

He grunted from the impact and my cheeks colored every shade of red in existence.

"Well," he chuckled, "this is interesting."

My eyes widened, and I hastily scrambled away, somehow pushing my hand into his chest, causing him to grunt.

"Sorry," I mumbled, falling back on my butt, only serving to embarrass myself further.

Trace laughed, shaking his head, and swung his legs over the side of the bed thing.

Despite the cold temperature outside, he was wearing a white wife-beater, loose jeans, and boots.

Standing, he reached down to help me up.

"Thanks," I mumbled sheepishly, looking anywhere but at him.

"You okay?" he asked, glancing over my body for any scrapes.

"Wonderful."

Trace chuckled. "You must be accident prone."

"Huh?" I finally looked at him, chewing on my bottom lip and nervously wringing my fingers together.

He ran his fingers through his short dark hair, flashing me a peek at a scripted tattoo on the inside of his bicep.

"Last night it was your tire—" he grinned, ticking it off on his finger "—and today you've already fallen, *twice*."

"Oh, uh, I'm not normally so clumsy," I explained.

Oh, God. I said uh, again. Why did every word in my vocabulary seem to leave me when he was around?

"Must be the shoes," he commented, pointing to deathtraps on my feet.

Looking down, I muttered, "Maybe."

"Where's your car?" He looked around, like he expected it to be in the garage.

"Outside," I pointed unnecessarily.

Trace nodded and wiped his greasy hands off on a rag sticking out of his back pocket.

I followed him outside and made a strangled noise in my throat when I saw Avery pressed up against the garage wall with the vest man attacking her mouth.

I covered my eyes, gagging. No one should have to see that much tongue in a public place.

Trace laughed. "Luca! Where'd you find this one?"

I blushed, letting my hand drop from my eyes. "She's my roommate."

"That right?" Trace glanced over his shoulder at me with a raised brow.

I nodded.

"She seems like a ... lovely girl." He smirked. "Keys?"

"Oh, right." I tossed him my car keys, and he caught them easily.

I stood out of the way while he drove the car into the garage and onto a lift.

"You can come in now," he said as he motioned me inside.

I glared at Avery, but she was oblivious. She was supposed to be helping me and not making out with a stranger! I'd already made a fool out of myself by falling *on top* of Trace. There was no telling what I would do next.

"I don't bite," Trace grinned, when I didn't step into the garage.

I forced each foot in front of the other and stopped next to him. He was already removing the spare tire and tossed it into the corner.

He grabbed a new tire from the front corner of the garage and lifted it into place like it weighed nothing.

"Are you from around here?" he asked, making small talk.

"No." I shook my head. "I'm from New Hampshire. I'm going to Shenandoah University so I guess this is kind of my home now. I certainly don't plan on going back."

"Why not?" He squinted when he glanced at me.

"It's not important." I shrugged. I didn't need to go into detail about my dad and his controlling nature. It would only sour my mood.

"Sorry, I'm prying." He smiled sheepishly. "If I ask you what you're studying, would that be too personal?" He tightened a bolt, holding the tire in place.

"I'm studying to be an English teacher, but I'd really like to write a book someday. I probably won't though." I shrugged.

"Why wouldn't you?"

I snorted. "I'm sure I'd suck at it."

"You don't know until you try," he replied and my eyes zeroed in on the muscles flexing in his arms.

My hormones seemed to go into overdrive when I was around Trace. I had never been attracted to someone, like I was with Trace. True, he was insanely good looking. But it was more than that. There was something about *him* that drew me in.

"I don't think I've experienced enough to write a book," I reasoned, toeing the ground.

Trace stopped working and turned toward me. "Isn't that the point, though? It's fiction; you make it up."

"But it still needs to be realistic," I rambled, waving my hands through the air as I talked.

"Olivia, you're overthinking this." He stopped what he was doing and crossed his arms over his chest, a wrench dangling between his fingers. "If you want to write a book, you just sit down and start writing."

I wet my lips and looked down at my hands to avoid his stare.

He finished putting the tire on, leaving me to my thoughts.

My car lowered to the ground and Trace popped the hood.

"What are you doing?" I asked, coming to life again.

"You're already here" —he shrugged—

"and according to the sticker in your car, you're due for an oil change."

"Oh, right," I muttered. "I forgot."

Trace grinned, sweeping his dark hair out of his eyes.

I grew quiet again as I watched his movements. It was clear that Trace knew what he was doing and he loved it. He smiled and whistled under his breath the entire time he worked on my car.

"You're good to go," he announced, closing the hood of my car.

"What do I owe you?" I asked, digging through the bottomless pit of my purse to locate my wallet.

Trace made a noise in the back of his throat and waved his hand through the air. "It's on the house."

"No!" I cried. "I can't let you do that!" I might not have been a car expert, but I knew enough to know that tires weren't cheap, and neither was oil.

Trace crossed his arms over his chest and leaned his hip against the side of my car. Grinning cockily, he said, "You can make it up to me by going out for lunch."

"With you?" I choked.

"Well ..." His smile deepened. "That was kind of a given."

I felt like I was being strangled. "Fine," I conceded, "but I'm paying for my own lunch," I pointed at him menacingly.

He snorted. "Nice try, but a *gentleman* never lets a lady pay for her own meal."

"This is the twenty-first century, for Christ's sake! I can pay for my food!" I was about two seconds away from stomping my foot but held myself back.

Trace watched me, not saying a word, waiting for me to calm down.

"You good now?" he asked after a moment.

"I'm good." I tugged on my sweater to have something to do with my hands.

"So, we can get lunch now? 'Cause I'm starving." He grinned, his eyes crinkling at the corners. He grabbed a green plaid shirt that hung on a hook next to the open garage door and shrugged it on.

"Yes," I snapped, and he straightened from his casual pose, "but I *am* paying for *my* meal."

"You just keep on thinking that." He brushed by me with a cocky grin.

Damn that grin and what it did to my insides.

I followed him outside and to the right of the rectangular building.

Handing me my keys, he informed me, "Your car will be fine in the garage. Luca will close and lock it when he leaves for lunch ... if he leaves, that is."

"Who's Luca?" I asked, standing next to the passenger door of Trace's sleek black sports car. It was definitely old but well maintained. However, with my limited knowledge of car brands, I had no clue what it was.

"I'm sure your friend will introduce you to him." He winked.

"Oh." I gulped, remembering him calling out that name when we passed them.

Trace slid into his car and motioned me to get inside.

I took a deep breath, hoping that this was a good idea. I mean, I didn't really know Trace, and I was getting into his car to go Lord knows where.

"You don't have to look so scared." He smiled when I slid inside, running my fingers over the buttery-smooth leather seats.

"I'm not scared," I scoffed. "Okay, maybe a little," I admitted. "This isn't something I normally do."

"Eat lunch?" He quirked a brow, a smile tugging his lips up crookedly.

"Ha-ha." I scrunched up nose. "No, what I mean is, I don't normally get into the car of a guy I just met."

He smiled again, the one that made panties drop everywhere. "But we didn't *just* meet. If I recall, we met last night."

"Why do I feel like I would never win an argument with you?" I grumbled.

"Because you wouldn't." He smirked, backing out. "I'm a Wentworth, and we never lose an argument. It's in our blood."

I laughed at his comment. "Where are we going?" I asked, watching Pete's Garage disappear behind us.

"To get lunch," he answered, rubbing his stubbled jaw.

I rolled my eyes. "Thanks, Einstein, but I knew that."

"Just a little sandwich shop. Nothing fancy."

We grew quiet, and I let out a giggle.

"What?" Trace flicked his gaze to me.

"Do you think they've come up for air yet?" I asked, picturing the way Luca and Avery had been going at it when we left.

Trace chuckled. "Probably not. If anything, ..."

"What?" I questioned.

"They're probably dirtying up the hood of his car," he snorted.

"Oh! Ew!" I covered my eyes, trying to block out the mental image he'd conjured up.

Having a preacher for a father, talking about sex had been

taboo in our house, making me a little squeamish on the topic. Even though I had lost my virginity at a party last year, it hadn't been that great, and honestly it had happened so quick that I couldn't quite remember it.

Trace chuckled. "You should see some of the dents in the hood."

"Trace!" I squealed.

"Don't hide your face." He grabbed my left hand and tugged it down. Reluctantly, I let my right hand fall as well. "Your face is far too beautiful to hide." His fingers skimmed over my chin before he gripped the steering wheel once more.

My cheeks flamed at his words, and a fire shot through my belly, heading south.

Trace parked against the curb, and I climbed out of the car, avoiding his gaze.

How could he make me feel so fluttery inside when I had just met him?

He dug some change out of his pocket and put it in the parking meter.

I followed him inside the building like an obedient dog. He ordered his sandwich, and then looked over his shoulder at me, motioning me forward to order.

I shook my head, the braid bobbing against my shoulder. "Nice try."

He glared at me, his green eyes darkening. "Olivia," he said warningly, "order something to eat."

"So demanding," I grumbled, stepping forward and ordering the first thing I saw off the menu.

He leaned against the counter, handing his debit card to the woman working there.

"My mama raised me right," he told me, "and that means you never let a lady pay for her own meal."

"I think you already mentioned that." I took one of the glasses of water the lady had placed on the counter.

"And, apparently," he said with a grin, slipping his wallet into his back pocket, "it didn't get through your thick skull." He tapped my forehead.

If he kept touching me, even if it was only silly little touches like this, I was going to melt into a puddle of goo.

He grabbed his own glass of water and we picked an empty table while we waited for our sandwiches to be made.

"I've been wondering something ..." I paused, searching for the right words to ask my question.

"Ask away." Trace tipped his chair back on two legs.

"Why did you stop to help me last night?" I bit my lip.

His smile widened. "Gentleman, remember?" He tapped his chest. "I wasn't going to leave you on the side of the road for anyone to stop when I could help you."

"Well, thank you." I took a sip of water, wetting my suddenly dry mouth.

"It's not a problem." He shrugged, gripping his glass of water. His fingers were long and elegant, his arms sinewy.

I didn't know what to say after that, so I chose to keep my mouth shut before something embarrassing came out.

Our food was brought out, and my stomach rumbled to life. That Special K Bar Avery gave me hadn't helped to satisfy my hunger.

"This is really good," I commented, after swallowing my first bite.

"I thought you might like this place." He took a massive bite of his own sandwich.

"It's delicious." I bit into the sandwich again. "And this place is really homey." I glanced around the café.

"I don't like to eat at the mainstream places." Trace took a sip of water, and my eyes followed the curve of his lips as they wrapped around the glass.

Oh, God. I was staring at his lips! What was wrong with me? I acted like I'd never been around the male species before! The one time I *needed* Avery and she ditched me! She was going to hear a rant from me later.

"They're too overdone," he finished, setting the glass back down.

I shook my head, forcing my eyes away from his full pouty lips.

"What's overdone?" I asked. "Oh, right, mainstream restaurants," I added. I *really* needed to stop looking at his lips, because I was getting flustered.

"You said you're going to Shenandoah University, right?" he asked, wiping his mouth with a napkin.

I nodded, tucking a piece of hair that had come loose from the braid behind my ear.

"Are you a freshman?"

"Sophomore," I answered. "Are you in school?" I asked. He didn't look much older than me, but one never knew.

"Nah." He let the napkin fall back to the table. "I was never big on school. Don't get me wrong, I love to read, and history is cool, but I never liked it. I went to a technical school to work on cars, but that was easy for me since I had been around cars my whole life." He shrugged his shoulders. "I don't like to study," he added.

"Who does?" I smiled.

"True." He grinned and finished off the last bite of his sandwich.

I had only eaten half of mine and I was already stuffed.

"I can't eat another bite," I mumbled, pushing my plate away.

"I'll get a box for you." He hopped up from the table and headed toward the counter.

A moment later, he returned with a small box, handing it to me.

"Thanks for lunch." I smiled gratefully, boxing the sandwich.

"It's no problem," he mumbled.

I tilted my head and studied him.

"What?" He squirmed under my gaze.

"You have a hard time saying you're welcome, don't you?"

He squirmed some more. "Maybe. It's just ... I don't *expect* a thank you. When I do something, it's because I want to, not because I want to be praised for it."

"Hmm," I mused.

"Are you sure you're not a psych major?" he questioned.

"I'm sure," I laughed. "I'm just observant. It comes from being shy."

He nodded. "Ah, I see."

I grabbed my purse and the to-go box before following him outside.

His car was low to the ground, and even though I was short, I felt like I had to perform contortions to get in there. I had no clue how Trace managed to duck his six-foot frame inside so easily.

"Am I going to see you again, after today?" Trace asked, glancing at me out of the corner of his eye.

"I don't know," I answered.

"I want to," he confessed, looking at me through thick sooty lashes.

I swallowed. Trace wanted to see me? Trace, with his cocky smile, and those *lips*, wanted to see me after today?

It didn't seem possible.

I was plain old Olivia who no one ever noticed. I was a wallflower. A nobody.

But Trace noticed me.

In fact, he saw *me*.

"I'd like to see you again," I admitted.

That cocky grin graced his full lips. "Good."

Trace parked his car in the same spot as it was before and we walked around to the front of the building. I was surprised to see that Luca and Avery weren't still against the building. Maybe they *had* moved onto the hood his car. I really hoped they were done, if that was the case.

Luckily, they were sitting inside the small office that was attached to the garage, and all their clothes were in place.

"Avery!" I called, waving her over. "Let's go!"

"Wait." Trace grabbed my arm, and a shiver skated up my spine. "What's your number?"

I rattled off my cell phone number and he entered it into his phone. "I'll call you," he said as he let go of my arm.

"Okay." I smiled, hoping he would but believing deep down that he wouldn't.

Avery made her way out of the office, making sure to sway her hips in a tantalizing rhythm for Luca's benefit.

I rolled my eyes at her and unlocked my Ford Focus.

"Thank you again," I told Trace.

"It's not a—"

"Problem, I know," I interrupted him.

He grinned as I climbed into my car. Before I closed the door, I heard him say, "I'll see you soon," and my heart soared.

Avery got into the car, grinning like the Cheshire cat. I gave her a look to keep her mouth closed as I backed out of the garage, praying I didn't hit anything. It *would* be like me to get into an accident while I was still at the mechanic.

Luckily, I managed to get out of there without making a fool of myself and poor Avery was about to jump out of her skin.

"How'd it go? Did you talk a lot?" she asked. "Or ... not a lot?" She waggled her perfectly sculpted auburn-colored brows.

"I think it went good," I told her, but in my overactive girl brain I was already over-analyzing everything. "We talked and he took me to lunch."

"That sounds promising." She fixed her lipstick in the mirror. "Did you get his number?"

"No, but he asked for mine." I bit my lip, hard enough that it started bleeding.

Avery squealed. "This is good news! He asked for your number, which means he's interested. Since you didn't ask for his, you don't seem desperate."

"What if he doesn't call?" I continued to nibble on my lip.

"Oh, he'll call." Avery smirked.

"How'd it go with Luca?" I asked, desperate to steer the conversation away from myself.

"Let me tell you, that man knows what he's doing." She fanned herself. "The things he can do with his tongue. *Wow.*"

"*Avery,*" I groaned.

"What? It didn't go *that* far. Stop imagining dirty things, Olivia," she laughed.

"Knowing you, I couldn't imagine it dirty enough." I eyed her.

"That's very true," she conceded. "Hopefully, I'll be seeing much *more* of Luca, if you know what I mean."

I wanted to bang my head against the steering wheel.

How Avery and I had ended up roommates and best friends was beyond me. We were so incredibly different. Sometimes, like now, I wanted to strangle the girl. But I couldn't imagine not having her as a friend.

"And maybe you can see more of Trace." She kicked off her heels and then brought her feet up to rest them on the dashboard. "And finally get laid so you'll stop bitching all the time."

I rolled my eyes. "Sometimes, I really think you're a guy."

"Hey, I have five brothers, so I practically have a dick."

"It doesn't mean you should act like you have one," I reasoned.

"Touché." She smirked, wiggling her red painted toes.

I parked my car in front of our dorm and grabbed my backpack out of the trunk. "I have to go," I told her, slinging the heavy bag over my shoulder. "I'll see you tonight."

"Later," she called, heading in the opposite direction for her own class.

My phone vibrated in my back pocket with a text.

I pulled it out and smiled when I saw it was an unknown number.

UNKNOWN: *Is it too soon to ask you out?*

I SMILED. *Trace.*

ME: *I don't know.*
   Trace: *What if I said I want to see you tonight?*
   Me: *Are you desperate?*
   Trace: *No.*
   Me: *Sorry, I didn't mean to offend you.*
   Trace: *I know. I just wanted to make you sweat a bit. ;)*
   Me: *You're mean.*
   Trace: *No, I'm a guy that you haven't said yes to seeing again.*
   Me: *Yes.*

I HOPED I didn't come across as desperate.

But he had been the one to text me, not the other way around. Besides, I'd never dated before so I was completely clueless on how these things were supposed to work. Was it normal for a guy you'd just met to ask you out? I'd have to ask Avery later.

. . . .

Trace: *Tonight?*

I BIT MY LIP. I was eager to say yes, but I knew that a mountain of homework was waiting for me tonight.

Me: *Friday night works better for me. How about the park?* I suggested, crossing my fingers that he wouldn't cancel.

My phone sounded seconds later with his reply. *Sounds good. I'll bring dinner. :)*

Me: *I'm looking forward to it.*
Trace: *Me too.*

I SMILED GOOFILY as I stuffed my phone into my pocket. I walked the rest of the way to class with a slight skip in my step.

CHAPTER THREE

I FINGERED THE WORN PIECE OF PAPER IN MY HANDS. I wrote it over a year ago, the edges were torn, and the once white paper had faded to yellow. I hadn't been able to bring myself to rewrite it. Maybe it was childish, but it felt special, and I didn't want to replace it. It was my ticket to freedom, if only I would stop being so shy, and *do* the things I had written down.

All the things on my *Live List*, as I called it, were things I had always wanted to do. But most of them I couldn't, because of my father. He had controlled every aspect of my life, and I let him, because I was scared of displeasing him. All I had ever wanted was to make him proud. By the time I started high school, I knew that nothing I ever did would please him. He was always striving for perfection—from himself, from me, from everyone and everything. But perfection doesn't exist, no matter how hard or how long we search for it.

So, why was I still looking for it?

I read over each item on my list like I did every night. It had become a sort of calming routine for me. By now, I didn't have to look at the list to know what was on it, but I did anyway.

~~Get drunk~~
Fly in a hot air balloon
Go to the carnival
Go to a concert (even if it's someone I've never heard of)
~~Go to a party~~
~~Lose my virginity~~
Dance in the rain
Go roller skating
See the ocean
Learn to paint
Get a dog...or a cat...or a rabbit. Any pet will do.
Sing in front of real people. Avery doesn't count.
Make more friends
Shoot a gun
Smoke
Get a tattoo
Learn to pole dance
Go skinny dipping
~~Pierce my belly button~~
Fall in love

I knew some of the stuff I had written down was silly, but I still wanted to *try* them. It was all about the experience and the chance to do something forbidden.

There were so many things I hadn't been allowed to do and I felt like I had missed out on a "normal" childhood.

I wanted, desperately, to do these things. But I was starting to believe it would never happen. A whole year had passed since I made my *Live List* and I had only done four things.

True, four was more than zero, but it seemed pretty pathetic to me, compared to all that was left to do.

I read over the items, yet again, nibbling on my bottom lip.

My *need* to do these things was growing restless.

Something inside me was saying it was now ... or never.

The dorm room door opened, and I hastily stuffed the piece of paper back into my pocket.

Avery dropped her backpack on the floor and promptly pulled her hair up into a ponytail.

I grabbed my textbook off my bed and placed it in my lap, pretending to be doing my homework so Avery wouldn't start questioning me about what I had been doing.

I had never explained my list to anyone, let alone *shown* them, but I was beginning to think differently. Avery was my best friend but I certainly didn't plan on showing her. She'd try to cross everything off in one night.

"Have you heard from Trace?" she asked, sagging into her desk chair, dejectedly. I guessed she'd had a hard time in class.

"He texted me." I shrugged, like it was no big deal.

"Annnnd?" she prompted, perking up.

"We're having dinner Friday," I answered.

"Aww, my little Livie is growing up," Avery cooed, batting her eyes, "and finding herself a man."

I rolled my eyes. "You're ridiculous."

"What? It's about time you dated, I was starting to think you were a lesbian and I should stop changing in front of you." She smirked.

I tossed my pillow at her but she easily deflected it.

"Or *maybe*," she laughed, "you're finally shedding that good girl preacher's daughter image. Let your inner woman out, girl!" She exclaimed, "Let her *roar!*" She clawed dramatically at the air.

I cupped my face in my palm. "Do you think *before* you speak?"

"Rarely." She grinned. "What do you think you'll wear for your date?"

"First off" —I held up a finger— "it's not a date. Secondly, do you only think about clothes?"

"Oh, it's a date. And no, sex comes before clothes." She grinned.

"Ugh," I groaned. "You act like a horny teenage boy."

"And someone sounds jealous." Avery twirled around in her pink swivel chair.

"Of the fact that you're practically a horny teenage boy? Hardly," I snorted.

"But seriously," she whined, still twirling, "what are you going to wear?"

She finally came to a stop and swayed dizzily.

"Probably jeans and a sweatshirt." I shrugged.

Avery made a strangled noise in the back of her throat. "*No!* You can't wear that!"

"We'll be in the park and it's cold out."

"You still can't wear that! A sweatshirt is completely unsuitable!" She gawked at me like I had grown three heads.

"I want to be comfortable," I reasoned.

"You can be comfortable when you're dead!" she squawked.

"Avery ..." I rolled my eyes. "Don't be dramatic."

"I am *not* being dramatic." She spun in her chair again. "I'm just telling you what everyone with a vagina knows about the rules of dating," she scoffed. "Everyone, except you, that is," she added.

"Why does there have to be rules?" I groaned. "It's stupid," I complained, falling back on my bed, the textbook on my lap falling to the side.

"There are rules for the sake of our sanity," Avery answered, striding across the room and sitting on the end of my bed. I kicked at her with my feet, trying to dislodge her.

"I'm wearing a sweatshirt," I mumbled, "whether you like it or not. I don't want to be cold."

"Olivia," she whined, "that's the point, you're supposed to get cold, so he can offer you his coat."

I sat up, staring her down. "What is this? The colonial age? I swear, what handbook are you reading this from?" I grumbled.

"The one that's been around since the dawn of time," she reasoned with a wave of her manicured hands.

"And that's exactly why it needs to be thrown away," I pointed out. "Women should be able to stand on their own and not depend on a guy. Let alone these stupid rules that are the so-called guide to dating. It's the dumbest thing I've ever heard."

Avery grinned. "I don't need to depend on a guy. I'm perfectly capable of taking care of myself. I just like to take a ride on their fun stick every now and then."

"*Avery!*" I blushed. "You did *not* just say that!"

"I did." She smirked, smoothing a finger over her red lips. "I love how when I say dirty things your little virgin ears turn red."

I reached up, grabbing my ears. "They do not!"

"Oh, they do." She nodded, grinning. "Back to the important matter at hand, these rules are a means to getting laid. To a guy, a sweatshirt is like practically wearing a chastity belt, telling him that these goods are not for sale."

"Oh, my God." I buried my face in my hands, my hair falling around me. "When did this turn into a mission for me to get laid? Besides, my *goods* are definitely not for sale."

"Girl, you're a sophomore in college, who's still a virgin. This has always been a mission to get you some sex, some *great* sex, and Trace is just the guy to do it. I can tell. It's in the way he walks."

I let my hands drop. "I'm not a virgin."

"What? I thought you—"

"Remember last year, at that party you dragged me to?" I asked.

Avery's mouth formed a perfect O. "No! Olivia! Not that guy! He looked like an ape!"

"He was pretty hairy," I snorted.

Avery shuddered. "There's no way that was a pleasant experience."

"It wasn't." I shrugged. "Is it supposed to be?"

She looked at me like I had completely gone off my rocker this time. "Yes! It's supposed to be amazing!"

"It lasted like two minutes, how is that amazing?" I asked, avoiding Avery's gaze by scrunching the bottom of my shirt in my hands.

Avery's eyes threatened to bug out of her head. "Two minutes? That's it?"

"Well, yeah."

"Oh, girl, you can do sooooo much better than that," Avery chuckled. "*So* much better," she reiterated.

"What did you mean by, it's in the way he walks?" I asked.

"What?" she asked, looking down at her hot pink nails.

"You said that you could tell Trace would be good in bed, that it's in the way he walks," I repeated her earlier statement.

"Oh!" she exclaimed. "Some guys have this *walk* they do. They don't even know they're doing it. If my experience speaks for anything, every guy that I've been with, that has *the walk,* knows exactly what he's doing." She rolled her hips and licked her lips to further drive home her point. "Trust me, Olivia, Trace can show you a good time."

I hid my face behind my hands again. "I think I've reached my sex talk quota for the day."

"Whatever." Avery hopped up from my bed, scampering to her side of the room. "You suck."

I turned my attention back to the homework I really needed to finish and forced myself to stop thinking about Trace's walk and wondering if Avery was right.

TRACE: *I no u said Friday but do you think we could do something sooner?*

I GAZED down at the text message from Trace, wondering what I should do.

I had some free time before my next class and planned to drive to Starbucks. So ... did I go on my own, like I had planned? Or did I invite Trace?

Finally, I sighed, and replied.

ME: *I'm getting Starbucks. Meet me there?*

WHAT WAS the harm in getting coffee with him?

TRACE: *See u there. :)*

MY STOMACH ROLLED NERVOUSLY. How could I be so affected by Trace? Why him and not another guy? What was so special about him? There had been plenty of guys in the last year who had tried to make a move on me, but I felt *nothing* for them while Trace caused a funny stirring in my stomach.

I tried not to think about the way he made me feel as I got in my car and drove to Starbucks.

He wasn't there when I arrived, and I stepped up to the counter, ordering a cinnamon dolce latte.

The guy handed me my drink and I slipped a cardboard sleeve on it.

Surprisingly, Starbucks was mostly empty.

I took a seat at the bar in front of the window. My eyes zeroed in on a sleek black car approaching and the butterflies started.

Oh, God.

Why had I agreed to this?

I had already been crazy nervous for Friday; agreeing to see him again was only serving to make my nerves worse.

I watched him slip from his car and pull off his sunglasses, folding them, and hooking them onto his shirt.

He opened the door and looked up, smiling when he spotted me.

His cheeks were dotted in day-old stubble and his eyes were a light green.

"Hey," he said with a grin.

"Hi," I squeaked, my eyes darting away from his and connecting with the tile floor.

"Save my seat." He winked before getting in line behind the few people that had trickled in.

I sipped slowly at my coffee so I didn't burn my throat.

The stool beside me pulled out and Trace dropped into it.

I didn't know what to say, so I stared awkwardly out the window.

He cleared his throat. "Olivia?"

I reluctantly turned to him.

"Are you okay?" he asked, looking me over.

I nodded. I couldn't tell him that it scared me the way my body responded to him. Already, I found myself scooting closer to him. It was like he was the sun and I was a flower, stretching up to reach his rays.

I knew I needed to say something and stop sitting here like a mute. "I'm glad you texted me," I squeaked.

"You are?" He tilted his head. "Because you don't look that happy."

I bit my lip. "You ... you make me ... nervous," I admitted.

He grinned. "I make lots of people nervous," he skimmed his fingers lightly over my hand that rested on the top of the bar. "It's a perfectly normal reaction."

I shivered in response to his words.

"Seriously, though ..." He pulled his hand away. "There's no need for you to be nervous around me. I'm just a guy."

I begged to differ. He was a freakin' Adonis. And he was nice. And caring. And—

I swallowed thickly.

I might not have known Trace for long, but I had always been able to read people well, and I knew he was a genuinely good person ... even if he was a little on the cocky side.

"Is your car doing okay?" he asked. "The tire's okay?"

"Huh?" I stuttered. "Oh ... yeah." I shook my head. "It's fine."

"Do I fluster you, Olivia?" He grinned, wetting his lips.

"No!" I answered too quickly.

"There's no reason to get defensive," he chuckled, rubbing his jaw.

I glanced at him quickly before my eyes flickered back to my cup of coffee, studying it intently.

I stared out the window, across the road at the strip mall, like it was the most interesting thing I had ever seen.

I shuffled my cup of coffee back and forth, scooting it along the tabletop, but then, it went flying from my fingers and tipped over. The contents spilled out on the counter and straight onto Trace's jeans.

He jumped from his stool to avoid more of the hot liquid. My cheeks flamed. This would only happen to me.

"I'm *so* sorry," I exclaimed, setting the cup upright and grabbing a wad of napkins to dry the mess I had made. Trace would have to take care of his pants because I wasn't going near that.

"It's okay," he assured me, wiping his jeans.

I bit down on my lip to hold back tears. I was the most embarrassing person on the planet.

I threw away the soiled napkins and frowned at the stain covering his jeans.

"Hey" —he grabbed my chin— "It's no big deal. They're only jeans. Look at them" —he pointed at the material "—they're already covered in grease stains. What's a little coffee?"

"Stop trying to make me feel better," I mumbled, stepping away from his touch.

He let his hand fall to his side. By now, the people gathered in Starbucks were watching us.

He shook his head, a small smile gracing his lips as if he was holding back laughter, and threw away his empty coffee cup.

"I have to get back to work." He slid his sunglasses on. "And change my pants," he chuckled. "I'll see you Friday."

"Friday." I nodded as my stomach twisted, amazed that he still wanted to see me after I spilled coffee on his jeans.

He smiled as he left, waving at me through the glass as he got into his car.

I watched him drive away and took a deep breath, feeling like I could breathe now that he was gone.

The way he made me feel scared me to death.

No one had ever made me feel the way Trace did.

A single look or touch from him sent my insides roaring.

I didn't know him, but it felt like I did.

He was one of those people that was easy to trust ... even if I did turn into a blubbering idiot around him.

My fingers sought my list in my jeans pocket. I touched the paper, biting on my lip.

I pulled it out of my pocket and threw my coffee away.

I unfolded the paper and stared at my *Live List*.

I made my list to try new things and be adventurous, so maybe it was time I took that leap and told someone ... Told Trace.

The worst that could happen would be he'd laugh in my face.

But my gut told me that he wouldn't do that.

The question was ... was I ready?

CHAPTER FOUR

I jogged across campus, toward my car, texting Avery to let her know my class had run late and I'd meet her at the restaurant in ten minutes.

Hurry up biotch.

I rolled my eyes at the text message and shoved my phone in my pocket. Leave it to Avery to come back with a smart-ass reply.

I unlocked my car and tossed my backpack onto the passenger seat. I was about to climb inside when I heard my name.

I looked around blindly.

No one ever called my name. I kept to myself, and my only friend on campus was Avery. I knew it couldn't be her, because she was waiting for me at Chili's.

"Olivia!" the voice called again.

Someone grabbed my shoulder, and I jumped, turning sharply.

"Sorry, I didn't mean to scare you," Grinning, Trace held his hands up in defense.

"It's okay," I mumbled, putting a hand over my racing heart.

"What are you doing here?" I asked, and a second later, blurted, "Are you stalking me?"

He chuckled. "You *wish* I was stalking you." Trace looked me up and down with a smirk, and I paled at his words. He pointed over his shoulder at a massive tow truck. "Some guy's car broke down, and we're towing it in."

How had I not seen that? I really needed to stop living in my own little world.

He shook his head, and blocked me in against my car, caging me with his arms.

He gazed down at me intensely for a moment, and I squirmed.

Flicking his dark hair out of his eyes, he questioned, "Why are you so awkward around me?"

My mouth flapped open. I hadn't been expecting him to ask that and it wasn't like I could really answer. What would I say? *You make me feel all fluttery inside and want to spill my guts to you.*

Um, no thank you.

He cupped my cheek. "There's no need to be uncomfortable around me."

I begged to differ.

Especially when he touched me like *that*.

I swallowed thickly as I looked up at him. I really wished he'd take his hand off and stop looking at me.

"You remind me of a frightened rabbit." He chuckled. "Your eyes are wide and you keep jumping. Relax." His fingers grazed softly over the curve of my cheek, causing my eyes to flutter closed.

"Are you ... petting me?" I asked, opening my eyes.

He grinned, wetting his lips. "I think the term is *caressing*, Olivia."

"Can you stop?" I begged.

His hand fell away. "I don't think anyone's asked me to stop before." He chuckled, cocking his head. "This is interesting." He rubbed his stubbled jaw, frowning.

"Good." I crossed my arms over my chest. "Your ego needs a blow or two."

"I'm always down for a blow or two ..." He smirked. "Not the kind you're talking about, though." He laughed.

Oh.

My.

Goodness.

He did *not* say that.

My cheeks colored, and my eyes darted to the ground, staring at my Converse.

"I was joking, Olivia." He grabbed my chin, forcing me to look at him. "I forget that you're easily embarrassed."

"*Do* you forget?" I eyed him.

"No." He chuckled, his eyes a light green. "I think you're cute when you're nervous."

Before I could reply, a guy was calling his name and waving him toward the tow truck.

"I've got to go."

"Okay," I squeaked.

He backed away, keeping his eyes on me. "Don't be nervous on Friday. Okay, Olivia?" He pointed a finger at me. "I don't want you to be embarrassed around me." His eyes grew serious as they narrowed.

"Uhm," I mumbled, turning around and reaching for the door handle.

His chuckle carried through the air.

I let out a deep breath when I got into my car.

All I had wanted to do was get in my car and drive to the restaurant, but *of course,* Trace *had* to show up and turn me into a blubbering idiot, once more. Why could I never hold my own around him?

I shook my head and started the car. As I backed out and pulled away, I was careful to avoid his intense gaze. Nevertheless, I *felt* it.

During the whole drive to the restaurant, my breath was erratic.

Trace had the ability to turn my insides to mush and make me feel completely safe at the same time. It was a lethal combination, and he knew how to use it to his advantage.

I parked my car and grabbed my wallet out of my backpack. When I stepped inside Chili's, Avery was pacing back and forth.

"There you are!" she exclaimed loudly. "You said ten minutes, Livie! Ten! Not twenty! I'm hungry!"

"Shh," I scolded, embarrassed by her behavior. "Keep it down. You'll never believe what happened to me."

She stopped her tirade and a slow smile spread across her face. "Now *that* sounds promising."

"Two?" the hostess asked us.

"Yeah." Avery nodded.

"Follow me." The girl led us through the restaurant, purposely placing us away from everyone so they wouldn't have to suffer from Avery's loudness.

"I already know what I want." Avery moved her menu to the end of the table after we sat down. "So, tell me what happened. I'm dying here."

I shrugged out of my jacket. "I was heading to my car when someone called my name—"

"Get to the interesting part," she urged.

I rolled my eyes. "I'm *trying* to."

She giggled. "Sorry."

"Anyway ..." I shook my head. "It was Trace."

"No!" she screamed. "Why was he on campus?"

"They were towing some guy's car." I ran a finger over the glossy menu.

"So, he talked to you, right?" she pressed.

I nodded. "You'll never believe what I asked him, though." I blushed.

"What did you do, Livie?" she shrieked, her hand twitching where it rested on the table. I was sure she wished she could knock some sense into me.

"I asked him if he was stalking me," I mumbled, staring at the tiled tabletop.

"Olivia!" she gasped.

"*What?*" I exclaimed. "It slipped out! I wasn't expecting to see him on campus and he surprised me!"

Avery shook her head at my stupidity. "You have so much to learn."

"You know what he asked me?" I inserted, tracing a fingernail around the designs on the tile.

"What?" she questioned with narrowed green eyes.

"He wanted to know why I was so awkward around him." I bit my lip.

"Livie! Really? I need to give you lessons on being normal around guys." She shook her head, pursing her red lips.

"And how would you do that?" I asked.

"I'd wear a dildo, of course." She chuckled.

"Avery," I groaned.

The waiter appeared, clearing his throat, and my cheeks colored knowing he'd heard what Avery said.

"What can I get you ladies to drink?" he asked.

Avery ordered water, and I asked for sweet tea.

When he was out of earshot, I hissed, "Can you *not* say stuff like that when we're in public?"

She rolled her eyes. "It's a free country. I'll say what I want, when I want."

"Ugh," I groaned.

"So" —she leaned forward, smiling— "you've still got your date on Friday, right?"

"It's not a date!" I cried, banging a closed fist against the table.

"Oh, it's a date." She smirked. "I hope you have some sexy lingerie hiding underneath your wimple."

"Avery!"

"What?" She shrugged. "I didn't use any bad words."

"How did I end up with you as a best friend?" I asked rhetorically.

"It was a match made in heaven." She giggled. "You tame me ... somewhat ... and I bring out the naughty in you."

The waiter brought our drinks and we ordered our meal.

"If you want me to be honest," Avery said, taking a sip of her water, "I think Trace is a good guy. I don't get any weird vibes off him or anything. And girl" —she pointed a finger at me— "I know my vibes. He seems like a good fit for you. As your best friend, it's my job to steer you away from the wrong guys, and there's nothing that strikes me as," she paused, tapping her lip, as she searched for the right word, "worrisome when it comes to Trace. I say go for it. You're only young once, it's time to live it up." She threw her hands in the air.

If only she knew her words had more impact on me than just pushing me toward Trace. They gave me the final nudge to know that I could tell him about my list. The question was *when?*

CHAPTER FIVE

Friday night, I reluctantly let Avery dress me for my "date" with Trace. I was starting to think I was her personal Barbie doll or something. She let me wear my jeans but paired it with one of her sweaters. Calling it a sweater was kind of pointless, though—it was so lightweight it would do nothing to protect me from the cold. It was orange with a pink heart on the front and one on each sleeve. It was cute, but not suitable for the weather. I was going to end up a Popsicle by the time the night was over.

"Sit down," she ordered, pushing me into her rolly chair.

"Can't you ask me nicely?" I grumbled as she pulled on my hair.

"I wasn't asking." She chuckled, braiding the front pieces of my wavy hair before gathering it into a side bun.

Thankfully, I had already done my makeup before she came storming into our dorm room like a woman on a mission.

"You're good to go." She gave the chair a nudge. "Oh, wait!

Don't forget these!" She tossed the deathtrap bootie heels at me, the ones I wore when I fell on top of Trace.

"I'll fall," I grumbled, purposely leaving out the part where I'd be falling *again*. I hadn't told Avery that I fell on top of Trace. She'd find it hysterical and then claim that it was a sign from the sex gods that I was meant to "fuck" Trace.

"No, you won't. Don't be a baby." She grabbed her phone off the desk.

I mumbled something unintelligible, sitting down at my own desk chair to put the shoes on and ditch my Converse.

Avery looked me up and down before nodding her consent. "Those shoes make any outfit look ten times hotter."

She was definitely right, but I'd never tell her that.

"Get out of here, you're already late," she scolded.

"Oh, crap." I looked at the clock on the small nightstand next to my bed. "I'll see you later," I told her, heading for the door.

"Stay out all night, I don't care." She laughed, and I turned in time to catch her wink.

Rolling my eyes, I left.

I held onto the stair railing like it was my life support as I made my way downstairs.

Outside, I spotted Trace's familiar black car.

I took a deep breath before heading his way.

He eased out of the car and rested his crossed arms over the hood. "Hey." He grinned. "I thought we could walk to the park but with those" —he eyed my shoes— "my guess is you're going to say no way."

"You've got that right," I replied.

"I've got it." Trace grinned, coming around the front of the car to open the passenger door before I could get there.

"Thanks." I smiled up at him as I lowered myself into the car.

"No problem," he mumbled, closing the door.

He slid inside, the car rumbling to life with a roar.

He exited the campus, turning right and then right again at the stoplight.

He drove the short distance, turning into the park's entrance, and then into the parking lot.

"I hope you're hungry," he commented, reaching into the back of the car for a large paper bag.

"Starving." I inhaled the scent of pasta wafting from the top of the bag.

"Good." He slid from the car, bag in hand, before continuing, "Because I made enough to feed your entire dorm."

"Wait, you made that?" I asked, hurrying out of the car after him, as fast as I could.

Trace stopped walking so that I could catch up to him. I was only five-two, and he towered above me.

"That's what I said." He grinned cockily.

I shook my head in disbelief. "What exactly did you make?"

"How about we find a picnic table and then you can find out?" he suggested with a wink.

We didn't walk far until we veered off the path and found a table. Trace set the bag down before sitting on the tabletop, his feet resting on the bench.

"Here, I brought you some blankets." He spread one out over the top of the table so I could sit down beside him and then draped one over my shoulders.

Just like the other day, he was wearing jeans, a wife-beater, and plaid shirt, only this one was red instead of green.

He reached into the bag and I noticed a tattoo on his wrist. It was small, maybe only an inch, and it was a solid black star.

He pulled out several containers full of food, a Thermos, two plates, and utensils.

"Geez, you're prepared," I commented, staring at everything. "Do this often?"

"No." He brushed his dark hair out of his eyes. Flashing me a crooked smile, he added, "Honestly."

I rolled my eyes. "I doubt that."

"To be honest with you, I've never done anything like this before." He waggled a finger between us. "I haven't always been a …" he floundered.

"Nice guy?" I suggested.

"Yeah," he sighed.

"I kind of figured that." I shrugged.

"Why?" He tilted his head, brows raised.

My cheeks flamed. I waved my hands at him and stuttered, "You've got that whole bad boy vibe. The tattoos, the hair, the boots, and that smile! It's pretty obvious that you've left a string of broken hearts."

He chuckled, the sound warm and husky, sending shivers down my spine. "I don't think it's *that* many broken hearts." Quieting his laughter, he opened one of the containers and said, "Besides, I'm *not* that guy anymore. I didn't like him very much."

"Is that a line or something?" I questioned, hugging the blanket closer to my chest as the sun went down and the air grew cooler. I really hoped Trace wasn't trying to use me, but I was beginning to question why he was wasting his time with me. I was nothing special.

"No." He handed me the container and I looked down to see a stuffed shell with tomato sauce. It smelled heavenly, the scent of garlic lingering in the air. "Some things happened in my life that sent me in a different direction, but now, I'm on the right path, and I plan to stay on it."

"Wow, that was deep." I laughed.

"Are you laughing at me?" He feigned anger.

"Yes." I stifled a giggle. "So" —I dug my fork into the pasta shell— "what was it that caused you to stray off your path?"

He sighed, looking out into the trees. "You know how the other day you didn't want to talk about something?"

"Yeah ..." My brows furrowed.

"Well, I don't really want to talk about it." His green eyes had darkened so that they shone like emeralds.

"Oh, okay, it's no big deal." I took a bite of the stuffed pasta shell and moaned in pleasure.

"One day, I hope to tell you, but not today." He shrugged. "Just like one day I hope you'll tell me why your smile's so sad but how you still manage to have this sparkle in your eye."

I started to choke on the pasta. I did the whole coughing-sputtering thing and no doubt my face turned an unattractive shade of red.

Swallowing a sip of the sweet tea he'd poured into the lid of the thermos, I asked, "Why do you say my smile is sad?"

"Because it is. You smile like you've been hurt and you're just holding the pain inside, not letting it go, but you want to ... You definitely want to be free." He pointed to me. "And that's where the sparkle comes from."

I tried to get my breathing back to normal after nearly choking to death.

I was completely shocked by what Trace said. Most people didn't notice the pain that I kept carefully hidden, and the fact that Trace had picked up on it so quickly blew my mind. I didn't think he'd noticed much about me. Apparently, he was far more observant than I gave him credit for.

I knew it was silly, since I didn't know him, but I found myself wanting to open up to him and tell him everything. It wasn't like I really had that much to tell and I felt like I *had* to tell someone.

"My dad," I whispered.

"Huh?" he asked, wiping tomato sauce from his lip.

I took a deep breath to steady myself. It wasn't like this was some big secret. My dad didn't abuse me ... at least, not physically, but I always found it hard to talk to people about him. I felt like they always thought I was making it up, since he was a preacher and supposed to be all about God, kindness, and whatnot.

"My dad, he's the reason I'm sad," I answered. "He's very controlling. That's why I came here for college instead of staying in New Hampshire. I needed to get away and find myself, but I haven't been doing a very good job." I chuckled humorlessly, plucking at an invisible piece of lint on my jeans. "I don't know why I've let it bother me so much." I shrugged. "It was just hard, growing up and always being told what to do, what to say, and how to dress. I was expected to be the perfect child and my mom the perfect mother, while he was the perfect preacher, father, and husband. But he's none of those things," I sneered, shaking my head. "He's mean and a bully. Maybe it was selfish, and maybe it was weak, but I had to get away. I have to *try* to find who I am, but what if I can't?" I looked over at Trace. "What if I'm just this broken girl that can never be put back together? What if I can never find who I *really* am?" I took a shaky breath, shocked that I had told him all of that. Maybe it was easier to tell him because he was a stranger and I didn't fear his judgment.

"Whoa." Trace's eyes widened. "That's some tough shit."

"Tell me about it." I shuffled my feet along the bench and took another bite of the delicious pasta shell. "I know a lot of people have to deal with a lot worse, so I feel bad complaining about it." I shrugged, looking away from his inquisitive gaze.

"Olivia." He grabbed my chin in his calloused hand and forced me to look at him. "It sounds to me like your father verbally abused you, and that's not something to be taken lightly. That's very serious, and people tend to overlook it, because it's not always as noticeable."

"It doesn't matter now." I smoothed my hands over my jeans. I wished he'd let go of my chin, because I was starting to feel warm inside, and pretty soon, I'd be begging him *not* to let go.

"Of course it matters, you've obviously been hurt by it." He finally released me.

Unconsciously, my fingers went to the piece of paper in my jeans that contained my *Live List*. I never went anywhere without it.

"Olivia," he murmured when I remained quiet, "I know you don't know me that well, and you have no reason to trust me, but you *can*."

I looked over at him, expecting his signature cocky grin, but it was missing. He was completely serious, and his green eyes were warm, inviting me to tell him everything.

Could I do it?

I had told him about my dad, but could I really tell him about my list?

I'd never shared it with anyone and it had almost become sacred to me.

For some reason, I trusted Trace. Which was odd. People should earn your trust and I hadn't known Trace long enough for that to happen. But I *did* trust him. There was something about him that made me feel ... safe. It was a feeling I wasn't used to.

He was right, though. I *didn't* know him that well. So, I had no idea why I was telling him everything.

I refused to tell him about my list; I wasn't ready.

But my fingers had a mind of their own, pulling it out and folding it into the palm of my hand.

Trace's eyes zeroed in on the piece of paper clenched in my hand and I knew there was no going back now. Even though I was tempted to stuff it back in my pocket and run away.

I took a deep breath, closing my eyes, shivering from fear and not the cool October night.

The things on my list were silly, none of them important, but they were things I had always wanted to do. I was beyond afraid that Trace would laugh in my face, and I honestly wouldn't blame him if he did.

Trace grew quiet as he watched me work through my inner turmoil.

I pushed down the scared girl I was on the surface and plastered on the face of a confident woman.

I could do this.

I could show Trace my list.

It was time someone besides me knew its contents.

"There's something I want to show you," I whispered.

"What is it?" he asked, still looking at my hand.

"It's a list ... a list of all the things I want to do," I answered, nervously fiddling with the piece of paper.

"*Okay* ..." His brows drew together. "Like a bucket list?"

"No," I whispered, "I call it my *Live List*. It has nothing to do with dying."

"Okay," he repeated, "what's on it?"

Slowly, I unfurled the folded pieces.

I stared down at the list in my hand. No one but me had ever seen these words, and now, I was about to hand it to someone who was practically a stranger. I couldn't explain what drew me to Trace and what made me trust him. Frankly, I didn't care.

I had written my *Live List* the day before I left for college. Growing up in the household that I did, I was expected to be perfect. There were so many things that I wasn't allowed to do. I vowed to live my life once I wasn't stuck under my father's roof. This list was the only form of rebellion I had. I never thought I would do any of the things on the list, even though I wanted to. I only made it for fun.

I read through it again before I handed it to him.

~~**Get drunk**~~
Fly in a hot air balloon
Go to the carnival

Go to a concert (even if it's someone I've never heard of)
~~Go to a party~~
~~Lose my virginity~~
Dance in the rain
Go roller skating
See the ocean
Learn to paint
Get a dog...or a cat...or a rabbit. Any pet will do.
Sing in front of real people. Avery doesn't count.
Make more friends
Shoot a gun
Smoke
Get a tattoo
Learn to pole dance
Go skinny dipping
~~Pierce my belly button~~
Fall in love

"Here's my list." I handed it to Trace. "Feel free to laugh." I sighed, even though I hoped he didn't. Those things had seemed so important when I made this list and now they seemed so silly.

Trace's eyes scanned over the wrinkled piece of paper. "You've never been to a carnival? Or a concert?" His piercing green eyes met mine.

"No." I shook my head. "My dad wouldn't allow it."

"Not even roller skating?" he asked in disbelief.

"No." I laughed. "I might have fallen and ended up with my legs in the air and my dad says that's not a respectable position for a lady."

Trace snorted. "Well," he said, "you've got four things crossed off. The first three are ... well ..."

I blushed, knowing exactly what those three things were. "Yeah," I groaned. "I kind of crossed those three off in one night."

"Really?" He raised a brow.

"Yeah." I laughed. "Avery dragged me to a party my first week here. There was beer, so naturally I had to try it, which led me to get drunk and thinking having sex with a stranger was a good idea. It was in the bathroom and it only lasted like two minutes. It wasn't really pleasant. I don't know why people seem to like sex so much."

"Olivia." He tilted my chin up, the green of his eyes searing my very soul. "I can assure you that sex can be very, very, good ... when it's with the right person." His thumb brushed my bottom lip, sending a shiver down my spine. "And" —he leaned forward, his lips brushing my ear, the stubble on his cheeks grazing my sensitive skin— "I also know with firsthand experience that it can last a lot longer than two minutes."

He pulled away and grinned knowingly at me.

Butterflies fluttered in my stomach and I looked away from Trace, trying not to think about performing the horizontal tango with him and wondering exactly how long it would last. I bet sex with Trace would be amazing.

Olivia! Stop! He's your friend! I scolded myself. *Or not really your friend, but still! Stop it!*

"So," Trace began, "you got your belly button pierced?" He waggled his eyebrows, staring at my shirt.

"Yep." I rolled my eyes. *Boys.*

"Show me." he grinned cockily.

I knew Trace didn't think I would, so that's exactly why I pulled my shirt up, making sure the bottom edge of my bra showed.

"Damn," Trace whistled, and he definitely wasn't looking at the piercing in my belly button.

"Are you staring at my boobs?" I asked with a smile and laugh in my voice, hoping he didn't notice the blush spreading up my chest, to my neck and cheeks.

I knew he was, but I wanted to hear him say it.

Trace ducked his head, his eyes landing on my stomach, before flicking away. "Sorry about that."

Boldly, I said, "I'm not."

Whoa, girl! Where did that come from?

I had never said or done anything like that in my life ... which was pretty sad, because that was tame compared to what most people did.

Trace grinned and went back to inspecting my list. "So, you want to learn to pole dance?"

I blushed at one of the more daring ventures I had scribbled down. "I've heard it's great exercise."

Trace flashed me his cocky grin. "And it's great viewing pleasure for men."

I pushed his shoulder and he laughed, but from the expression on his face, I knew he was imagining me shimmying up and down a pole. Hopefully, I was doing a good job in his mind, because I knew that if I did cross that one off my list, I'd probably bruise my butt in the process.

"These are definitely doable." He scanned over the list once more.

I was relieved that Trace hadn't laughed at me and took my list seriously.

"I want you to help me cross all of these off," the words tumbled out of my mouth. "I know you don't know me that well, but I've been too scared to do them on my own. I don't want to be scared anymore, Trace." I bit my lip to stop the floodgate of words I was spewing.

"Of course I'll help you," he responded immediately, not even giving it a second thought. It had become obvious to me that he was just that kind of guy, always willing to help. He kept reading over my list, and I swallowed, wanting to snatch the piece of paper from his hands so he would stop scrutinizing it.

"Can I keep this?" he asked.

No! I wanted to scream. But instead, the word that left my lips was, "Sure."

"Thanks." He grinned, tucking it into his left breast pocket.

I looked down at the half-eaten dinner sitting in my lap, looking pitiful in its container. I really hoped he couldn't see how badly I was freaking out.

Now not only had I told him about my father and my list, but I was letting him keep it? Had my common sense taken a hike? This was only the fifth time I had seen Trace and I was telling him things that even Avery didn't know!

"It's getting late," Trace commented.

I looked up and realized night had descended upon us.

The sky was clear, thousands of stars gazing down upon us. They were so magical with the way they sparkled in the sky. When I was little, I always thought it looked like they were winking at me.

I found myself setting the food aside and leaning back on the table, my legs dangling.

Trace did the same, cupping the back of his head with one hand.

"They're so pretty," I whispered, reaching a hand up like I could capture one of those white shimmering dots in my hand. "It amazes me that the stars we're looking at right now could actually be dead, but because it takes so long for their light to reach the Earth they're still shining for us."

"It's an amazing world we live in," he murmured, his free arm brushing mine.

My heart thundered in my chest.

Keep it cool, Olivia! I scolded myself.

I gasped when I saw a shooting star. "Oh, my God! I've never seen a shooting star before!"

"Make a wish then," he whispered, turning on his side to face me, propping his elbow on the table, his head in his hand.

I closed my eyes and wished for everything, anything, and nothing at all.

CHAPTER SIX

It had been two weeks since I had seen Trace in person, but we were constantly texting.

Every time a text from him popped up on my phone, I smiled goofily, or at least that's what Avery told me. I wasn't sure if she could be trusted, though, because she was miffed that she hadn't heard from Luca.

"Seriously," she whined for the thousandth time today, "why hasn't he called or text me?"

"Avery." I laughed, spinning around in my chair to face her, where she sat on her bed. "I have never seen you so worked up over a guy before."

"He was amazing, Olivia! I've never kissed anyone like that before! Excuse me if I want to see what else he has to offer!"

I snickered quietly. "I'm seeing Trace tomorrow. I can ask him about Luca, if you want me to."

"You are? And you would do that for me?" Her eyes sparkled to life.

I hid my giggle. Normally, Avery would have told me that asking a guy's best friend about him was breaking the dating code, but obviously she was getting desperate.

"Yep," I replied to her first question. I had no idea what we'd be doing though. All Trace had told me was that we'd be crossing something off my list. Unfortunately, that sounded ominous to me, because he could have picked any of the sixteen things left. "And of course I would do that for you. That's what best friends are for."

She nibbled on her fingernail. "I'm not sure. I don't want to seem desperate."

I hated to inform her, but she had passed *desperate* a long time ago.

"You won't seem desperate," I replied, because that was the nice, best-friend thing to say.

"No, no." She shook her head, a grin spreading across her face. "I have a better idea."

"Oh Lord," I muttered, turning back to my computer and the homework that wasn't going to do itself. "With that smile, I'm a bit worried for Luca's wellbeing."

"Don't worry, he'll be fine." She giggled behind me. "After all, I need all his parts intact and in perfect working order for what I want to do. I just need to find a really short skirt and some 'fuck-me' heels. No guy can resist that."

I knew there was no point in scolding her or trying to talk her out of whatever her plan was.

"Have fun plotting," I muttered. "I need to finish this." I pointed to my computer.

"Mhmm," she mumbled, already scheming poor Luca's demise. He didn't stand a chance against whatever Avery was coming up with. When she set her sights on a guy, she didn't give up, which is why I found it odd that she had waited this long for *him* to take action. Maybe she really did like him.

I looked over my shoulder at her as she typed away on her laptop; her long hair fell around her like a curtain and her red lips were pursed.

This was definitely an interesting development.

"ARE you going to tell me where we're going?" I begged, peering out the windshield of Trace's car.

"No," he snorted. "If I'm going to help you cross these things off, we do it on my terms, which means you'll never know which one we're doing."

I swallowed thickly, starting to regret that I told him about my list. I didn't like the idea of not knowing what thing I would be doing. He could've picked anything. There were some I could easily eliminate though. Like riding in a hot air balloon, or skinny-dipping, or falling in love. But that still left too many possibilities for my liking.

I wrung my fingers together, nibbling on my bottom lip nervously.

I knew I shouldn't be nervous, it wasn't like he was making me do anything that I didn't want to do. I mean, I'm the one that made the stupid list!

"You look really pale," he commented.

"I do?" I squeaked, looking over at him.

"Don't worry, I'm taking it easy on you. We're doing one of the simpler things," he explained, but I still didn't feel any better. "It's okay, Olivia," he added, comfortingly.

"I just don't like *not* knowing which one I'm doing," I whispered, picking at my chipped blue nail polish.

"Hey," he said softly, tugging on the beanie he was wearing with one hand, "you made the list. You said that every single one is something that you want to do. It'll be fine."

"You're right," I swallowed, "I'm freaking out over nothing."

Trace exited off of the Interstate and onto Route 7.

His change of direction still didn't give me a clue as to where we were headed.

I was tempted to sit on my hands so I would stop fidgeting. I didn't like feeling this antsy.

Trace came to a stoplight, turning on his left blinker.

I bit down on my lip so that I didn't ask him where we were going *again*.

"Hey ..." He grabbed one of my hands, steadying the dance it had been doing across my leg. "This is an easy one, no strip poles or skinny dipping is about to go down. Relax."

Sadly, I still wasn't relaxed.

"Olivia" —he glanced at me out of the corner of his eye and released my hand "—you trusted me with your list and you can trust me now."

He had a point.

I nodded. "Okay. You're right," I conceded, but my nerves didn't ease.

The stoplight turned green and he drove a short way, passing a strip mall and a Dodge dealership on the left.

He turned suddenly onto an unmarked dirt road. I gripped the side of the car, holding on, and he chuckled at me.

I glared across the car at the side of his face. "You could've warned me!"

"And where's the fun in that?" He peered at me through his aviator sunglasses, his cheeks and chin covered in stubble.

I grumbled something unintelligible, only serving to entertain him further.

We came to a stop in front of a large rectangular building. My eyes lit upon the words *skating rink* and I breathed a sigh of relief.

Trace removed his sunglasses, beanie, and leather jacket.

Underneath his jacket, he wore a light blue plaid shirt,

buttoned about halfway up his chest, and a white wife-beater underneath. I was beginning to think all he owned were plaid shirts. I had yet to see him in anything else.

"What?" he asked, looking down at his shirt. "Is there something on it? I swear, I got it out of the clean clothes pile," he grumbled, picking at the bottom edge of the shirt, looking for a stain.

"Nothing's on it," I promised, "I was just thinking about how you only wear plaid shirts."

He grinned, letting his shirt fall back in place. "I like plaid."

"I can tell." I laughed.

"I also" —he leaned close to me, which wasn't hard in his car, and his breath skimmed across my bare collarbone— "*really* like these shoes you keep wearing." His fingers grazed over my knee and I held my breath so I didn't start hyperventilating.

"They're Avery's," I squeaked, "but she gave them to me."

"You'll have to thank her for me," he whispered, brushing my hair off my shoulder, and my pulse accelerated.

"Mhmm, I can do that." My eyes followed his fingers as they skimmed down my neck.

He leaned even closer, and I thought *this was it, he's going to kiss me.*

But instead, he grinned that cocky grin and slid back to his side of the car. "We've got some roller skating to do."

I squished my eyes closed and took a deep breath.

Damn him for getting me all worked up like that. It wasn't fair.

When I opened my eyes, he was already out of the car and closing the door.

I scurried after him as fast as I could.

He held the door for me and I followed him to where we paid for our skates.

Luckily, I outsmarted him by cutting in front of him to pay for my own roller skates.

"That won't happen again," he whispered in my ear as we walked away from the counter. "I'm onto you." He narrowed his eyes as he walked backwards past me.

I sat down on a bench and pulled off my shoes then realized I didn't have socks. I sighed in disgust.

"I'm not wearing socks and that's not exactly something I carry around in my purse," I grumbled, glaring at my bare feet, and then at the skates I knew were far from sanitary.

"Don't worry, I've got you covered," Trace winked, sitting down beside me and handing me a pair of socks. "They're clean but they'll be a little big on you."

"I'll make do." I smiled gratefully at him, taking the wadded-up ball of socks from his hand. "I hope you're prepared to handle my suckiness." I looked out onto the rink where a group of teenagers was skating. It was clear they knew what they were doing and that scared me further. I'd fall flat on my butt as soon as I set foot on the rink.

"That's what the beginner's rink is for." He pointed to a different rink on our right.

It was full of small children and their parents.

"Great." I rolled my eyes. "This is going to be wonderful."

"You're the one that wanted to do it, so stop complaining." He bent to lace up his skates. "We'll have fun, and I won't let you fall."

He was probably right. I wouldn't fall. Why? Because I'd be crawled halfway up his body, holding on for dear life.

I had put roller-skating on my list because I'd always wanted to do it when I was younger. Now, looking at the four wheels on the bottom of the skates and the slippery wood floor, I didn't think it was a good idea. I had already proven myself to be clumsy around Trace, and this would make it worse.

"Ready?" he asked me.

There was nothing I could do to stall.

"Yeah," I mumbled reluctantly.

Trace held out a hand for me, and I placed mine in it. His hand was warm and rough from hard work.

"I won't let you go," he promised, guiding me across the carpeted floor.

This wasn't so bad, but I knew the carpet was giving me false hope.

Trace stepped onto the rink first and my heart began to race in fear.

I did *not* want to fall and bruise my butt. Not only would I embarrass myself, but I'd also be sore.

"You can trust me," he coaxed. His green eyes were encouraging.

I placed one foot onto the hardwood rink and immediately felt myself slip. I reached out, grabbing the half-wall that separated the rink from the carpeted area.

"Olivia," Trace warned.

I whimpered, letting go of the wall, and latched onto his arm.

I'm sure we looked strange, with him holding my left hand in his right, and me gripping his right forearm.

Trace made a face as my nails dug into his skin.

"I told you I won't let you fall." He looked into my eyes. "Relax," he added, soothingly.

Unwillingly, I let go of his arm.

I instantly felt even more off balance.

Why on Earth had I ever wanted to go roller-skating? I think I'd rather be pole dancing!

I held onto Trace's hand like ... Well, like it was the only thing holding me up, which it was.

"It's okay, Olivia." He squeezed my hand, studying my tense face. I'm sure I looked like someone who just spotted a giant ass spider, but I couldn't wipe the look of fear off my face. I hated that Trace was seeing me freak out like this. He didn't know me well, and I didn't want him to think I was a scaredy cat ... which I was. But my father had made me that way by sheltering me so much. Things that seemed normal to most people were completely foreign to me.

I eased off a bit on the death grip I had on his hand.

He smiled encouragingly.

I looked at the children around us. For most of them, this was probably the first time they'd been roller-skating. If they could do this without holding onto their moms and dads, then I could do this without hanging onto Trace.

I let his hand slip from mine and began to wobble.

His large hands clasped me by the waist before I could fall.

"I've got you," he hummed, his chest pressed against my back.

I smiled in relief even though he couldn't see. "Thank you," I whispered.

"I told you I wouldn't let you fall and I meant it. I'm a man of my word, Olivia," he murmured, and my stomach fluttered.

I had been attracted to plenty of guys over the years. I even had a few schoolyard crushes like everyone else. But no one had ever made me feel the way Trace did. The nerves and heart fluttering I felt around him were entirely new.

"How does this feel, Olivia?" he asked, resting his chin on my shoulder.

"Like freedom," I smiled, closed my eyes, and let him guide me.

TRACE DIDN'T MAKE me skate for long, which I was grateful for.

It was okay, but I didn't like it that much. Maybe, if I had tried it when I was younger I would have enjoyed it, but not now.

He helped me back to the carpeted area and I sat down on the nearest bench, yanking off the skates.

"You did good for a first timer." Trace grinned, mussing his hair.

I laughed. *Who was he trying to fool?*

"I'm pretty sure I drew blood from squeezing your arm. I don't call that good."

He sat next to me and rolled up the sleeve of his shirt.

Sure enough, there were five very red, half-moon indents. A trickle of blood had escaped one of the marks and dried on his arm.

"Told ya." I picked up the skates and headed to where I'd left my shoes.

Trace followed behind me, his skates dangling from his fingers.

"I still think you did good," he stated and I saw him shrug out of the corner of my eye.

"You're such a liar," I scolded him, sitting down to put my shoes on.

He smirked, his lips upturned on one corner. "Okay, maybe I am, but I'm not lying now."

I rolled my eyes and wadded up Trace's socks. "I'll wash these before I give them back." I tried to put them in my purse, which I had grabbed from the cubby my shoes had been in, but Trace reached out and snagged them from me.

"I know how to work a washing machine, Olivia." He grinned. "I promise," he added. "I even know how to add fabric softener. Smell, it's Mountain Spring," he said sarcastically, holding the end of his shirt under my nose.

"Fine, wash them." I stood. "It's not like they're dirty from my feet or anything."

"I'm not afraid of your dirty socks, Olivia." He grinned, leaning against the wall. His green eyes sparkled with carefully contained laughter.

"Technically, they're *your* dirty socks." I walked over to the counter to return the roller skates.

"Ah, they may be my socks, but you're the one that dirtied them."

"Why are we still talking about socks?" I stopped, throwing my hands in the air, and he ran into me. "I told you that I would wash them."

"I like messing with you." He made his way around me, sauntering up to the counter and dropping his skates loudly.

I returned my skates as well and followed Trace out the door.

He made sure to hold each door for me, and I thought it was sweet.

Back in the car, he slipped his beanie on and perched his sunglasses atop his elegant nose.

I clasped my hands together so that I wouldn't reach over and run my fingers along the stubble grazing his jaw.

"I'm hungry," he announced.

"Okaaay," I drew out the word.

"Wanna go to Sonic?" he asked, and I remembered passing one before we got here.

"Sure." I shrugged. "I've never been there."

His jaw dropped. "You've *never* been to Sonic?"

"Nope, never. I don't think there were very many in New Hampshire," I explained. "Plus, my dad wouldn't let us eat out. We always had home-cooked meals."

Trace looked at me like I had spoken a foreign language. "There are so many things I need to show you. You haven't experienced anything."

I blushed at his words and hid my face behind the curtain of my hair.

"Don't do that," he murmured, reaching up to brush my long hair behind my ear. "Never hide your face from me."

My breath came out in short gasps. He'd said something similar the day he took me to lunch.

He smoothed his thumb over my cheek and let his hand drop.

"*This* is Sonic?" I asked, looking around the parking space he'd pulled into that was surrounded on both sides by a menu. Other cars were parked in different spots, all with the same setup.

"Yep." He grinned, turning off his car, and manually rolling down his window.

"This is weird." I glanced at the two different menus.

Trace chuckled and I whipped my head in his direction. "What?" I snapped.

"Your face is priceless," he snickered.

"This is kind of overwhelming." I looked from the menu on his side of the car and back to the one on mine.

"Relax, it's really not. This is the food menu," he explained, pointing to the menu on his side, "breakfast, lunch, dessert, the whole shebang. That one" —he pointed to the one beside me— "is just for promotional stuff."

"Oh." I nodded, feeling relieved. I tended to overreact whenever I was presented with something new.

I leaned toward Trace, careful not to touch him, so I could read the menu.

"You have to try their tater tots, they're the best," he commented.

I scooted back to my side of the car. "Just order me whatever you're having."

"You sure?" He raised a brow.

"I'm not picky." I smiled.

"Okay." He hesitated for a moment before pushing the red button and waiting for someone to respond.

After he ordered our food, I looked over at him and probed, "Tell me something about yourself. You know about my dad and my list, but I really don't know anything about you. That doesn't seem fair."

He grinned, flashing only a small amount of his straight white teeth. "What do you want to know?"

"Anything you want me to know." I relaxed into the seat.

"Hmm," he mused. "I have a little brother, Trent. He's seventeen and a senior in high school. We're close despite the fact that I'm five years older."

"So, you're twenty-two?" I asked.

"Someone knows their math," he joked.

"Is there anything else you'd like to tell me?" I pestered, curious to find out more about Trace. I had opened myself up to him, for some reason, and I wanted him to do the same with me. I wanted to know the real man behind the cocky, panty-dropping smile.

He grew quiet and I could hear the wheels turning in his head. He snapped his fingers and grinned. "I like to dance."

"Dance?" I questioned, my brows raised. Trace didn't strike me as a dancer.

"Yeah," he replied. "I suck at it, but I enjoy it. I dance while I work on cars, I dance while I cook, you never know when it's gonna happen."

I put a hand over my mouth to stifle my laugh as I pictured Trace dancing in the middle of the grocery store or some other odd place.

"That's very ... uh, interesting," I giggled.

"Hey, you're the one that wanted to know something about me."

"Right you are." I smiled as a girl appeared on Trace's side of the car with a tray full of food and drinks.

Trace sat up, pulling his wallet out of his back pocket. I didn't even bother fumbling through my purse for mine. I knew Trace wouldn't accept any money for my meal. Stubborn man.

He took the food and drinks, placing them on the bench seat in his car.

He handed her a bill and waved her away.

"Raspberry tea for the lady." He handed me a Styrofoam cup. Since there were no cup holders, I held it between my knees. "Tater tots and a hotdog." He placed the items on the seat with a wad of napkins, before pulling out identical items for himself. "And" —he pointed to the two extra cups— "these are our dessert."

"What is it? A chocolate shake?" I inspected the top of it.

Trace grimaced. "No, it's a chocolate malt. There's a big difference. Prepare to have your world rocked." He chuckled, ripping open a packet of ketchup and dumping it on his tater tots. "Want some?" He held up another packet.

I shook my head. "I hate ketchup."

He gasped. "How is it possible to hate ketchup? It's one of the single most delicious food items *ever*."

"It's gross." I glared at the red goo covering his tater tots.

"Suit yourself." He popped one in his mouth.

I happily ate a plain, non-ketchup drenched tater tot, and Trace chuckled.

"You are one interesting girl, Olivia Owens," he commented, wiping his mouth with a napkin.

"Interesting is always better than boring." I smiled, biting into the hotdog. "This is really good." I pointed to the food.

He stretched his arm along the bench seat. "Told ya."

We finished eating and stayed parked to drink our chocolate malts. It was thick but delicious. Trace kept smiling at me as I drank the malt.

"What?" I asked.

"Nothing." He grinned, shaking his head. His dark hair fell over his green eyes and he promptly pushed it back.

"No, you're thinking something," I insisted. "Tell me."

"It's just ... who would've thought that the girl I stopped to help with her flat tire would be sitting in my car right now. I'm just ... I'm glad I met you."

I smiled. "I'm glad I met you too."

"I'm sure you are."

I rolled my eyes. "You're so cocky."

"No, I'm confident. There's a big difference in confident and cocky." He winked, taking the straw into his mouth, and my eyes followed the movement of his lips. *Those lips should be illegal and I hadn't even had a taste yet.*

I blushed at my thoughts and turned away from him.

"Why do you do that?" Trace asked, perplexed.

"Do what?" I questioned, reluctantly turning to face him.

"Blush and then look away. I know you're still blushing even if I can't see you." He leaned against the driver's side door to face me fully.

"I don't know." I shrugged. "I guess it's a defense mechanism."

"Why do you need to be defensive about blushing? It's a perfectly normal reaction." He licked a drop of chocolate malt from his lip and my heart stuttered in my chest.

I took a deep breath and stuck my finger into the whipped cream. "You don't understand the kind of home I grew up in," I reasoned, licking off the whipped cream.

His green eyes darkened as he watched my finger. I blushed again. I wished I could turn off the blushing, but around Trace my cheeks seemed to have a permanent rosy hue.

"Then make me understand," he insisted.

"Not today," I sighed. "I'm having a good time and I don't want to ruin it by talking about things that I wish would stay in the past."

"Fair enough." He grinned, changing the subject by talking about random things like music and favorite colors.

I liked how Trace understood when not to push me. He would let me tell him about myself on my terms. It was nice not having someone trying to pry information out of me.

I smiled the rest of the afternoon we spent together and even late into the night. Not even grumpy Avery could sour my mood.

CHAPTER SEVEN

"Where are you going?" Avery asked, pushing away from her desk as I headed toward the door.

"I have plans with Trace. I'm supposed to meet him at the garage. He gets off work soon," I explained, lifting my purse onto my shoulder.

"Oh." She frowned.

"Still upset over Luca?" I asked.

"No," she answered hastily, turning away from me.

I grinned. "You are."

She turned back around and my smile faded. Avery truly *was* hurt.

"I just ... I thought I understood men, but Luca seems to be entirely different. I can't read him at all." She played with the ends of her hair. "Normally, I know when a guy's into me, but with Luca, I'm clueless. I can't tell whether he hates me, tolerates me, or actually likes me. He doesn't say much," she mused.

I felt bad for her, I did, but I also found her situation funny too, because it wasn't like her to be this worked up over a guy. Avery's confidence level was through the roof, but something about Luca made her insecure.

"Maybe that's because you're too busy kissing each other to carry on a conversation." I laughed, crossing my arms over my chest.

Avery had finally met up with Luca and, apparently, they'd ended up doing the deed on the hood of his car. At least, that's what Trace told me, because he said he walked in on them. Avery had told me nothing, which was unusual. Normally, she told me everything, even the gory details that I had no desire to hear. I was really starting to think she had feelings for Luca, which made me all kinds of excited. I wanted Avery to find a guy she loved and stop fooling around. She needed to learn that someone could truly care about her for *her*. I knew from what she had told me that her parents were wealthy and had only looked at her and her brothers as an accessory. Which led her to believe that no one could ever love or want her.

"That could be it." She laughed. "But I *have* tried to talk to him before and he gives me grunts for answers."

I snorted.

"He's a total caveman," she giggled, "but I kinda like that about him. Plus, he has these big man hands, and you know I love me some man hands."

"Avery, you're something else." I laughed. "I've really got to go, though, can we talk later?"

"Sure." She spun in her chair. I swear, one day I was going to find a way to mess up that chair so it couldn't twirl. "I don't have any plans for tonight. I'll just be here, all by myself, while my so-called best friend ditches me for a hot piece of ass."

"Bye," I called over my shoulder, rolling my eyes.

"Have fun, Livie!" she hollered as I closed the door.

I let out a sigh of relief, dashed down the steps, and out of the building.

I walked quickly to my car, holding on tightly to the mace on my keychain. You never knew when a creeper could pop up.

I giggled to myself as I got in my car; I certainly hadn't been reaching for the mace when Trace pulled up behind me.

Shaking my head, I drove to Pete's Garage, and parked beside Trace's car.

I walked around to the front of the building. The large garage door was open, exactly like when I'd been there to get my car fixed.

Music was playing loudly, the lyrics saying something about blowing the roof off the place.

I stepped inside, looking around, hoping that Trace didn't scare me like last time.

I walked around a car and saw him.

He was completely oblivious to me, and I put my hand over my mouth, to stifle my giggle. He was dancing like ... well ... there were no words to describe Trace's dancing style. It was interesting, to say the least. In fact, I wasn't sure if it could be considered dancing.

He held a metal car part in his hands while shaking his whole body.

This was not dancing; it was more like a seizure.

I kept my mouth covered so that I could watch him longer.

It would be cute if it wasn't so funny.

He hadn't been lying when he said he liked to dance, but he was right when he said he sucked. The man had no rhythm whatsoever.

He turned and spotted me.

And holy hell, I had been too taken by the dancing to notice he was shirtless.

Shirtless and coated in a sheen of sweat.

I had never seen a man's chest like Trace's. It was lean and tan, but muscular, just like his arms. A light dusting of dark hair started at the bottom of his naval and disappeared under the edge of his boxers, that I spied above the edge of his jeans.

I covered my eyes and turned around like I had caught him naked.

I was the epitome of smooth.

Not.

His chuckle rumbled through my body and I let my hand drop. Slowly, I turned back around to face him.

He'd turned the music down, and leaned against the car he was working on, grinning cheekily at me.

"You're early." He pushed his hair out of his eyes. I was discovering it was a nervous habit for him.

"And you're naked," the words slipped out of my mouth before I could stop them.

His smile grew. "I'm not quite naked yet, but if you'd like to help me get there, that's fine by me."

Oh. My. God.

"I'm kidding, Olivia," he added when I stood there with a stunned look on my face. "You're definitely a preacher's daughter," he commented. "But you're going to have to get used to my sexual innuendos if you're going to spend time with me. I can't help myself."

Lord, help me. Please.

"Got it," I replied awkwardly.

My parents really should have made Awkward my middle name. It suited me better than Camille.

Olivia Awkward Owens—it had a nice ring to it.

Trace wiped his hands on his jeans and moved around the front of the car with the part he'd been dancing with.

I followed him, watching as he fiddled easily with the car parts.

It looked complicated to me, but he made it seem easy.

"I'm almost done here." He glanced over his shoulder at me. "And then we'll cross off something else."

"Uhmm," I replied, trying not to look at his muscular back and the way his muscles rippled as he worked on the car. Why did he have to be so good looking?

I turned away, bobbing my head to the music. I needed to stop thinking about how good he looked. He was my ... friend, and it was wrong to have these kinds of thoughts about him.

"All right, I'm done for now," Trace announced and I spun back around. "The owner won't be by to pick it up till tomorrow night, so I have time to finish it."

"Are you sure?" I asked, tapping the toe of my right heel on the concrete floor.

He grinned. "Yeah, I'm sure."

A noise sounded at the front of the garage and I turned rapidly.

The sudden movement caused me to lose my balance and I started to fall.

"Whoa." Trace grabbed my arm to steady me.

"Sorry," I mumbled, fiddling with a strand of hair.

"I didn't mean to scare you," Luca mumbled in his deep voice. He was dressed much like he was the first time I saw him. Jeans, vest, and a fedora. Apparently, Luca and Trace stuck to very rigid dress codes. Except when Trace was making me drool by *not* wearing a shirt, although, he was definitely drool-worthy fully clothed.

Luca pulled a pack of cigarettes out of his pocket and lit one.

I wasn't sure if he ever actually smoked one, they seemed to be a part of the whole look he was going for. I still hadn't figured out what the vests meant, though.

A grin spread across Trace's face, and he grabbed me by the hand, dragging me over to Luca.

"Looks like we can cross two things off tonight." He smirked.

"Huh?" I was confused.

"Luca, give me one of those." Trace held his hand out for a cigarette.

"But you don't smoke," Luca grumbled, "and these are expensive."

"Luca," Trace groaned. "Just do it."

Luca mumbled something unintelligible but handed over a cigarette.

"Lighter," Trace continued to hold out his hand.

Luca slapped the lighter into his palm. "I expect *that* back."

Trace led me outside and released my hand.

It was chilly outside, in the forties, but Trace was still shirtless. I was sure he was doing it on purpose because his bare chest was all kinds of distracting.

"Here," he handed me the cigarette.

I glanced down at it, perplexed.

"You put smoking on your list so stop looking at it like it's going to bite you," he told me.

"I don't know how to hold it," I explained.

"Oh, like this." He fixed my fingers around the slender white cigarette.

He motioned for me to hold it up and I did.

He lit the end of it and waited for me to do something.

"I don't know what to do!" I exclaimed, terrified that the thing was going to burn my fingers.

Trace chuckled and motioned for me to bring it up to my lips. "Just inhale."

I did and it was horrible. Smoke flooded my lungs and I felt like I was being suffocated. I dropped the cigarette and Trace stomped on it to snuff it out.

Coughing, I gasped, "That was horrible."

My eyes watered and I felt like I couldn't breathe.

Either I'd done it wrong or other people were nuts for sucking on those things. It was awful.

"You okay?" Trace asked.

"I'll be fine." I wiped my eyes and struggled for air.

I couldn't get the horrible taste out of my mouth.

Trace took my hand and led me to the other side of the building, the side I had never been on, and up a flight of steps.

He pulled a key out of his pocket and unlocked the door.

"This is my place," he explained, leading me inside, and straight into a small kitchen area. He grabbed a bottle of water and handed it to me.

I swirled the water around my mouth and spit it out in the sink. I did that several times before rinsing out his sink.

"Better?" he asked, leaning a hip against the linoleum countertop.

"Much." I smiled. "But I am *never* doing that again."

He laughed. "I figured you wouldn't."

"Why do people like that?" I asked, wiping my mouth on the back of my hand.

"Beats me." He shrugged. "My grandpa used to smoke a pipe all the time, and let me tell you, that thing smelled horrible."

I finished off the bottle of water.

Trace took it from me and tossed it in a recycling bin then handed me another.

"I'm going to shower" —he nodded toward the door that led to the bathroom— "and then we can get out of here."

"'Gonna tell me what we're doing?" I coaxed.

"Nope." He grinned. "I told you before, you're never going to know which one I've picked. It makes things exciting." He motioned to a nice beige couch. "Sit down and relax. Watch TV. I don't care." He headed into the only bedroom.

"Okay," I mumbled, sitting down, and looking around at the darkened space.

In front of the couch were two crates flipped upside down to create a makeshift coffee table. A bowl of Skittles sat on top. Across from the couch was a nice sized flat-screen TV.

Trace came out of the bedroom with clothes in his hands and flicked on a light. "You don't need to sit in the dark, Olivia. Make yourself at home." He smiled and closed the bathroom door.

I heard the shower turn on and breathed a sigh of relief.

My feelings for Trace were quickly escalating and even though, at this point, we'd known each other for almost a month, it seemed too quick to be falling for someone. But could you put a time limit on something like that?

This was bad.

I couldn't fall for Trace. He was my friend and he could do *so* much better than me. He could have any girl he wanted, not just because of his looks, but because of his personality too, and I needed to stop pining over someone who would never be mine.

Friends, I told myself. *We. Are. Just. Friends.*

I buried my face in my hands.

I couldn't let Trace know I liked him. There was no way he returned my feelings and he'd just give me some song and dance about how we'd never work. That's what most guys did, right? I didn't have any experience and was basing my assumption off of movies. Which was stupid because movies always got it wrong.

I took a deep breath before I had a panic attack.

I used to have them all the time as a child but I had grown out of them. Now would be the worst time *ever* for them to return.

The door to the bathroom opened, steam billowing out, effectively cutting off my internal tirade.

Droplets of water clung to Trace's dark hair, making it appear black instead of brown. He'd shaved, but short prickly stubbles of hair still remained. I liked that he was never clean-shaven. I always thought that the guys with smooth cheeks looked babyish.

"I'm ready," he announced, running his fingers through is hair rapidly, trying to dry it.

"Okay." I stood, running my hands down the front of my jeans.

He locked the apartment behind us and led me to his car.

"I can drive." I pointed to my car.

"Nice try," he said as he grinned, "but I'd have to tell you where we're going and that's not going to happen."

"Fine." I slid into his car. "I don't care." Which was a lie. I did care, very much. It seemed completely unfair that he wouldn't tell me where we were going. But I knew there was no point in arguing with him.

He hadn't driven far when he stopped in front of a small building in the old part of town.

"That was fast." I looked up at the building, reading the sign.

It was an art gallery.

"I'm learning to paint?" I grinned, excitedly.

"Yeah." He eased out of the car and jogged around to open my door.

"This is going to be so much more fun than roller skating!" I squealed and Trace chuckled in response.

"I SUCK AT THIS!" I exclaimed, causing the other people in the room to turn and glare at me.

It was mostly older people there, aside from Trace and me.

"It's not that bad." Trace glanced from his canvas to mine.

"It looks nothing like it!" I pointed to the purple blob I had painted and to the purple vase it was supposed to look like. "Yours looks good compared to mine!"

Which was pretty sad, because his sucked too.

"You can't expect to learn to paint in one evening." The teacher breezed over to me. She looked at what I had done and wrinkled her nose. "Then again, there are those who can *never* learn."

"I take it I'm in the never category?" I huffed.

She didn't bother to answer.

I tried to pretty up the mess I had made on my canvas, but it was hopeless. Completely and utterly hopeless. It was obvious I didn't have an artsy bone in my body. At least, when it came to painting and drawing. I could write pretty well. But then again, it was impossible to judge yourself.

I was tempted to say, "Screw it, let's get out of here," but I knew that wouldn't fly with Trace.

Plus, he was completely engrossed in talking with the old man beside him. Apparently, the man had served in one of the wars and was telling a curious Trace all about it.

I cleaned my paintbrushes off and then placed the canvas on a drying rack.

"You done?" Trace asked when I sat back down on the stool.

"Yeah," I sighed grumpily. "I'm never going anywhere near a paintbrush again. I'm an insult to artists everywhere."

Trace chuckled. "That's not true and this is only a beginner's class. I think you're supposed to suck."

I frowned.

Trace swiveled in his stool to face me and leaned down to my level. "You don't have to be perfect. It's okay to suck at things."

His words were like a stab straight to my heart, even though he hadn't meant them that way.

He was right. I didn't have to be perfect. But when you've been striving for perfection all your life, it's hard to let it go.

"Hey," Trace whispered, lifting my chin up. "Don't be sad. I didn't mean to hurt your feelings or anything."

"I know," I mumbled. "And you're right. I don't have to be perfect but with my dad …"

"You've always tried to be," he added. "It's okay to mess up though. I thought you wanted to live? You can't live if you don't mess up. Life's all about mistakes, and sometimes, those things you *think* are mistakes turn out to be the thing you were searching for."

I nodded at his words. They made sense.

"Life isn't about perfection," he added, "perfection doesn't exist."

"I know," I replied, playing with the ends of my hair.

"Do you?" he questioned, his green eyes studying me. "Because I'm not sure you do."

———

I KEPT TURNING Trace's words over in my mind.

I *knew* that perfection didn't exist, but since my dad had always expected it, I strived for it.

My list was supposed to be my chance to make mistakes, so why was I holding myself back?

I *wanted* to mess things up and live a little, but when you had worked so hard to be perfect for so long, it was hard to let that go.

But I was going to, because if I didn't, I would never find the *real* Olivia Owens.

We were back in the car but we hadn't pulled away from the building.

"You may not be the next Picasso," Trace began with a grin, causing me to smile in response, "but you tried, and that's what really matters."

He pulled a pen and piece of paper out of his pocket.

I quickly realized it was my list.

He carefully unfolded it and held the crinkled piece of paper out to me, along with the pen.

"Would you like to do the honor?" he asked, eyes sparkling.

I didn't bother to reply, I took both items from his hands, crossing off smoking and learning how to paint.

~~Get drunk~~
Fly in a hot air balloon
Go to the carnival
Go to a concert (even if it's someone I've never heard of)
~~Go to a party~~
~~Lose my virginity~~
Dance in the rain
~~Go roller skating~~
See the ocean
~~Learn to paint~~
Get a dog…or a cat…or a rabbit. Any pet will do.
Sing in front of real people. Avery doesn't count.
Make more friends
Shoot a gun
~~Smoke~~
Get a tattoo
Learn to pole dance
Go skinny dipping
~~Pierce my belly button~~
Fall in love

It was so rewarding seeing two more things crossed off my list. I had been too scared to do them on my own. But with Trace's help, it was finally happening.

I was living.

CHAPTER EIGHT

"We're going out," Avery announced, bouncing into our dorm room.

"No," I responded, even though it hadn't been a question.

"Yes, we are," she sang, stripping off her clothes, and changing into clean ones. "Luca invited me to go out and he said Trace would be there, so you're going."

I perked up at Trace's name but I had a pile of homework. The professors were laying it on thick before Thanksgiving break.

I frowned. "I can't."

Avery sauntered over to me. She reached out and tweaked the corners of my lips up. "Stop frowning, it doesn't suit you. Instead, smile and say, 'Yes, Avery, I'll go out with you, Luca, and Trace'."

"I *have* to get this homework done," I whined.

"It's not like it's going anywhere. Do it tomorrow." She padded back across the small room, to her closet and flicked through the various items.

"And that's the kind of philosophy that gets people in trouble," I commented, pointing a finger at her turned back.

"Livie," she pleaded, "please, for me?"

I sighed. I *had* been spending a lot of time with Trace and even though we'd be out with the guys, Avery would be there. "Fine," I conceded. "But I want to know where we're going."

"Just out to eat, I think Luca said he wanted to go to B-Dubs, so that's why you have to go."

"Oh, I see." I laughed. "Luca invited Trace so it wouldn't be a date. But if I tag along, then it makes it a double date."

"Exactly." She smirked.

"You play dirty, Avery Callahan." I shook my head. "Poor Luca doesn't know who he's dealing with."

Avery laughed, throwing her head back. "You've got that right." She winked.

I closed my laptop with a sigh and changed into something more presentable than sweatpants.

I ended up in a pair of jeans and a red sweater. Avery eyed me disapprovingly.

"What?" I squawked. "There's nothing wrong with this!"

Avery rolled her eyes, crossed her arms over her chest, and looked me up and down. "It's just so ... boring."

"You're the one that's dragging me away from homework which I *need* to do. I'm sorry if I'm not very concerned with how I look," I snapped.

"*Please*, make an effort, Livie. Trace is going to be there, and you don't want to go walking into the restaurant covered up like that." She gave me pleading puppy dog eyes.

"It's *cold* outside and I want to wear a sweater. What's wrong with that? At least it's not a sweatshirt," I snapped. "I'm not going to be walking around in booty shorts when there's frost on the ground in the mornings." Avery lit up, so I quickly added, "And I won't be wearing booty shorts in the summer ... or *ever*, for that matter."

Avery frowned. "But you don't always have to wear jeans and a sweater when it's cold outside. There are other options. Please, let me dress you," she pleaded, pouting her bottom lip.

"Fine," I groaned, stripping off my sweater, and throwing it at her head.

"Thank you!" she shrieked, running across the room to her closet.

"Would you like to lay out clothes for me to wear in the morning, Mother?" I snarled.

She laughed. "Maybe I should. You always look fabulous when I dress you," she said flippantly, but with a grin. "Change into these." She tossed a pair of black skinny jeans my way.

I made a face of disgust. I *loathed* skinny jeans.

"Olivia," Avery scolded, looking over her shoulder, noticing my scowl. "Put the pants on before I force you to the ground and do it myself." She narrowed her dark green eyes at me.

I knew she would. Avery was a woman of her word.

Reluctantly, I removed my jeans and wiggled into the skinny jeans. I was really beginning to hate having a roommate that was the same size as me.

But then, when I turned and saw the way the jeans hugged my curves, all hate was forgotten.

"Nice, huh?" Avery smirked, studying my reaction.

I groaned at being caught smiling. "They're okay."

"You're such a liar. Don't liars go to Hell?" She grinned saucily.

I threw a pillow at her. "I know sinners do."

She caught the pillow and hugged it to her chest. "Then there's a special place in Hell with my name on it" —she winked — "and a majority of the population of the world. Everyone is a sinner when it comes to something."

"So," I drawled, "I assume you're going to give me a shirt to wear. I don't think they'll let me eat in just my bra."

"Oh, right." Avery shook her head and grabbed a lightweight sweater off of her bed. "Here."

It was oatmeal colored and the bottom of it hung in different lengths. I was surprised by how soft it felt, like a blanket you'd give a baby.

I pulled it over my head and adjusted it so that it hung right.

"Seriously, Olivia, you're so pretty." Avery looked me up and down. "It's not fair."

Avery was calling me pretty? What planet was this?

Avery was drop-dead gorgeous with red hair that hung halfway down her back, pouty lips, and insane curves. She had the kind of body girls desired and guys drooled over. She wasn't big but she wasn't small, either. I thought she was the perfect healthy size.

She grabbed a leopard print scarf off her closet door and fixed it around my neck.

"These will look great too." She handed me a pair of brown leather boots that looked like the kind you'd wear to go horseback riding.

I sat down and pulled them on. They almost came as high as my knees.

"Almost perfect," Avery appraised her handy-work.

In a matter of seconds, she had my hair hanging down one side in a fishtail braid.

"Now, you're perfect." She grinned.

I laughed, shaking my head at my best friend.

Avery had changed into a gray dress with black tights, heels, and a red jacket. She looked gorgeous. No matter what we were doing, Avery always looked like a knockout. I don't think I had ever seen her look rumpled or frazzled.

"Let's get outta here." She grabbed her gigantic purse and

slung it over her shoulder. Sometimes I wondered what she smuggled in there. No one needed a purse that big.

"Right behind you," I replied, taking a deep breath.

AVERY PARKED her red Volkswagen Beetle in front of Buffalo Wild Wings.

Her phone chimed and she read the text.

"That's Luca, he says that they're already inside." She tucked her phone in her purse.

I followed her inside, not saying a word.

I was extremely nervous and I didn't know why. I had been spending a lot of time with Trace, but this felt different. Maybe, it was because we were meeting up to do something that wasn't on my list. Or *maybe,* it was because I knew he didn't know I was coming and I was scared of his reaction. Yeah, I was pretty sure it was that.

Avery spotted Luca instantly, and what do you know? He was wearing a vest again with a fedora perched atop his head. I was really beginning to wonder what he had against shirts, or maybe he just wanted to show off his impressive muscular physique. More than one woman was eyeing him appreciatively.

My eyes moved away from Luca and locked on Trace's intense green stare.

He wasn't checking me out like most guys would. Instead, he was looking into my eyes, as a smile graced his face. And not just a little smile either; it was a big happy one that showed me all of his perfect white teeth.

My heart leapt.

Trace was happy to see me.

Avery and I took the chairs across from the guys.

"Hey." I smiled lightly at Trace, hoping the dim lighting of the restaurant hid my blushing cheeks.

"Hey." He leaned toward me, his eyes glowing.

Trace's eyes were always expressive. I was beginning to read his moods just by the variance in shade. The sparkle in his eyes told me he was feeling playful. I liked playful Trace ... well, when he wasn't making me blush.

"I didn't know you were coming" —he tilted his head to study me, grin widening— "but I'm really glad you're here."

A gust of air fled my lungs.

"I'm glad to be here," I spoke softly.

"Don't go getting shy on me now, Olivia." He smirked.

Avery, clearing her throat loudly, had me turning to face her. I blushed an even darker shade of red when I saw that a waitress was standing there, waiting for our drink orders.

I stammered that I wanted sweet tea and Trace ordered a beer.

I picked up the menu, using it to block my reddened face from Trace's powerful gaze.

I settled on an order of eight boneless wings with sweet BBQ sauce. That seemed safe enough since I wasn't a fan of spicy food.

When the waitress came with our drinks, I ordered my food quickly.

Trace kept watching me, and the feel of his eyes skating along my body, was igniting a fire inside me.

For something to distract myself, I grabbed another packet of sugar, and added it to my already sweet tea. It wasn't like you could ever make anything too sweet.

I was taking a sip of my tea when Avery leaned over, and whispered in my ear, "Trace is undressing you with his eyes. He wants to do you, right here, right now."

I choked, spewing sweet tea across the table, and coughing so hard my sides began to hurt.

Avery giggled, beating my back.

"Are you okay?" Trace asked, wiping up the mess I had made. Thank God none had gotten on him or I would've melted into a puddle of embarrassed goo.

"Fine," I croaked, my voice hoarse from all the coughing.

I glared at Avery and she hid a smile behind her hand.

Luca seemed oblivious, but I wondered if he was really as aloof as he acted. He was a weird guy. I guess that's why he was perfect for Avery.

"You sure you're okay?" Trace questioned, dropping the soiled napkin where the waitress could grab it.

"Yeah." I took a breath and it burned my raw throat. If Avery was sitting across from me, I would kick her so hard in the knees, she wouldn't be able to walk for days.

Trace took a sip of his beer, eyeing me. He really needed to stop with the whole staring thing. It was turning me into a nervous wreck.

"Get any homework done?" he asked, deciding that was a safe topic.

"No." I rolled my eyes. Pointing at Avery, I added, "This one dragged me away before I could accomplish anything."

"What can I say?" Avery flipped her hair over her shoulder. "That's what best friends are for."

"Failing grades?" I turned to look at her with a raised brow.

She rolled her eyes and turned her attention to Luca, who only seemed to grunt in reply to anything she said.

Trace shook his head and chuckled. "You two are complete opposites."

"I know," I laughed, "but I love her." I poked Avery's side, and she glared at me before resuming her conversation.

"I know what you mean." Trace chuckled. "Sometimes I wonder why I'm friends with this weirdo." He slapped Luca on the back.

Luca chuckled, "It's 'cause I make things interesting."

Oh, my God, he spoke more than two words!

"That's for sure." Trace laughed. "Your stories about California are the best."

Luca took a drink of his beer, gazing out into the restaurant. I guessed he had used up his word quota for the day.

"Luca was a professional surfer in California," Trace explained, since Luca had turned into a mute once more.

"Why'd you quit?" Avery asked.

Luca huffed a sigh, leveling Trace with his eerie pale-blue eyes. Reluctantly, he removed his fedora and pushed his shaggy, light-brown hair off his forehead showing us a jagged white scar that marred at least an inch of his forehead and disappeared into his hair.

Avery's eyes widened and her mouth formed a perfect O. "What happened?"

Luca glared at Trace and then met Avery's eyes. "Surfing accident, the scar's about six inches long. I lost a lot of blood and almost lost my life. After that, I didn't have the passion for the sport anymore, so I quit." He pulled his hair down to hide the scar once more and replaced his hat.

"Wow," Avery gasped.

I wondered if she was saying wow about his surfing accident, or at the fact that he spoke a whole freakin' paragraph.

The waitress came with our food, but Avery was too busy staring at Luca to notice.

I rolled my eyes, choosing to ignore them.

I tried to eat my dinner as quickly as possible. I wanted to go. I felt so incredibly awkward, more awkward than I normally felt. I was able to talk to Trace easily now, but something about having extra company there scared me. I was afraid I'd say something to Trace, Avery would overhear me, and proceed to tell me that I should talk about something else.

I really needed to stop being so insecure.

Trace's eyes twinkled and his lips quirked with barely contained laughter.

"What?" I asked, automatically reaching up to touch my face.

Oh, shit.

I had BBQ sauce all over my mouth. I pulled my hand away, staring at the stickiness now covering my fingers.

I bit down on my lip, trying not to cry. This was so *embarrassing!*

"Here." Trace tossed one of the wet wipes at me.

That only made me want to cry more. I felt like a child.

I was really beginning to hate that I was so shy. Avery would have brushed this off as if it was nothing. But I couldn't do that.

I ripped the packet open and hastily wiped my mouth and fingers clean, vowing to *never-ever-not-in-a-million-years* eat BBQ wings again. Nope. Never.

"Hey ..." Trace leaned across the table. "It's okay."

No, it most certainly was *not* okay. I was about to cry in front of a room full of strangers ... and Trace.

I nodded, avoiding his scrutiny. I stared at the basket of chicken. I'd only eaten two of them, but suddenly, I wasn't hungry. In fact, I was pretty sure I would never be hungry again.

I pushed my basket away and covered them with a napkin.

Trace watched my movements, not missing anything, before doing the same and motioning the waitress over.

She scurried quickly to the table. "Is there something I can get you?" She looked down at the food we'd barely touched. "Did you not like the food?"

"We're not very hungry," Trace explained with a grin. Pulling his wallet out of his pocket, he handed her money. "This should cover our meals" —he pointed to himself and me— "and a tip for you."

"All right." She accepted the money. "If you didn't enjoy your meal I can speak to my manager and—"

Trace held up a hand to stop her. She tucked a piece of blonde hair that had fallen out of her ponytail behind her ear.

"That's not necessary," he told her.

"Okay," she said softly, skittering away, but glancing back over her shoulder at Trace.

"Did you drive?" he asked me.

"No." I shook my head. "Avery brought me."

"Good." He grinned, tapping Luca on the shoulder. "We're gonna head out. Get Avery to take you home."

Avery grinned like the cat that ate the canary. "Don't expect me back tonight," she informed me.

I rolled my eyes. Avery was cocky enough to be a guy. There was no one else on the planet like her.

Trace stood and shrugged his lean shoulders into his leather jacket. I raked my eyes over him—I'd been too nervous earlier to see what he was wearing. Surprise, surprise, he wore a purple plaid shirt.

"Come on." He reached for my hand and led me outside.

I noticed that there was an area for people to eat outside but it was currently closed for the winter months.

Trace led me to a black car that definitely wasn't the one he'd been driving.

"New car?" I asked, as he used a push button to unlock it. *Definitely a new car.*

"Yeah. I've had it a few months. I don't like to drive the other one much."

"Hmmm," I mused, sliding inside, and then rubbing my hands along the black leather seats. *How did he afford this?* "What kind of car is this?" I asked.

"Dodge Charger," he answered, backing out.

I grew quiet as he drove down the road and turned left at the stoplight, driving past the CVS and Payless, before turning sharply into the Dairy Queen parking lot.

My body slammed into the door. "Oomph," I groaned.

Trace chuckled.

"You really like slamming me against your car door," I groaned, rubbing my shoulder.

Trace waggled his eyebrows and put the car in park. "What can I say? Slamming you into things has a certain kind of appeal." He looked me up and down.

I gulped, my eyes widening like a cornered rabbit as I grappled for the door handle.

Trace chuckled. "I was just kidding ... unless you're into that kind of thing." He winked.

Oh, my God! He needed to stop it before I did something stupid, like tell him he could slam me against anything he wanted.

My cheeks flamed at my thoughts. Apparently, after a year, Avery's ways were finally rubbing off on me. She'd be so proud.

Trace continued to chuckle as he got out of the car. I climbed out, and followed him into Dairy Queen, my legs shaking like limp noodles. All Trace had to do was suggest something remotely sexual and my body immediately responded. As Avery liked to say, he was the kind of guy that could make you have an orgasm just by talking.

I covered my cheeks with my hands, willing the heat in them to leave. Maybe Avery could give me a lesson in *not* blushing. In all the time I had known her, she had never blushed, while I seemed unable to turn it off.

"What do you want?" he asked, motioning for me to order.

"Oh," I mumbled, stepping up to the counter, scrutinizing the menu. "Um, I'll have the double fudge cookie dough blizzard," I mumbled and stepped back. I didn't see how I could go wrong with that.

Trace ordered a pineapple sundae and we stood off to the side and waited.

Once we were handed our ice cream, we took a seat on the other side, away from the commotion of the counter.

The seats were old fashioned with blue and red shiny cushions. A mural of various ice creams and candies decorated one wall, while the opposite wall was made entirely of windows.

We sat down at one of the tables next to the windows. It was dark outside, but it seemed brighter with the light from inside the Dairy Queen and the various shops across the street.

"Pineapple?" I raised a brow as Trace took a bite.

"I like pineapple, therefore pineapple *and* ice cream are a winning combination. I can also delude myself into believing it was semi healthy when I feel guilty later."

I laughed. "You sound like you have a vagina."

He snorted. "I don't, but feel free to check it out if you want."

"I'm good." I looked away, taking a bite of my ice cream. "So, you don't eat a lot of sweets?" I asked.

He frowned. "I *try* not to, but Skittles are my guilty pleasure."

I laughed, remembering the bowl of Skittles on his coffee table.

"I try to eat healthy, not like most guys living on their own," he explained. "My mom made sure that my brother and I could cook."

"Those stuffed shells you made were delicious." I licked my lips free of ice cream.

He grinned. "I knew my stuffed shells would impress you."

I rolled my eyes, silently scolding my cheeks for flaming at his words. "How do you manage to make everything sound dirty?"

He smirked cockily. "What can I say? It's a gift."

"That's some gift." I laughed.

"Not everyone can be this talented." He winked and then swirled his tongue around the spoon, licking away every drop of ice cream.

I think my ovaries may have exploded.

Heat rushed through my body, and I knew not even the ice cream I was currently eating could smother it.

Damn Trace Wentworth.

He finished his sundae and waited patiently for me to finish mine.

"I'm sorry about earlier. I didn't mean to embarrass you." He leaned back in the chair.

Ugh, couldn't he have just kept quiet about that?

Men.

I waved my hand in dismissal.

"I really am," he added.

"Can we just not talk about it?" I pleaded.

"Sure." He shrugged, clasping his fingers together. "Whatever you want."

"Thanks," I mumbled, staring down at the ice cream like it was the most interesting thing I had ever seen.

"You get embarrassed easily, don't you?" he questioned.

I sighed, looking up to meet his eyes. "Yeah. I like to believe it's a byproduct of being raised by my dad and not just me ... being me."

"*Everyone* gets embarrassed now and then," he replied.

"Even you?" I looked at him in disbelief.

"Even me." He chuckled. "Just not as much as I used to when I was an awkward tween," he winked.

I doubted Trace had *ever* been awkward or as easily embarrassed as I was. It seemed impossible. He was always calm, cool, and collected.

I finished my ice cream and Trace drove me back to the dorms.

"Well," he said, grinning and looking over at me, "goodnight."

Goodnight." I smiled back, opening the car door.

I was closing the door when he exclaimed, "Oh, Olivia!"

"Yeah?" I opened the door wide and leaned my head inside.

The panty-dropper smile graced his lips, causing a fire to erupt inside me. "I hope you dream of me."

My heart skipped a beat, and he chuckled, having caused the desired effect.

"And I hope we're doing all kinds of naughty things," he added and then began to laugh at my bug-eyed reaction.

"I hate you," I hissed

"Hate is such a passionate word, Olivia." He reached up to push his dark hair out of his eyes, causing my mouth to water. *I* wanted to be the one pushing that hair out of his eyes.

I eased my head back out of the car, but before I closed the door, I hissed, "And I hope *you* dream of me *passionately* shoving my foot up your cocky ass."

I slammed the door closed but it did nothing to hide his booming laughter.

I stomped up to my dorm room cursing his name, because I knew now that I would certainly dream of all the naughty things I wanted to do with him.

CHAPTER NINE

I kicked at random pebbles as I strode up to Pete's Garage. I had no idea if we were doing any of the things on my list today. All Trace had said was, "We'll hang out for a while and see what happens."

That sounded ominous to me.

Any number of things could happen.

We could play Yahtzee or end up egging someone's house or—

I really needed to stop thinking before my thoughts moved on to dangerous ideas.

I stepped into the garage, and Trace looked over at me, a smile lighting his face.

He waved me over and then motioned for me to sit on a stack of tires.

"It may not be the most comfortable thing ever, but it's better than sitting on the floor." He shrugged, pointing to the concrete floor riddled with stains from leaky cars.

"True." I smiled. "So, what are we doing?"

Trace waggled a grease-covered finger at me. "I'm not telling."

"Shocker," I deadpanned, causing him to laugh.

He grinned and pointed at the car on the lift. "I'll be done in no time."

"All right." I sighed, kicking my feet against the stack of tires. "How come no one ever seems to be here but you and Luca?"

"I prefer to work late. The other guys are usually gone by four o' clock."

"Huh," I commented, cupping my face in my hands and leaning forward, watching as Trace expertly began rotating the tires.

When it came to cars, everything seemed to be as easy as breathing to him.

He lifted one of the tires off, and I wouldn't have been a female if I wasn't affected by the way his muscles flexed and rippled, glistening with sweat.

Even dirty, covered in grease and sweat, Trace was the sexiest man I had ever laid my eyes on.

I looked over at his car, the older one, parked outside the garage, and a question popped into my mind.

"Trace?" I voiced.

"Yeah?" he asked, looking over at me, those green eyes rendering me speechless for a moment.

Shaking my head, I asked, "Your car ... I'm no expert, but isn't that a classic?"

"Yeah, it is." He grinned, lighting up. Trace truly loved cars, had a passion for them, a passion that a lot of people didn't have for anything. "My dad and I fixed it up together. It was a hobby of his, restoring old cars. It's where I got the knack for it. He gave it to me for my eighteenth birthday. Best day of my life." He stared off into the distance, remembering something. "My dad was a mechanic too. Some might say it's not a glamorous job" —he spread his arms wide, encompassing the garage— "but it's rewarding to fix something. I especially love restoring cars, like we did with that one." He flicked his head toward his car. "There's something so satisfying in taking this broken piece of metal and turning it into something beautiful."

I looked down at the ground. "Is that why you want to help me? Are you just wanting to fix me and make me beautiful again?"

Suddenly, he was in front of me, his boots blocking the ground I was staring a hole in.

With a finger under my chin, he lifted my face up to his. "Olivia, you're already beautiful, and you're definitely not broken. Lost? Yes. But not broken."

"What's the difference?" I asked.

"A broken person wouldn't have this spark of life that you have," he spoke fiercely. "You're just lost, like so many others, trying to find your way in this world. Trying to find who you are."

"Who am I, Trace?"

He grinned. "That's what we're going to find out."

He stepped away, going back to work on the old Subaru.

"You were talking in the past tense," I noted.

"Huh?" He looked over his shoulder at me, his brows knitting together.

"About your dad. You said he *was* a mechanic."

"Oh, right," Trace mumbled, taking a deep breath, and bracing a hand against the side of the car. "He died four years ago. Motorcycle accident. Truck didn't see him." His eyes were dark. "I used to have a motorcycle," he mused, "but after that, I haven't been able to go near one."

I felt the pain and the sadness that accompanied what Trace was telling me. Obviously, he had been close to his dad, and the loss was still hard on him. I wanted to hug him, just wrap my arms around him and tell him that everything would be okay, but I wasn't sure if he would be okay with me doing that. So, instead I stayed where I was, sitting on the stack of old tires.

"I'm sorry," I murmured. "I can tell you were close with him."

"He was my best friend." Trace smiled sadly. "He was the greatest dad anyone could ever ask for, and he was taken away too soon. I was angry for a long time." He sighed, and I was surprised that he was talking so openly about this. From his stance, and the way his eyes had darkened, I knew this was a difficult topic for him. "I didn't like being that angry. It made me hurt the people I was closest to, the ones that mattered the most."

"How did you stop being angry?" I questioned, wondering if I could ever get rid of the anger bottled up inside me that was caused by my dad.

He pondered my question for a moment. "The hate I felt was eating me alive. I didn't like the person I was becoming. I didn't like being someone my mom and grandparents were disgusted by. I decided that I wasn't going to be that guy anymore. My dad didn't raise me to act like that. He raised me to be a good man and I was spitting on his memory. In order to cope with my dad's death, I lashed out at those closest to me. I did some horrible things, Olivia. Things I'm ashamed of." He shook his head, his eyes far away in another time and place. "I realized that I needed to be the man I was before, the man my father knew and respected, in order to *truly* heal. I decided that I couldn't let my pain consume me anymore. My dad wouldn't have wanted that for me. So, here I am" —he pointed to his chest— "being me."

I smiled. "Well, I like who you are."

"Good." He grinned, grabbing one of his many tools. "And, in case you were wondering, I like who you are too," he said with a wink

My heart soared as Trace turned back to the car.

I hated that I was so pathetic that only a few kind words from him sent my heart racing.

"Done," Trace announced a few minutes later, lowering the car.

I hopped off the tires and made my way outside, leaning against the building as I waited for him.

He parked the car he'd been working on outside, closed the garage door, then I followed him upstairs to his apartment.

Since I felt more comfortable this time, I studied the place as Trace showered.

It was surprisingly clean and tidy for a guy. There wasn't anything sitting out that could be considered clutter ... unless you counted the bowl of Skittles.

The apartment had an industrial feel with high ceilings and exposed beams and pipes. The back wall and the wall across from the couch were painted an ocean blue-gray color, while the other two walls and kitchen area were painted beige.

I made my way over to the window, the wood floors creaking under my steps.

I expected to look out and see a junkyard of old cars out back, but I was pleasantly surprised to see woods and even a small creek. I was sure that during the summer when the leaves were green it was breathtaking.

Turning around, I took in a round metal column that separated the kitchen from the living room.

The apartment was nice. Homey, even. It was the last thing you'd expect from a twenty-two-year-old guy.

I started over to the couch, my feet sinking into a plush rug, as I waited for Trace to get ready for ... whatever it was we'd be doing.

The door to the bathroom opened and steam billowed out,

followed by Trace with only a small gray towel wrapped around his waist.

Oh, sweet baby Jesus.

I watched as a droplet of water trickled down his chest, into the dips and curves of his abs, and finally disappeared into the towel.

My eyes roamed over his tattoos and my tongue flicked out to moisten my dry lips.

Trace chuckled and I blushed, turning away, embarrassed that he caught me staring. I wished I could be bold all the time, like when I showed him my belly button piercing, but those moments were few and far between.

His bedroom door clicked closed and I breathed out a sigh of relief.

The door opened again and my heart stuttered in my chest. He came out in a clean pair of jeans, a white V-neck tee that showed off his tanned collarbone with the edge of the tattoo over his heart peeking out, and shrugged into a red and blue plaid shirt.

He ran his long fingers through his damp hair, trying to dry it. He fixed the collar of his shirt and nodded at the door.

I stood, following him outside and around back where his newer car was parked.

We were both quiet as he drove, getting on the Interstate, and heading north.

Trace got off at the exit that led to Target and a strip mall. But instead of turning right to head toward that area, he went left.

We passed a Denny's on our right and a Sheetz on the left. Neither of which gave me a clue as to where we were going.

I glanced over at Trace, who was staring straight ahead at the road, a smirk lifting his lips.

I kept quiet, wiping my sweaty palms on my jeans as we turned and headed into a part of town I'd never been to before.

He pulled into the packed parking lot of a restaurant called Backseat Bar and Grill.

"We're here," he announced, as if I hadn't figured that out already. The question was *why* were we here? The mischievous grin Trace wore told me that we weren't here to eat.

I trailed along behind him, trying not to reach up and slap that smirk right off his face.

He held the door open for me and I stepped inside, my eyes greeted by red and white old-fashioned tiles and booths.

"This way." Trace nodded to the other side of the restaurant where the bar was.

My eyes lit upon a sign. I read the words carefully. Once. Twice. Three times.

"HELL NO!" I backed away, but somehow Trace had moved so he was no longer in front of me. Instead, he was behind me, and I bumped into his chest, his hands gripping my upper arms.

"Don't even think about running away, Olivia," he whispered in my ear. "I will chase your ass down and drag you back in here."

"But ... but—"

"You're getting up there, and you're singing," he responded.

I took a deep breath. I really had to stop freaking out every time we did something on my list.

The problem was, I was *scared* to do those things, which was why I had wanted to do them in the first place. Maybe that was strange, but I was sick of being sheltered.

My dad wasn't holding me back anymore.

I was.

Straightening my shirt, I steeled myself for what I was about to do.

"I've got this," I muttered, striding forward, past the leering guys sitting at the bar.

I felt rather than saw Trace's grin at my words.

Finding an empty table, I slid into the booth. Trace slid in across from me, still grinning widely. Did he *ever* stop smiling?

I glanced over my shoulder at the area where the karaoke was set up and gulped down the lump in my throat.

"It'll be fine," Trace crooned.

"You're not the one that's going to have to sing in front a bunch of strangers!" I hissed.

"That's true," he chuckled, leaning back in the booth as a waitress appeared.

Her dark hair was pulled back in a messy bun and her pen was poised against a notepad.

"Can I get you anything to eat or drink? Do you need some more time to look at the menu?" she asked.

I looked down at the red and white menu, that had been on the table when we sat down, with a picture of a girl from the '60s and a classic red convertible. I hated to inform her, but I hadn't even cracked open the menu.

"Sweet tea," I answered, "and I'm not very hungry." I picked up the menu and handed it to her.

Actually, I was hungry. But if I was going to sing, it had to be on an empty stomach or I'd end up throwing up on the floor in front of everybody.

"A chocolate milkshake. That's all," Trace replied.

"I'll be back with that, and if either of you change your mind and want something to eat, let me know." She smiled before heading for the kitchen.

"Ready?" Trace asked, nodding to the karaoke setup.

"No!" I shrieked, practically jumping out of my skin. "Give me a few minutes to talk myself into this!" Nervous beads of sweat were forming on my forehead; I reached up, wiping them off with the back of my hand.

He narrowed his eyes. "Are you talking yourself *into* it or *out* of it?" He leaned forward as he asked the question, the booth squeaking.

"In! I'm talking myself *into* doing it!" I squawked.

"Sure you are." His eyes narrowed further and dammit if that didn't make some part of me want to show him that I wasn't scared.

I slapped my hand on the table and stood up.

Trace grinned and leaned back. "Challenge accepted?"

"You betcha'." I pointed a finger at him.

I strode over to the karaoke station, my nerves beginning to catch up with me, but I pushed them down.

I could do this.

I sang at home all the time—even my dad had praised my voice and tried to talk me into joining the choir at his church. That was one thing I refused to do to please him. I was too shy, and he wouldn't have taken kindly to me throwing up on his patrons. The only non-family member who had heard me sing was Avery. Which happened by accident when she walked into our dorm early and I was singing. But even Avery had complimented my voice.

I took the microphone from the man working the machine and told him the song I wanted to sing.

"You sure, darlin'?" he questioned me in a thick Southern accent, something even more Southern than Virginia.

"Positive." I gripped the microphone tightly in my hand, my knuckles turning white.

I swallowed down the bile in my throat as the first notes of the song filled the air while everyone in the restaurant turned to see who was singing.

I closed my eyes but promptly opened them, locking my gaze

on Trace's. If I looked into his eyes and at no one else, I could do this.

He smiled encouragingly as the song reached the part where I was to start singing.

I sang the opening lines of LeAnn Rimes' "I Need You", and everyone grew silent. My voice was shaky at first but quickly grew stronger as I blocked everyone out and focused solely on Trace.

Trace's jaw dropped open and his eyes widened at the sound of my voice.

My mom always told me that I had a soft but powerful voice. Whatever that meant. I just liked to sing ... as long as no one else was listening.

But right now, *everyone* was listening. The patrons, the bartender, the waitresses, even one of the cooks.

But most importantly, Trace was listening to me sing, and I didn't feel sick.

I felt ... happy.

My eyes never wavered from his as I sang, like he was holding me up and giving me the power to do this, and maybe he was.

I still wasn't able to explain what drew me to Trace and what made me trust him.

There was just ... something about him.

The song ended and the place erupted into applause, causing my heart to soar. I smiled, bowing to the crowd gathered.

I had done it.

I sang in front of people. Real. Live. Breathing. People. That weren't family or Avery.

"Sing again!" someone hollered out.

I blushed.

I wasn't sure I could do that again.

But then, Trace was stepping in front of me, "Sing with me," he pleaded, and I found myself nodding in agreement.

Trace named off a song to the guy, but I was back to freaking out, so I didn't hear what it was.

I was about to sing a duet with Trace Wentworth. If I thought my stomach was in knots before, this was ten—no, a hundred—times worse.

The lyrics came up on the screen.

Oh, God.

We were going to sing "Just a Kiss" by Lady Antebellum.

I began singing first, and instead of looking at the crowd gathered in the restaurant, I found myself facing Trace. It got to the first part he was supposed to sing, and holy cow! The man could sing!

Was there anything that he couldn't do?

He stared into my eyes as he sang every word, and surprisingly, I didn't blush. But I did swoon.

We joined in, singing the chorus together, and our voices blended together like the song was meant for us to sing.

Every time Trace sang the word *kiss*, my heart soared.

We leaned toward each other, smiling as we sang each word. His green eyes sparkled with pleasure.

I had never felt happier than I did in that moment.

I sang each word with every ounce of passion I had in my body, portraying through lyrics what I couldn't say, and I knew Trace was doing the same. He picked this song for a reason.

When the last note came to a close, Trace and I were oblivious to everyone else; we only had eyes for each other.

A grin lit his face and he cupped my cheek with one hand. My chest rose and fell with labored breaths.

"I knew you could do it, Olivia," he whispered, his thumb grazing over my bottom lip.

"You did?" I asked breathlessly.

"Okay, maybe not." He chuckled, leaning his forehead against mine.

I laughed too. "You mean you thought I might suck?"

"Well, yeah." He shrugged, his hand still cupping my cheek, and his impossibly green eyes seared me to the spot. "I don't expect you to be perfect at everything, Olivia. I mean ..." He grinned. "You definitely were horrible at painting."

I poked his side.

"Ow!" He feigned pain, because I definitely hadn't poked him that hard. Still grinning, since he never seemed to stop, he said, "You were amazing, honestly."

"So were you," I replied. "I didn't know you could sing."

Trace opened his mouth to say something when a throat clearing over his shoulder interrupted our bubble.

"Uh, if you two are done, there are other people that would like to sing," the man running the karaoke machine told us.

I blushed and was sure Trace felt the heat infusing my cheeks where his palm rested against one.

"Sorry, sir." Trace chuckled, taking my hand, and leading me back to our table.

My sweet tea sat in its glass, and I slurped at it greedily. Singing always made me impossibly thirsty.

Trace picked up his chocolate shake, stirring in the whipped cream. I saw that he'd already drank about half of the massive thing.

"I didn't know you could sing," I repeated.

"Oh." He waved a hand. "I don't."

"I beg to differ." I eyed him. "Your voice is amazing."

He rolled his eyes. "It's average, there's a big difference."

I snorted. "If you think your voice is average I'd love to know what you think is extraordinary."

He snapped his fingers together. "Steven Tyler has an extraordinary voice," he reasoned. "Aerosmith is one of the greatest bands ever."

"Says the man who was dancing to a song talking about blowing the roof off the place." I shook my head.

"Hey, variety is the spice of life." His eyes sparkled. "I can't help it that I enjoy different styles of music. Old rock and techno happen to be my favorites." He grinned and took a sip of his shake.

"You're nuts," I muttered.

"Sanity is overrated." He winked, flashing me his cocky grin. "So" —he licked his lips— "think I can convince you to sing another song?"

"No." I shook my head. "I'm done ... for now," I added.

"As long as I get to hear your voice again. It's beautiful." His lips wrapped around the straw. I had no idea how Trace made the simplest of things seem sexy.

"Uhmm," I muttered in agreement, finishing off my sweet tea.

Trace placed his empty shake glass at the end of the table.

He pulled his wallet out and left enough money to cover everything.

"Ready to get out of here?" he asked.

"Yeah." I smiled, sliding out of the booth.

As we made our way to the door, more than one person stopped to tell me that I had a beautiful voice.

One older man stopped Trace and said, "She's a keeper, lad. A forever girl, that one." He pointed at me. "Don't let her get away like I did." He nodded before slapping Trace across the back and waddling away. We didn't have a chance to explain that we weren't a couple.

I burst into laughter when we finally made it outside. "A forever girl?" I giggled.

Trace stuffed his hands in his pockets, brows knitted together, suddenly serious. I wasn't used to serious Trace.

"But you *are* a forever girl," he murmured, halting his steps.

I stopped too, waiting for him. "What does that even mean?"

He looked up, tilting his head to study me. "You're not the kind of girl that guys fool around with, Olivia. You're the kind of girl that when a guy finds her, he'll do everything he can to keep her."

My breath hitched.

Trace strode by me, straight for his car, leaving me standing there reeling.

His jaw was tense and his eyes were serious when I finally managed to get in the car.

He drove me straight to the university.

"My car—"

"Don't worry, I'll make sure it's here in the morning," he replied before I could even finish my sentence.

Okay, then.

I went to get out of the car but Trace's hand closed around my arm.

"Wait," he pleaded, so I did.

He didn't say anything for a moment, just studied my face, almost as if he was searching for something.

"Take a walk with me," he murmured.

"It's cold," I whined.

He unbuckled his seatbelt, and reached into the backseat, handing me a sweatshirt. "Wear this," he commanded.

I slipped on the sweatshirt, wondering what was going on in his head. Trace was rarely so serious.

I followed along beside him as we walked on the sidewalk.

He stopped when we reached the pavilion.

It was one of my favorite places on campus. It was beautiful with its copper top and the water surrounding it. Peaceful. Avery thought it was weird, but I often read out there and even did my homework on occasion. I liked being outside. Something about the outdoors always made me feel at home. I loved the smell of the freshly-mowed grass and the lilies in the spring. Even on days like this when it was cold and blustery, I still found a reason to enjoy being outside.

Trace leaned against the railing, separating the pavilion from the water.

I stared at the fountain in the middle of the manmade pond, waiting for Trace to say something.

Even though it was late, students were still milling around campus, but the pavilion was empty except for the two of us.

Trace clasped his hands together and his jaw was rigid. He turned his head toward me, and I studied his handsome face like it was the last time I'd see him, which I was sure it was. I was convinced that he was about to tell me that he couldn't help me with my list anymore and that he never wanted to see me again.

He looked so sad and serious, I knew nothing good could come from whatever he wanted to say.

"I enjoyed singing with you tonight," he murmured, standing to his full height so he towered over me.

"I enjoyed singing with you too," I stuttered, looking at the ground, waiting for him to shatter my heart.

He stepped forward, so his boots were in my line of vision, butted right up against my Converse.

"Olivia," he murmured, and I shivered at the way he said my name, his voice a husky whisper.

Slowly, I looked up, and my eyes connected with his.

Every time Trace looked at me like this, I was convinced he was seeing straight through me, right to my very soul, and uncovering all of my hidden secrets.

"There's something I've wanted to do ever since I met you," his voice grew softer, but every word was like a shout to me as he lowered his head and his mouth came closer to mine.

"What?" I asked, like an idiot, just before his lips pressed against mine.

A fire erupted inside me, a fire only Trace created, and I found myself wrapping my arms around his neck, reaching up on my tiptoes to kiss him thoroughly.

His lips were soft, a direct contrast to the stubble on his cheeks rasping against my sensitive skin, and I was tempted to beg him to never stop kissing me. It felt so good.

I knew that this is what kisses were supposed to be like.

Magical.

I pressed my body firmly against his. Even through the thick sweatshirt I was wearing, I felt the hard ridges of his body, and I trembled.

His tongue skated against my bottom lip and my mouth opened in response.

One of his hands cupped the back of my neck while the other ventured over my shoulder, down my arm, and over my back, before settling at my waist and pressing me firmly against him.

Holy Hell.

I gasped against his mouth and he groaned in response.

My body moved against his like it was programmed to respond to everything he did to me.

He lightly nipped my bottom lip, and I cried out in surprise.

That seemed to shock him, and his hands dropped from my body, his lips leaving mine.

I suddenly felt very cold.

My fingers touched my lips, finding them to be surprisingly tender.

Then again, I had never been kissed like that, so maybe they were supposed to be sore.

Trace's eyes had darkened with lust, but he looked tormented; his jaw was clenched once more and his hands were fisted at his sides.

"I'm sorry, I shouldn't have done that," he groaned. "I'm sorry," he repeated, before turning around and walking away, as fast as humanly possible.

What. The. Hell?

I had just been given the most amazing kiss of my life, of *anyone's* life, and he was apologizing and walking away?

Had I done something wrong?

Was I a bad kisser?

A million thoughts tumbled through my mind as I began to cry, standing there, willing him to come back and tell me this was a joke.

But it wasn't.

Trace had kissed me, and now he was gone.

CHAPTER TEN

I wiped my tears away as hastily as they fell. I had never been so hurt or humiliated in my entire life. I felt like Trace had ripped my heart right out of my chest and stomped on it.

How could he do that to me?

I spotted his car, still parked in front of my dorm, but he wasn't in it.

The sight of his car caused even more tears.

I walked up the steps, heading for my dorm room, blinded by my tears.

I opened the door and was greeted with a cheery, "How did it go?" from Avery, and then, "Oh, my God! Are you crying? What did he do to you? Do I need to chase his ass down and cut his dick off then force feed it to him?"

Not even Avery's sick sense of humor could get me to crack a smile.

"Olivia," she whispered softly as the door clicked closed.

I couldn't see her through my blurry eyes.

I felt her arms wrap around me in a tight hug as she pulled me over to my bed.

"I'm sorry, Livie," she whispered, cradling me against her like a mom would with her small child. I must have looked *really* pathetic.

I sniffled, taking deep breaths.

"What happened?" she asked, running her fingers through my long hair.

I sniffled in response, and she rubbed my back.

"Shhh," she whispered, "it's okay. Cry. You can tell me later, because you *will* tell me." She continued rubbing my back. "I need to know if I have to castrate him," she muttered the last part under her breath.

When I composed myself to the point where I could talk, I told her about the kiss and Trace running away from me.

Avery giggled. Giggled! She plucked at the sweatshirt I was wearing. *Trace's sweatshirt.* "I told you a sweatshirt was like wearing a chastity belt. It scares guys off every time."

"It's his sweatshirt," I whined, yanking it off as quickly as I could, making sure to wipe my snotty nose on it so that if I ever had the guts to return it, it would be covered in nastiness. It would serve him right for what he did. *What's a little snot compared to a broken heart?*

"Sorry." Avery smoothed her fingers through my hair again. "I was trying to make you laugh."

"I know," I mumbled. "But I don't really feel like laughing right now."

"Fair enough." She shrugged, wrapping her arm around me again. I leaned my head on her shoulder and she rested hers atop mine.

Avery was a lot of things, but there was no best friend as great as her, I was sure of that.

"I still think you should let me hunt him down and cut his

balls off. Serves him right for doing that," she muttered, wiping tears from my cheeks. I couldn't seem to stop crying, no matter how hard I tried.

I knew it was silly.

It was *one* kiss and it wasn't like Trace and I were dating. We were ... friends, I guess.

But it seemed that in the past month, I'd started falling for him, and when he kissed me it felt ... perfect.

Obviously, it didn't seem perfect to him.

I started crying again, harder, and Avery got up and returned with a box of tissues.

"Thank you." I forced a smile a few minutes later for Avery's benefit.

The tears seemed to be over for now.

"No problem. That's what best friends are for." She hugged me, before hopping off of my bed and climbing into hers. "Get a shower and go to sleep. You'll feel a lot better in the morning."

"I'm afraid I'll *never* feel better," I mumbled.

Avery frowned. "You will," she promised.

I stood, gathering my pajamas and bath products.

A knock at our dorm door sent the items falling to the ground with a loud bang.

Avery sat up. "What the fuck?"

"I'll get it." I waved for her to lie back down.

I opened the door, expecting to see the R.A., coming to investigate all the crying.

But no.

I didn't have normal people luck.

I had Olivia Owens luck.

And it wasn't the R.A.'s pale brown eyes that I was looking at it.

It was emerald ones.

I opened my mouth to say I don't know what, but Trace didn't give me a chance.

His hands closed around my arms like steel bands as he stepped inside the dorm, pushing me against the empty expanse of wall beside the door. His mouth descended on mine, his lips moving against mine like they were dancing.

The rational part of my mind told me to slap, kick, or bite him.

But I couldn't react; all I could do was feel.

And God, did I feel *everything*.

My hands roamed across his chest, they couldn't go any further since he held my arms prisoner, and my lips responded to every movement of his.

"Oh, my God!" Avery shrieked. "You look like you're about to make babies with your tongues!"

Her words were like a bucket of ice water being poured over me.

I hastily turned my face away so Trace's lips connected with my cheek.

He groaned as he let me go.

"You have about ten seconds to explain yourself before I dredge up my long-buried karate skills and kick your ass," Avery fumed from behind Trace. I peeked over his shoulder to see Avery standing there, hands on her hips, and her hair flaming around her shoulders.

Trace groaned, and I resisted the urge to kick him for leaving me, making me cry, and then storming into my dorm room like a maniac and kissing me senseless.

He pulled away, and I would have fallen if it weren't for the wall holding me up.

Ignoring Avery, he said to me, "I'm sorry, Olivia."

Those words were like a slap.

He'd said the same thing when he kissed me the first time.

Was I *really* that bad?

"No! No!" he exclaimed at my pained expression.

"Tracey, you better hurry up and explain what that sorry is about." Avery tapped her foot against the floor, giving him the evil eye.

He licked his lips and looked from Avery to me.

"Can we talk in private?" he pleaded with me.

"No," Avery answered him, but his eyes never wavered from mine.

"Avery," I pleaded.

"Fine!" She threw her hands in the air. "But I will be right outside that door," she told me. "And if *you*" —she thrust a finger roughly into Trace's chest— "try *anything*, I will come in here and forcibly remove your balls from your body then stuff them down your throat," she seethed, storming outside, and slamming the door closed.

"Whoa." Trace looked from the closed door to me. "I take it you told her?"

I crossed my arms protectively over my chest and nodded.

He rubbed his jaw, nodding.

"I really am sorry," he whispered.

"I know," I snapped, looking at the ground. "You've said that a bunch of times now. I'm sorry you kissed me too, now get out."

Score 1 for Olivia.

His face fell. "That's not what I meant."

I ground my teeth together.

I steeled my shoulders, the words tumbling out of my mouth before I could stop them. "Kissing me, apologizing, and then running away kind of speaks for itself, Trace."

"I'm sorry—"

"Stop saying that!" I shrieked, stomping my foot in the process.

I hadn't been this mad or hurt in all my twenty years of life.

"Olivia—" His hand came up to cup my cheek and I flinched.

My body felt hot and cold all at the same time, and I hated him for it.

How dare he do what he did then come into my dorm room and *kiss* me *again*! And then my traitorous body had to go and *enjoy* it!

"I want you to leave," I spoke softly, the fight draining out of my body. I felt exhausted.

"*Please*," he begged, "let me explain. I thought you kicked Avery out so I—"

"I asked her to leave so you didn't lose your man parts, I was doing you a favor, now get—"

His lips crashed against mine and I was pushed against the wall once more.

I pushed against his chest but it did no good, he was too heavy.

When he didn't appear to have any intentions of stopping anytime soon, I bit down on his lip.

"Ow!" He pulled away. "I guess I deserved that, but it was the only way I could think to shut you up so I could talk to you."

"You can't really talk when your lips are otherwise occupied!" I snapped.

"Everything okay in there?" The door opened a crack and Avery stuck her head in.

"It's *great*," I replied sarcastically.

"Watch yourself," Avery warned Trace. "You hurt my best friend and I'll hurt you."

"Believe me, I know," Trace sighed. "I can see my chances of fatherhood dwindling away by the second." He looked between Avery and me.

"I've got my ..." she paused "ear on you," Avery pointed from her ear to the door. With one last warning glare at Trace she closed the door.

"Can I *please* explain myself *now* without you trying to kick me out?" he asked.

I crossed my arms protectively over my chest and skated around him, making sure I didn't brush against him.

I sat on my bed and advised, "You can talk, as long as you stay far away, over there." I motioned to the wall across from my bed, which really wasn't *that* far away in the small dorm room.

"Deal." He moved back two steps and I breathed a sigh of relief. "I should've known this was your side," he commented, nodding at my bed.

I guessed it wasn't that hard to figure out which side was mine. My side was neatly organized while Avery's side of the room was an explosion of junk. Makeup, clothes, and textbooks, everything spilled forth onto her bed, floor, and desk.

While I kept everything carefully hidden, and while my side was far from bland, it wasn't like Avery's side.

My bedspread was yellow, my favorite color, with a white flowery design on it. On the wall, I had hung framed glass words for a bit of decoration. *Love. Laugh. Dream.* I looked at the words every day, wishing I had more of all three in my life.

My side was simple, but I liked it.

Simple wasn't a word in Avery's vocabulary though.

Her bedspread was pink and orange cheetah print and the wall on her side of the room was covered in a huge poster of the rapper Drake.

The poster kind of freaked me out; it always looked like he was watching you, but Avery refused to remove it no matter how much I pleaded.

Above her bed, Avery had put peel and stick letters, spelling out her name.

I shook my head, looking across my bed at the very tall man currently standing in my room, studying me like I was the most interesting thing he'd ever laid eyes on.

"You can talk, but if you say you're sorry again, I'll let Avery have at you." I narrowed my eyes.

He chuckled, but I was being serious.

When I didn't crack a smile, he sobered.

"I shouldn't have done that," he whispered.

"Kissed me? I know, you said that already," I muttered, drawing my knees up to my chest, willing him to leave and end this torture. I felt like I was dying on the inside.

He flinched. "I'm-" He swallowed. "That's not what I meant. I mean...I shouldn't have walked away. It was wrong."

"You snuck into my dorm to tell me *that*?"

"No." He shook his head, rubbing his jaw. "I snuck into your dorm to kiss you again and apologize for leaving you there." His lips threatened to turn up in that cocky grin.

"That makes no sense whatsoever!" I cried.

His eyes darkened as he looked at the door.

Good, leave.

His lips had narrowed into a thin line when he turned back to face me. "I'm saying this all wrong." His eyes pleaded with me to believe him.

I opened my mouth to interject some smartass comment, but he continued.

"What I said earlier is true, Olivia. You're a forever girl and fuck if I don't want you to be *my* forever girl. But I don't deserve you. But I had to kiss you, I had to know what your lips tasted like, and one taste isn't enough. I never want to stop kissing you." I swallowed thickly at his words. I hadn't seen him move, but he was now on my bed. "When I kissed you ..." he paused. "*No* kiss has ever felt like that before but I know you deserve better than me."

I leaned up on my knees, cupping his face in my hands, forcing him to meet my eyes.

My anger had melted out of my body at his words and the

expression on his face. He looked so sad. His brows were drawn and a frown marred his perfect lips.

"Why don't let you *me* decide who's good enough for me?" I asked.

He swallowed, his Adam's apple bobbing. "What if you decide I'm not good enough?"

"What if I know you *are*?" I countered.

His tongue flicked out, wetting his lips. He swallowed again, his eyes bright with hope.

"I wish I hadn't left you standing there," he whispered.

"You shouldn't have," I replied, "but you did and if you promise to never do it again, I might be able to forgive you." My eyes studied his face, waiting for any sign that he was going to run away again.

"I'll never leave you standing anywhere alone, again," he vowed.

"That's all I ask," and this time I was the one who initiated the kiss.

A slow simmer started low in my belly, quickly reaching a boiling point.

I don't know how it happened—whether I moved on my own or he moved me—but I was straddling his lap, my fingers tangling into the short hairs at the nape of his neck.

"Olivia," he gasped against my lips, and my body shivered at the sound of my name and the huskiness in his voice.

"Please, don't stop," I begged.

"Never," he responded, deepening the kiss. His tongue rubbed against the sensitive skin just behind my teeth and I moaned.

The door to my dorm room burst open. "*Really?*" Avery shrieked. "Olivia! I didn't know you had this side to you!" Despite the exclamation, she sounded proud.

I eased off of Trace's lap, blushing profusely, not just at being caught, but also at my behavior.

Trace grinned at me and dammit if my cheeks didn't turn redder.

"It's time for you to leave." Avery pointed at Trace. "And if you so much as try anything as stupid as you did tonight with her, you better sleep with your eyes open, Tracey-poo, 'cause I will hunt your ass down. No one can hide from Avery Lyn Callahan for long!" she declared.

Trace stood and turned to me. "Tracey-poo?" he mouthed.

I shrugged.

"Come on." Avery ushered him to the door. "You can kiss her senseless another day."

"Avery!" I exclaimed.

"What?" she replied.

I shook my head.

"Bye." Trace grinned.

"Bye." I nodded, waving. I was afraid if I got up and walked him out, I'd end up pressed against another wall. But, then again, maybe that wasn't such a bad thing.

Avery closed the door and let out a deep breath. "What the fuck was that?"

"I don't know," I answered honestly.

"In all the time I've known you, I've never seen you act like that," she motioned to where I sat on my bed, hair mussed and lips swollen. "Trace turns you into a raging ball of hormones."

"Says the girl with a dick," I muttered.

She grinned. "That's true."

"Seriously, though" —she sat down on the end of my bed— "did he explain what happened outside?"

I told her what he said and she sat there, chewing on her bottom lip. "Huh. Interesting."

She scurried over to her own bed and I asked, "What are you thinking?"

"Guys are just so weird," she said with a frown, "and confusing. Nothing they do makes sense."

"Do you think he meant what he said?" I rolled over on my stomach, propping my chin on my hand.

"Words are one thing, Olivia. Anyone can say anything, at any time. It's actions that matter, not words," she warned, leveling me with her green eyes.

I pursed my lips.

"Just ... don't get too attached," she whispered. "Attachments cause broken hearts."

I hated to tell her, but it was too late for that.

CHAPTER ELEVEN

Trace and I sat outside on one of the various benches dotting the campus grounds. It overlooked the pond and a cool wind swarmed around us. I bundled my jacket tighter against me, and Trace slung his arm across my shoulders, pulling me against his warmth.

I burrowed my cold face against his neck.

"Should we go inside? I don't want you to get sick." His lips brushed against my forehead.

A week had passed since the incident at the pavilion. Neither of us had mentioned it, all that needed to be said had already been spoken, and there was no point dwelling on it.

But like Avery had mentioned, actions spoke louder than words, and I could tell Trace was trying.

He showed up a few days ago, on campus, and I spotted him easily. Trace wasn't hard to miss. He waved me over to his car and we ate lunch together, laughing at random things, and getting to know each other better. When I went to get out of his car, to head to my next class, he handed me a single pink peony. I smiled the rest of the day.

"No, I don't want to go in," I answered his question. "I like being outside."

"Me too," he replied, his lips brushing against the top of my head again.

"I don't want to go home tomorrow," I confessed.

"Stay here." He played with the wavy ends of my hair.

"I can't." I frowned. "Residence halls close tomorrow."

"You can stay at my place," he replied.

I snuggled closer to his warm chest as a blast of wind hit us.

"I don't think we know each other well enough for *that*. Besides, my dad would hunt me down, and drag me home. He's all about *appearances*," I sneered the word.

"When will you be back?" he asked.

"Sunday," I ground out the word.

Because of drive time, I'd only be at my parents' house for four days, but that was four days too long.

"I'm sorry," he whispered, letting my hair fall from his fingers. "I wish you didn't have to go."

"Me too," I replied.

He grew quiet and I listened to the steady beating of his heart against my ear.

"I think when you get back, you should get a tattoo," he murmured, running his finger down my neck.

"Really?" I asked. "So, is that what I'm doing next? I thought you weren't going to tell me what we're crossing off the list."

"Yeah, well ..." He scratched his chin. "A tattoo is forever. I want you think about it while you're on break. I want you to be one hundred percent sure of what you want."

"How many tattoos do you have?" I asked.

He chuckled. "You mean, you don't know?"

I blushed, figuring he was talking about the day I was ogling his bare chest.

"No," I replied, glad he couldn't see me blush. I still hadn't figured out a way to stop blushing.

"Well, I have *Never Regret* on the inner bicep of my left arm. A star on my wrist—" he showed that one to me. Rolling up his jacket and shirtsleeve, he showed me a cluster of overlapping triangles on the inner part of his right forearm. Some of them were colored in while others were blank. One of the triangles even had a watercolor look. They were beautiful. "There's more, but I think I'll let you find those on your own." He grinned, rolling his sleeves down.

If I had been drinking something, it would have spewed out of my mouth at his words. Trace never ceased to shock me. You'd think I'd be used to all kinds of comments living with Avery, but no.

"What do you think I should get?" I asked.

"Whatever you want, it's your body," he replied. "No one else can tell you what to get. It just has to mean something to *you*."

I mulled over his words, wondering exactly what his tattoos meant to him.

CHAPTER TWELVE

I pulled into the driveway of the large white colonial-style home with black shutters.

I should have felt like I was home, since this was where my parents lived, instead I felt like I had arrived at prison.

"Four days, Olivia. Four days. You can do this," I coached myself.

I eased out of my car, as slowly as humanly possible, and stretched after the ten-hour drive. I had stopped a few times, but I wasn't used to being in the car for a long time, and it had taken its toll on my body.

Normal parents would have probably run out to greet their child that they hadn't seen since August.

Not mine.

No, my mom had probably slaved away over the *perfect* dinner and was cleaning up from that, while my dad sat in his leather chair, reading the paper for the second time today.

With a sigh, I grabbed my suitcase and glumly made my way to the front door.

I knocked on the door since I didn't have a key.

I heard the telltale slapping of my dad's slippers against the hardwood floors and I flinched. I had hoped my mom would get the door.

"Olivia," he said my name like it was the dirtiest word in the dictionary. "You're late. Based on the time when you called, and where you were at, you should've been here ten minutes ago." He looked at his watch. His black wire-framed glasses were perched on his nose, his gray hair was longer than the last time I saw it, and his beard thicker.

I closed my eyes. "Sorry, traffic—"

"That's no excuse, you should have called to tell us you were running late," he snapped, while I still stood outside.

"I know." I resisted the urge to roll my eyes. "I apologize."

He stepped inside. "Stop standing outside. Your mom saved you a plate of dinner. It's in the microwave. I expect you to eat it all and clean your plate after."

"Sure thing," I mumbled. My dad still treated me like I was an incompetent toddler. He even treated my mom the same way.

"What was that, Olivia?" he questioned and I felt his dark eyes searing a hole into my back.

He'd never wanted a child, he told me that all the time growing up, but he *needed* one for *appearances*. Other than that, I was a hindrance.

"Yes, sir," I managed to sound semi-polite, even though I wanted to chuck my suitcase at his bowling-ball-sized head.

I left my suitcase by the stairs, praying he wouldn't yell at me for that.

I waited, but he said nothing and, eventually, I heard the clacking of his slippers as he walked into the family room.

Taking a shaky breath, I stepped hesitantly into the large kitchen.

My mom was hunched over the large farmhouse sink, scrubbing away at pots, pans, and dishes by hand. We had a dishwasher but my dad wouldn't let her use it. He claimed that they never got the dishes clean enough.

My mom looked up, sweeping a lock of dark hair from her face, forcing a smile.

She had aged so much in a short amount of time; the toll of my father was heavy on her shoulders.

Her once bright smile was all but extinct and her shiny chestnut hair was dull and lifeless. Even her eyes, the eyes she gave me, were the same way, their copper color gone.

I hated looking at my mom knowing what my dad had done to her. I didn't know what to do to help her. As a child, I begged her to leave him, but she was scared. I knew that's why most people stayed in abusive relationships. Fear was crippling.

"How's school, Liv?" she whispered my nickname. My dad hated for me to be called anything but Olivia.

"It's great." I sighed, reaching into the sudsy water to help her clean.

"You don't need to help me." She scrubbed at a dish that looked pristine to me "Eat something. I'm sure you're hungry." She nodded toward the microwave.

"I'm fine, let me help you," I pleaded.

She didn't reply, and I took that as my cue to continue cleaning.

I helped her dry off the dishes and put them away.

"I better get in there with your dad," she said when the last dish was put away, her voice was barely above a whisper.

I nodded. He'd come looking for her soon. After she finished cleaning the dishes he expected her to sit in the family room with him.

I warmed up my dinner and the smell of homemade food elicited a growl from my stomach.

I sat down at the dining room table with my plate.

The table was so clean that I was pretty sure those CSI guys wouldn't be able to find a fingerprint on it.

I ate my dinner slowly, because if my dad thought I had eaten too fast, I'd be scolded for that.

He was always looking for things to complain about.

A piece of lint.

A pea in his carrots.

You name it and he'd find a way to whine about it.

I made sure to eat every morsel on my plate, which wasn't hard, because it was delicious, like everything my mom made. But I'm sure my dad didn't bother to tell her it was good; he never did. He only told her what she did wrong, not what she did right, and the same with me.

He couldn't be pleased, simple as that.

I cleaned, and dried my plate, stacking it in the cabinet. Although, I was tempted to put it in the dishwasher just for spite, but since I was afraid of his reaction, I didn't.

I stepped into the family room, my hands clasped behind my back.

My mom didn't look up from whatever it was she was knitting, which was normal. She was expected to be a meek submissive wife.

My dad flicked the newspaper down, eyeing me.

I knew I wasn't allowed to speak first, so I waited for him to address me.

"Yes?" he finally spoke, his voice booming.

"I finished my dinner and cleaned my plate. I'd like to be excused for bed," I said, staring him right in the eyes.

He flicked a hand, and just like that, I was dismissed.

I walked slowly until I was out of his line of vision, and grabbed my suitcase, carrying it upstairs.

I closed my bedroom door for a moment of peace. The only time I was allowed to have my door closed was when I was changing.

I checked my phone and there was a text from Trace.

Hope u got home safe. If it gets bad come home. I'll let you sleep in my bed. I promise to sleep on the couch like a good boy. ;)

I smiled. Something I rarely did when I was stuck behind these walls.

I'm here. Getting ready for bed. Miss u.

Miss u 2. Think about that tattoo and I'll think about mine.

Ur getting another 1?

U can never have 2 many tattoos.;)

I had to agree with that. I loved Trace's tattoos.

Night, Olivia. And seriously, my place is yours if you need it. He texted a few seconds after his previous message.

Night. I'll keep that in mind. :)

I could tell he was worried about me being there, even though it was only for a few days. When I left early that morning, I was shocked to find him outside my dorm, leaning next to my car. He kissed me over and over again, like with each kiss he was trying to convince me to stay. It almost worked, but fear got the better of me. I didn't want my dad driving all the way to Virginia and tracking me down.

I turned my phone off since my dad frowned upon texting and tossed it onto my bed. It got lost in the sea of frilly white and pink blankets. My room hadn't changed since I was five.

The walls were a pale pink, teddy bears cluttered a corner, and white curtains kept anyone from peering into the large windows.

This room should feel like an oasis, but I was more comfortable in my dorm room. At least it reflected *me*. This room was who my father wanted to pretend I was.

I grabbed my pajamas from my suitcase and walked across the hall to shower.

I wasn't in there long, because my dad would have ended up banging on the door, yelling about all the water I was wasting. But by the time I got out, they were both in bed.

"Olivia!" my dad called out before I could tiptoe across the hall to my room.

"Yeah?" I replied, cursing everything I could think of.

"Leave your door open," he warned.

I rolled my eyes since he couldn't see me. "I know," I muttered.

I made sure to leave the door wide open, not cracked, and climbed into bed.

But I couldn't sleep. I never could when I was there. I don't know what I was waiting for, but it was something.

MY DAD HAD the Kirkpatrick family, who were members of his church, over for Thanksgiving dinner.

"Sit there and look pretty," my dad had told me before they showed up.

It was no surprise when Kevin Kirkpatrick sat down beside me. He was a year older than me, and my dad had planned our wedding and named our children by the time I was four and he was five.

I had news for my daddy-o: I would rather stab myself in the eye than marry Kevin. All he talked about was himself. If I had to hear one more time about how he did this ... or that ... I was going to scream bloody murder.

Finally, for my sanity's sake, I tuned him out, and pretended to listen, inserting a nod here and there. Kevin didn't even notice that I wasn't paying attention. Pretentious jerk.

I ate my dinner slowly as my dad played the part of the perfect husband and father. Telling those gathered how well I was doing in college. He didn't even know what I was studying to be.

Kevin's hand brushed against mine and I scooted a teensy bit farther away.

I didn't want him touching me.

There was only one man I wanted to touch me, in any way, and he was ten hours away.

Kevin tapped my shoulder. "You're not listening to a thing I say, are you?"

"Of course I am." I pretended to be hurt that he thought I was ignoring him. "You were talking about how you play tennis."

And just like that he started talking again. He was so egotistical that I almost felt sorry for him.

I zoned out again, ignoring not only Kevin, but everyone around me. I wanted this to be over. Not only today but the whole weekend. I was desperate to get back home.

I was probably the only college student who thought of her school as home, but that's what it was. Once I graduated, I had no plans to move back to New Hampshire.

Kevin's arm brushed against mine, and he was lucky I was a nice person and didn't stab him with my fork.

I heard my dad mention something about dessert and I breathed a sigh of relief. This Hell on Earth was almost over.

I helped my mom clear away the plates, thankful for the respite from Kevin, and helped her carry out the various pies.

I swear, she must have made one of each.

French silk. Apple. Cherry. Pumpkin.

They were all there.

I waited until everyone else had gotten theirs before snagging a giant piece of homemade French silk pie.

It was so delicious that I wanted to moan in ecstasy, but my dad would kill me if I started making sex noises at the table.

"Thank you for the lovely meal, Nora," Kevin's mom, Linda, said. "I'm sure it took you hours."

"It was no bother," my dad replied, because apparently his name was Nora now.

Linda sported a tight-lipped smile as she looked between my dad and mom. "Yes, well, thank you as well for inviting us, Aaron."

He nodded. "You and your family are welcome here anytime." He lifted his wine glass in salute.

He wouldn't let my mom drink wine, the controlling bastard.

"Are you enjoying school?" Linda asked me with a bright smile. I had always liked her, but right now, I was irritated with her son and therefore her. I wanted her, Kevin, and her husband to leave so I could wash the dishes and hide in my bedroom until tomorrow morning.

"It's great," I answered, sipping at my glass of water, because my dad didn't let us drink soda or my favorite, sweet tea. I had never had sweet tea until I moved to Virginia for school, but after trying it, it had become my favorite drink.

"That's good to hear." She wiped her mouth free of pie crumbs.

She was the same age as my mom, but she looked ten years younger. Her light blonde hair glowed and her blue eyes were bright. A few wrinkles crinkled the corners of her mouth and eyes, but they weren't that noticeable.

"What was it your dad said you're studying?" Linda asked.

I scooted a little bit farther away from Kevin, whose leg had just brushed mine, before answering her. "He didn't," I mumbled low enough that no one heard. "I'm studying to be an English teacher."

"Oh, isn't that ... nice." She smiled.

I wanted to growl. It was like everyone looked down at you when you said you wanted to be a teacher. I guess it all came back to that saying; those who can, do. Those who can't, teach.

"What grade are you thinking about teaching?" she asked.

"High school, I haven't decided on what year yet, though." I shrugged.

"I told Olivia that she should follow in her old man's footsteps." My dad chuckled.

I snorted and he glared at me. I'd pay for that later.

"Teaching is a very rewarding and respectable career," I countered. "I'll be teaching people, just like you do, father." I smiled cheerfully at him, even though cheerful was the last thing I felt.

"No, not like I do, Olivia." He narrowed his dark brown eyes at me, peering at me above the rim of his glasses. "I teach people about the meaning of faith and God. You'll be teaching people useless information that won't help them to reach heaven come judgment day."

Somebody stab me in the eye. My father was one of the most ungodly men to ever walk the planet. Who was he to preach? I wanted to tell him we'd see where he went come judgment day. I'd bet money it wasn't to heaven.

"Yes, well," I muttered with a shrug. I knew I better stop talking before I got myself in trouble ... Well, into more trouble than I was already in.

"Kevin's studying to be an architect," Linda's husband, William, informed me.

"I think he mentioned that already," I replied, my sarcasm falling on deaf ears.

Thirty minutes later, the Kirkpatricks left, and I wanted to dance for joy.

"Olivia," my dad's voice boomed as he came into the kitchen. My shoulders tensed as I leaned over the sink, my fingers raw from scrubbing. "Your behavior tonight was unacceptable, a downright embarrassment."

I swallowed thickly, shoving my hair out of my face.

"What exactly did I say that was unacceptable, sir?" I steeled my shoulders.

My mom had stiffened beside me, but she went on scrubbing, like nothing was happening.

"You completely ignored poor Kevin; the boy's infatuated with you, Olivia. The least you could do is carry on a conversation and see where it goes," he reasoned.

My hands clenched into fists beneath the water—thank God I wasn't holding a knife, or I would've sliced my hand open.

"We were talking," I argued. "Kevin was telling me all about his time at school and his volunteer work. It was *fascinating*," I snapped.

His eyes widened. "Don't sass me," he barked and I flinched.

I held my breath so I didn't cry.

"When you're under my roof," he roared, pointing to the ceiling, "you are to act a certain way! I knew letting you go off to college that far away was a bad idea! You should have stayed here where I could've supervised you! God only knows what kind of trouble you've gotten yourself into. You're a disgrace, Olivia. This is why I wanted a son," he ranted. "A son would never disappoint his father this way! But a daughter," he growled, striding over to me, and grabbing my hair. I yelped, tears burning my eyes. "A daughter is nothing but trouble."

He had never grabbed me like this before; he preferred to hurt me with words.

"Let me go, please, let me go," I begged.

He did, giving me a shove so that I went sprawling onto the floor.

He stomped out of the kitchen, his steps echoing through the house.

Air crawled through my chest, escaping in strangled gasps. I wrapped my arms around my legs, holding myself together.

My mom sank to the ground beside me, wrapping me in her arms, and gently rocking me back and forth. Her fingers smoothed through my hair.

She didn't say anything and I didn't, either.

There was nothing we *could* say.

But we still sat, united, both victims of a man we should trust.

I PULLED into the parking lot of my dorm and a weight lifted off my shoulders. I was finally home and I could *breathe*.

I felt like I had been holding my breath the entire time I had been away.

I carried my suitcase up to my dorm and found Avery sitting on the bed.

She immediately hopped up, hugging me. "I missed you, Livie."

"I missed you too," I replied, letting go of my suitcase. "Did you have a good Thanksgiving?" I asked, stepping out of her embrace.

"My parents weren't home." She shrugged like it was no big deal. "And my brothers didn't bother to come home, either."

"You mean you were alone in that big house the whole break?" I unzipped my suitcase and started putting things away.

"Well ..." She laughed. "I wasn't really alone."

"Luca?" I questioned, turning around to face her.

She smiled, completely enamored. "I don't know what it is about him, Livie. He makes me feel ..." she trailed off. "I can't explain it."

"That's nice." I forced a smile, even though I wasn't quite sold on Luca. He reminded me of a barbarian. A hot barbarian, but still.

"I think I'm really falling for him," she murmured wistfully.

I made a strangled noise in the back of my throat as I choked on my own saliva.

"Really?" I asked with a high voice.

"Yeah." She ran her fingers nervously through her hair. "You don't know him like I do. He doesn't talk much when he's around other people, but he's really started to open up to me, and I ..." She blushed. Avery *never* blushed.

"Are you falling for him, or have you already fallen?" I raised a brow.

She swallowed, biting her lip. "I don't know. What about you and Trace?"

I took a deep breath. "I don't know, either. It seems like it's impossible to fall for someone so quickly, someone you barely know." I shrugged.

"I know what you mean," she breathed. "This whole love thing is so confusing," Avery pouted.

"And I have a feeling it never gets less confusing," I mumbled, putting the last of my things away.

"Jesus Christ! Don't do that!" I exclaimed as I stepped outside my dorm and found Trace leaning against the building. "I think I almost peed my pants."

He chuckled and his voice rumbled, "We can pick up some Depends on our way to the tattoo shop."

"Tattoo?" Avery asked from behind me. I had completely forgotten she was there. "Are you getting a tattoo, Livie?"

"Um, yeah," I mumbled, stepping back, looking from her to

Trace. I knew I had probably paled at least ten shades and I felt sick to my stomach.

"Can I come?" she asked, looking between Trace and me. "I've been wanting to get one but I haven't had the chance to go. I mean, feel free to say no. I don't want to be intruding—" she rambled.

"It's fine with me." Trace looked at me, making sure I was okay with that.

"It's not a problem," I assured her.

"Great," she beamed. "I was supposed to meet Luca, but let me call and tell him there's been a change of plans." She grinned, walking off, with her phone glued to her ear.

"So ..." Trace grinned crookedly. "Have you thought about want you want to get?"

"Live," I answered. I honestly hadn't thought about my tattoo at all while I was at home, but as the word left my lips I knew it was perfect.

"Live," he murmured. "That's perfect for you."

I smiled.

Avery walked up to us, her phone tucked back in her purse. "Can you give me a ride?" she asked Trace. "Luca will meet us there, then he'll drive me back here after we have dinner."

"That's not a problem," Trace replied.

"Thank you!" Avery clapped her hands together. Entwining one of her arms through mine, she exclaimed, "We're getting tattoos, Livie!"

Avery climbed into the backseat of the old Camaro while I sat up front with Trace.

He drove into old town Winchester, parking in front of the tattoo shop. He'd held my hand the whole way. Trace could tell I was nervous. Heck, the way I kept chewing on my fingernails *anyone* could see that I was nervous.

He inserted change into the parking meter and motioned Avery and me to follow him inside.

As soon as the bell above the door chimed, a guy covered in tattoos looked up, grinning. "Hey, Trace, I knew you'd be back soon." He called into the back, "Brian! Trace is here!"

Trace turned to me, explaining in a hushed tone, "This is Justin. I went to high school with him and Brian."

"Yeah," Justin piped in, rubbing a hand over his buzzed cut scalp. "We used to get into all kinds of trouble back in the day."

"It wasn't *that* long ago." Trace chuckled. "Stop trying to make me sound old."

"Longer than you think." The guy I assumed was Brian entered the room. He had dark wavy brown hair and tattoos covered both of his arms. "What can we do for you today?" he asked. "Ladies?"

"Hmm," Trace mused, "why are we here again? I forgot."

"Always a smartass, this one." Justin pointed to Trace but he was looking at me. "Watch yourself with him."

"I think I can handle him," I spoke up, causing Justin to laugh.

The door opened behind us and Luca stepped inside. The guys greeted Luca before leading us to the back.

"How're we going to do this?" Justin asked, eyeing all of us.

"We'll take a room and they'll take another," Trace replied, gripping my hand. Justin's eyes narrowed on our clasped hands before he grinned. "I'm sure you will. Brian, think you can handle those two?" Justin nodded at Avery and Luca.

Brian chuckled. "I can handle anything." He flipped a light on in a room and motioned them inside. Justin led Trace and me to the next room.

Shrugging out of his leather jacket, Trace asked, "Do you want me to go first?"

"No." I shook my head. "I'm afraid if I watch you, I'll chicken out."

"Fair enough." He grinned, sitting down in a vacant chair.

"Do you know what you want?" Justin asked.

"Yeah," I replied, figuring he was expecting me to say I wanted a butterfly or something like that. "I want the word, live, here," I pointed to the outside part of my left forearm.

"Pick your font." He pointed to a poster.

I made a face. I hated all of them.

Justin chuckled at my expression.

"Can I get my friend to write it down?" I asked. I had heard of people getting tattoos in a person's handwriting and I knew Avery's handwriting was nicer than any of these fonts.

"Sure." He shrugged. "I'll be right back." He grabbed a pen and paper, leaving Trace and me alone.

"The fonts are kind of sucky," he commented.

Justin returned in no time, holding up the piece of paper for my inspection. "Perfect," I replied, and he went to work transferring the word onto another type of paper.

"What are you getting?" I asked Trace.

"Wouldn't you like to know?" He chuckled.

"I told you what I was getting!" I cried.

"You're just going to have to wait and see." He smiled. "Patience."

"Ready?" Justin asked suddenly.

I sat back in the chair. "Yep." I held out my arm for him to place the word on my skin.

"Is this where you want it?" he asked, before pressing it in.

I looked in the mirror and instructed him to move it a little bit. "Perfect," I told him.

"What color ink do you want?" he asked, putting on gloves.

"Black," I answered.

I took a deep breath as he got everything ready.

"Ready?" he asked again, holding the tattoo gun in one hand and sliding a stool over.

I took a deep breath, closing my eyes, and felt Trace's hand grip mine.

"Look at me," Trace commanded, "it'll be over before you know it."

I nodded at Justin to start and then locked my eyes on Trace. He distracted me by talking about random things, and at one point, he started kissing me, which Justin scolded us for, because I started wiggling.

"Done," Justin announced, laying the gun down on a table. "Want to see?"

"Of course," I replied giddily. I stood up and he closed the door, revealing a floor-length mirror. I held my arm up and couldn't help the goofy smile that formed on my face. "It's perfect. Thank you."

The tattoo was small and simple, but I loved it. It was perfect for me and the meaning behind it was what mattered. All I was doing, was trying to live my life, and this tattoo would remind me of that every day.

live

I knew that I couldn't have picked anything more important to put on my body.

When I finished looking at it, Justin rubbed some kind of ointment over it then taped a bandage around it, going over the rules for keeping it clean.

He finished and I turned around to see Trace removing his standard plaid shirt and then yanking off his white t-shirt by hooking his thumbs into the back collar.

His back muscles rippled and flexed, causing my heart to stutter.

Unlike the last time I saw him shirtless, I forced myself not to get distracted.

I noticed that there was a fleur de lis tattoo between his shoulders. Low enough that it didn't peek out of his shirts, and small, maybe only three inches. There was also some kind of script on top of his shoulder but I couldn't read what it said from where I stood.

"What are you getting today?" Justin asked, disinfecting the equipment.

"A four-leaf clover," Trace answered, taking a seat.

I stepped closer to him, leaning down, to peer at the tattoo over his heart.

The words, 'To live in the hearts you leave behind is not to die,' formed the shape of a heart with the initials, T.W., inside.

"For your dad?" I asked shakily.

"Yeah," he replied, studying my face.

"And what does this one say?" I pointed to the tattoo in small script on top of his shoulder.

"Inhale the future, exhale the past," he answered.

"Hmm," I murmured.

"What are you thinking?" He raised a dark brow.

"I honestly don't know," I whispered, my eyes roaming over the tattoos and his chest.

"Is this good?" Justin asked. I had completely forgotten he was in the room. Trace appraised the design and nodded. "And where do you want it?"

"Here." Trace pointed to a spot on his right side, below another line of script. I couldn't read that one, either, and something told me not to ask what it said.

Justin pressed the design into Trace's skin and scooted the stool to Trace's side.

Trace grinned up at me from where he sat as the needle roared to life. "Hold my hand? I'm scared." He winked, reaching out for my hand.

I rolled my eyes but placed my hand in his anyway. "I'm sure you're *really* scared," I replied sarcastically.

"Terrified." His lips quirked as he withheld laughter.

"Are you guys dating?" Justin asked, eyes intent upon his work.

"Uh—" I stuttered.

"Yes," Trace replied and my eyes widened.

Justin chuckled. "I think this is the first time I've seen you date a girl since Aubrey."

My whole body stiffened at the sound of another girl's name.

Trace's hand tightened against mine and his jaw clenched. "When you know it's right, it's right."

"Yeah, well" —Justin shrugged, wiping away excess ink— "I still thought no one would ever tie you down again."

Trace made a face of disgust, and turned away from me, but he didn't release my hand.

Justin finished the tattoo and went through the same procedure with Trace as he did with me.

We each paid him, because I demanded that I pay for my own, and headed back to the front.

Avery and Luca were already waiting there for us.

"I wanted to see your tattoo before we left," Avery explained. "Especially since it's in my handwriting." She danced.

I peeled back one side of the wrapping and showed her.

"It came out so pretty!" she exclaimed.

"What did you get?" I asked.

She turned to the side and lifted a tiny bandage behind her ear, showing me an anchor, no more than half an inch big.

"Isn't it cute?" she asked, her green eyes wide like she was afraid I was about to tell her it was horrible.

"Oooh, I love it," I told her.

She smiled in response, putting the bandage back over it. "I'll see you tonight." She smiled, taking Luca's hand, and headed outside.

I waved goodbye to Justin and Brian.

Trace was quiet as we got into the car but I wasn't about to let him stay that way.

"Who's Aubrey?" I asked. I had to know and couldn't keep quiet about it any longer.

Trace sighed and pinched the bridge of his nose. "I was really hoping that you would forget about that," he mumbled.

"I'm a girl, we forget nothing," I retorted. "Now, answer the question."

"She's my ex." He rubbed his jaw.

"Care to elaborate," I snapped.

Trace glanced at me, then back to the road. "We dated in high school," he muttered.

"How long?"

"Do you really need to know all of this?" he asked, staring at me for a moment, with darkened eyes.

"You said we were dating, I think that gives me a right to know who, and what my competition is," I whispered, feeling insecure.

Trace sighed. "We dated for four years before it ended. We grew apart and there was no spark anymore. I'm not sure there was a spark to begin with." He shrugged. "We were young. It's in the past. And just so you know, there is no competition."

"You haven't ... dated anyone since her?" I asked.

"No." His hands tightened on his jaw.

I could tell he was holding back, so I pleaded, "Please, Trace."

He took a deep breath. "We were still together senior year of high school, but when my dad died, the last thing I wanted was a relationship." He wet his lips and continued, "I quit the baseball team and turned to alcohol and random sex to fill the void inside me."

My heart constricted at his words. I was no longer concerned about faceless Aubrey, he was obviously over her, but I felt compelled to know more.

"Did you?" I asked.

"Did I what?" He glanced at me with a furrowed brow before his eyes darted back to the road.

"Did you fill the void?" I questioned.

He looked at me significantly, sending a shiver of pleasure down my spine. I didn't understand how Trace could affect me so much with just a look and a few words. "Not with that, but I think maybe I've finally found something to fill it."

"And what would that be?" My breath escaped from between my lips with a tiny sigh.

"You," he answered.

I swallowed, waiting for him to crack a joke or flash me his signature cocky grin, but he didn't.

He was serious, and I was flabbergasted.

"Me?" I squeaked, causing him to chuckle.

"That's what I said." Now he was grinning, but his eyes were still serious.

"Stop looking at me, you're going to crash the car!" I exclaimed, needing a reprieve from the intensity of his stare.

He laughed. "I'm not going to crash."

Maybe not, but he was certainly going to give me a heart attack.

He pulled into the campus parking lot and before I could talk myself out of it, I asked, "Do you ... want to ... uh ... come up to my dorm ... I mean—" I stuttered.

He silenced me with a kiss.

"Is that a yes?" I asked.

"That was definitely a yes." He winked. My eyes widened, hoping I hadn't given him the wrong impression. "And no, Olivia, I don't expect anything, so stop looking at me like that."

"Sorry." I blushed, and got out of his car as quickly as possible, walking briskly to the dorm entrance.

"Don't be sorry." He caught up to me easily and his arm wrapped around my waist.

He followed me up to my room and I stopped at the door, turning to look up at him, a question arising in my mind. "How did you get in the dorm that night and figure out which room was mine? They keep the main doors locked."

He grinned, the panty-dropping one, and replied, "I have my ways."

"Oh, I'm sure you do," I mumbled, opening up the door, and quickly closing it behind him.

"It's pretty nice in here," he mused, looking around, taking everything in.

"For a dorm, yeah. Avery and I tried to make it homey." I shrugged, kicking my shoes off, and letting me feet sink into the fluffy yellow rug we had purchased to hide the tile floors. "I wish she'd take that down." I nodded to the Drake poster.

Trace chuckled. "It is kind of ... large."

I removed my jacket and hung it on the hook attached to the door. "Make yourself at home." I motioned to the small space. "No need to just stand there."

"Does this mean I can make myself comfortable on your bed?" He raised a dark brow, and his stare caused a fire to roar through my body.

"Anywhere you want." I swallowed and took a step back.

"Anywhere?" He stepped forward so that the distance I had created was affectively cut off.

I nodded as he removed his jacket.

I kept backing up and he kept following until I bumped into the desk next to my bed.

His arms caged around me, locking me in.

I gulped, staring up at him with wide eyes, feeling like a cornered animal.

He leaned down, his lips brushing the sensitive skin below my ear, as he said, "I can see your pulse racing." His hand cupped my neck and my heart skipped a beat in response. "I like that you're affected by me." His hand trailed lazily up and down my neck. I shivered, eyes closing. "I really missed you while you were gone," he whispered huskily, his lips brushing over my cheekbone.

"Y-you d-did?" I stammered.

"Very much," he murmured, cupping my chin and tracing my bottom lip with his thumb. "You're special to me, Olivia."

"I-I am?" My voice faltered.

"Mhmm," he hummed, skimming his nose along my jawline. "I'm going to kiss you now," he whispered.

"O-Okay," I stuttered and then gasped as his lips descended on mine.

My hands fisted in his shirt as I plastered my body against his. I couldn't get close enough to him.

His hands had somehow moved from my face, to rest below my breasts, and they were moving lower. His fingers skimmed over the flare of my hips, and gripped me, lifting me effortlessly so I could wrap my legs around his waist.

He deepened the kiss, his tongue begging for entrance, as his hands glided under the edge of my shirt. The feel of his hands on the bare skin of my stomach made my heart race faster.

He turned, backing me into the bed, and laying me down on top. He maneuvered me, without breaking the kiss, so that my head was cradled on my pillow.

He held himself above me, one hand on each side of my head.

Ten minutes ago, I had been freaking out about him mistaking my intentions for inviting him into my dorm room, and now I was clawing at his shirt, desperate to remove it. If he didn't take it off himself, I'd find a way to rip it off. That was the power my raging hormones had over me.

He rose up, yanking his plaid shirt off and the t-shirt below it, tossing them to the floor.

My hands roamed over his bare chest as my lips sought his once more.

The warmth of his body heated me further. I was sure I was sweating, but I was so absorbed in everything that I was feeling, I didn't even worry about it.

My hands slid up his stomach, exploring his abs, before settling on his chest. His heart beat steadily underneath my right palm, and when I circled one of his nipples with a finger, it skipped a beat.

He hummed in satisfaction, his tongue stroking mine.

I cupped his neck with one hand and the other ventured south once more. Back over the ridges of his abdominal muscles and lower, to the V and the trail of hair that I knew disappeared beneath the waistband of his jeans.

My fingers seemed to have a mind of their own as they yanked at his belt buckle.

Abruptly, he withdrew his lips, and he clasped his hand over mine. He didn't move it right away, just held it.

"No, Olivia," he said sternly, his green eyes nearly black as he looked down at me.

"But—" I could feel his erection pressed against me and I felt like I was ready. I had had sex before, what was the big deal?

He swallowed, looking pained. "In the parking lot you were scared that I'd read into you inviting me up here. You may think you're ready, but you're not, Olivia. When I make love to you, you'll be ready, you'll be begging, and—" he bent to whisper huskily in my ear "—you'll be wet for me." I wanted to tell him that I was sure my panties were soaked now. Raising back up, he murmured, "And I'm *definitely* not having sex with you in your dorm room where everybody can you hear you scream my name." An impish grin lifted his lips. "On second thought, that could prove interesting."

I smacked his shoulder.

"I was kidding," he said with a chuckle. "Unless you're into that sort of thing." He nuzzled my neck, whispering, "When I finally make love to you, you're going to be in my bed, and I'm never letting you leave."

His fingers tangled in my hair and I gasped in pain as he touched the tender part of my scalp where my dad had pulled my hair.

He pulled away, slowly, untangling his fingers from my hair. He tilted his head questioningly, "I know I didn't pull your hair."

"You didn't," I confirmed.

"Then?" he questioned.

"It's sore," I mumbled, turning my head away from him.

"Sore from what?" he hissed.

"My dad yanked me by my hair," I whispered, biting down on my bottom lip.

Trace gripped my chin, forcing me to look at him. "He hurt you," he stated.

I nodded, swallowing thickly.

"Olivia," he pleaded. "Why didn't you tell me?"

"It's my burden to bear," I whispered.

"No, it's not," he growled, sitting up and pulling me on his lap. He gently probed the back of my skull and I winced again. "No one should ever have to endure something like this."

"He's never hurt me physically before—"

Trace put a hand over my mouth, his eyes steely. "*Do not* make excuses for that bastard. He hurt you. I remember what you said about your dad, and I'm sure he hurt you more than just physically while you were home."

I nodded.

Trace closed his eyes and swallowed. "I can't stand the thought of anyone hurting you in any way. I don't even know the man but I want to hunt him down and rip him apart. I want him to hurt worse than he's hurt you."

I burrowed against his warm, still naked chest.

His hands rubbed up and down my back comfortingly. "Does he hurt your mom?"

I pulled back. "Verbally? All the time. Physically? I-I think so. I saw bruises on her arm this time." I bit my lip to hold back tears. "She didn't mean for me to see them but when I was leaving to come back to school, she reached out to hug me and her sleeve slid up. They ... They were in the shape of fingerprints," I swallowed.

Air hissed through his teeth. "Why doesn't she leave?"

"Fear," I replied instantly. "My dad's highly respected in our small town. He'd paint her in a bad light if she left and everyone would believe him. But to be honest with you," I paused and swallowed thickly, "I'm afraid that if she did try to leave him, he'd get angry enough to kill her. His temper is ... volatile."

"I'm so sorry you've had to grow up in a household like that. If I could change it for you, I would." He pressed his forehead against mine, our noses brushing together.

"If I hadn't, I wouldn't be here with you," I whispered, cupping his cheeks, stubble rubbing against my palms. I forced a smile and added, "Even if I was here, we probably still wouldn't have met. Things happen for a reason, Trace, and it's usually so we can find greater things in life. There can't be good without bad and vice versa. I wouldn't wish away my life, because then I wouldn't be here, and I think *here* is a pretty good place."

His soft chuckle shook my body lightly.

"How about I reword that?" he asked rhetorically. "I wish you didn't have to grow up with a dad like that, but I don't regret meeting you. I don't regret anything with you." He lifted one of my hands from his cheek and kissed my palm. "I wish I could take your pain away, but I would never wish *you* away.

"That makes me happy," I murmured.

"All I ever want to do is make you happy." His hands rubbed up and down my back. "I never want to see you frown or cry because of me."

I couldn't help but smile. "I didn't know you could be serious."

He chuckled. "It's rare, but it happens."

I sobered. "I'm sorry for pestering you about Aubrey, I just ... I needed to know."

"I understand."

I didn't want us to dwell on his ex, so I grinned, "You played baseball?" I asked, remembering him mentioning that he had quit after his dad died.

He groaned, banging his head lightly against the wall. "Yeah."

"I bet you looked cute in that uniform." I ran a finger over his collarbone.

He pretended to be angry. "Cute? Baby, I was *hot* in that uniform."

"Hmm," I hummed. "Is that something I might see?"

He smirked. "I might be able to make that happen."

CHAPTER THIRTEEN

"Rise and shine!" Avery chirped, tapping my foot.

Why was I on top of the covers? And why was I lying on something hard and warm?

I rose up, cracking my eyes open, and discovered that Trace was asleep in my bed.

Oh, crap.

Since it was only large enough for one person, I had ended up cradled against his chest. I really hoped I hadn't drooled; that'd be beyond embarrassing.

"Next time," Avery said with a wink, "hang something on the door to warn me."

"Avery!" I shrieked, startling Trace. "We didn't do anything!"

"I know," she cackled. "I just wanted to watch your ears turn red."

Trace sat up, rubbing his eyes, and stretched his arms above his head. The muscles in his chest flexed with the movement.

"Sorry," he yawned. "I didn't mean to fall asleep. Where's my shirt?" He looked around.

"The floor," Avery answered, grinning from ear to ear.

"Right," he drew out the word, smirking. "Someone wanted me to take it off."

My face flamed.

Avery held out a Starbucks coffee cup for each of us. "I don't blame her." She laughed as Trace took the offered cup. "It's a nice chest."

I spit out the coffee I had taken a sip of.

I was going to have to stop drinking liquids around Avery. It was proving dangerous.

She laughed at my reaction. "Just because I'm with Luca doesn't mean I can't look."

"It should," I grumbled, glaring at the droplets of coffee now staining my bed.

"Thanks for the coffee." Trace saluted Avery as he hopped out of my bed and bent to pick up his shirts. He placed the cup on my desk as he pulled them on. He was adorably bedraggled and if Avery wasn't there, I might have begged him to stay. "I'll call you later," he whispered in my ear and then pecked me on the lips. He grabbed the coffee cup and opened the door. "Later, Avery," he called over his shoulder as he eased the door shut, "and thanks for the coffee."

"Not a problem," she hollered after him. Looking back at me with a smirk, she shook her head. "Look at you, Livie. Letting a boy sleep in your bed. I would have went crazy ginger on your ass, but since it was obvious no hanky panky went down, I decided to let it slide." She pulled her desk chair out and sat down.

"I'm sorry, we didn't mean to fall asleep," I mumbled, running my fingers through my tangled hair.

"Really, it's okay," she chirped, spinning in her chair. I didn't know how she managed not to spill her coffee. "I was kind of surprised when I opened the door and found you both curled up like that. It was cute."

"What time did you get in?" I questioned, sipping at my caramel latte.

She grinned. "Late."

"I should've known." I laughed lightly.

"We can't all be a goody two-shoes like you," she mumbled.

I rolled my eyes. "I'm far from that."

"Olivia, if there was a picture next to the word perfection in the dictionary, it would be you." She finished her coffee and tossed it at the trash can, missing.

I gritted my teeth. There was that word again. Perfection. The single thing I had strived to be my whole life and now, I felt angry that Avery was telling me I was perfect.

"There's no such thing as perfect," I muttered quietly, picking at a loose thread on my comforter.

She did another spin in her chair. "I know that. I was only picking on you. Sometimes, you don't know how to take a joke." She wrapped a piece of hair around her finger.

I finished my coffee and stood. "I'm going to take a shower and then I have a lot of work to do, what with finals being this week."

My stomach clenched at my own words. Campus would be closed for a whole month.

A whole month trapped in New Hampshire with my dad. Four days had been too long. Four weeks would kill me. But I had no choice. There was nowhere else for me to go.

Avery pretended to gag. "Ugh, finals." I opened the bathroom door and Avery said, "Hey, before finals are over, and you head home, we should have a girls' day."

I smiled. "Sounds great."

FINALS WERE KICKING MY BUTT.

Then again, I had thought the same thing last year and passed with flying colors.

I walked out of the classroom, breathing a sigh of relief. Finals were done, but tomorrow I had to go home.

My phone rang and I pulled it out of my pocket. "Hey, Avery," I answered.

"Are you almost back to the dorm? It's time for our girls' day," she sing-songed.

"I'm walking back now." I cradled the phone between my ear and shoulder as I adjusted my grip on the books in my arm.

"Drop your stuff off and then meet me at my car," she commanded and hung up before I could reply.

"So bossy," I snapped at the dead line.

I left my books and backpack in the dorm, and while I was there, I pulled my hair back in a ponytail, desperate to get the long strands out of my face.

My phone rang again and I wasn't surprised to see that it was Avery calling.

"I'm coming," I growled into the phone.

"Just checking. I was afraid you might have chickened out on me," she chimed.

"Nope, I'm leaving the dorm right now."

I hung up and speed walked outside before she came after me.

"Took you long enough." Avery laughed when I slid into her red Beetle.

Buckling my seatbelt, I snapped, "You are so impatient. I had to drop off my stuff."

"I've learned that patience never gets me what I want," she chortled.

"What is it, exactly, that you're subjecting me to on this girl's day?" I asked.

"We're getting our nails and toes painted."

"Avery!" I groaned. "You know I hate getting my nails done! The last time I went with you that guy made me bleed!"

"It was one time, Olivia." She shook her head. "I highly doubt he'll cut you again."

"We're going to the *same place?*" I shrieked.

"Well, duh, I always go to the same place." She merged into the right lane as the strip mall came into view. I saw the sign for the nail place from there and squirmed in my seat.

"Honestly, Olivia, you act like I'm sending you in front of the firing squad. This is supposed to be relaxing and I wanted to talk to you. I feel like we're both either studying or out these days. You go back home tomorrow and I won't see you for a whole month."

"You're right." I sighed as she parked in front of the nail salon.

We stepped inside the small salon and the smell of acetone permeated the air.

Avery explained what we wanted done and one of the ladies working there got two of the pedicure chairs ready.

"Pick your color." She pointed to rows upon rows of nail polish.

Avery didn't think twice before picking a shade of red.

I picked out a bright sky-blue.

I took the seat next to Avery and rolled up my jeans. Placing my feet in the warm water, I handed the color I had chosen to the nail tech.

"How are things with Luca? Are you guys … serious?" I glanced over at her. I didn't want to make her uncomfortable by probing. Then again, I didn't think *anything* made Avery uncomfortable.

"We haven't put a label on our relationship but neither of us are seeing other people." She shrugged. "I really like him."

I grinned. "It's about time and it sounds pretty serious to me. Normally, you're like a guy, and the minute the chase is over, you're done."

She sighed. "I am normally like that ..." She smoothed her hands over her jean-clad legs. "Luca is different. Most guys don't *want* to get to know me. They're happy to fuck and leave." She shrugged, not at all concerned that the people around us could hear every word she was saying. "But not Luca. I thought he'd be like all the others, but he wanted to get to know me and, Olivia ... I found myself opening up to him, and that's not something I do."

"I'm happy you've found someone, Avery." I reached for her hand and gave it a light squeeze.

"I am too." She smiled but it didn't reach her eyes.

"What is it?" I asked. "You look worried about something."

"It's just ... How long can it last?" She looked over at me with wide green eyes. I had never seen Avery look so upset before.

"We never know how long anything can last. We have to decide if it's worth the risk," I explained.

She nodded. "He's worth it."

A WEIGHT HAD SETTLED in my chest and it wouldn't go away. I didn't want to go back home. I didn't want to deal with my father, and I didn't want to watch my robot mother.

The summer months I had spent at home had drained me completely, and I knew the next four weeks would take their toll as well.

What was supposed to be a break for students wouldn't be for me. I would spend the whole time on edge, waiting for my dad to blow up.

I zipped my suitcase closed. We had only been back on campus for a week after Thanksgiving break and now I had to leave again. I wished I could hide in my dorm.

"Hey," Avery said softly behind me, "you can come stay at my house. My parents probably won't even be there."

I turned around slowly to face her. Avery knew about the verbal abuse, but I hadn't told her about my dad yanking me by the hair. "Thank you for offering, Avery. Really. You don't know how much it means to me, but I can't impose myself on you like that."

"It's no trouble at all, honestly." She moved her bags closer to the door. Avery's family lived local to the college but she insisted that she stay on campus. When I asked her about it once, she said that she couldn't stand being in that big house by herself. It reminded her of how alone she really was.

"I'll be fine." I took a deep breath.

"Will you?" she asked with a raised brow and tilted her head.

"Yeah, of course," I replied, praying she would drop it.

The truth was, I would have loved to stay with Avery, but since my dad was expecting me home, staying wasn't an option.

"All right," she sighed and hugged me. "Call or text me, anytime."

"I will." I hugged her tighter.

She pulled away and grabbed her bags.

The door clicked closed behind her and I was alone.

I sat down on my bed. Everything was packed and I really needed to get on the road. It would be late when I finally arrived at home but I couldn't make myself leave just yet.

The door opened and I didn't bother to look over. Avery was always forgetting things. "What did you forget this time?" I laughed.

"I didn't forget anything."

"Trace," I gasped and looked up to see him standing in the doorway. "How do you keep getting in here?"

"Avery let me in." He grinned crookedly. "I was afraid you had left already but your car was still here." He came in the rest of the way and closed the door behind him. "I wish I had seen more of you this week, but I knew you were busy with finals."

"Yeah," I sighed.

I knew Trace and I were dating, but I had wanted to leave before I saw him. This was making it even harder to go. I didn't want to say goodbye to him. If we were still together by the time classes ended for the year, I was sure it would kill me to leave him.

"Hey," he breathed, his eyes narrowing as he strode across the room, and pulled me off of my bed and into his arms. "Don't look so sad."

"I don't want to say goodbye to you," my voice cracked.

He pushed me back a little so he could stare into my eyes. "This isn't goodbye, Olivia. This is just ... see you later. Okay? I'm not going anywhere." He swallowed thickly. "I can see in your eyes that you think I'm going to be gone when you come back, but that isn't true. I'll be waiting for you." His lips skimmed over the curve of my ear. "I like spending time with you and" —his lips lightly brushed against mine— "kissing you. I like hearing the small little gasps you make when I touch you in certain places." To prove a point, his fingers glided down my neck, and over the curve of my breast, eliciting a gasp from me. Grinning, he added, "Plus, we still have things to cross off that list of yours." With a husky chuckle, he whispered in my ear, "I'm especially looking forward to the pole dancing."

"I'm sure you are," I gasped, my eyes fluttering closed as he pushed my shirt off my shoulder, and kissed the skin beside my bra strap.

"I really hope this" —he plucked at the strap— "comes off."

He stepped back, grinning boyishly.

I swayed unsteadily and his large hand gripped my waist to keep me from falling.

I expected some cocky remark about his effect on me, but

instead, his lips crashed against mine. I leaned into the kiss, standing on my tiptoes to reach him better. His tongue flicked against my lips, seeking entrance, and I was happy to oblige. He growled low in his throat as one of my hands sought his hair and tugged lightly while I fisted his shirt in the other.

He wrenched his lips from mine, breathing raggedly and panted, "That's me *not* saying goodbye."

Before I could recover, he walked away from me and out the door.

Holy hell, I think liked *not* goodbyes.

CHAPTER FOURTEEN

My mom and dad were asleep when I arrived home. I half expected my dad to still be awake, pacing the halls, waiting for my arrival. I let myself in and went straight up to my room to go to bed, leaving my suitcase in the trunk of my car.

It was morning now, late morning.

Dad never let me sleep in.

I stepped out of my room and looked around, expecting him to come running at me, with a shaking fist, cursing me for sleeping in.

But nothing happened.

I quietly descended the steps, looking for him.

I tiptoed into the family room and saw my mom sitting there, drinking a cup of coffee, and watching a news show.

She never watched TV or drank coffee when *he* was around.

"Dad's gone," I stated.

"Some church thing." She smiled pleasantly and patted the spot next to her on the striped couch. Whenever he was gone, she became a whole new person, more vibrant and alive. "He won't be back until late tonight; we'll probably be asleep. There's some breakfast left over if you'd like some or we could go out and get lunch."

I smiled brightly. My dad would never let us eat out, so on the rare occasions that he was gone, my mom would treat me to lunch out.

"Lunch would be great," I beamed.

"Good." She patted my knee. "And I can't wait to hear all about school without your dad around."

"I'll go shower and get dressed," I stood. "Where do you want to go for lunch?"

We always had to drive out of town so that one of dad's church members didn't see us.

"I'm not sure yet." She sipped her coffee. "We'll think of something while we drive." Her eyes widened and zeroed in on my arm. "Is that a tattoo?"

"Oh." I looked down. "Yeah."

"I like it." She smiled. "But you better not let your father see it. You know how he is."

"Yeah, I know," I grumbled with a dramatic sigh, rubbing my still sleepy eyes.

I went outside and carried my suitcase in before getting ready.

Since I was home, I dressed in a worn pair of jeans and a sweatshirt. Avery would have a conniption if she knew, but I wasn't trying to impress anyone.

"Ready!" I called as I bound down the steps.

She grabbed her keys and I followed her out to the garage.

I slid into the beige leather seat of her Lexus sedan. Even

though it was a few years old, it was in pristine condition and still smelled new.

We were quiet during the ride, enjoying the peace.

"How does that place look?" My mom pointed to a restaurant after driving for almost an hour.

"Looks good to me. I'm not picky." I shrugged.

She glanced at me, a smile curving her lips. "I'm really happy you're home, Olivia. I know you were just here," she said as she swallowed, "and you'd probably rather be at school, but I want you to know that I love when you're home. I hate that we don't get to spend much time together."

I took her hand in answer.

"THIS IS SO YUMMY." I took a bite of a sweet potato fry before slurping on my second glass of sweet tea. I'd added a ton of sugar packets to it. No one up North knew how to make it sweet enough.

"Mhmm," my mom hummed in agreement.

A text message vibrated my pocket and I reached down to read it. It was a message from Trace.

TRACE: Miss u.
Me: I miss u 2
Trace: Oh. I was supposed to send that to someone else.
Me: I hate you.
Trace: ;) U no I like 2 mess with u.

. . .

I READ his text and decided that I wasn't going to write back. Two could play this game. It was time for Trace Wentworth to shake in his boots.

TRACE: Olivia?

THE TEXT CAME a minute after the previous one.

TRACE: I was kidding.
This one came a few seconds later.
Trace: R u ignoring me?
Trace: I guess I deserve it.

THIS TEXT CAME two minutes later. I decided to let him off the hook.

ME: Sweating yet?
Trace: U suck. I thought you were really mad at me.

I COULD PICTURE Trace letting out a sigh of relief.

ME: Nah. I just wanted to get back at u 4 that comment. I have to go though. Having lunch w/my mom.
Trace: Have fun. If I was there, I'd be...well I'll let you imagine what I'd be doing to u right now. ;)

. . .

I GULPED as my mind went rampant, imagining Trace running his hand up and down my thigh, then higher.

I put my phone back into my pocket and looked up at my mom.

"So ..." She eyed me. "Who's the guy?"

Immediately, my cheeks reddened. "What makes you think there's a guy?" I squeaked.

She tilted her head, giving me a don't-play-dumb look. "Girls don't smile like that over nothing, Liv." She pointed at my face with a fry.

I clapped a hand over my mouth.

"Tell me about him. I know he has to be special to have captured your attention."

"You're not going to tell Dad, are you?" I asked shakily.

She narrowed her eyes at me, those same eyes that I saw every day in the mirror. "There are a lot of things I don't tell your father, Liv. Remember that."

"His name is Trace," I supplied.

She smiled, biting into her burger. "And how'd you meet?"

"I ... uh ... got a flat tire." I looked down at my plate. "He stopped to help me."

"That's nice. Is he in college?" she asked, playing with her straw as she waited for my reply.

"He's a mechanic." I bit my lip.

"Is he ... older than you?" she questioned cautiously.

I rolled my eyes. "He's twenty-two."

"Oh," she breathed a sigh of relief. "I can tell you really like him."

"I do," I admitted. "He's great."

She sighed. "I wish I could meet him."

I swallowed. "Why don't you leave dad?" The words tumbled from my mouth. I knew the real reason why she wouldn't leave, but I wanted to hear what she had to say.

She put her burger down and studied me. "How could I leave him, Liv? I have no money of my own. I have nowhere to go or stay. I have *nothing* and he made sure of that," she whispered the last part under her breath. "And honestly, Liv" —tears shone in her eyes— "I'm afraid of him."

I was shocked that she admitted to me that she was afraid of him but I was careful not to let it show.

I reached across the table and took her hand. "I don't like that you have to live like this, Mom."

"It is what it is. He won't change and I can't leave. I'm stuck. It's better if I pretend like I'm happy and everything is okay." She rubbed her eyes. "I shouldn't talk bad about him, he's your father, but ..." she paused. "Once, when you were about five, I had been putting money away. He'd give me money for groceries and I'd keep the change; hide it away, that sort of thing. One day, he found the box I was hiding it in. He got so angry. So angry," she repeated, her voice barely above a whisper. "After that ..."

"You stopped trying to find a way out," I supplied.

She nodded. "It wasn't worth it."

"How-How did you meet Dad?"

A wistful look stole across her face. "In high school. He was a senior and I was a sophomore. He was ... so handsome and charismatic. I could talk to him for hours. He was *nothing* like he is now."

"What changed him?" I picked up a sweet potato fry.

"He changed after we got married," she said. "He turned into a completely different person. I felt like I was living with a stranger. He had fooled me and I was stuck."

"Why didn't you leave then? Why stay and get pregnant with me?" I wasn't sure I wanted my questions answered but I had to know.

Tears glassed her eyes. "It's time you know the truth, Liv." She bit her lip, crumpling the napkin between her fingers.

Panic coursed through my body. "What? What truth? What are you talking about?" I stuttered. What was going on? She was looking at me seriously and the tears were starting to trickle down her cheeks.

I began to sweat, feeling like a bomb was about to be dropped on me. I wanted to run but my feet wouldn't move. I gripped the slick wood table in my hands.

"Early in my marriage with Aaron, I volunteered at the local library. That's when I met Derek." She smiled longingly and I began to shake my head at her words. "He was even more handsome than your father. Dark wavy hair and his smile ... It lit up the room, Liv." Her eyes grew clouded with the distant memory. "All of the ladies that worked at the library were infatuated with him, even the older ladies. He was so charming that he was impossible not to fall for." My need to run was steadily increasing but I still couldn't *move*. "He was at the library almost every day to study. He wanted to be a doctor. I found myself making excuses to go by there, even when I wasn't volunteering." Her smile waned. "One day, we got to talking and ..." She looked down at the table, taking deep breaths. This was hard for her. "I was craving companionship but Aaron was too busy studying to be a preacher. It started out innocently. I just wanted someone to talk to, I needed someone to listen to me." She reached across the table for my hand and I gave it to her. "I fell in love with him. I didn't mean to, but I did." Her eyes pleaded with me to understand. "I was going to leave Aaron for him—" She shook her head back and forth, fighting for composure.

A part of me wished I could go back in time and undo what she was saying. I didn't want to hear this and I had a pretty good idea where this was headed.

"Derek and I were going to move in together and after the divorce was final with Aaron, we'd get married. I saw a lawyer and had the papers ready to give Aaron. I was waiting for the right moment. That's when … That's when I found out I was pregnant, with you."

"Mom," I croaked, "no. Don't say it. Please, don't say it."

"That was also the same day," her voice cracked, "that Derek got into a car accident."

"No, no, stop," I begged. I wanted to cover my ears but I couldn't make my hands move. I was paralyzed.

"He didn't make it and I never got the chance to tell him about you," she sobbed.

"Please, stop," I cried.

I knew I should be happy, and a part of me was, that Aaron Owens wasn't my biological father. But everything I knew was being shattered to pieces by a few words.

"Derek is your dad, Liv, not Aaron." She squeezed my hand. "Aaron knew. There was no way you could be his, and I'm so sorry, because he hated you for it. I tried to leave for *you*. I did, Livie. I tried so hard." Her sobs could be heard through the restaurant. They probably wanted to kick us out. "This is all my fault."

I was shocked. I didn't know what to do or what to say.

I sat there and watched my world crumble around me.

I HADN'T SAID anything as we finished eating. Or *attempted* to finish eating, I should say. Neither of us really had much of an appetite after the shit-storm of lies that made up my life were revealed.

We were almost home when I spoke up, "Is that why Dad—er—Aaron, has treated you so badly? Is it because of me? Because I'm not his?"

"No, sweetie." She reached over and patted my cheek. "He was like that before … that's why I—"

"Cheated?" I supplied angrily.

"Yes," she sighed, gripping the steering wheel, bowing her head. "You have to understand, I didn't do it maliciously. It just ... happened. I love Derek. Or loved, rather." Her eyes pooled with tears as she gazed at the road. "I miss him every day of my life. I miss what we had and what we could've been. I miss him so much, Liv, but he gave me *you*." Her voice was fierce. "He gave me the greatest gift a man can ever give a woman. You're so much like him and you don't even know it. When you smile, it's *his* smile. When you laugh, it's *his* laugh. When I get sad, and miss him, I know it's okay, because there's still a part of him here on this Earth."

"Why did you decide to tell me? Why now?" I questioned.

The air left her lungs in a gust. "When you were little, I thought I'd never tell you, and especially with the way Aaron treated you—us—I thought it was better to keep you in the dark. But a few years ago, I decided to tell you. I didn't know when, I just knew I had to." She swallowed thickly, gazing out at the road. "You deserved to know the truth and Derek isn't some dirty secret I'm trying to hide from the world. He was the love of my life, Liv, and it wasn't fair to spit on his memory by keeping the truth from you. He was a good man." She quieted and then added, "The way you were smiling at your phone when you were talking to that boy, that's how I smiled when I was with Derek."

"What was his last name?" I asked. I don't know why I needed to know, but I did.

"Wynn. Derek Wynn," she answered immediately.

"Olivia Wynn," I whispered quietly. "Do his parents know about me?"

"No." She shook her head. "After he died ... I didn't believe there was any point in telling them. They knew about me and they didn't approve. Not that I blame them. I was married."

"Are they still alive?"

"They are." She glanced over at me.

I was still in a state of shock, but the questions kept pouring from me. "Do you have a picture of him? Of Derek?"

She swallowed thickly. "Yes."

"Can I ..." I paused. "Can I see it?" I asked as she pulled into the garage.

"Of course." She looked at me like I was crazy for thinking she would say no.

I unbuckled my seatbelt mechanically.

"Liv ..." My mom reached for my arm, grabbing it before I could get out.

"Yes?" I looked over my shoulder at her.

"Do you hate me for what I did?"

I studied the broken woman before me and thought of all the years of torment she had endured from my father—Aaron. How could I hate her for trying to find happiness with someone else?

"No, Mom, I could never hate you. I ... I feel very confused right now," I answered honestly, shaking my head as I gazed at my lap.

She released my arm. "That's understandable."

I followed her inside and upstairs to the master bedroom.

She opened the bottom drawer to her dresser and dumped out the contents.

Once everything was cleared, she lifted out a false bottom. Beneath it was pictures, a whole stack of them.

She smiled sadly and began handing them to me.

I stared at the stranger in the picture who really *wasn't* a stranger.

I clearly saw the resemblance. It was indisputable. I had his lips and just like my mom had said, I even had his smile. His hair was wavy, bordering on curly, and I assumed that was where I got my natural waves.

She handed me more, and I flipped through them, finding more of myself in him.

Finally, the last picture she handed me was one of her with Derek. It was a close-up and you could see Derek's arm as he held out the camera to take the picture. My mom was curled against his side. Neither of them was looking at the camera, though. They were looking at each other, and the love on both of their faces was unmistakable. I had never seen that look on my mom's face in all my twenty-years of life. I think a part of her must have died that day with Derek.

I flipped through the pictures, again and again, memorizing his features, and imagining how different my life could have been if Derek Wynn hadn't died.

But ... if Derek hadn't died, and I hadn't grown up with Aaron as a father, I would've never been desperate to get away.

I would've never met Trace.

Like I had told Trace that night in my dorm room, we can't undo the past, and I wouldn't change it for anything.

Those bad things led me to Trace.

Every decision, every moment, has the opportunity to change the course of our lives.

One moment can change everything.

For me, that moment was when I met Trace.

For my mom, it was when she met Derek.

We were similar in that regard.

"Can I keep one?" I held up the pictures, surprised to find that I was crying.

"They're all for you," she whispered, draping an arm over my shoulder. I hadn't realized she had sat down on the floor beside me. I had been too taken with discovering a piece of me that now only existed in these photographs. "I can't bear to look at them. It hurts too much. They're for you, Liv. They've always been for you."

I bundled the photos into a neat stack and cradled them close to my heart, crying for a man that I would never know.

CHAPTER FIFTEEN

I woke up and the first thing I did was look through the photos again. Unfortunately, the photos didn't reveal much about Derek. After all, they were only photos. They couldn't tell me what his voice sounded like, or his favorite color, or his hobbies.

I did notice that a lot of them were taken outside and I wondered if Derek—my dad—enjoyed being outside like I did.

I'd always rather be outside, soaking in the sun, than stuck indoors.

A banging on my door startled me.

I glanced at my bedroom clock.

It was nine o' clock in the morning; I should've been up two hours ago to avoid this wrath.

"Olivia Owens! Open this door right now! You know you're not allowed to close your bedroom door!" My dad's voice bellowed throughout the house.

I hopped up from my bed like it was made of hot coals, and bound across the room in two large steps, swinging the door open.

"You may sleep in late at that school of yours but that's not allowed in my house!" he bellowed.

"I'm sorry." I reached up, pushing my ratty hair from eyes.

"What's this?" he hissed, his large meaty hand capturing my arm. He gripped it tightly and I cried out as he held it up for inspection. Cold eyes glared at me. "What is this on your arm?"

Oh, no.

I swallowed.

When I didn't answer right away, his grip tightened.

"What is it, Olivia?" He shook me roughly, hard enough that my teeth clanked together.

"It's a tattoo," I cried.

His fingers dug painfully into my arm. His face reddened as his teeth clamped together. It felt as if he held me like that, for minutes, but the logical part of my mind knew that wasn't true. My adrenaline had already clicked in.

He released me roughly and I fell, sliding across the hardwood floor, where my head smacked into the wall. I reached up and fingered the tender part of my skull, half expecting there to be blood.

He glared down at me, and I flinched, waiting for him to strike.

My breath came out in ragged gasps, like I couldn't get enough oxygen.

"You're nothing but trouble." He glared at me with eyes that were anything but human. He was a monster. "Your mother should've had you taken care of."

Surprising words from a man who preached about the sins of abortion.

He stood there, seething, his chest rising and falling as his hands flexed at his sides.

For some reason, he looked around my room, and his eyes landed on the pictures on my bed.

"No," he growled softly. "*No,*" he screamed, storming over to my bed, reaching for the pictures.

I knew that he was going to ruin the pictures, the only thing I had tying me to a man I had only learned about yesterday, and that spurned me into action.

Those pictures were the key to a life I knew nothing about and I wasn't about to give it up.

With energy I didn't know I possessed, I stood.

He picked one of the pictures up and crumpled it into his hand, yelling unintelligibly.

I jumped on his back, wrapping my arms tightly around his neck, as he reached for another picture.

"Those are mine!" I screamed. I wouldn't let him ruin them.

"She was never supposed to tell you!" he roared, rearing back in an effort to dislodge me. I may have been small but adrenaline was on my side. I wouldn't be easily thwarted.

My arms tightened around his neck, I wasn't really trying to choke him, I only wanted him to stop destroying the photos. They were the only things I possessed that made Derek real.

"Stop it!" I shrieked when he reached for another. "Those are mine!"

"I raised you! You're my daughter!" he yelled, his spit landing on my arm.

"I was never your daughter!" I screamed shrilly. "Never!"

He started to rip the photo and time slowed down further.

I found myself letting go of his neck with one arm and clinging tightly to his waist with my legs as I reached for the heavy light on my bedside table.

I yanked the cord from the outlet and hurled the lamp at his head.

He grunted and fell slack, falling to the side.

I fell with him, my knee harshly colliding with the hardwood floor. He landed on my leg, passed out, and I pushed at him.

Blood poured from the gash on his head. It wasn't fatal, but he'd need stitches, and he'd definitely be out of it for a while.

"Oh, my God."

The words didn't come from me. I turned to find my mom standing in the doorway of my bedroom. She clutched her chest as she looked from Aaron to me.

"Oh, my God," she repeated, rushing to my side, and falling to her knees. "Liv, oh, my God. Oh, my God. Oh, my God. I heard the yelling and then the thump. Oh, my God. Is he?"

"No." I shook my head. "He's not."

I rose unsteadily to my feet. I had to leave before he woke up. If he woke up and I was still there … The consequences would be disastrous.

I didn't know where I'd go and that didn't matter. I had to get away.

"I need to leave," I whispered, scurrying around my room, gathering up my things. I hadn't removed much from my suitcase so it didn't take long. "He was going to ruin the pictures, Mom. I snapped. I'm sorry. I couldn't let him destroy them," I rambled.

He had already destroyed a part of me, a long time ago, there was no way I was letting him destroy my only connection with my real father.

"I have to go, Mom. I can't stay here," I rambled, gathering the photos from my bed, and the ones that had fallen on the floor.

I looked down at Aaron, the man who I had believed to be my father. I had never loved him, only feared him. But shouldn't I have felt some kind of remorse for hurting him? Instead, I felt relieved.

"I have to go, Mom," I repeated, because she kept standing there with shocked, wide eyes as she looked at Aaron passed out on the floor.

Slowly, she looked up at me.

"And you need to go too," I pleaded. "He's going to be livid when he wakes up."

"I can't, I can't." She shook her head, "I can't."

I grasped her hands in mine. "Please, Mom. For me. You have to. He'll kill you." I looked down at the broken lamp and the gash on his head. "He'll blame *you* for this," my voice cracked. "You have to leave."

"There's nowhere for me to go, Liv! Nowhere!" She was flustered, fanning her face, and fighting hysterics.

"Find a place," I begged, taking her hands in mine to soothe her. "I can't lose you too. Come to Virginia. I'll get a job and so will you. We can find a place and live together. If you stay here, you'll die."

I knew in my heart, that if Aaron woke up, and she was still here, he'd kill her ... just like I knew he'd kill me.

His anger had been growing progressively worse over the years. I had blocked a lot of what he had said and done, in order to cope, but if I really started digging through my memories, I knew I would find that Thanksgiving wasn't the first time he'd grabbed me like that.

Acting on instinct, I grabbed her long-sleeve shirt and yanked it up. "Look at this!" I pleaded, looking at the purple, yellow, and green bruises on her arm in the shape on his fingers. "If you think this is bad, what happens when he wakes up will be worse. Don't let him control you anymore!" I begged. "Where's that woman I saw yesterday? Huh? The woman that was going to leave her husband for Derek? Where is she, Mom? Find her! Find her and hold onto her! If you were going to leave dad for Derek, you can leave him for *me*."

Her whole body shook from crying, and she kept looking from me to Aaron, and back again.

"You can do it, Mom. Find that woman Derek fell in love with. *Please*," I sobbed.

She nodded. "Okay, okay. I know where he keeps some money hidden. I—"

"Just hurry, Mom," I begged. "Get rid of your cellphone and anything he can use to track you. Leave your car. I'll drive. Grab necessities only. Got it?"

She nodded mechanically and dashed down the hall to the master bedroom.

I eyed the small pool of blood that had gathered on the floor from Aaron's wound. It wasn't a dangerous amount of blood, I knew that, but the sight of it still upset my stomach.

While my mom was gathering her things, I changed from my pajamas into clothes and brushed my hair, quickly braiding it.

I stepped over Aaron's slumped form and tore my dresser apart. I had hidden money in each drawer from all the summers I had worked at the local ice cream shop. I knew I would never be coming back to this house.

This house wasn't my home; it was a prison, and I wanted none of these things, because they would only keep a part of me chained here.

I was glad that I had bought most of my things. I'd even saved and bought my car and I had managed to get into college with a full scholarship.

Once I stepped out the front door of this house, nothing would tie me to this place.

I would be free to float.

Free to wander.

Free to find myself.

CHAPTER SIXTEEN

My mom and I dashed out of the house, quickly loading my car with our meager possessions.

I drove away as fast as I could, not even bothering to look back at the house.

"What if he finds me?" she kept repeating over and over again.

I took her hand in mine. "Then we'll handle him together, Mom. Okay?"

She nodded.

I knew she was scared, but I honestly didn't think he had the guts to try and find her. If she stayed, he would hurt her ... probably kill her *but* he didn't strike me as the type to hunt her down.

Men like Aaron didn't have the guts to chase someone. They liked to control you behind closed doors and act like nothing was wrong when you were outside them.

We had a long drive ahead of us, but I didn't mind. I had my mom beside me and I would never let her go back to that man. It was time she found the freedom that I had been searching for, and I was pretty sure I had found it in Trace.

IT WAS LATE when we crossed the state line into Virginia.

An hour before, I had called Avery, and asked her if my mom and I could stay at her parents' house. She was quick to agree and I was so incredibly thankful that I had a friend like her.

I turned into Meadow Branch, Avery's neighborhood, and started making the turns she had described.

I found the house and pulled into the driveway beside her red Volkswagen Beetle.

"Mom, we're here." I shook her shoulder.

She startled awake. "Huh?"

"We're at Avery's house," I explained, "this is where we'll stay."

"Oh." She rubbed sleepily at her eyes. "She's your roommate, right?"

"Yeah."

"And she doesn't mind?" she asked, surprised.

"No, Mom. I called and asked her," I unbuckled my seatbelt.

The garage door opened and Avery stepped outside. She was dressed in her pajamas and her hair was pulled back in a sloppy ponytail. She waved her hand for us to come inside.

"Go on ahead, Mom, I'll get our stuff," I sighed.

I watched as she made her way to Avery. She looked so small and broken. I felt responsible for her, even though it should have been the other way around.

I carried our suitcases inside and sat them down in the mudroom area that you walked into from the garage.

"I already showed your mom her room," Avery said from the shadows, startling me. "Your room's ready too. My parents will be back in time for Christmas, but once they get back, they won't mind if y'all stay here."

"Thank you, Avery. I can't begin to express to you how much this means to me," I cried softly.

"Hey," she whispered, hugging me. "I'm happy to help, but what happened?"

"I can't talk about it right now. I'm sorry," I sobbed, covering my face with my hands.

"It's okay." She rubbed my back. "I know you'll tell me when you're ready. It was something with your dad, though, wasn't it?" she questioned.

I nodded; she didn't need more of an answer than that.

"He's worse than what you told me, isn't he? Did he hurt you, Livie?" She pulled away, looking me over.

My whole body was sore and I knew my arm would be bruised come morning.

"In more ways than what you're thinking," I whispered.

"Oh, Olivia." She hugged me again. "I'm so sorry you've had to go through this."

I hugged her back, tightly, thankful again, and definitely not for the last time, that I had a friend like Avery. She could say crude things and get on my nerves sometimes, but at the end of the day, she had my back and I had hers. If that wasn't friendship, I didn't know what was.

She released me, wiping at her tear-streaked face. "Let me show you your room."

I followed her through the massive house and up a sweeping staircase.

"This is my room." She pointed to an open door. "Don't hesitate to wake me up if you need anything or just a shoulder to cry on." She smiled lightly. Opening a closed door at the end of the hall, she announced, "This is your room."

It was a large, nicely decorated guest room. The walls were

painted a light brown color with carpeted floors in a similar shade. The bed coverings were all white and the furniture was black.

"You're probably going to want to sleep in, so I should warn you, my brother Nick will be here tomorrow. Don't be surprised if you see a guy walking around in his boxers, scratching his balls. It's normal."

I laughed. I could always count on Avery to make a serious situation not so dark.

"Thank you again," I told her.

"Not a problem. I'm going back to bed." She padded down the hall and into her room. "See you in the morning," she chimed and closed the door.

I knew I should grab my suitcase and try to go to sleep, but I didn't want to.

I wanted Trace.

I wanted to tell him everything.

I wanted him to make me forget.

I FOUND myself running up the steps, leading to Trace's loft apartment, and banging on his door.

I kept knocking and knocking. I started to question whether he was even there and then I began to worry, what if he *was* there but otherwise occupied?

Trace would never do that to you.

The door opened underneath my banging fist, and I tumbled inside, captured by warm strong arms.

"Whoa." He steadied me. "Olivia, what are you doing here? I thought you were in New Hampshire." He gazed down at me and the intensity in his eyes caused me to shiver. I saw worry there too, swirling in the green depths. He knew something bad had to have happened to send me running here.

"I just ... I needed you," I whispered. "I have to tell someone. I have to."

"Hey, hey, it's okay," he crooned, wrapping me into his arms when I began to cry.

He swept my legs out from under me and we settled on the couch.

"What happened?" He wiped away my tears with his large thumbs.

"So much," I croaked.

For the first time, I noticed that he was practically naked, wearing only a pair of plaid boxers. At any other time, I would have snorted. *Of course he wears plaid boxers.*

"Tell me what happened," he pleaded. "I can't help you if you don't tell me."

The whole thing, everything that happened in the past forty-eight hours, and what had happened years ago, spilled from my mouth. I didn't hold anything back. Memories I had long ago suppressed bubbled to the surface, and I told those too, like the time we were in the park and my dad—Aaron, pushed me off the swing, claiming I fell on my own and I ended up with cuts on my hands and knees.

There was another time, when he was teaching me to ride a bike, where he purposely let go of me so that I fell into a ditch full of large rocks.

As I grew older, he switched to solely using the verbal abuse on me, but in the back of my mind, I remembered walking in on him beating my mother.

So many years and so much abuse. I had been able to block a lot of it, but I was sure my mother hadn't been able to do the same. She had to remember everything, and I wondered how she made it through each day without crumbling to pieces. I guess she was stronger than I thought.

Trace didn't say he was sorry, he simply held me, and that's all I wanted.

To feel safe.

SOMETIME LATER, I pulled away from his embrace. He looked me over carefully with those inquisitive green eyes.

"Thank you, for telling me," he murmured, "and for trusting me. I know it was hard for you to tell me." He played with my braid and his tongue flicked out to moisten his lips.

"I'm so lucky I met you," I whispered, resting my head on his shoulder.

"Flat tires come in handy sometimes." He chuckled as his lips brushed against the top of my head.

"Mhmm," I murmured and kissed his bare chest.

"Olivia," he warned.

"Trace," I smiled at his tone and kissed a spot on his collarbone.

"What are you doing?" he asked as one of my hands roamed over his chest.

"I think ..." I leaned up and kissed his neck. "It's called seducing." I draped one of my legs across his and sat on his lap so I faced him. I placed my hands on his stomach, just above his boxers, and then moved them up slowly. They lingered on his chest, then wound around the back of his neck, and settled on his ears.

He squished his eyes closed. "It's working. Then again, you don't have to seduce me."

I rubbed my fingers down the back of his ears. "Don't make me beg," I whispered.

His hands came up to grip my waist. "Olivia," he said as if pained, "don't do this to me."

"I want you." I sat back on his lap, staring into his eyes, trying to get him to *see* that I needed him.

His hands tightened on my waist. "I want this to be perfect with you," he murmured fiercely. "I don't want this ... sadness, clinging to you. I want it to be only about you and me. No one else. I don't want you to use me to erase your pain."

"I'm not." I kissed his chin. "This is about no one else, but you and me, and the fact that I want you in every way."

"Olivia, I've wanted you since the moment I saw you." He pulled me against his hard length. "Don't make this any harder on me."

I grinned. "I don't think you *can* get any harder."

He groaned. "You're really trying to kill me."

"Ah, but what a pleasant death it would be." I ran a finger from the indent of his collarbone, straight down, hooking it into the edge of his boxers.

His hand closed around mine. He swallowed thickly. "It's too soon, Olivia. But I want to, so bad."

"Then don't hold back," I coaxed. "I'm ready."

His hands flexed against my waist as I watched an internal battle rage across his face.

I was about to resort to begging, but before I could open my mouth, his lips were on mine as he resigned to the inevitable.

I wrapped my arms around his neck as I pressed against him, closer, closer, *closer*. I knew I wouldn't be close enough until our bodies had melded together, and even that, I was sure, wouldn't be close enough.

He pulled back and lifted my sweatshirt off of my head, throwing it to a far corner of the room. My long-sleeved t-shirt quickly followed and I was left in only my bra and jeans.

He kneaded my breasts through the thin cups of my bra before undoing the clasps and tossing it as well.

He pulled me against him so that we were chest to chest. I felt his heart racing as quickly as mine and I was pleased to know I wasn't the only one affected by this. I wasn't naïve; I knew Trace had loads of experience in this department.

"You can still tell me to stop," he panted breathlessly.

"I'm not asking you to." I ran a finger along the curve of his jawline. "And I *won't* ask you to."

"Okay," he whispered, standing. My legs wrapped around his waist and he held me tightly against him, his hands clasped below my butt. "I've got you," he assured, nudging his bedroom door open further and laying me down on the mattress. The covers were pushed down to the bottom of his bed from his haste to answer the door when I arrived.

He stood, gazing down at me, and I blushed shyly as he scrutinized my body. I was still wearing my jeans, but the way he looked at me made me feel as if I was bare everywhere else.

"You're beautiful, absolutely beautiful," he crooned.

He leaned down and I closed my eyes, expecting to feel the light pressure of his lips meeting mine. Instead, I felt a slight tug, and the ponytail holder holding my braid in place came undone. He fanned my hair around my head and appraised his work. "You're absolutely breathtaking, Olivia," he whispered.

I reached for his arm and felt the muscle flex at my touch.

"I'm getting lonely down here." I pulled him slightly closer and he moved the rest of the way.

"I can't have you getting lonely, can I?" He grinned. He scooted me up the bed until I lay in the center and covered my body with his. His fingers rubbed against my jean-clad center and I arched against his touch. He popped the button with deft fingers and eased the zipper down. My breathing accelerated.

My only experience with sex had been nothing like this.

That time had been clumsy and fast while this was slow and

intimate.

Trace's eyes met mine when the zipper could go no further.

He scooted down in the bed, placing tender kisses along my breasts and stomach as he went.

He spread my thighs apart, and not taking his eyes from mine, he blew a gust of hot air against where I needed him the most.

This was torture.

The sweetest, most delicious, kind of torture, but torture nonetheless.

He hooked his fingers through the belt loops of my jeans, tugging them down slowly. Trace kissed each piece of skin my jeans uncovered. Not a centimeter was left untouched by his lips.

I heard my jeans fall to the floor and then we were both left in only our underwear. He moved back up my body, kissing his way there.

When he reached my face, he clasped both of our hands together and stared into my eyes.

"Don't be afraid," he whispered.

"I'm not."

He released one of my hands and smoothed his large thumb over the skin between my brows. "This wrinkle here suggests otherwise."

I swallowed down the lump in my throat. I didn't know how to express to Trace exactly what I was feeling. I wasn't scared about the actual sex ... I was scared that sex with Trace would only make me fall harder for him.

"I am a little nervous," I admitted reluctantly.

"Don't be nervous with me, ever, Olivia," he whispered, staring intently into my eyes.

"Okay," I replied but his words had done nothing to ease my racing heart. I feared that it might gallop right out of my chest.

He kissed the dip between my breasts before releasing my hands and palming them.

"You have the most perfect breasts I've ever seen." He gazed down at them. I squirmed under his scrutiny. He pressed one hand against my stomach, stilling me. "Don't do that," he scolded. "There's no need to be embarrassed I'm just ... enjoying the view."

I nodded.

His hands skimmed lower and then came back to my breasts.

Goosebumps broke out across my skin from pleasure and my head rolled to the side.

He gripped my chin and forced my head back.

"Don't look away from me and keep your eyes open. I want to see you," he rasped.

I nodded, my voice leaving me, and he placed a tender kiss on the end of my nose.

"Look at me," he warned again when my eyes threatened to flutter closed.

I opened them wide and he smiled.

His head dipped down and he began to kiss my neck. Then moved down to my breasts where he spent an exceptionally long time and over my stomach. His tongue flicked out, playing with my belly button ring.

"I can't believe you're mine," he whispered so low that I couldn't be sure I heard him correctly.

His fingers hooked into the edge of my panties but he didn't pull them down.

One hand ventured inside the elastic and he hissed through his teeth when he found how wet I was.

One finger slipped inside, pumping in and out.

"Trace," I gasped.

Just as I was getting accustomed to the feeling, he removed his finger and pulled my panties down, kissing my thighs and calves as he went.

His eyes flicked up to meet mine before his tongue delved into me.

"Trace, don't," I cried, but it was too late.

His tongue swirled over my sensitive nub and I bucked against him. His chuckle vibrated against me, and if I had half a brain left, I'd be blushing.

He lapped at my aching core and I was a willing prisoner to the feel of it.

His tongue swirled inside my entrance, and my hips lifted up off the mattress, desperate for more.

I mewled in protest as he rose up. "Enjoying yourself, baby?"

I nodded woodenly, but what I wanted to say was, *Oh, yeah*.

He grinned and dipped his head back down. His mouth closed around my clit and tingles zinged through my body. I knew I was close to reaching that peak everyone talked about.

He sucked harder and I came apart.

I'm pretty sure I saw stars at that moment, or maybe it was heaven, because I could have died and never known.

My fingers tangled into the soft strands of his hair.

He lifted up and smiled at me. His lips were slick, and instead of being disgusted, it only made me want him more.

"That's just orgasm number one," he murmured promisingly.

My body hummed at his words.

More?

Is that possible?

He moved back up my body, kissing me deeply, as his erection pressed against me.

I gripped his boxers and pulled them down. He removed them the rest of the way and rested between my thighs, his hot length pulsing against me.

My heart stuttered, knowing what was about to happen.

I hadn't known Trace very long but this felt *right* with him.

He twisted his fingers in my hair, gazing down at me.

He looked like he wanted to say something, but kissed me instead, our tongues tangling together.

My legs wrapped around his waist, pulling him against my core.

"Not yet," he rasped.

He flipped to his back, taking me with him so that I straddled his hips and gazed down at him.

He may have called me beautiful, but he was wrong. Trace was the beautiful one, inside and out, not me.

His fingers trailed gently up my back, causing me to shiver.

He sat up and took one of my breasts in his mouth. I cried out, gripping the short dark hairs at the base of his neck to steady myself.

All of the nerve-endings in my body seemed to react to his touch.

His body was warm against mine and slightly damp with sweat.

His arms wrapped around me, hands clasping around my back, bringing our chests flush against each other. I bent my head, kissing his lips, chin, and neck.

He felt perfect against me. I knew, then, that Trace was it for me. There would never be anyone else that made me feel this way. It wasn't possible for more than one person to make you feel this ... complete. *This* was once in a lifetime and once you found it, you held onto it with everything you had.

He flipped me over so my back rested against the mattress and my head was cradled on his pillow.

He reached for his night table and opened the drawer. Pulling out a foil packet, he laid it beside my head.

He held himself above me, his eyes roaming over my body, and I did the same to him.

His body was muscular and masculine, the hard length of him jutting proudly out of his body.

I reached down, and gripped him in my hand, feeling him twitch.

He swallowed thickly as I smoothed my hand up and down, rubbing my thumb over the sensitive pink head. A small drop of liquid coated my thumb and I swirled it around.

He gazed down at me and a small smile graced his lips.

"So beautiful," he murmured, reaching for the condom packet.

He ripped it open and together we fixed it onto his length.

"Ready?" he asked.

"I've been ready," I panted, "you're the one that insists on dragging this out."

He chuckled huskily. "Perfection takes time, baby, and you deserve nothing less."

"I thought you said perfection doesn't exist?"

"It doesn't, but that doesn't mean it isn't worth searching for." He reached between us and guided his thick length to my entrance. He squeezed inside, just an inch and stopped. "Oh, God," he moaned.

My heart beat faster at the intrusion. Trace was large, and I had only had sex once before, my body still unaccustomed to the foreign feeling.

He slid inside slowly, the rest of the way, and stopped there.

He looked down at me and panted, "I was wrong. Perfection does exist and it's right here. With me inside you."

I gasped as he pulled out and then rolled his hips forward, slamming firmly back into me.

I clawed at his back, desperately seeking something to hold onto and anchor myself.

He reached around and undid my hands from his neck, then entwined our fingers together once more as he slowly rocked in and out of me.

This was making love.

"You're so tight, Olivia," he panted before frantically seeking my lips and sealing them with his own.

The temperature in the room rose and I wondered if we were

close to lighting the small apartment on fire with the friction we were creating.

Sweat dotted his skin and dampened his hair.

He released my hands and gripped the wooden headboard in his hands.

The change in position left me gasping in pleasure. "Right there," I encouraged, raking my fingernails up and down his back.

His jaw tightened and he squeezed his eyes shut.

"Look at me, Trace," I pleaded like he had with me earlier. I needed to see him. I *needed* to know that he was feeling all the same things that I was.

He complied, bright green eyes connecting with my own.

"It's never felt this good before," he confessed and peppered my face with kisses.

A low moan built in his throat and he reached between us, rubbing his thumb over my clit.

My body arched as my hips lifted to meet his.

He rocked in and out, still rubbing that spot, and I felt my body tighten.

He let go of the headboard and raised my hips, adjusting the position again, and it felt like he was filling every part of me.

With a scream, my orgasm tore through my body, and I cried his name.

He silenced me with his mouth, sucking on my lower lip.

"I love the way you scream my name," he growled.

He pumped in and out a few more times, and then I felt him twitch inside me, growling as he came.

"Oh, holy fuck, Olivia," he roared, the veins in his neck popping out.

He slumped forward, careful to hold his weight above me, and pressed his face into the crook of my neck.

Tender kisses were exchanged, both of us shaking slightly, until we finally passed out from exhaustion.

CHAPTER SEVENTEEN

Light spilled into the bedroom and across my bare chest, warming me.

I glanced to my left at Trace. He was sound asleep, on his stomach, the sheet barely covering his bottom. His heavy arm was draped over my stomach as if he had tried to pull me closer during the night.

I studied the way his long dark lashes fanned across his angular cheekbones. His lips were slightly parted as he breathed deeply in and out. His cheeks were dotted with stubble and my thighs were chafed from where his cheeks rubbed against them.

My body was sore, but not overly so. Despite the tenderness from over-worked muscles, I had never felt better.

Last night had been ... perfect. I didn't regret a moment. I knew, now, what Avery was talking about. Sex was wonderful, when it's with the right person. Not to mention, Trace knew exactly what he was doing. Maybe that should have bothered me, but for some reason, it didn't.

I sat up, gently placing Trace's arm on the bed as I slid out. I sat on the edge of the mattress, trying to run my fingers through my knotted hair, but it was futile. Only conditioner and patience with a comb would remove the knots.

I peeked over my shoulder at his sleeping form before standing and gathering my panties then the rest of my clothes from the living room.

I couldn't contain my laughter when I picked up my sweatshirt.

So much for Avery's theory of a sweatshirt being a chastity belt.

I rolled my clothes into a ball and opened the door to the only bathroom.

It was surprisingly clean, like the rest of his apartment. There was a razor sitting on the sink, and an open tube of toothpaste, but that was as messy as it got.

I dropped my clothes on the floor and started the shower. I searched through the small cabinet underneath the sink for a towel. I almost expected him to have plaid towels, but they were a light solid gray, and super soft.

The bathroom quickly filled with steam, and I pushed the shower curtain back, stepping inside.

The hot water felt like heaven on my sore muscles. I closed my eyes and let the hot water work out the kinks in my muscles.

I yelped in surprise when the shower curtain slid open.

Trace grinned, eyes raking over my body. "How are you feeling?"

Deliciously sore. "Fine," I replied with a smile.

He wrapped a hand around my waist, pulling me away from the spray. He pecked me on the lips, and my fingers tangled in his sex-rumpled hair.

"Let me wash you," he murmured huskily, reaching for his soap.

I swallowed as my heart rate quickened.

He opened the shower curtain and reached out for a cloth. He slid the curtain back into place and the hooks rattled against the metal rod.

The cloth was the same light gray color as the towel and he reached behind me to lightly wet it.

He squirted a dollop of soap onto the cloth and rubbed the ends together until it foamed.

"Come here." He took my hand and switched places with me so that the spray of water was beating on his back and not mine.

He gently rubbed the cloth over my shoulders, up my neck, and down my chest. He paid special attention to my breasts and when he reached my stomach he dropped to his knees. He kissed the apex of my thighs before soaping that area as well. Trace scrubbed both of my legs thoroughly, and then warned, "Hold on."

I grabbed ahold of the metal shower curtain bar as one of my legs was yanked out from under me.

He placed light kisses on each of my toes and then carefully rubbed each one with the soapy cloth. He lifted my foot and steadied me with a hand on my opposite leg when I swayed.

"You okay?" he asked.

"I'm good," I squeaked.

When he was sure I had my balance again, he massaged the bottom of my foot, and cleaned it as well.

He did the same thing with my other leg.

When he was finished, he swirled his finger in the air, motioning me to turn around.

He cleaned the back of me and stood again, lifting my hair off my neck and tenderly kissing the exposed area.

I fell back against his chest and his hands rested on my thighs.

We stood like that for a few seconds, and then he turned me around so we were facing one another.

He stepped back, forcing both of us under the spray of water.

"Trace!" I squealed. "A little warning would have been nice!"

He chuckled and the sound vibrated through my body.

"It's just a little water, baby." He grinned, rubbing me to make sure all the soap was gone. "Let me wash your hair." He coaxed my head under the water.

Once every strand was wet, he rubbed his woodsy scented soap into my hair.

He massaged my scalp and I found myself moaning in pleasure, which only served to make him laugh.

"Don't laugh at me," I scolded.

"I'm not. I'm laughing at myself," he muttered.

"Why?" My eyes popped open as he guided me under the water once more and began to work the soap out of my hair.

"Because, this was about you. I wanted to please you in a completely non-sexual way and" —he looked down significantly — "you had to go and make those sexy noises."

I looked down at the thick length arching beautifully out of his body.

"Hmm," I murmured. "I think we're going to have to do something to fix that."

I QUIETLY OPENED the door from the garage that led into Avery's house. I had text Avery before I arrived and she gave me the code so I could get inside the house.

I turned around, easing it closed, and locking it with a soft click.

"Well, well, well, look who's doing the walk of shame and it's *not* my little sister," a guy chortled behind me.

I turned around, biting nervously on my bottom lip.

Even though it was almost noon, he was only wearing a pair

of black boxer briefs. He was drinking straight out of the bottle of orange juice and scratching his crotch.

I snorted. This had to be Nick.

He had shaggy strawberry-blonde hair that hung just past his ears and he was huge. His height dwarfed my small size and he was built like a stocky football player. He had to be at least six foot four.

"You must be Nick," I responded, a slight squeak to my voice.

"And you must be ... Actually, I don't know."

"Olivia," I answered.

"My sister's roommate?" He raised a brow. "What are you doing here?"

"Family troubles," I replied. No way was I telling him all about the soap opera my life had become.

"Gotcha." He scratched his chiseled chest. "Avery wouldn't tell me." He winked. "I thought if I played dumb you might give me more information. So ..." He looked between the door and me. "If you're having family troubles, and staying here, where have you been?"

I pressed myself flat against the door, wishing I could slip right through it.

"Leave the girl alone, she was getting her brains banged out by a sex-god." Avery smirked at her brother as she stood in the hallway outside of the mudroom. "And she better tell me all about it."

"Avery!"

"Don't deny that you went to him last night. I have radar for these things." She eyed me, disappearing into the kitchen.

I scurried after her so that I wasn't left alone with Nick again.

I sat down at one of the barstools while Avery made a bowl of cereal.

Nick pulled out the barstool beside me and I bristled.

"Hungry?" Avery asked, holding the gallon jug of milk in her hand.

"I already ate," I told her.

She grinned. "I bet you did."

"Avery!" I exclaimed again.

She chuckled, grabbing a spoon from one of the many drawers. It would take me years to explore every nook and cranny of this large house.

"After your all-night sex-a-thon you should probably eat something with some protein. Build up your endurance." She winked and sat down on the other free stool beside me. She leaned around me and leveled her older brother with a glare. "Nickolas, leave," she warned.

"No." He smirked. "I want to know what girls talk about when guys aren't listening."

"I guess you better spontaneously grow a vagina because we won't be talking about *anything* in front of you," she snapped. "Come on. I'll eat in my room." She grabbed my arm, dragging me behind her and upstairs.

She opened the door to her room and I found that it was pretty similar to her side of our dorm room in the fact that it was a mess. Clothes were strewn everywhere and junk was stacked on her tables, dresser, and bookcases. I wondered how she ever found anything.

The walls were painted in a bright kelly-green and her comforter was the same color. All the furniture was white.

Avery swiped her hand across two chairs, that I hadn't seen in all the mess, dislodging the clutter that had been sitting on them.

I took a seat on one of the chairs and she took the other.

"Tell me" —she munched on her Frosted Flakes cereal— "did you have sex with him?"

I blushed and looked away.

"You did!" she shrieked and I heard the sound of her cereal

and milk sloshing over the lip of the bowl. "Shit," she muttered, looking at the mess she had made. "Oh, well." She shrugged. "So," she said with a grin, "how was it? Did he have big dick? I bet he did."

I did not want to share this kind of information with Avery, best friend or not; it was personal.

"I don't want to talk about it," I muttered. "And I am definitely *not* telling you that."

"Give me a range here, please?" she begged. "Good? Bad? Off the charts? This big or *this* big." She held up her fingers in different lengths.

"Shut up, Avery! I'm not talking about *that* with you!" I waved my hands back and forth. "As far as how the sex was, I don't think I'm the right person to judge it," I mumbled. "I don't have a lot of experience."

"That doesn't matter, trust me," she finished what was left of her cereal since most of it had ended up on the floor.

"Off the charts," I reluctantly answered since I knew she wouldn't drop it until she got some sort of answer out of me.

She squealed shrilly. I was surprised the windows in her bedroom didn't shatter.

"My little Livie is all grown up." She pretended to wipe away a tear.

"Oh, please." I rolled my eyes.

"I really am happy for you, though." She smiled. "Now," she eyed me seriously and continued, "I think you owe me an explanation as to why you're here."

"You're right." I sighed and began to divulge everything about Derek being my real dad and what had happened with Aaron. It was wrong of me to keep Avery in the dark, even if I wanted to. She was a good friend, and she deserved to know the truth of why I had called her in the middle of the night, desperate for a place to stay.

"Holy fucking shit," she whispered when I had finished.

"That makes no sense," I mumbled.

"I couldn't think of any other words to express what I'm feeling right now." She shook her head back and forth, still trying to absorb the information. "This is ..." She pulled at her hair. "Shocking."

"I'll be right back." I stood.

She narrowed her eyes. "You better."

"Don't worry. I only want to grab the pictures." I smiled.

Once in the guest room, I flipped through the photos again. I didn't think I'd ever get used to the fact that the man in the pictures was my real dad.

I made my way back to Avery's bedroom before she hunted me down.

I handed her the stack of pictures and her jaw dropped open. She looked from the pictures and back to me.

"Holy shit," she whispered. "He's definitely your dad. You look just like him, Livie. I can't believe this." She flipped to the picture of Derek and my mom. "She looks so happy and young." Avery smiled. "They really loved each other."

I looked at the pictures in Avery's hand and finally managed to say the words that had been stuck in my head since my mom told me. "This changes everything."

CHAPTER EIGHTEEN

I walked out of Avery's room and nearly collided with my mom.

"Sorry," I apologized, holding a hand out to steady her. I looked over her disheveled appearance. "Are you just now waking up?"

By now, it had to be close to one in the afternoon.

"Yeah. I can't tell you the last time I've slept this late. I guess I really needed it."

"Whoa," Nick muttered from somewhere behind me as a door clicked closed. "Too much estrogen in here."

"Shut up," Avery sneered, coming out of her bedroom, dressed for the day.

Nick stepped forward, looking my mom up and down, grinning appreciatively.

Um ... ew.

"It's nice to meet you." He held out a hand to my mom. "I'm Nick."

"Nora," she squeaked, her eyes connecting with his bare chest.

I gagged, glancing at Avery.

She looked as shocked as I did.

"Well, Nora" —he grinned and a dimple popped out in his right cheek— "if you need help with *anything* don't hesitate to ask me. My room's right there" —he pointed— "and you can come get me *anytime*."

I think I just threw up in my mouth.

She blushed. "Oh, well."

I wanted to slap my hands over my eyes but I didn't want to call attention to myself.

After everything that had happened, the last thing I wanted to see was Avery's twenty-two-year-old brother trying to finagle his way into my mom's pants.

"Mom," I spoke up, finding my voice. "Why don't you shower and get ready? I'll take you to lunch," I suggested.

"Okay." She smiled gratefully, making her way back to the guest bedroom.

Nick's eyes never left her. When the bedroom door closed behind her, he turned to me.

"Your mom's fucking hot." He shook his head back and forth like he was in a daze. "Can I come with you to lunch?"

"Absolutely not!" Avery and I exclaimed simultaneously.

"Honestly, Nickolas." Avery reached up to slap the back of his head. "What is it with you and older women?"

She didn't wait for him to answer. She bounced down the stairs and I was left alone with Nick. I crept around him and ran for the stairs.

I heard him mumbling under his breath as he went back into his room.

"I am so sorry about that," Avery began when I set foot in the kitchen.

"That was weird," I admitted.

"Nick's always had a thing for—uh—older ladies," she mumbled. "It's gotten him into a lot of trouble over the years."

"It's gross," I grumbled. "Keep him away from my mom."

She laughed. "I'll try, but once Nick sets his mind to something, he doesn't give up easily ... At all, actually."

"This is too much." I collapsed onto one of the stools as Avery washed her bowl and wiped down the counters. "My brain's already on overload with the whole Derek and Aaron thing, plus what happened with Trace last night, and now this? I don't have time to worry about your brother seducing my mom." I crossed my arms on the countertop and dejectedly laid my head on top.

Avery began laughing and I couldn't help but join in.

Wiping tears away, she giggled. "This is nuts!"

"You're telling me! It's my life!" I laughed hysterically.

"Am I interrupting something?" my mom asked, stepping into the kitchen.

"No." I wiped my face dry with the backs of my hands. "You ready?"

She nodded in reply.

I pulled my car keys out of my pocket and left through the garage.

"Oh! Wait!" Avery called over the roaring of the garage door. She scurried down the garage steps and opened one of drawers in the built-in cabinets along the wall. "Here." She tossed a black rectangular device my way.

"What's this?" I looked down at it stupidly. I quickly realized what it was but Avery was already answering.

"It's a garage opener," she replied. "This way, you don't have to worry about me or Nick being home, and you don't have to get out and enter the code like you did this morning. We have a security system but it's turned off right now."

"Okay." I flipped the device over in my hands. "Thanks."

"Not a problem. I'll see you guys later. And Mrs. Owens," she called out to my mom, "watch out for my brother."

A bunch of gibberish came out of her mouth, which made Avery and me laugh.

"I'M NOT MAD AT YOU," I stated, drenching my waffle in syrup. "I want you to know that."

My mom looked up from her plate of food, studying my face. When she found that I was telling the truth, she let out a sigh of relief.

"I know I should have told you the truth a long time ago; it never seemed like the right time, though." She shrugged and took a bite of her egg sandwich.

After a lengthy discussion about where to eat for lunch, we ended up deciding on Waffle House.

"I'm glad you waited to tell me. I don't think I would've handled it well if you told me sooner. It's been hard to process now, it would've been even worse if I was younger." My eyes strayed to my purse where I had placed the pictures of Derek. I wanted to keep them with me at all times. I think I was afraid that if they were separated from me for too long, they'd disappear. "Can you tell me more about him?"

I hadn't wanted to listen when she first told me, but now, I was ready to know more about my real dad.

"I don't know where to start." She took a sip of water.

"Start wherever you want," I told her.

She grew quiet as she thought. "He loved to be outside." She smiled, her eyes far away. "I can't begin to tell you how many times I found him outside the library, stretched out on one of those small benches with a book in his hand. He was a serious student, but he was funny, the kind of guy that was always cracking a joke. He loved his family and friends, to the point that he was almost loyal to a fault. But I loved that about him. He would have been the greatest father to you, Liv, and I'm so sorry that you missed out on that, sweetie."

I swallowed thickly, wondering if I would have made Derek Wynn proud. *Would I have been enough for him?*

"Do you think Aaron will try to find you?" I whispered.

She released my hand and sat back, staring out the window at the traffic going by. "I honestly don't know. He's ... unpredictable."

I really didn't think Aaron would try to find her, but I still worried.

"*Please*, if he finds you, don't let him take you from me, again," I begged.

"Never," she answered fiercely. "I'll never go back to that, Liv. I would rather have *nothing* than live with that man. I wish I would've left sooner, but I didn't think I could. I was scared. But now that I'm gone, nothing will ever send me back. I can promise you that."

I breathed out a sigh of relief.

She continued, "As soon as I get a job and find a place of my own, I've decided to file for divorce."

My eyes widened. "I don't want anything tying me to him. Especially a marriage." She removed her wedding band to drive home her point. "It's time for me to move on and live my life."

"I'll be here every step of the way," I assured her. "You don't have to go through this alone."

She smiled, tears glassing over her eyes once more. "I know I haven't been the best mom and that I should have stopped Aaron. I shouldn't have let ... I shouldn't." She grabbed a napkin and wiped her tears away. "I shouldn't have let him hurt you like he did. I'm sorry I wasn't strong enough for you. I hope you'll let me make it up to you."

"Mom," I said fiercely, "there's nothing to make up for. I *understand*. I was scared of him too. I know he treated you worse than he did me. This isn't your fault. I'm happy you're out of that house now. I promise you, there's nothing you need to make up for. You're my mom, you always have been, and you always will be."

We stared at each other for a moment, and I expected her to say something serious, but instead, she cracked a smile and asked, "So, when do I get to meet this guy of yours?"

"You want me to meet your mom?" Trace asked incredulously over the phone.

I coughed into the phone trying to hide my discomfort. "She wants to meet you."

He sighed. "It's been a long time since I did the whole, meet the parents thing, but for you, I will."

I bristled, knowing he was referring to his ex, Aubrey.

"I'm sorry, I hate asking you, but she keeps bugging me about it," I grumbled, tugging on the strands of my hair.

For the past two days, she had asked me incessantly about Trace. I knew I couldn't put off this meet and greet forever and preferred to get it over and done with.

"Don't apologize," he replied. "It's not that I don't want to meet your mom, I'm just not very good at this. I know what kind of house you grew up in. Is she going to think I'm some tattooed criminal or something?" He sounded insecure.

I snickered. "That was my dad—er, Aaron—that's like that. Not my mom. She'll like you, I promise."

"All right," he mumbled and I heard the sounds of him pacing as his shoes shuffled along the carpet of his bedroom. "When am I supposed to meet her?"

I coughed again. "Tonight," I squeaked.

"Olivia," he groaned and I was sure he was pinching the bridge of his nose. "This isn't a lot of notice."

"I know and I'm sorry." I bit my thumbnail.

"What time do you need me to be there?" he asked, sounding resigned.

"Is five o' clock okay?" I suggested. That gave him three hours to get ready and pep talk himself.

"Yeah," he huffed. "Where do I need to meet you guys?"

"Avery's house," I answered, rattling off directions. "She'll be gone tonight and so will her brother. My mom wants to cook."

"Sounds good." He sighed. "I know I don't sound happy, but I'm really nervous."

"It's fine. I totally understand. I wouldn't be too happy if you sprung something like this on me," I told him.

"I'll see you tonight. And, Olivia?"

"Yeah," I replied reluctantly.

"You owe me big time."

THE DOORBELL RANG and I ran out of the kitchen like my butt was on fire.

I had been pacing the length of the kitchen for a solid twenty minutes as I waited for Trace to arrive. My mom continued to cook, pretending she didn't notice me nervously walking back and forth.

I swung the door open and forced a smile.

Trace was freshly shaved with his dark hair brushed back and a beanie on top of his head. He wore a dark pair of jeans and a tight white V-neck shirt, with a long-sleeve button-down yellow and black plaid shirt on top. His leather jacket and boots completed the look.

"Hey." He grinned. "I'm sorry about the way I acted earlier on the phone." He pulled a bouquet of flowers from behind his back and handed them to me. "Forgive me?"

I narrowed my eyes, making him sweat it a bit longer. "Are flowers supposed to make me feel better?"

He squirmed. "Well, no."

"I'm kidding." I smiled genuinely this time. "They're beautiful." I inhaled the fresh scent. "Get inside, it's starting to snow." I opened the door wider.

He stepped inside and I saw that he had a similar bouquet clasped in his other hand. "For your mom," he explained at my staring.

"Oh." I nodded. "That was nice of you."

He chuckled. "I *am* a nice guy."

I rolled my eyes, closing and locking the door.

He took a deep breath and removed his beanie. I could tell he was nervous and trying to lighten the mood.

"It'll be fine." I stood on my tiptoes to place a light kiss on his lips.

He kissed me back and grinned fully when I pulled away.

I took his hand and led him into the kitchen.

My mom's back was to us. She hummed as she stirred a pot on the stove and then wiped her hands on her apron.

I cleared my throat and she turned around. "Mom, this is Trace. Trace, this is my mom."

"It's nice to meet you, Mrs. Owens." Trace let go of my hand and reached out to shake my mom's.

She surprised him by reaching up and giving him a hug. "Please, call me Nora."

"Nora, these are for you."

She smiled as she gazed at the flowers in his hand. She took them from him. "These are lovely. Thank you. Olivia, why don't you look around and see if you can find two vases?" She eyed the bouquet in my hand.

I looked around at all the cabinets and grumbled, "Where do I even start looking?"

Ten minutes later, I gave up on locating a vase and stuck the flower arrangements in regular drinking glasses. Problem solved.

Trace was helping my mom set the table when I placed the flowers in their makeshift vases at the center of the table.

"Nice," Trace snorted, looking at the drinking glass vases.

"Sometimes, you have to be resourceful."

Once all the food was on the table, we sat down to eat. My mom sat across from Trace and me.

My mom had made a batch of her cheesy potatoes, my favorite, among several other side dishes, and she had grilled steaks since the Callahan's had one of those fancy indoor grills.

"This is fantastic," Trace told her.

"Thank you." She smiled, her eyes crinkling at the corners. "Do you cook?"

"I love to cook."

"Really?" Her eyes widened. "That's nice to hear." Turning to me, she whispered under her breath, "He's a keeper."

"Mom," I grumbled.

Trace chuckled, eyeing me over his glass of ice water, and I knew he had heard her.

"So," she continued, "what do you like to cook, Trace?"

He shrugged. "All kinds of things. My mom made sure that my brother and I could cook for ourselves, do laundry, and all kinds of domestic things. She didn't want us to be clueless."

"Your mom sounds like a wonderful person," she commented.

Trace beamed. "She's the greatest. I don't know what I would do without her and my grandparents. Family is everything."

My heart soared at his words.

That was one of my favorite things about Trace, he cared deeply for his family, and wasn't afraid to express that.

"Maybe I'll get to meet them one day." She looked between the two of us.

"Mom, please," I hissed. If I didn't watch her, she'd be asking Trace to propose before he left.

"Sorry," she chuckled. "I'm getting a bit carried away."

"Yeah, you are," I agreed.

"Olivia, it's fine. I would love for my family to meet you." He looked at my mom. Turning back to me, he added, "But I would like for Olivia to meet them first."

Oh, crap.

The color drained from my face.

Me, meet Trace's family?

Trace chuckled huskily and whispered in my ear, "It's payback time. Not really, though, they'll love you."

His words did nothing to comfort me. I had never met a guy's family before.

My chest felt tight and I idly wondered if this was what a heart attack felt like.

He laughed again before pulling away.

"I think it would be nice for Liv to meet your parents," my mom spoke to Trace. "After all, you've met me, it only seems fair." She smirked at me.

Who was this woman? She certainly wasn't the meek mother I was used to.

I cleared my throat and forced a bite of potato into my mouth. Swallowing, I asked, "When exactly would this be?"

Trace stretched an arm across the back of my chair, his early nerves about meeting my mom, completely gone. Now, *I* was the nervous one.

"Hmmm." He tapped his stubbled chin and pretended to think. "Soon, I think. They live in the area."

"That sounds ... wonderful." I swallowed a gulp of water. Actually, a lobotomy sounded less frightening than meeting Trace's family. I was beginning to regret caving to my mom and inviting him to meet her. This was causing *me* nothing but trouble.

"Don't be worried," he winked and gave my shoulder a squeeze.

"I'm not," I squeaked.

"You should know by now," he murmured, brushing a strand of hair from my shoulder, "that you can't lie to me."

I completely forgot that my mom was sitting at the table with us and blurted, "You were nervous to meet my *mom!* Now, you want me to meet your whole family!"

He chuckled. "It would only be my mom, brother, and my grandparents."

"And I only asked you to meet my mom! One person, not four!" I cried.

My mom laughed and scolded, "Stop freaking out, Liv. Your shyness will only get you in trouble."

I opened and closed my mouth repeatedly.

"It's not that I have anything against meeting your family," I explained. "I just know how I am and I'll end up doing something stupid. Like ... falling in a hole."

Trace threw his head back and laughed. "I'll call beforehand and make sure all the holes are filled."

"You know how clumsy I am," I defended.

"I don't think you're that clumsy. I think you just get" —his fingers skidded down my neck and my pulse jumped— "nervous around me."

"It's kind of hard not to get nervous when you do things like that!" I hissed and flicked my gaze in my mother's direction.

"I can't help it that you're so affected by me, Olivia," he crooned.

I covered my face with my hands. "Can we not talk about this right now, with my mom sitting right *there*?" I nodded my head in her direction for emphasis.

"Whatever you want, sweetheart." He smirked, sitting back casually in his seat, like as if he hadn't just made my stomach do somersaults from his touch. "But you *will* be meeting my family *very* soon."

My temperature rose and I grabbed my glass of water, downing it.

"Liv always did get worked up over the littlest things," my mom explained.

"I've noticed that." Trace grinned at me. "It doesn't take much to get her ... excited."

My closed fist connected with his thigh, but he laughed it off, his green eyes glowing with mirth.

My mom moved the conversation to less ... stomach-churning topics, asking me about school, and Trace about being mechanic.

At the end of dinner, I volunteered to clean the dishes, and Trace offered to stay and help me so that my mom could go on up to bed.

"Are you sure?" she asked, eyeing us.

"Absolutely positive," I assured her, already stacking the dirty plates.

"All right." She stood. "Thank you." She hugged me and then Trace. "I hope I get to see you again soon. You're a nice young man, perfect for Liv."

I rolled my eyes.

"I'd like to see you again too, Nora. Maybe you and Olivia can come for dinner at my place," he suggested.

"That would be lovely," she beamed. "Night you two. Don't get into trouble now." She looked between us.

I waved her off and then picked up the heavy stack of dishes to carry to the sink but Trace snatched them from me.

Grinning, he said, "Can't have you dropping these, Olivia."

"Oh, no, that would be tragic." I laughed, following him to the sink.

I turned the water on and added soap.

The Callahan's had a fancy dishwasher but I was scared to work it. It had way too many buttons and I was afraid I might break it.

Trace and I worked in silence. He cleaned the dishes and I dried them before putting them away.

"We make a good team," I joked, bumping his hip with mine.

"We do." He grinned down at me. "I hated saying goodbye to you the other morning," he whispered, staring into my eyes. "I wanted to keep you in my bed all day."

My body hummed at his words and the promise behind them.

"I didn't want to leave," I confessed.

He hooked his fingers into the belt loops on my jeans, and pushed me into the edge of the counter, staring down at me.

"And why would you want to leave?" He smirked. Pushing his hips into mine, he added, "I'm *spectacular*."

"You're so full of yourself," I groaned but couldn't keep the smile off my face.

He lifted me up onto the counter so that we were closer in height. "When you're as wonderful as I am, there's no point in sugar coating it."

I rolled my eyes and opened my mouth to retort, but he covered my reply with his lips. I hummed in satisfaction. His fingers edged under my shirt, rubbing across my stomach, and then venturing up my back, stopping on the clasp of my bra

He pulled away and smiled crookedly. "I better stop before I take you right here."

I paled at his words, imagining my mom walking in on us. That would be beyond embarrassing.

He chuckled at my reaction. "I love embarrassing you."

"You're mean," I groaned, leaning my forehead against his hard chest.

He cupped my cheeks, pulling my head back so that I was forced to look at him. "I really do want you to meet my family," he whispered huskily, "and it has absolutely nothing to do with getting back at you."

"What if they hate me?" I pouted.

"They won't," he assured me, "and even if they did, it wouldn't change the way I feel about you." He leaned forward, taking one of my earlobes between his teeth, and giving it a light nip.

I swallowed thickly. "When do you want me to meet them?"

"I'm supposed to have lunch with them in two days. Is that too soon?" he questioned.

"It's perfect," I squeaked.

CHAPTER NINETEEN

I knocked lightly on Avery's closed bedroom door. I was supposed to be meeting Trace's family today, but at the rate I was going, it would be the next century before I was ready. I had tried on everything in my suitcase and wasn't happy with any of my clothes. I wanted to look nice and make a good impression, but everything I owned fell flat.

"Come in," Avery replied to my knock.

I pushed her door open and found her lying on the floor of her room flipping through a magazine while the TV blared in the background.

"What's up?" she asked, turning a page of the magazine.

"I'm supposed to be meeting Trace's mom, brother, and grandparents," I replied, nervously biting on my lower lip.

"Whoa, lover boy is bringing out the big guns. Grandparents, huh?" She smirked, sitting up.

"I know, right? I'm super nervous," I admitted.

"I bet you are." She looked at me sympathetically.

"I was hoping" —I kicked a spot on the floor— "that you would help me get ready. I can't find anything to wear."

Avery grinned. "Of course I'll help you." She hopped up from the floor and opened her closet doors, motioning for me to follow her.

"Geez, Avery," I remarked, looking around her spacious closet, "it looks like a mall in here."

Everything was perfectly organized with shelves, drawers, and racks lining the space. It was exceptionally neat; nothing at all like her closet in our dorm room, which consistently looked like a bomb had went off.

"I have a lot of stuff." She shrugged, rifling through one of the color-coded racks of dresses.

"It's very—uh—organized," I mumbled.

Avery glanced at me and rolled her eyes. "My mom is a control freak and makes the maid keep it neat. If it was left up to me ..." she drifted off with a small shrug of her shoulders.

"It would be a hot mess?" I supplied.

"Yeah, that about sums it up." She smirked. "What do you think of this?" She held out a flowered print wrap dress.

"I think I'd be cold," I muttered.

She sighed. "Do you want to make a good impression or not?"

"Of course I do." I glared at her.

"Then you'll wear the dress, with black tights" —she rummaged through the drawer, and pulled out a pair— "and this blazer," she added, pulling it off of its hanger.

I took the clothes from her and mumbled, "I don't want to look *too* dressed up."

"Trust me, Olivia. You want to make a good impression on them and a dress says that you're a good girl," she explained.

"As per usual," I muttered, "your logic is whack."

"You'll be thanking me later." She placed a hand on her hip. "And stop pouting, you're the one that asked for my help."

"You're right. I'm sorry. I'm really—"

"Nervous," she finished. "I know. Change into that and I'll do your hair and makeup."

My eyes widened.

"I promise not to make you look like hooker." She flounced out of the closet. "I'll keep the red lipstick far away."

I sighed as she closed the closet door.

If I was this nervous now, what would I be like by the time Trace picked me up?

"I TOLD you I wouldn't make you look like a hooker." Avery spun me around to face my reflection.

She had managed to keep my hair and makeup simple. My eyes were shadowed in different shades of light grays and my lips were slick with a pale pink gloss. She had added a light amount of blush and bronzer to my cheeks. My hair was pulled back in a messy, but stylish, side-bun.

"Avery, you're a life-saver," I breathed. "Thank you."

"I try." She smiled and did a little curtsy.

I turned away from my reflection and hugged her. "I seriously don't know what I would do without you as my best friend."

"You wouldn't have nearly as much fun."

I pulled away. "That's true."

"What time is Trace supposed to get here?" she asked.

I picked up my cellphone, which I had placed on her bathroom counter, and read the time. "Any minute," I groaned as my nerves shot through the roof and straight to outer space. "I'm going to go say goodbye to my mom." I knew it was silly, but since we had escaped Aaron, I kept checking on her to make sure she was still here. I was afraid that she'd disappear.

Avery winced.

"What?" I questioned from the doorway of her bathroom.

"Your mom isn't here," she muttered quietly.

"What? Where did she go? Why isn't she here?" I went into panic mode, assuming the worst, which was that Aaron had found her.

She eyed me sheepishly. "My brother took her to lunch."

"*What?*" I shrieked.

"Apparently my brother has the hots for your mom." She giggled but quickly sobered when she saw that I didn't find it funny.

"Your brother's twenty-two. That's disgusting."

"I told ya Nick liked them older. Besides, your mom is really pretty."

Even though we had only been here a week, my mom looked like a whole new person. Her eyes were bright and she smiled more. She had bought new clothes that weren't so frumpy and she'd even gotten her hair cut and styled. She looked nothing like the woman I'd called mom in New Hampshire.

I shuddered. "My mom and your brother. I can't even." I shook my head rapidly back and forth.

Avery made a face like she had sucked on a sour grape. "That was not a pleasant visual I just got in my head."

"Ew! Avery!" I shrieked.

She giggled. "Sorry, I'm a visual person."

"Stop." I covered my eyes. "Please, stop. I *cannot* be thinking about this right now."

At that moment my phone beeped, saving me from the nasty seed Avery had planted in my head.

Unfortunately, I wasn't quite saved.

TRACE: *I'm here. U ready?*
Me: *I'll be down in a minute.*

. . .

"Wish me luck," I told Avery.

"You don't need any," Avery tsked. "They'll love you. You're every parents' dream for their son. You're pretty, smart, and nice." She ticked each attribute off on her fingers.

"Thanks." I took a deep breath. "I'm sorry to run out and leave you here—"

"It's no big deal. I'm going to Luca's."

I sighed. "I should've known."

"You better get out of here before Tracey-poo comes in here after you."

I rolled my eyes. "Can you please stop calling him by that ridiculous name?" I asked, striding out of her room.

"Nope!" she called after me.

I sighed and grabbed my purse from the guestroom before making my way downstairs and out through the garage.

It was snowing again; a good inch already coated the ground. Growing up in New Hampshire I was used to heavy snows but people in this area flipped out if there was even a dusting of snow on the ground.

"Hey." I smiled lightly, climbing into the car.

"You look nice. Who are you trying to impress? It's certainly not me," he joked with a small chuckle.

I tugged on the end of the dress and buckled my seatbelt. "Hmm, who could I want to impress?"

"They're going to love you." He reached for my hand and gave it a small squeeze before letting go to back out of the driveway. "Don't worry. I was nervous to meet your mom, and she liked me, *right?*"

"That's because you're extremely likable," I groaned. "I'm the quiet shy girl that everybody overlooks because they think she's standoffish. I don't want your family to think I'm rude."

"They would never think that." Trace sighed, glancing both ways before turning out of the neighborhood.

"How do you know?" I sulked. My nerves were getting the best of me. I had *never ever* met a guy's parents, because I had never dated before. This was completely new for me. I didn't know what to do or what to say.

"Because, I know everything." He winked.

I fanned my face. "It's really hot in here." I wiggled in my seat. "I think my butt's on fire."

Trace chuckled and pushed a button. "Sorry, the seat warmers *are* kinda hot."

"How far away does your mom live?" I asked, chewing nervously on my fingernail.

Trace grabbed my hand and pulled it away from my mouth. "Not that far."

"That's vague." I frowned.

"About fifteen to twenty minutes from here."

"And your grandparents will be there too? Are they your mom's parents or your dad's?" I rattled.

"They're my dad's parents and they—uh—live with my mom and brother. Or my mom and brother live with them. Whichever way you prefer to look at it." He ran a hand through his hair.

"Um-okay, because that's not confusing at all," I muttered.

He chuckled. "It used to be my grandparents' house but they gave it to my dad. They continued to live there though."

"Gotcha," I mumbled, staring out the window at the snow falling.

We both grew quiet and I silently coached myself that everything would be okay, and I wouldn't make a complete and total fool out of myself.

I never did well with meeting new people and I knew my anxiety would be ten times worse with meeting Trace's family.

I chewed nervously on my bottom lip, and it began to bleed,

but I didn't care. It distracted me and that's exactly what I wanted. I'd chew right through it if I had to.

We drove deep into a thickly wooded area with large houses every few acres or so.

Finally, Trace came to a plain black mailbox, and turned in the driveway, but I still couldn't see the house. The forest surrounded us and I was afraid the craggily branches on the nearby trees would scratch the shiny black finish of the car.

The driveway, or maybe it was a road, went on *forever*. We still hadn't come to an end five minutes later.

"Are you really taking me to your mom's house or did you just drive me out here to murder me where no one can hear me scream?" I gulped.

Trace's laughter filled the car. "You're funny."

Actually, I was being serious. We were in the middle of nowhere and the snow was coming down in thick white flakes that blanketed the ground like a fluffy blanket. At this rate, it would snow six or eight inches. In this area, that was rare and akin to the zombie apocalypse.

But seriously, if Trace wanted to off me, all he'd have to do—

"Oh, my God," I gasped as the trees finally opened up.

High up on the peak of the hill we were currently driving up to was the biggest house—no, mansion—I had ever seen. Avery's house was huge but could have easily fit inside this one *twice*.

It was huge ... gymungo ... gargantuan ... imposing. And I was all out of words to describe it. It was all brick with tall windows. A high fence hid the backyard but I was sure there was a massive pool back there and whatever else rich people put in their yards.

My mouth was hanging open and I was pressed as close to the glass of the windshield as possible.

"This isn't real," I muttered.

I couldn't get over the sheer size of the place. I had seen big houses before but never anything like this. It looked like something that should belong to a celebrity not a normal person.

"*This* is where you grew up?" I squeaked.

"Yeah," Trace replied, chuckling at my reaction.

"People live here?" I gasped.

He snorted. "That's typically what people do, you know, live in houses."

"But it's so *big!*" I exclaimed, squinting my eyes, as if that alone would make the mansion smaller.

Trace scratched the back of his head and muttered, "I know."

"I thought you said your dad was a mechanic?" I accused.

"He was ... but it wasn't his job, just a hobby." He parked the car in front of a four-car garage attached to the mansion. There was another four-car garage detached from the house with what looked like an apartment overhead.

"*Who are you?*" I glared at him. I felt like he had lied to me. I thought Trace was just a normal guy, with normal parents, a normal childhood, and *this* was anything but normal.

He ground his teeth together and yanked the keys out of the ignition, fiddling with them. "I knew you would react like this and that's exactly why I didn't tell you."

"This is a big thing to keep from me!" I pointed to the house. "You-you're-ugh!"

"This" —he pointed to the mansion— "changes *nothing*, Olivia. I'm still me."

"But," I gasped, "you were raised by Daddy Warbucks or something!" I exclaimed, still gaping open-mouthed.

He pinched the bridge of his nose. "I don't know how to explain this to you."

"How about you use your words for starters!" I was getting angry now. I had been nervous enough to meet his family; toss in this, and I was close to having a heart attack. This was completely unexpected and it made me realize just how little I really did know about Trace. If he had kept this a secret, what else was he hiding?

He licked his lips and took a deep breath. "I come from old money—"

"That makes me feel so much better!" I snapped sarcastically, crossing my arms over my chest.

"Are you going to listen to what I have to say or not?" He waited for me to nod before continuing. "Like I said, I come from old money. It goes back several generations. I was never that interested in our family history so I don't know how many greats it might be. Anyway, Great-Granddaddy-Whatever made his fortune during World War I when he invented some new way to make bullets or some shit like that, and it made him a lot of money, and the business boomed from there."

"This is insane," I whispered.

"I am not this." He pointed to the house. "I am me" —he shoved a finger into his chest— "and my family history does not define me. I can't change where I come from, Olivia, and I wouldn't want to." He pulled at the ends of his hair. "I have a good, loving, family that is nothing like the uppity people you're thinking of," he growled. "They're normal everyday people. Don't you think I'm normal?" he pleaded.

I nodded.

He took a deep breath. "I don't want you to look at me differently because of this. I thought springing it on you would be the best route, but I can see now I was wrong."

"I'm sorry." I placed a hand on his cheek and forced him to look at me. "I shouldn't have reacted like that. It upset me because I feel like I've shared so much with you, and if you didn't tell me about this, what else are you not telling me."

"Fair enough," he whispered. "But *please* go inside and don't freak out. I know it's a big house and it seems overwhelming, but my family is perfectly normal. In fact, we might be a little bit redneck."

"I doubt that." I rolled my eyes and a small laugh escaped my lips.

"You'd be surprised. We better get in there before they come out to see what's taking us so long."

"You're right." I looked at the time on my phone and saw that we had been talking for ten minutes.

"Oh, and Olivia?" he asked, leaning toward me.

"Yeah?" I replied feeling a little sick knowing I was about to meet the Rockefeller's of Virginia.

"I've thought of something that might distract you from your nerves," his voice had grown husky and his eyes were a dark forest green.

"What?" I squeaked.

"This," he murmured, and grabbed the back of my neck, pulling my lips against his. He kissed me thoroughly, leaving me flustered when he pulled away.

"Was that sufficient?" His lips turned up in a lopsided grin.

"What?" I muttered.

"Yep, it worked." He hopped out of the car and jogged around to open the passenger door.

I stepped onto the driveway, my feet sinking through three inches of snow, and the little white fluff balls quickly gathered in my hair and on my shoulders.

Trace looked up, sticking out his tongue to catch a flake. I watched one fall onto his eyelash where it immediately melted and he wiped it away.

Once he was successful in catching a snowflake, he grinned at me impishly, like a small boy.

"I had to." He chuckled and held out his hand for me to take.

We hesitantly made our way to the garage, cautious of the slippery ground. Trace flipped open a panel and entered a code. A second later, one of the garage doors began to raise.

I took a deep breath, tempted to beg him to kiss me again. My heart had plummeted to my stomach and my stomach had dropped entirely out of my body and was currently flopping around on the ground.

"Breathe," Trace reminded me.

I let out a gust of air.

"Breathe," he repeated as he twisted the knob on the door and leaned over to push a button that closed the garage door.

With a firm grip on my hand, he led me into the house.

It didn't take long for me to get confused. The house was massive. We passed by so many open and closed doors that I quickly lost count.

The wide hallway opened up and we stood in a large foyer with the highest ceiling I had ever seen and a shiny marble floor. I turned around, taking in the two massive staircases, and tilted my head back to gaze at a chandelier that was bigger than my car.

"Wow," I gasped in awe. "Are you sure we're still in Virginia?"

"I'm sure," he chuckled.

"This place belongs in Beverly Hills," I murmured, turning around to face the massive front door. "I've never seen a house like this before. Only on TV and in magazines." My mouth was open in awe.

"It's all right." He shrugged with a laugh.

"All right?" I smacked his shoulder.

He grinned. "Okay, maybe it's *more* than all right."

"I'd say," I whispered, peering to the right of the staircases where there was a living room. A gas fireplace was lit there, and I watched the flames for a moment, admiring the way they illuminated the room with an orange glow.

"Enough gawking." Trace grabbed my hand, leading me to a different part of the house. I think he was purposely trying to get me lost so that if I decided to run, I wouldn't be able to find my way out.

Suddenly, Trace stopped, and I would've fallen over my feet if he hadn't had a firm hold on my hand.

"I really am sorry that I didn't tell you." He cupped my cheek with his free hand.

"It's okay," I sighed. "I understand why you didn't." I glanced around at the spacious hallway and expensive fixtures. "It's a bit much."

"Still, you were right. You've been honest with me, Olivia, and I didn't return the favor." He rubbed his thumb over my cheek. "I won't make that mistake again."

"All right," I breathed, my eyes fluttering closed as his thumb skirted over my lips.

He kissed me lightly, and I jerked back, eyes popping open. "Trace! Someone might see!"

"You're so shy. It was just a little kiss."

"Yeah, a kiss that your mom, grandma, grandpa, or brother could've walked in on." I ticked each of them off on my fingers.

"You worry too much. Live a little." He grinned and pushed open the double doors we had stopped in front of.

The doors opened into a formal dining room, that much was clear, but I couldn't look around. Instead, my gaze was focused on the four people sitting at the table, looking right at me.

Trace cleared his throat. "Hi, Mom."

She smiled at her son and then smiled at me. "You must be Olivia. Trace can't seem to stop talking about you."

My cheeks colored at her words and my eyes darted to the ground.

"Mom," Trace groaned.

"Don't Mom me." She eyed her son. "It's true and it makes me so happy that Trace has finally found someone he cares so much about," she addressed me.

"Thank you," I squeaked.

"Stop being rude, boy," a gruff man with thinning gray hair said from the end of the table, "introduce us to your girl."

Trace coughed. "Olivia, that old geezer is my Gramps, Warren."

"Just call me, Gramps." Warren smiled. "No need to get all fancy."

Trace pointed to the distinguished older lady beside his grandpa. She had curly, shoulder-length, graying blonde hair. Her eyes and smile were kind when she looked at me. She had a calming affect that instantly put me at ease. "And that lovely lady is my Grammy, Eleanor."

Eleanor smiled and surprised me by scooting her chair back to hug me. Trace released my hand and I hugged his grandma back. "It's so nice to meet you, sweetie." She held me at arm's length. "Call me Grammy or Ellie, it's up to you."

"It's nice to meet you too, Ellie." I smiled back.

She took her seat and Trace pointed to his mom. "That's my mom, Lily."

Lily, like Eleanor, stood to hug me. She was on the shorter side with straight dark brown hair and bright blue eyes.

"It's nice to meet you, Lily," I whispered when she pulled away. My voice had all but completely left me.

"And that fucktard—"

"*Trace!*" Lily and Ellie screamed while Warren chuckled.

"—is my brother, Trenton." Trace grinned.

"But everyone calls me Trent," the guy spoke up. He looked a lot like his brother, with dark hair and expressive eyes, but while Trace's were green, Trent's were a bright blue like his mom's. A black baseball cap sat atop his head and he had black gauges in his ears. His grin was infectious, with small dimples indenting each cheek, and I was sure that the girls at his school dropped at his feet. Trace had the whole hot bad boy thing going for him but

Trent had it even more. The sleeves of his blue sweatshirt were rolled up to his elbows and at the edge of the fabric, I saw the start of a tattoo that I was sure went up the rest of his arm.

I waved. "Hi."

"Now that introductions have been made, you can sit down and eat," Warren said.

I followed Trace to the side of the table where his grandma and Trent were sitting. He pulled out the chair beside his brother and flicked his hand in a gesture for me to sit down. I did and he pushed the chair into the table.

"I knew there was a gentleman in there somewhere," Warren chortled.

"Gramps," Trace muttered, "quit it."

"A little teasing never killed anyone." Warren winked and took a sip of red wine. "Cecilia!" he called through a doorway I hadn't noticed. An older Hispanic lady came scurrying into the room. "We're ready for lunch."

Cecilia brought out each of our plates and drinks for Trace and me. She paused by Warren's chair, waiting for instruction.

"That'll be all," he said, "please help yourself to a plate in the kitchen. There's plenty."

She smiled and scurried out of the room, her short black heels clacked against the marble floors.

I took a bite of the roasted chicken. It was coated in a citrus glaze with a hint of basil and the flavors exploded across my tongue.

I was swallowing a bite of garlic-mashed potatoes when Lily asked, "Did you grow up around here?"

"No." I shook my head. "I grew up in New Hampshire. I came here for college."

"Oh, what are you planning to major in?"

"I want to be an English teacher," I answered nervously.

She beamed. "I was a science teacher before I met my husband. I miss it."

"Really?" I asked, shocked.

She nodded. "It's a rewarding job when you're in it for the right reasons. So," she cleared her throat, "are you planning on staying here after you graduate or going back to New Hampshire?"

Before I could answer her, Trent nudged my arm. "That's her backwards way of asking if you're going to take my brother away. He's her favorite." He grinned boyishly. His smile and looks were so similar to Trace's that it was disarming.

Trace chuckled beside me at his brother's words and his mom was blushing. "Trent," she scolded.

"What?" He shrugged his shoulders. "It's all true."

I laughed, starting to feel more at ease. I looked across the table at Lily. "I plan on staying in the area. I like it here."

Trace squeezed my knee under the table.

She smiled. "Good, it's nice here."

"It is." I smiled back. "And the people" —I looked over at Trace— "make it even nicer."

CHAPTER TWENTY

"I told you they were nice." Trace grinned, showing me around the palatial mansion.

"They're great," I agreed.

Trace pushed open a set of double doors and dragged me inside.

I stopped in my tracks, looking around the empty room with tables and chairs for events stacked against the wall and a stage in the corner. Crystal chandeliers dotted the ceiling and gold sconces were affixed to the walls. The walls shimmered with ivory and gold wallpaper, accented by the shiny marble floors.

"A ballroom? You have a freakin' ballroom in your house," I gasped.

"Not my house."

I rolled my eyes. "According to what your grandpa said, it *will* be yours."

"Yeah." He shrugged, leading me out to the middle of the floor. "But I never plan on living here. I mean, I grew up here, and

I turned out fine, but ... it's kinda ... cold. I want a *home*. I don't want to raise my kids in a palace. I want them to have a normal life, with a dog, and white picket fence."

I smiled. "You want kids?"

"Well, yeah." He scratched his head. "Not now, but eventually. Until then" —he leaned down to whisper huskily in my ear— "I'll have lots of fun practicing."

I shivered and he chuckled.

Changing the topic completely, he held out a hand for me, and asked, "May I have this dance?"

"But there's no music, and you suck at dancing."

"You wound me," he winced but with a smile. "Maybe, I just want an excuse to hold you for a little while."

I shook my head but placed my hand in his outstretched palm. He took advantage and pulled me flush against his body. With his free hand, he pressed my waist against his, and I gasped aloud when I felt the prominent bulge.

I blushed and gazed up at him. With a very bad, fake British accent, I gasped, "Mr. Wentworth, I'm scandalized."

He laughed. "It's your fault you always look so damn hot. Now," he said and his green eyes shimmered, "stop talking and just enjoy the music."

"But there is *no*—"

He began to hum and we swayed back and forth.

With a light laugh, I laid my head against his chest, listening to the steady beating of his heart.

"Now there's music," I murmured.

I didn't know how much time had passed but it wasn't long until the doors of the ballroom opened.

I reluctantly pulled away from Trace and faced Warren, who was leaning against one of the open doors, with his hand on a cane.

"What is it, Gramps?" Trace sounded concerned.

"I wanted to let you two lovebirds know that you're snowed in," he muttered. "I called the snow removal company I use and they can't get here till morning. That's what we get for living in the boonies." He thrust a finger in the air. "Regardless, it's snowing something fierce out there and not fit for driving. You'll both stay here tonight."

"No," I gasped, "I can't."

"Of course you can, darlin'." Warren covered a cough.

I looked beside me, at Trace, nervously chewing my lip.

"Looks like we're snowed in." He grinned, rubbing his hands together. "This is going to be fun."

IT WAS OFFICIAL. I had the worst luck *ever*.

Honestly, who goes to meet their boyfriend's family, and ends up snowed in at their McMansion?

This girl, that's who.

Trace and I ended up hanging out with his brother and watched movies for most of the afternoon before eating dinner and heading upstairs to go to bed.

Trace opened the door to what I assumed was a guestroom, but when he flicked the switch and the room was illuminated, I knew it *had* to be his bedroom. The walls were painted a light gray and the bedspread on the king-sized bed was charcoal and red stripes. The tip-off that it was Trace's room was the baseball memorabilia scattered around.

"Nope." I bumped back into his chest. "Nope, nope, nope, *nope!* I can't sleep here." I turned around and tried to escape out the door, but he was blocking it.

"Yes, you can." His eyes darkened. "It's my room, and it's my bed, and I want *you* in it."

I gulped. "But your mom and—"

He snorted. "They're not from the dark ages, Olivia. Besides, their rooms are all on the other side of the house, and Trent's room is in the middle. Even if that wasn't the case, these walls are *really* thick."

"Trace!" I shrieked.

He answered with a chuckle and picked me up by the waist, tossing me over his shoulder.

He ran across the massive bedroom and dropped me on his bed.

He gazed down at me and wet his lips. "Now I have you right where I want you."

"Trace," I warned but he silenced me with his mouth. He was really good at doing that.

He hovered above me, careful to keep his weight from pressing against me.

I pushed at his shoulders lightly, and he pulled away, gazing at me quizzically.

"We really—"

He cut me off with another kiss.

He pulled away again and pressed his hand against my mouth. "I'm going to keep kissing you until you give in."

I glared and stuck out my tongue in an effort to lick his hand.

He grinned and wiped his hand on his jeans.

"Try that again, buddy, and I'll bite your hand," I cautioned.

"Promise?" he asked with playful wide eyes.

"You're so weird." I pushed his shoulder, and he rolled off me onto his back, and pulled me with him so that I was straddling him.

He reached up and cupped my cheek. "We don't have to do anything, Olivia. I'm perfectly content to lay here and hold you in my arms."

I snorted. "Yeah, it *really* feels like you're okay with that." I ground my hips against his.

He chuckled. "I can take a cold shower. Problem solved."

Conflicted, I bit down on my lower lip.

I *wanted* Trace, badly. The slow ache building in my core was proof of that, but the thought of his family being in the same house, freaked me out.

"Hey …" He reached up and tugged my lip from between my teeth, wiping away a smidgen of blood I had drawn. "It's okay."

"Are you sure?" I asked hesitantly.

He sat up with me in his lap, cradling my bottom in his hands. "Absolutely, Olivia. I would never force you to do something you're uncomfortable with."

I leaned my head against his chest and nodded. "I want to … I do … but I can't."

He forced my head back so that he could stare into my eyes. "I understand." He kissed me sweetly. With a grin, he added, "I wouldn't feel comfortable with your mom around hearing you scream my name."

I ground my teeth together and narrowed my eyes. "Do you think before you talk?"

"Of course" —he fingered one of my loose curls— "but I enjoy watching your reactions to the things I say. A blush here" —he grazed his fingers lightly over my cheek— "or there" —he brushed the curve of my ear. "But my favorite" —he looked into my eyes— "is when you blush right *here* …" He skimmed his fingers lightly over my breasts.

My breath stuttered out in short little gasps as I tried to get air to my oxygen-deprived brain.

Trace held out a hand to me. "Want to shower?" My eyes widened and he chuckled. "I promise to be good boy and go down the hall to take my shower, separate from you."

"Sure." I nodded. I knew if Trace got in the shower with me, neither of us would be able to hold back.

He led me through a short hallway in his bedroom. There was

a door on the left that he said was his closet and the door to our right was the bathroom. I could see through the archway in front of us that there was even a living room attached to his bedroom.

Trace opened the bathroom door with a flourish.

I stepped inside, looking around at the shiny black floors and countertops, gray walls, and all the fancy finishing touches. My eyes zeroed in on the massive shower that looked more like a car wash. It could have easily fit six people inside.

The amount of knobs and showerheads was scary.

"I'm never going to be able to work that." I pointed to the shower.

"It's not as hard as it looks." He chuckled. "But I'll get it going for you."

I watched as he turned several knobs, water spraying out of a rain showerhead and body sprayers. He checked the temperature and closed the glass shower door.

"I'll grab you some of my old clothes to wear. I doubt that would be comfortable to sleep in." He plucked at my dress. He grinned impishly. "And if you sleep naked, I can't be held accountable for my actions."

Before I had the chance to reply, he strode out of the bathroom and into his closet. He returned with an old high school baseball team shirt and a pair of boxers. He laid them on the counter then dug underneath the cabinet, pulling out a cloth and towel. He placed those on the counter and continued to look for something.

"Aha!" he finally chimed and held out a new toothbrush and toothpaste triumphantly. "You should be all set." He looked around the bathroom, which was quickly filling with steam.

"Thank you." I smiled, suddenly feeling bashful.

He kissed my cheek, as if sensing my sudden shyness, and closed the door behind him.

I wasn't in the shower long; just enough to clean my body, and scrub my face free of makeup. I could wash my hair in the morning. I had always hated washing my hair at night and going to bed with it wet.

I dried off, wrapped the towel around my body, brushed my hair out with a comb I found on the counter, and then brushed my teeth.

I pulled on Trace's shirt and it hung down past my butt but not quite to my knees. I grabbed his boxers and pulled those on as well so I wouldn't feel so exposed.

I cleaned up the counter and then padded back into his bedroom. He wasn't back yet and I breathed a sigh of relief. I pushed the covers back and sighed in pleasure at the feeling of the soft sheets rubbing my skin.

The door cracked open and Trace tiptoed inside.

"I'm not asleep." I grinned.

"Oh." He chuckled, running his fingers through his damp hair.

I sat up and studied him in the dim light of the bedroom. "Are you wearing glasses?"

"Oh, um, yeah," he stuttered. "I can't sleep in my contacts."

"I didn't know you wore glasses." I tilted my head and smiled at him. "I like them."

"They're so dorky," he groaned, sliding in beside me.

"I don't think so." I laid back and turned on my side to face him in the bed. The glasses were thick black-framed retro looking ones.

"You're just saying that."

"I'm not lying, you look good in them. You should wear them more often." I cupped my hands under my head.

"I didn't know you had a fetish for glasses," he snickered.

"You're impossible." I rolled over to my other side and faced away from him.

He turned out the light on his side of the bed. The sheets rustled as he wiggled around and settled beside me.

"Are you mad at me?" he asked. "Or can I hold you?"

"You can hold me," I whispered. The bed dipped down behind me, as he scooted closer until my back was spooned to his front, and his arm was thrown across my body.

"Good. I wanted to make sure before you bit my arm off or something."

"We have all night," I warned.

"I love it when your spitfire side comes out," he whispered.

I snorted, and closed my eyes, resolving not to reply so that I could get some sleep.

I was close to drifting asleep when Trace whispered, "Olivia?"

"Yeah," I replied softly.

He paused. "Why did you tell me about your list?"

I had often asked myself the same thing. *Why so soon? Why Trace? What made him different?*

"I-I don't know. You ... made me feel ... safe," I stuttered. "A part of me didn't want to tell you ..." I paused. "I was afraid of what you would think of me. But something made me take that leap. I guess ..." I searched for the right words to explain how I felt. "I guess I was tired of being the girl hiding in the shadows. I wanted you to show me the light."

"Regardless," he whispered huskily, his breath gusting against my ear, and the curve of my cheek, "I'm glad you did."

"Me too," I replied, but the words were barely above a whisper.

I WAS SHAKING.

Why was I shaking?

"Wake up," Trace coaxed and I felt something soft press against my lips.

Slowly, I opened my eyes to see Trace hovering above me. He

grinned like a little boy. "I knew kissing you would do the trick, just like Cinderella."

"You're thinking of Sleeping Beauty." I yawned, covering my open mouth with a hand.

"Whatever." He rolled off of me.

"Are you always this ... *chipper* in the mornings?" I groaned.

"No, I'm usually horny."

I tossed a pillow at his face. He caught it and tucked it behind his back.

"It's not that I'm not horny this morning," he continued much to my dismay, "I just figured you wouldn't appreciate waking up with me between your legs."

I moaned, and it wasn't in irritation. His words had sent tingles of pleasure straight through me.

Damn him.

He licked his lips and leaned closer. "Based on that little moan of pleasure, I'm guessing you wouldn't have objected."

His hand skimmed over the side of my hip, and he nuzzled my neck, kissing it tenderly. I pushed his shoulder so he ended up sprawled across the other side of the bed. He looked excited, no doubt he was thinking I was about to hop on, and take a ride. Crazy man. "Down, boy," I warned.

"Ugh, you're mean," he pretended to wince.

"And you're driving me insane." I sighed.

"Are my ploys working?" He gazed at me with a smirk.

I rolled my eyes and climbed from the bed.

"I'm going to shower," I called as I walked away.

"You can run but you can't hide," he sing-songed and I heard rustling as he climbed from the bed.

"Don't even think about joining me, bud. I know what your agenda is and it's *not* happening," I snapped.

"Fine," I heard him say before I closed the bathroom door. "I'll just take you back to my place and handcuff you to my bed. Problem solved," he cackled.

I washed my long hair in record time, afraid that Trace was going to pop in the bathroom any second. He was driving me insane with all his innuendos, and I was close to taking him up on it, but the thought of being in his family's house was too awkward for me to get over. Especially, since I had only met them last night.

If he kept it up, though, I *would* be begging him to chain me to his bed.

What had Trace turned me into?

I dressed quickly in the same outfit I wore yesterday which I had left folded neatly on the counter.

When I walked back into the bedroom, Trace was dressed, and the bed was made.

"Hungry?" he asked. "Cecilia made breakfast."

"Starving." I smiled graciously.

I followed him through the maze-like house and into the dining room. We were the first to arrive and Cecilia was starting to bring out different dishes of food.

"Do you guys always eat your meals in here?" I asked, looking around at the grandeur dining room.

"Yeah, Gramps likes to eat in here. He says if we're going to have a fancy dining room we might as well use it. There's an eat-in area in the kitchen but it's never been used."

"Huh," I mused quietly. "I would think there would be a lot of unused spaces in this house."

"Gramps is weird." Trace shrugged.

"Respect your elders, boy," Warren snapped as he came hobbling into the dining room. He stopped behind Trace and smacked the back of his head with a surprising amount of strength.

"Sorry, Gramps," Trace muttered.

"You gotta watch this one." Warren chuckled as he sat down,

and addressed me, a finger pointed at his grandson. "If he gets outta line, you've just got to give him a little smack." He swatted at the air for emphasis. "That'll straighten him right up."

I laughed. "I'll keep that in mind."

The rest of the family strolled casually into the dining room.

I grabbed a bagel and slathered it in cream cheese and added two scoops of mixed fruits onto my plate.

Cecilia brought out champagne flutes filled with orange juice and a slim orange slice along the rim.

"How did you sleep?" Trace's mom, Lily, asked me.

"Well, thank you." I took a sip of orange juice.

"I'm glad the guestroom was to your liking." She smiled.

"Wait, what?" I gasped.

Trace snickered beside me.

I glared over at him.

"Way to go!" Trent fist bumped Trace.

"Oh, God." I hung my head in my hands.

"I—uh—take it you didn't sleep in the guestroom." Lily chuckled.

"This is so embarrassing," I mumbled

"Don't be embarrassed," she said as she shrugged, spearing her scrambled eggs, "you're both adults."

"Still ..." I glared at Trace. "You're such a little liar."

"I told you she wouldn't care."

"Ugh," I groaned, praying a hole would open up and swallow me.

Warren cleared his throat, drawing everyone's attention to the head of the table. "I was able to speak with Cameron who owns the snow removal business we use, and he said that they should be able to clear the driveway this afternoon."

I smiled gratefully and then paled. "Oh, my God!" I stood up from the table. "I forgot to let my mom and Avery know we got snowed in. They're probably so worried." I started to dart away from the table but Trace caught my arm.

"I talked to your mom last night, you were in the shower, and your phone rang," he explained. "I answered and told her what had happened."

"Oh, thank goodness." I put a hand to my racing heart and sat back down.

Trent snickered from across the table. "Did you seriously say, 'Thank goodness'?"

"Um, yeah," I replied.

He laughed quietly. "Grammy says that."

"That's because Grammy's cool." Trace slung his arm across the back of my chair.

"Grammy's not cool," Trent snorted.

Ellie glared at her youngest grandson. "Who was it that went snowboarding with you during winter break last year?"

"You did," Trent squeaked.

"And what did you say then?" She raised a brow, waiting for his response.

"That you were the coolest grandma ever," he mumbled, looking down at the shiny wooden table.

Ellie smiled. "Now that that's settled, let's all enjoy this lovely breakfast."

"Okay." I held up a finger. "So in the basement, there's a movie theater, a game room, a basketball court, and a bowling alley. What else do you guys have?"

"Well" —Trace collapsed on the huge sectional couch in the family room— "in the backyard, there's a pool with a diving board, slide, and waterfall. There's a hot tub too. And if you don't mind walking, we have a tennis court, because back in the day,

Grammy played and Gramps added that. We also have a couple of tree stands for hunting scattered around the property."

I stood, looking around the gargantuan family room.

Trace grabbed my arm and pulled me on top of him. He smoothed my hair away from my eyes and cupped my cheek. "You look like a little kid in a candy store with your mouth hanging open like that. Should I find you a lollipop?"

I rolled my eyes. "It's kinda unbelievable that you grew up here and your family is great. They're not stuffy at all. I love your grandpa," I thundered on, ignoring his statement about lollipops.

"I told you, and they love you."

I snuggled against his warm chest and closed my eyes. "I love them too," I murmured, before the calming symphony of our breaths sang me to sleep.

CHAPTER TWENTY-ONE

I hugged Warren tightly. I had never met my grandparents and I found something in Warren that I connected with.

"Come back and see us," he whispered in my ear. "Don't worry about being with Trace. Come anytime, ya hear?"

I pulled away and nodded. "I will."

He smiled and his eyes crinkled at the corners.

My eyes lit upon a picture behind Warren. "Is that—"

He turned and smiled sadly. "Trace's dad?" he supplied.

I nodded.

"It is. The resemblance is uncanny. Trey marked both of those boys. There is no doubting they're members of the Wentworth family. Trace looks the most like him, though," Warren explained. "That boy loved his daddy something fierce. He did some bad things after Trey died in the accident. He was like a different person. Somehow, he found his way back to the light, and I'm so thankful for it," Warren breathed. "For a while there, it was like we lost two people. Did Trace tell you that he was with his dad when he died?"

"No," I gasped, tears automatically welling in my eyes.

"He doesn't like to talk about it but they were out goofing around on those bikes and a semi-truck slammed into Trey. Bastard didn't even stop. Trey was in front of Trace, so poor Trace saw everything. There were body parts scattered everywhere."

Sobs raked my body. "Th-That's h-h-horr-ible," I stuttered.

I couldn't imagine the kind of pain that one would experience from an event like that. No wonder Trace had gone off the deep end. Anyone would.

"Don't cry, sweetie." Warren hugged me to his robust chest. His hand rubbed up and down my back soothingly. "I didn't tell ya to make ya cry. I just wanted to help you understand my grandson better. He pushed everyone away after his dad died and I don't want to see him do the same thing to you because, Olivia, you're the best thing that's happened to him in a long time." He swallowed thickly. "If he grows distant, you're going to have to push him, don't let him retreat into that dark hole he disappears to inside himself."

"I won't," I vowed, remembering the first time Trace kissed me, and how he walked away from me. I understood now why he did. When you lose someone you care about that much, it's hard to connect with someone, for the fear of getting hurt again.

Warren continued to hold me until all my tears had been shed.

"Better?" he asked, as I swiped underneath my eyes.

"Yeah." I nodded, my voice a little shaky. "I'm glad you told me. It was just a lot to take in."

"Of course," he replied as the others joined us in the foyer.

"Why are you crying?" Concerned, Trace ran to my side and began looking me over.

"I'm fine." I squirmed under his gaze.

"No, you're not. You're crying, and in my book, crying never means someone's fine or okay. Tell me what's wrong so I can fix it," he pleaded.

I looked at Warren pleadingly for him to come up with an excuse.

"I was just telling Olivia," Warren started, "that I may not know her well but I consider her as much my granddaughter as you are my grandson and that she's welcome here anytime. She just got emotional, that's all. Women cry for no reason sometimes, boy, get used to it." He clapped Trace on the shoulder before disappearing behind a door I had been told led to his home office.

"You see, I never had grandparents." I shrugged, trying to explain away my tears further. I didn't think Trace would take too kindly to the fact that his grandpa had told me how his dad died.

"Oh." He nodded, absorbing my words. "Okay."

I breathed a sigh of relief.

I said my goodbyes to the rest of Trace's family and followed him out through the garage.

The snow had been completely cleared. I only hoped the actual road was as snow free as the driveway.

Luckily, no one seemed brave enough to be out driving, so we practically had the road to ourselves, which was nice. I didn't have to worry about us hitting a spot of ice and slamming into another car.

Trace pulled into Avery's driveway.

"I'm sorry we got snowed in," he said softly.

"I'm not. It gave me more time to get to know them." I smiled.

He reached for my hand. "They all love you. You were great."

"I'm happy I didn't throw up on myself." I laughed. "I was really nervous."

Trace chuckled. "I think Gramps wishes he could replace Trent and me, with you."

"I doubt that." I rolled my eyes. "I better get in there—" I pointed to the door. In fact, I was kind of surprised that Avery hadn't come running out to assault me with questions.

"All right." He leaned over to kiss me deeply.

"On second thought," I breathed, cupping his chin in my hand, "I can stay."

"Nice try." He smiled, running his thumb over my lower lip.

He pecked my lips once more and I slipped out of the car. He waited for me to enter the garage code and go inside. It didn't escape my attention that there was a new car in the garage. I wondered if Avery's parents had arrived home or if another one of her brothers was here.

I opened the door that led into the mudroom and was greeted by a flustered Avery. "Olivia! There you are!" She grabbed my arm and dragged me into the kitchen. "My parents are here," she hissed in my ear warningly. "Mom, Dad," she called to the two people standing at the center island with their backs to us. "This is Olivia."

They turned around slowly. I was expecting glares and orders to get out of their house. Instead, Avery's redhead mother came striding toward me with open arms. "It's so nice to meet you, Olivia. I'm so sorry about what happened with your dad. You and your mom are welcome to stay here as long as you need to. I mean that," she insisted, holding me at arm's length. Avery looked like a younger version of her mom but with plumper cheeks and lips. Her mom was very thin and tall. Tall enough that I was sure she could have been a model. "Oh, and I'm Theresa, but just call me Resa. And this" —she motioned to the man beside her— "is my husband, Galen."

I waved awkwardly. "Hi."

"It's nice to meet you," he replied. His blonde hair was cut short and styled to perfection. His light blue eyes seemed to miss nothing. "Avery speaks highly of you," he added, peering down at me over his thin aristocratic nose, which appeared to be the only thing his daughter had inherited from him.

"Okay, great." Avery grabbed my arm again. "Now that introductions have been made, I really need to talk to my best friend."

Before her parents had a chance to respond, she pulled me out of the kitchen. I looked over my shoulder at them apologetically.

Avery led me upstairs and into her room, closing the door behind us.

"Spill girl," she demanded. "How'd it go?"

"It went good." I shrugged.

"Good?" She perched on the end of her bed and I collapsed into a green beanbag chair. "I need more details than that."

"I really liked them and I managed to not do anything stupid," I answered. "His grandpa is great."

"So, what kind of house did they live in?" she asked, twirling a lock of red hair.

"They didn't exactly live in a—uh—house," I muttered.

Her brows furrowed together. "So, where'd they live? A trailer?"

"Um, not quite." I nervously chewed on a hangnail, and wiggled, causing the balls in the beanbag chair to make a funny swishing sound.

"You're being vague, Olivia. Speak," she commanded.

"You see—well—I don't know where to begin," I stuttered, still biting on that stubborn hangnail.

"Here's a wild idea," she snapped sarcastically, "start at the beginning."

"It's a mansion, Avery," I finally managed to find the words, "and when I say a mansion, I mean a *mansion*."

"Bigger than this house?" She raised one brow.

"It makes this house look like a trailer," I replied.

She whistled. "Holy crap. Wait ..." She eyed me. "What did you say his last name is?"

"Wentworth."

"Oh, my God." She stood and began to pace across her bedroom. "I can't believe I never connected the dots before. I'm so stupid!" She smacked her forehead. "I should've known he was one *those* Wentworths. It's not like there are many around and that family is practically like royalty in this area. I just assumed he couldn't be related because why would someone worth billions be working at a mechanics shop."

"*Billions?*" I screamed shrilly. "No one said anything about billions!"

She stopped and gave me a 'duh' look. "Of course they're billionaires, Olivia, or at least pretty damn close to it."

I couldn't breathe. "Billions?" I gasped again.

It had been hard enough for me to swallow the unexpected news of Trace's family being rich, but billions went beyond rich. That was ... insane. I couldn't begin to imagine what a billion dollars even looked like or what on Earth you'd do with it.

"Hey." Avery knelt down in front of me and pulled my hands away from where they clutched my cheeks. "Are you okay? Is this what a panic attack looks like? Where's my stupid brother Ben when you need him?"

"Why do you need Ben?" I asked.

"He's a doctor." She shrugged. "Are you okay?" she repeated, looking me over.

"I don't know if I can do this," I choked.

"Do what?"

"This-This relationship with Trace—" I waved my hand dramatically. "He didn't tell me about his family being rich and now, you're telling me they're worth billions! How can I compete with that! I'm a normal girl from New Hampshire, Avery! Not the Hamptons!"

"Hey, hey, hey." She grabbed my flinging hands, and brought them down to my sides, holding them in place. "This" —she pointed her finger in my face— "is exactly why lover boy didn't tell you. Frankly, I don't blame him. You do have the tendency to overreact." I opened my mouth but she shushed me. "Trace is still the same guy he was before you found all this out."

"That's exactly what he said," I mumbled reluctantly.

She smiled. "It seems to me that Trace has tried to distance himself from that lifestyle. He works as a mechanic and lives above the garage, it seems to me that he's trying to make his own life not based on his family's name."

"It's just ... weird," I pleaded with my eyes for her to understand me. "I have *nothing* to my name and he has *everything*."

"Hey." She shook me lightly. "Money is *not* everything. Money does not buy you happiness, Olivia. A shiny new toy doesn't make up for mommy and daddy being gone all the time. It doesn't fill an ache inside you. All that matters is how you feel about Trace and how he feels about you."

I swallowed down the lump in my throat. "You're right."

"Of course I'm right," she scoffed. "I'm always right."

I scooted over and made room for her on the beanbag chair. I lay with my head on her shoulder.

"You were talking about your mom and dad, weren't you?" I asked quietly.

She nodded. "It's not that they're bad people, they're just not very good parents. They've both always been too focused on making money and traveling just the two of them. We didn't matter to them. It's sad, but true. They tried to make up for being gone all the time by giving us gifts. But that wasn't enough."

"I'm sorry, Avery," I whispered.

"It was a long time ago. I know they love me and I love them, but it's a different kind of love. It's not the way it should be. I hardly know them." We both grew quiet and then she pleaded, "Don't let your insecurities make you miss out on the greatest thing to ever happen to you."

"I won't," I sighed. "I'm in too deep."

I had fallen too far and too deep to swim back to the surface now.

I was sunk—hook, line, and sinker into Trace Wentworth.

CHAPTER TWENTY-TWO

It was Christmas day at the Callahan house, which meant it was awkward central for my mom and me.

I made my way down the curved staircase and I heard the whole family in the living room. The sounds of wrapping paper being ripped, met my ears, and I was sure they were all gathered around the massive Christmas tree.

I tried to tiptoe by them into the kitchen for a glass of orange juice, but since I had the crappiest luck *ever*, Avery spotted me.

"Olivia! Come in here!" she called, and her whole family stopped what they were doing to look at me. Her remaining four brothers had arrived a few days ago. They seemed nice but I hadn't talked to them much, preferring to stay out of the way, unnoticed. Unfortunately, Nick had a knack for finding my mother. *Gag*.

Ben, the brother that was a doctor, smiled kindly at me. "Don't stand there, come in." He waved me into the room.

"Uh." I stepped into the room and faced all of them. "I was

going to get something to drink and go back upstairs. I promise I won't be in your way."

"Olivia, please, sit down. It's Christmas," Galen said. I was surprised he had spoken. He hadn't said much to me since him and his wife arrived, he hadn't been mean to me or anything, but he certainly didn't go out of his way to make conversation.

"I feel like I'm intruding." I tried to back out of the room.

"Sit, Olivia," Avery demanded and like an obedient dog I listened. Dammit.

"That-a girl," she patted the top of my head.

"I will so get you for this," I hissed.

"Don't be such a baby. It's Christmas!" she chimed, throwing her hands in the air with excitement.

I glared at her and then began to giggle. "Why are you wearing an elf hat?" I eyed the monstrosity on her head.

"It's tradition!" she exclaimed.

I looked around and realized that Galen was wearing a Santa hat, Resa was wearing a Mrs. Klaus bonnet or whatever you wanted to call it, while Avery and the guys all wore elf hats, pointy ears included.

A giggle bubbled to the surface, and escaped my lips. At the sound of my laugh, I couldn't hold back full-blown hysterics.

"I need a picture of this." I wiped tears from my eyes and grabbed my phone from my pocket, snapping a picture of Avery before she had the chance to react. "This is so going in our dorm room." I laughed, waving my phone around.

When her brother's caught sight of the picture, they began to laugh. Pretty soon, even Resa, Galen, and Avery were laughing.

Once our laughter had ceased, Avery smiled menacingly. "Luckily, we have an extra hat." She stuck one of those ridiculous elf contraptions on my head. "Now, we can continue with presents."

"What's going on?" I turned around to see my mom standing in the doorway.

"Olivia's making everyone laugh." Nick grinned at my mom. "Join us." He patted an empty spot of carpet beside him. I watched as she made her way across the room, to Nick, and sat down beside him. He leaned over and whispered something in her ear, which made her smile and blush at the same time.

Avery and I exchanged a look and shook our heads. I had no idea where that was heading, and frankly, I didn't want to think about the possibilities.

When they started making lovey-dovey eyes at each other I wanted to point a finger at my head and yell, "Mom! Look at me! Your daughter! Over here! Stop staring at the guy young enough to be my brother!"

Nasty.

I didn't understand how she'd become so smitten with Nick so soon. I would've thought that after finally getting the courage to leave Aaron the last thing she would have been interested in would be another guy. I guess I was wrong.

"I got you something," Avery beamed and plopped a box in my lap. It was large, but light, and wrapped in shiny green paper with stockings on it.

"Avery, you didn't have to get me anything," I told her.

"I know." She shrugged, smiling at me while she played with a strand of red hair.

"I feel bad." I frowned. "I didn't get you anything."

"Don't. Besides, Christmas is about *giving* gifts not *receiving* them."

"Are you sure you're Avery Callahan?" I tapped her forehead.

"Yes." She rolled her eyes. "I do have a heart, you know. Now open it!"

I smiled and began tearing off the wrapping paper. It was just a plain brown box, taped down on all four sides. I used the edge of my fingernail to rip off the tape and then took the lid off.

I pushed aside the red and green tissue paper to find a stylish infinity scarf in different shades of blue and a navy button down pea coat.

"Avery," I gasped, pulling the items out of the box. "They're beautiful."

"I knew you'd love them!" She clapped her hands together. "As soon as I saw them, I knew you had to have them. There's a hat too." She shuffled more tissue paper aside and pulled out a beanie in one of the lighter shades of blue from the scarf.

"Avery, this is too much. I can't accept this," I whispered.

"You can and you will. You're my best friend, Livie, and I wanted to get you something nice, for putting up with all my crazy shit."

"I-I ... Thank you," I stuttered, completely taken aback by the sweet gesture.

"You're welcome," she beamed.

I hugged my best friend to my chest. "I'm so lucky to have someone as wonderful as you in my life," I confessed. I didn't tell Avery enough how much she meant to me. A lot of people were less than happy with their roommate, but I had found a lifelong friend with mine.

"I didn't know a coat would make you this happy." She giggled. "I only wanted you to stop wearing those sweatshirts."

We both dissolved into a fit of giggles.

"My sweatshirt sure didn't stop Trace," I whispered in her ear.

"Oh, my God." She laughed. "Livie! Too much information!"

"You're the girl who asks me a million and one questions about my sex life, and gives me the explicit details of hers."

"True." She put a hand over her mouth to stifle her laughter. "I do like me some details."

After that, it was hard for us to reign in our laughter.

Once every present was opened, I insisted on helping clean up. After all, they were letting my mom and me stay there for free. It was the least I could do.

Two trash bags were filled to the brim with wrapping paper and I was finally sure I had gotten everything.

I tied the bags shut and carried them to the garage, dropping them into the trashcans.

On my way back inside, my phone buzzed.

I pulled it out and saw that I had a text message from Trace.

Trace: I'll b there in 10 min. B ready.
Me: Ok.

I couldn't help smiling.

I dashed upstairs and changed out of my pajamas and into a pair of jeans and a long-sleeved sweater with an owl on it. I cut the tags off of my gifts from Avery and put them on as well. I spotted the heeled booties she had given me at the beginning of the school year and sat down on the end of the bed to put them on.

I opened the door and was greeted with a low whistle. "Lookin' nice," Dylan, the brother closest in age to Avery, said. He towered above my small frame and his blonde hair waved on the ends. His eyes were the same shade of dark green as Avery's.

"Thanks," I mumbled.

"Where you goin'?" he asked, crossing his arms over his massive chest. All of Avery's brothers were huge, tall, and muscular.

"Out," I replied casually. It's not like I owed him a lengthy explanation or anything.

"Dylan!" Avery yelled up the steps. "Leave, Livie alone. She's not going to suck your dick for you, so give it a rest!"

"Avery!" I shrieked.

"It's true!" she hollered.

With a quick glance at Dylan, I ran away from him, and down the steps before Avery could say anything else embarrassing.

I met Avery in the foyer and she assessed my outfit. "I knew that would look good on you."

"I love it." I did a little twirl and the ends of the coat flared around my knees.

"I take it Trace is coming to get you." She smiled and we started toward the garage.

"Yeah." I blushed. "Was I that obvious?"

"No, you just smile differently when Trace is involved." She opened the door that led to the garage and leaned inside to push the button that raised the garage door.

"I'll see you later. Or maybe not." She winked.

I shook my head. "Thank you again for the coat and-"

"You're welcome, Livie. I'm happy you love it so much." She pulled me into a quick hug.

I stepped outside and she closed the garage door behind me.

Trace was pulling into the driveway and I scurried inside his car before the cold penetrated my coat.

"Excited to see me?" He grinned crookedly at my speedy entrance.

"I didn't want to get cold." I laughed.

"Aw ..." He put a hand to his chest. "And here I thought you were excited to see me. I'm hurt."

"Hmm." I leaned over and kissed his stubbled cheek. "How can I make it up to you?" I whispered.

His eyes met mine and the green had darkened to a mossy gray color. "I'm sure I can think of a few different ways."

"That sounds ..." I paused, messing with him. "Exciting."

"Oh, it is." He grinned and backed out of the driveway.

"Where are we going?" I asked, looking at the snow-covered lawns.

"My place," he answered. "Unless you don't—"

"No, no, that's fine," I interjected.

"Good." He smiled and adjusted his grip on the steering wheel.

CHRISTMAS MUSIC PLAYED SOFTLY in the background, and the smell of hot chocolate permeated the air, along with the scent of freshly-baked snickerdoodle cookies. Not only could Trace cook, but he could bake as well. *Was there anything he couldn't do?*

"How many marshmallows do you want?" he asked from the kitchen.

I sat on the couch and turned so I could watch him. "Are they minis?"

"No, the big ones." He looked up at me, and held the bag aloft, shaking it for emphasis.

"Two, then."

He fixed the hot chocolate in coffee mugs and added the marshmallows then carefully carried them to where I was. He placed them on the coffee table and winced. "They're a little too hot."

Before he sat down, he went back to the kitchen to grab the plate of cookies.

He held the plate out to me and I took one of the cookies. It was cooked to perfection, and every bite was chewy, just the way I liked them.

"You're Betty Crocker." I laughed.

"It's not like I made them from scratch or anything," he

defended, sitting down beside me so that the sides of our legs touched. "It's not that difficult to heat up the oven and stick 'em in. You just have to watch them so they don't burn."

"They're delicious." I finished off the first and reached for a second.

"I'm glad you like them, but you haven't tried my hot chocolate yet. Now, *that* I do make from scratch." He grinned, a cookie crumb sitting on the corner of his mouth.

I couldn't help myself. I leaned over and licked it away.

When I pulled back, his eyes were closed, and his Adam's apple was bobbing.

"That wasn't nice," he whispered and opened his eyes. The green was light and playful.

He pounced on me and my second cookie fell to the floor as I squealed.

He pressed me into the couch as he hovered above me.

"Fair is fair." He pinned my wrists to my sides as I squirmed against him. He bent and licked the side of my mouth in the same spot I had licked his.

"Now we're even." He gazed down at me and pressed his hips into mine.

"No, we're not. I didn't have any cookie crumbs on my mouth," I panted.

"I can fix that." He folded both of my hands into one of his and lifted them above my head. With his free hand, he reached for a cookie. He broke a corner off of one and held it above my mouth, crushing it in his palm, and letting go so that the crumbs covered my mouth and cheeks. I'm pretty sure a few went down my shirt but I wasn't telling him that.

He appraised his handiwork, and before I could come back with something snappy, he covered my mouth with his, sucking the crumbs away.

My body responded and my mouth opened underneath his. I

felt his tongue nudge its way inside and I welcomed it. He growled low in his throat and released my hands so his fingers delved into my hair.

I grasped his ears in my hands, forcing him closer to me.

"Olivia," he gasped my name.

"Don't stop," I begged, clutching at his shirt.

He nodded and sat up, hooking his thumbs through the back of his shirt, pulling it over his head. He tossed it behind him and then covered my body once more with his.

My hands skated over the smooth hard muscles of his chest, and his hands skimmed under my shirt.

He sat up, pulling me with him, and in record time, my shirt was off.

"That's better." He kneaded my breasts.

I moaned his name and pressed my face into the crook of his neck.

I hugged my arms around his chest and kissed the edge of his chin. "Bed," I gasped breathlessly.

He stood and grabbed my hand, leading me into his bedroom. He ripped the covers back and they pooled on the floor.

He sat on the edge of the bed and yanked his boots off. I used the doorway for support and removed my shoes as well.

I felt his eyes gliding over my body but I refused to blush.

"Come here," he crooned huskily.

I stepped quietly across the room until I stood in front of him. He hooked his index fingers in each side of my jeans and tugged until I was straddling him.

"That's better."

He kissed me, and the taste of cookies still lingered but Trace's own unique taste was more prominent. Our hands were everywhere and nowhere at the same time. He sucked at a spot on my neck and I cried out.

"Please," I begged. The ache that only he created inside me

was growing stronger by the second. I needed him to fill me.

"Not yet," he whispered, ghosting his lips along my collarbone. I shivered in response and clung to his shoulders, my knees on either side of his hips.

He kissed over the curves of my breasts and then released the snap holding my bra in place.

I lifted my arms from his shoulders and let the bra fall away.

He gently palmed them in his hands, and little mewling sounds escaped my lips as I rubbed my hips against his. I felt his hardness pressing against me, and knew he was more than ready, but he insisted on taking it slow.

"Olivia," he warned, placing a kiss on my lips.

"I want you," I pleaded.

"I know," he whispered. "I want you too."

"Then, please—"

"Not yet," he repeated.

What is he waiting for? Does he want me to come in my pants? If that was the case, I was pretty close.

He gripped my hips and pushed me off so that I was standing in front of him once more.

I cried out in protest, but he stood, and silenced the noises I was making with another kiss.

He pulled his lips away and dropped to his knees. With a quick flick of his fingers, the button of my jeans popped, and he slid the zipper down slowly. He gazed up at me and placed a kiss on my stomach, then removed my jeans, kissing each part of my legs the fabric exposed.

He helped me step out of them but left my panties on.

"You're beautiful," he murmured into the darkened room.

I had felt like a plain Jane before I met Trace, but he made me see that I was beautiful.

When I was sure that he was only going to look up at me, and go no further, he made his move.

He was still on his knees and grasped me around the hips, pulling me up until my legs were over his shoulders.

Somehow, I ended up with my back against the wall as he pushed my panties to the side and closed his mouth over my aching center.

I cried out, grabbing at his hair.

"Trace," I pleaded for no reason.

The sensations running through my body were more intense than the first time with Trace. Could it get better each time? It didn't seem possible, but this was definitely better.

His tongue lapped at me and I held a hand over my mouth to quiet my cries.

His tongue flicked back and forth against my clit.

"I'm coming," I gasped breathlessly. I closed my eyes and my body shook. My hands grappled for anything to hold onto.

When I opened my eyes, I found that I was on the bed, with no clue how I got there. I really hoped I hadn't passed out. That would be embarrassing.

I heard Trace opening the drawer on his night table along with the ripping sound of a foil packet.

My body tightened in anticipation.

"Ready?" He hovered above me and I felt him at my entrance. If I raised my hips just a little ...

"Yes," I gasped. I was more than ready.

He kissed me and lifted my hips, sliding all the way in, in one hard thrust.

I cried out and he stilled. "Did I hurt you?" Worry filled his eyes.

"No." I tried to steady my breathing. "Just surprised me. It feels good. Keep going," I encouraged.

"Are you sure?" He pushed my hair off my forehead. "I don't ever want to hurt you."

I nodded. He moved his hips, slowly at first, and then gradually grew faster. Sweat dripped off his body and he gritted his teeth.

I held onto his arms and wrapped my legs around his waist as my toes curled.

He reached between us and rubbed his thumb over my clit, sending me over the edge once more.

I repeated his name as all other words left me.

His fingers dug into my hips.

"Oh, fuck," he gasped. "I'm close."

He pumped faster and I felt my core tightening again.

At the same time, we cried out each other's names and collapsed into a tangle of arms and legs.

He kissed the end of my nose tenderly, and pulled me against him so we were chest to chest, facing each other.

"I think my couch is proving dangerous to us. That's twice it's led to us ending up in bed together."

I laughed, trailing my finger down his chest. "I think I like your couch."

"It has its perks." He kissed my forehead. "Our hot chocolate's going to be cold now."

"How can you think about hot chocolate right now?" I giggled.

"Because" —he rubbed his nose against mine— "it's hot chocolate. The greatest drink on the planet. I mean, how can you go wrong with liquid chocolate?"

"I can't argue with that." I circled a finger around the tattoo over his heart.

"I'll get it and bring it in here." He stood, disposing of the condom, and pulled on his boxers. He grabbed a long-sleeve plaid button down shirt from his dresser and threw it at me. "Here, put this on."

"Why?" I asked, sitting up, shrugging my shoulders into the shirt. The material was soft and warm. It smelled of Trace—like leather and mint, mixed with detergent.

"If you keep laying around naked I won't be able to control myself." His eyes narrowed. "And I like to take my time with you, to savor every inch."

I shivered as I buttoned the shirt.

"I'll be right back." He tapped the door on his way out.

I scooted back on the bed and propped one of the pillows up so that my back wouldn't be digging into the wood headboard.

I heard the sound of the microwave whirling and the smell of hot chocolate infused the air once more.

Before the microwave dinged, I heard him open it and remove the cups. He came strolling into the room with the two mugs. He looked absolutely delicious with his hair mussed and his boxers hanging low on his hips. I had thought Avery was crazy when she called guys delicious, but I understood now.

"I tried not to get it too hot." He handed me the black mug with the yellow Batman logo on it. He kept the bright green one that had Yoda on one side and said, 'May the force be with you,' on the other side.

I took a hesitant sip. Despite what he had said, I was worried it would be scalding, but it was the perfect temperature.

"This is the best hot chocolate I've ever had," I informed him with a smile, leaning back against the pillows. "I don't normally like it, but this is really yummy."

He gasped, stretching his legs out in front of him. "First ketchup and now hot chocolate! I don't think I can date you anymore."

"First off, I said this was good" —I pointed to the mug in my right hand— "and secondly, ketchup is disgusting."

"Don't say that. Ketchup is delicious." He grinned over the rim of his mug.

I pretended to gag. "It's so nasty."

"How can you be American and not like ketchup? It doesn't add up." He shook his head.

I took a sip of the steaming liquid. "I just don't. Do you like everything you eat?"

"No, but it's *ketchup!* It's impossible not to love," he exclaimed dramatically.

I eyed him. "You do realize that we're two adults, sitting here, arguing about ketchup."

"But it's ketchup!" he repeated. "It deserves to be argued for its tomatoey goodness!"

I laughed. "Tomatoey isn't even a word."

"Well, it should be," he huffed, shaking his head back and forth. "Especially when used in the defense of ketchup."

We finished our hot chocolate and Trace insisted on cleaning the mugs while I lounged in bed. I wanted to help, but he refused. Trace was stubborn like that. I stretched out in his bed, suddenly feeling tired, even though it couldn't be later than six o' clock in the evening.

Trace came back into the bedroom and rummaged through his top drawer.

He pulled out a small white box and sat down on the bed beside me, stretching his long legs out.

"I got you something," he whispered softly.

"Trace, you didn't—"

"I know." He put a finger over my lips. "It's not for Christmas or anything. I saw it and it made me think of you. I had to buy it."

I took the box from his outstretched hand, and pulled the lime green ribbon off, before lifting the lid.

Inside, was a necklace with a delicate gold chain, and a small star charm that was no bigger than the nail on my pinky finger.

"It's so pretty," I gasped, lifting it out of the box. I wasn't one to wear jewelry ... ever, but I would make an exception for this.

"You really like it?" He seemed unsure.

"Trace, I love it." I clasped it in my hand, tightly; like I was afraid he might take it back.

"Good," he breathed out a sigh of relief.

I glanced down at the necklace again. "Why a star? I love it, I do, but I'm just wondering."

"Because, you're a star, Olivia. Even though you can't see it, you are. You shine so brightly and captivate everyone with your light and brilliance. Also," he paused growing bashful, a rare state for Trace, "it made me think of that night, on the picnic table, after you told me about your list, and we saw the shooting star." He brushed his fingers along my chin.

"I-I—" I didn't know what to say. I couldn't believe he had put so much thought into a gift for me. "Thank you," I finally gasped.

"You're welcome." He kissed my cheek and I waited for a sexual innuendo or something snarky to come out of his mouth. But it didn't happen. Trace was oddly serious ... for the moment, at least. I wouldn't put it past him to begin arguing the virtues of ketchup again.

I brushed my hair to the side of my neck and fumbled a few times with the clasp, since I wasn't used to them, but I finally got it on.

Trace fingered the necklace, purposely brushing my chest in the process.

"Perfect." He smiled at me. "By the way, you look really hot in my shirt, and it's not helping me control myself."

"What should I do then?" I asked, playing along.

His eyes darkened and he climbed on top of me, dragging me down the bed, so that I was flat on my back.

"I think you should take it off," he whispered huskily.

"And I think you should take it off for me." I played with the top button.

"Is that so?" He raised a brow.

I nodded.

His eyes sparkled with mischief. "Challenge accepted."

CHAPTER TWENTY-THREE

"It's New Year's Eve," Trace whispered, skimming his fingers down my bare arm while I curled against his side.

"Mhmm," I murmured. "I know."

"Have any plans?" he asked casually.

I pretended to think. "Not that I know of."

"I know it's super last minute" —he trailed his fingers over my shoulder and collarbone— "but I was hoping you'd accompany me to my family's party."

"Is it fancy?" I questioned.

"Well, yeah," he replied reluctantly.

"How fancy?" I asked nervously.

"Like, I'll be in a tux, fancy," he winced.

"Trace!" I exclaimed, sitting straight up, bringing the sheet with me to hide my chest. "It's not like I keep a ball gown stashed in my suitcase! Why didn't you ask me sooner?"

He grinned like a little boy and tucked his right arm behind his head. "Because I knew it would give you more time to think of an excuse not to go. I was going to ask you yesterday, but I got distracted," he pulled the sheet from my feeble clutch.

"How do you expect me to get ready for something this fancy on such short notice?" I growled angrily.

He chuckled. "Your best friend comes in handy sometimes."

"Avery knew! How? That girl can't keep a secret to save herself!" I cried.

"Apparently, she can."

"Ugh," I groaned and flopped back on the bed dramatically.

"She should be here soon, to help you get ready." He slid from the bed and pulled on his boxers and jeans. He left the belt undone.

"I hope you're prepared for your apartment to be turned into a beauty salon," I whined, covering my face with my hands.

How did Trace expect me to be comfortable at some fancy New Year's party? I would be completely out of my element, with a bunch of strangers, and I was one of the shyest people on the planet.

I heard Trace pad across the room and then the bed dipped down beside me as he sat.

He pulled my hands away and gazed down at me. "I'll be by your side the whole night. I promise. You have nothing to worry about. I don't want to go but I'm expected to be there. Excuse me for wanting my girlfriend with me."

I bit down on my lip. *When he put it like that ...*

"Okay. Fine. I'll go and I'll be happy about it." I forced a smile.

"You don't look very happy." He chuckled. "Maybe, I should —" He leaned down, kissing me thoroughly, and took my bottom lip lightly between his teeth. He placed smaller kisses along my neck and my body arched into his.

"Trace," I gasped his name out in a small cry.

His chuckle vibrated against my skin as he pulled the sheet completely off of me and moved lower.

Then, someone had to go and knock on the stupid door.

Trace cursed quietly, and climbed off of me, quickly covering my body with the sheet. He ran his fingers through his hair. "That has to be Avery. I'll get the door while you get dressed," he mumbled, striding from his bedroom.

I slipped out of the bed and dressed in record speed.

I was zipping my jeans when Avery busted into the room.

"Good, you're dressed." She dropped a garment bag on the bed, along with what looked like a suitcase full of supplies. "I was afraid I might see a nipple or something."

"Then why would you come barging in here," I snapped, mad that my best friend had known about this stupid extravagant party and I had not.

"It's the excitement that drives me." She winked, opening the suitcase, dropping hair supplies and makeup on the bed. "It smells like sex in here. Y'all weren't gettin' it on when I knockety knock knocked, were you?" she asked, pretending to knock the air.

I rolled my eyes.

"You were!" she gasped. "Olivia Owens! You naughty girl." She smacked my side.

I looked toward the doorway of the bedroom for Trace, silently pleading for him to swoop in and save me from my best friend.

"I sent lover boy away," Avery cackled. "There's no one here to save you."

"Ugh," I groaned.

"Come on." Avery grabbed me by the shoulders and pushed me out of the bedroom and into the bathroom. "Shower time."

I half-expected her to strip me down and force me inside the shower, but she didn't. She simply smiled and closed the door.

I knew I was in for it.

I washed my hair and scrubbed my body until my skin was raw and pink.

Frankly, I wasn't trying to get super clean, I was stalling for time.

When Avery started pounding on the door, I knew I had overstayed my welcome. I twisted the squeaky knob and the water shut off.

I dried my body with one of the fluffy gray towels and dried the ends of my hair as well, then redressed in what I was wearing earlier.

Avery was raising her hand for another round of knocking when I opened the door.

"'Bout time." She smirked, grabbed my hand, and pulled me back into the bedroom. "Sit." She pointed to the bed.

I grumbled but did as she said.

She turned a blow dryer on and grabbed one of those huge round brushes with the spiky bristles. I cringed. Those things always hurt like hell when they touched your scalp.

Avery used the blow dryer to aid in straightening my hair but since it couldn't get rid of all my natural waves, she ended up having to use a flat iron as well.

Once each strand of hair was straightened to perfection, she brushed it through and started my makeup.

"I'm going for a dramatic look here, so don't freak out," she warned.

"Telling me *not* to freak out instantly makes me freak out," I grumbled.

"Just go to your happy place, Livie. Think of rainbows, and butterflies, and unicorns ... and ..." She grinned wickedly. "Fun times with Trace."

I frowned. "I hate you so much right now."

"You won't hate me when you look so hot that Trace comes in his pants when he sees you," she chortled.

"Filter yourself, Avery. *Filter*."

"Eh." She shrugged, rummaging through her ginormous

makeup bag. "I think not. I prefer to say what I want to say, when I want to say it. Now close your eyes," she warned.

I whimpered, glaring at the makeup brush in her hand. "What color are you using?"

"It's plum, chillax. It matches your dress."

I closed my eyes and kept my mouth shut while she worked.

She finished my eyes and patted a light layer of concealer on my face. I felt her swipe a streak of blush across my cheeks and prayed that I didn't look like a clown.

"Pucker up," she warned and I felt lipstick touch my lips. She wiped the excess off and said, "Open your eyes."

She held a mirror in front of me and I gasped in surprise at my reflection. I looked like an actress ready for her red-carpet appearance. My hair and make-up was flawless. All I was missing was the dress.

"Wow," I gasped. "I look—"

"Drop dead gorgeous," Avery inserted. "I think I should've been a cosmetologist."

"I-I—" I stuttered.

"I'm still waiting for a, 'thank you, Avery'," she said with a hand on her hip.

"Thank you, Avery," I replied mechanically, fingering my straight hair.

"You're welcome." She did a little twirl and began gathering up her stuff. "Oh! I almost forgot. Wanna see your dress?"

I nodded.

Grinning, she unzipped the garment bag. I watched with wide eyes as she pulled out the most beautiful dress I had ever seen.

It was floor-length with cap sleeves and the rich plum color was beautiful. It cinched in at the waist, with jeweled detailing, that surprisingly, didn't take away from the beauty.

"That's the most beautiful dress I've ever seen," I gasped. "Is it yours?"

She nodded. "I got it for an event I had to attend with my parents. I only wore it once."

I fingered the silky fabric. When it moved, it shimmered in the light.

"Are you sure I can wear it?" I asked.

She laughed. "Of course."

The door to the apartment opened and Trace called out.

"We're in here!" I hollered.

He appeared in the doorway and his eyes widened when he saw me. "You look beautiful, Olivia."

"You haven't seen her in the dress yet." Avery smirked.

Trace stalked forward and wrapped a hand around my waist. "I don't think the dress will make a difference," he replied. "I still think you're the most beautiful, with no makeup, and walking around my apartment in my shirts," he whispered into my ear.

I blushed and he moved to kiss me, but was cut off by Avery stepping between us and pushing his chest.

"Nuh uh! I'm not letting you ruin all my hard work!" she warned.

"All right, all right," he grumbled. "I need to get ready anyway."

He moved around Avery and opened his closet door. He pulled out a tux and started for the door.

"I'm guessing you didn't rent that." I laughed and he stopped in the doorway.

"No." He chuckled. "This is mine."

"You go to these fancy parties all time, don't you?" I questioned.

"Maybe." He winked and left the room. A moment later, I heard the bathroom door close.

"What time is it?" I asked Avery.

She glanced at her phone. "Six o'clock."

I guffawed. "You mean, you've been playing beauty stylist all day, and I didn't even notice?"

"Um, yeah. I've got major skills."

My stomach rumbled with the reminder that I hadn't eaten breakfast or lunch or dinner.

I headed for the kitchen and Avery trailed behind me.

I opened the refrigerator and a freakin' monkey jumped on my back.

"Avery," I groaned, trying to dislodge her. "Get off."

"No! Not a morsel of food shall pass through your lips and ruin my creation!" She tightened her hold on my neck.

Dear Lord, the girl was going to choke me.

"Ave—" I reached up and tried to pry her arms from my neck. "Let go," I gasped.

"Never!"

"You're choking me," I gurgled, digging my fingernails into her arms.

"Sorry." She loosened her hold but still didn't let go.

"Avery, I'm *hungry!* Let me eat something! You'll only have to fix my lipstick!" I pleaded.

"Fine." She dropped to the ground. "Eat. Ruin all my hard work. See how much I care." She pouted, sticking her nose in the air.

"Thanks for caring that I'm hungry, Avery," I mumbled.

"I'm sorry. I'm being really insensitive."

"Ya think?" I raised a brow incredulously.

She grew quiet while I made a bowl of cereal.

I sat down on the couch with my bowl of Fruity Pebbles, and Avery sat beside me, chatting excitedly about her plans for the night with Luca. I tuned her out when she mentioned an edible bra and panties.

I finished my cereal and cleaned the bowl, reluctantly letting Avery drag me into the bedroom to get in the dress.

She pulled it out of the bag, and I stripped out of my clothes, letting her help me into it. She zipped it in the back and appraised me.

"Looking good, girl." She turned around and grabbed a pair of black heels off the bed. "But these will make you a showstopper."

I sat down on the bed and slipped the shoes on.

"Oh, yeah." Avery nodded. "My work here is complete." She hugged me and stepped back. "I feel so proud." She pretended to wipe away a tear. "Oh, and here's a clutch." She grabbed a sequined black clutch out of her never-ending bag of supplies. The girl thought of everything.

The bathroom door opened, and a moment later, Trace stepped inside the bedroom.

We both stood staring at one another.

Trace looked impeccable in his smooth black tux. His hair was brushed back from his eyes and his normally stubbled cheeks were shaved clean. He looked nothing like the scruffy fun-loving mechanic I was used to, and looked exactly like the billionaire grandson he was.

"I thought you were beautiful before, but damn ... that dress." He shook his head.

"Thanks," I squeaked, still shocked by his transformation. "You look good too."

You look good too? That's the best you could come up with, Olivia. You're pathetic.

"I mean—"

He chuckled. "I know."

"Come here." Avery grabbed us both by the elbows and forced us side by side so she could evaluate us together. She tapped her index finger against her lips and smiled. "You two make one sexy couple."

"Avery," I groaned.

"What? I'm just being honest." She smacked my butt and started packing up her stuff.

Trace ventured out into the living room area and I was left alone with Avery once more.

As she gathered up her various items, she rambled, "I know you're really nervous, but don't be. Enjoy tonight and don't overthink it. Okay?"

"Okay," I agreed to shut her up. I knew it would be impossible for me to relax.

"Good." She smiled, and slung her bag across her shoulders, leaving the garment bag behind. "I'm sure you'll be playing doctor with Tracey-poo later, so I'll just leave that."

She didn't give me a chance to complain about her comment. She hugged me quickly, whispered, "Good luck," in my ear and headed out the door.

The door had barely clicked closed behind her when Trace announced that it was time for us to go.

He held my hand as we descended the steps while I silently prayed I didn't fall and cut my head open.

He stopped when we reached the bottom step, instead of rounding the corner, and heading toward his car.

I looked up, away from my feet, and gasped.

"A limo? We're going in a freakin' limo," I mumbled.

"Of course." He smiled crookedly as the driver held the door open.

Trace helped me inside and slid in beside me.

"Unfreakinbelievable." I gazed around the limo. I had never been inside one before, and found myself mesmerized by the many seats, and the ceiling that glowed with small lights meant to look like the night sky.

Trace straightened his tux jacket, and sat back, holding my right hand tightly in his.

After I had committed every piece of the limo to memory, I relaxed.

My nerves were beginning to bubble to the surface again and I took deep breaths so I didn't get sick.

"Calm down." Trace smoothed a thumb over my hand. "Everything will be fine. It's just a little party."

I snorted. I doubted this was just a *little party*.

My suspicions were confirmed when the house came into view, along with a gazillion limos and town cars.

The circular driveway in front of the house, which I hadn't noticed before, since it was hidden with snow, was filled with limos and cars pulled up to let guests out.

Our driver pulled up to the front and opened the door for us.

Trace slipped outside and held his hand inside the limo to help me out.

He drew me tightly against his side and nodded at the driver before walking inside the open double doors.

We followed the other guests to the massive ballroom.

The tables and chairs that had been stacked against the walls the last time I was here were now set up with white tablecloths covering them and white slipcovers over the chairs. A large area in the middle was cleared for dancing, which many people were taking advantage of, and a band played on the corner stage.

People that weren't dancing, were either sitting, or walking around mingling.

"Thank God you're here," a voice said from behind us and we turned around to come face to face with Trent. "If one more person asks me about the holes in my ears I'm going to blow up."

Trace laughed. "Guess you shouldn't have gotten the gauges."

"You have tattoos!" Trent cried.

"So do you." Trace shrugged. "Just ignore these people." He indicated the whole room.

"Ugh," Trent groaned. "I'll try. But mom wants me to 'be nice' and 'make connections'." He held his hands up in air quotes. "Whatever the fuck that means. I'd rather be in my room. There aren't even any hot girls here. Just stuffy old people with no sense of humor."

"I feel you, man. But we have to do what we have to do."

"Whatever." Trent cracked his neck. "I hope you two don't mind company, because I'm about to be a fucking leech and latch on and never let go."

"I don't mind." Trace shrugged. "Olivia?"

"I don't care." I smiled at Trace's younger brother.

"Thanks." Trent grinned and stood on my other side.

I felt even shorter than usual, despite the heels I was wearing, standing next to the Wentworth brothers.

A waiter with a tray of food passed us and my stomach rumbled. The cereal I ate earlier had done little to quench my appetite.

I eyed the food longingly and Trace chuckled. "Hungry?"

"Starving." I bit my lip.

Trace sought an empty table and pulled out a chair for me, taking the seat to my right while Trent took the one to my left.

We hadn't been seated for long when a waiter appeared with menus in hand and glasses of water and champagne.

We each scanned the menu and made our choice out of the three options. I opted for the steak since it seemed like the safest option.

I took a sip of the champagne and gagged. The bubbly liquid tasted disgusting. I couldn't figure out exactly what the flavor was, I just knew I hated it.

Trace and Trent got quite the chuckle out of my reaction. Neither of them seemed to mind the overly bubbly liquid, but it wasn't passing through my lips ever again, that was for sure.

What felt like an eternity later, our food was brought out.

I ate it like someone was going to come steal my plate before I had the chance to finish.

"Slow down," Trace chortled, "you're going to choke yourself."

"At least if she chokes herself the party will end early," Trent mumbled.

Trace glared at his brother. "Thanks for your concern."

"Hey" —Trent put his hands up in defense— "the sooner these stuffy old farts get out of my house, the sooner I can get the fuck out of here, and to the real party." An older man glared at Trent as he passed. "Yes, Melvin, you're one of the stuffy old farts I was talking about," Trent added loudly to the older man.

The man, Melvin I assumed, shook his head and shuffled away.

"At least there will be fireworks at midnight." Trent took a bite of asparagus. "That'll be fun."

"Hey, boys," I heard Trace's mom, and turned to find Lily striding toward us, from a few feet away. "Olivia," she added, smiling at me.

"Hi."

Trace grinned. "Mom."

Lily stopped beside Trent's chair and glared at her youngest son. "Melvin Cross just came up to me and—"

"I'm out of here." Trent jumped up from his chair and ran away.

Exasperated, Lily threw her hands in the air and scurried after him.

Trace looked at his fancy silver watch. "All this excitement and it's already nine o' clock. What's next?"

"I THOUGHT YOU COULDN'T DANCE." I pouted as Trace led me across the dance floor.

"I can't. Not really. But I can *act* like I know what I'm doing." He grinned down at me as my dress swirled around my feet.

I tried to mimic the way other people were dancing, but I wasn't exactly the most coordinated person on the word, and Trace wasn't very good at leading.

Finally, I gave up, resting my head on his shoulder.

Golden lights sparkled around us, illuminating the room in warm glow.

I felt Trace's lips brush against my forehead, and I smiled, the innocent gesture warming my heart.

The first song bled into the second and third and so on.

My feet were starting to get tired and I asked Trace if we could take a break.

"Sure thing." He smiled, and started to guide me back to our table, with a hand on my waist.

"Trace Wentworth, funny running into you here," a twinkling female voice stopped us in our tracks.

"Fuck," Trace whispered under his breath, low enough that I, and the girl behind us, were the only ones who heard.

Trace's hand flexed against my waist and his jaw tightened as he turned around slowly.

"Aubrey," he ground out. "This is my family's home. I'm supposed to be here. *You* are not."

Aubrey ... Aubrey ... Aubrey.

Where had I heard that name?

Oh, my God. I gasped aloud.

Trace's ex.

The petite blonde girl glared daggers at me with her dark blue eyes. She was pretty, as in model pretty, with slim features and body, and fair, blemish free skin.

She wore a strapless pale pink dress that hung straight down her narrow body. Her light blonde hair was pulled back in a low bun and a few pieces framed her pretty face. I had never seen a person that looked so flawless.

Her pale pink lips were pouted and fake tears watered her eyes.

"Just because we broke up doesn't mean you need to shut me out of your life." Her lower lip trembled for emphasis.

"Aubrey—"

"I've been a part of your life since we were children, Trace. I spent as much time here, as you spent at my house. We shouldn't shut each other out. I miss you." She reached for his hand and he recoiled. Anger flared in her eyes. "I still love you, baby." She tried to grab his arm, but he stepped back, dragging me with him.

"That's a lie." He pointed a finger in her face. "And even if it wasn't, I don't love *you*."

"*You're* lying." Her navy-blue eyes narrowed. Her gaze flicked my way. "You think this white trash bitch is better than me? It's clear she's not from money," My mouth gaped open at her words. She looked me up and down, a sneer marring her pretty face. "She can't understand you the way I do." She grabbed his tux jacket, but Trace shook her off as easily as if she was a pesky fly.

"If you were a guy I would punch you in the face for what you said about Olivia—"

"*It* has a name?" She batted her eyelashes innocently.

I flinched at her tone.

"You're asking for it, Aubrey," Trace warned. "I *will* have you escorted off of *my* property, no questions asked, if you keep this up." She opened her mouth but he cut her off. "I don't give a fuck who your daddy is, Aubrey, *you are nothing*."

A fire burned behind her eyes. "*I* am *nothing*? You sure didn't think I was nothing when you dated me. You talked about marrying me and having kids with me." She pointed at her bony chest. "What changed? Did your dad dying mess you up that bad that you're willing to settle for *her*?" She stabbed a manicured finger in my direction.

"People grow up, Aubrey. They grow up and they outgrow each other. We weren't right together. Surely, you can see that," Trace reasoned. "And I am *not* settling with Olivia. I would be settling if I was still with you. Last names aren't everything, Aubrey, and I know that's the only reason you wanted me. So, shut the fuck up and stop acting like I meant everything to you, because I didn't. I was nothing but a means for you climb up the mother-fucking social ladder!" he yelled.

"You did! I loved you! I still love you! This bitch isn't your future, Trace! I am!" she squealed shrilly.

By now, we had drawn quite the crowd.

I felt Trent step up beside me. "Oh, fuck, this isn't good," he whispered.

"If you make one more comment about Olivia, you will be escorted from this house, and you *won't* be coming back," he warned. "I don't care how much money your daddy throws our way," Trace seethed.

Aubrey's nostrils flared and her lips pursed. Her tiny hands were fisted at her sides as she glared at the three of us.

"Fine," she sighed. "Whatever. I'm not done with you, though." She pointed a finger in Trace's face. "*Do not* think this conversation is over. As soon as your pound puppy is out of the way, we're talking."

"No, we're not," Trace snapped. "We were done talking years ago. Come on." He released his hold on my waist and grabbed my hand. We melted out of the crowd and Trent followed.

Adrenaline was fading from my body and being replaced by sadness. Aubrey may have been a bitch, but Trace belonged with someone like her, not *me*. Someone beautiful and from the same lifestyle, someone with money, and status, someone that he grew up with. I was none of those things.

"Who invited the fucking ice queen?" Trent asked when we stepped outside the ballroom and around the corner.

"I have no clue," Trace snapped angrily, running his fingers through his hair. "Mom, Gramps, and Grammy wouldn't do that to me. She had to tag along with her parents or someone else." He released my hand so he could punch the wall. When he calmed down some, he turned to me. "I'm so sorry, Olivia. I would've never brought you here if I knew she was going to be here. She's a bitch and I never wanted you to have to know—"

"Know what?" My lip trembled as I fought back tears. "Know that you loved someone as cold-hearted as that? Know that you belong with someone like her? Someone with money and status? I have none of that. I can't give you what you need. I'm sorry," I sobbed, backing away from him and his brother.

"Olivia!" he called after me as I ran, but I didn't look back.

I had to get away before my emotions got the best of me.

I FOUND the staircase leading to the basement and ran down them. I had ditched my shoes a few minutes ago and carried them in my hands.

I picked a door to a room I knew I had never been shown, hoping that would give me more time to get my emotions in check, since I knew Trace would look for me in all the rooms I had toured.

"Holy shit," I gasped as the door closed behind me.

I looked around, dazed.

"Of course," I muttered, inhaling the scent of chlorine. "They *would* have an indoor pool."

The floors were made of some kind of pebbles and three of the four walls were solid glass windows.

The night sky reflected into the room and the full moon lit it.

I dropped my heels and they clattered to the ground.

I pulled the dress up to my thighs and sat at the edge of the pool, dangling my legs into the heated water.

I took deep breaths to quiet my sobs.

I don't know why I had freaked out so bad. I'd like to blame it on being a girl and stupid insecurities. I had already felt uncomfortable and Aubrey had made me feel even more out of my element. I didn't belong here, while she did. She fit in with these people. She was gorgeous and from a rich family like Trace. I would never, no matter what, fit in with these people.

When Trace had shown me around and introduced me to people, I had let him do all the talking. I wasn't good around strangers, never had been, add in the lifestyle difference, and I was a fish out of water. I didn't know how to talk or act around them. Did they have a book titled, *Talking to Rich People for Dummies*? If it existed, I needed it.

I sighed and kicked my feet through the water, watching the bubbles I created float to the surface and disappear.

I wiped at my cheeks and my hand came away black.

I sighed again. There went all of Avery's hard work.

I reached down and used the pool water to clean my hand. I stood and went in search of a towel. I opened several different cabinets, full of various pool related items, before I finally located the towels.

I wiped my face clean of the smeared makeup and tossed the soiled towel in the hamper beside a bathroom.

Still sniffling slightly, I made my way back to the spot I had been sitting in before, dipping my legs back into the warm water.

It seemed weird to be sitting with my feet in pool water when there was snow flurrying outside.

My tears finally stopped and my hiccups quieted.

I continued to kick the water and watch the ripples while biting on my fingernails.

The door behind me opened, and I turned slowly, praying it was Cecilia or anyone I didn't really know.

"Hey," Trace said nervously, shoving his hands in his pockets. He had ditched his tux jacket and his hair was mused with the many times he had run his fingers through it.

"Hi." I turned away and stared down into the blue depths of the water.

"I've been looking for you," he murmured and his dress shoes clacked against the pebbled floor. "I was getting worried."

"Well" —I spread my arms— "here I am."

"You mean everything to me, Olivia. *Everything*," he pleaded. "These people and their money, means *nothing*," he growled, spreading his arms. "Why would you think I wanted to be with someone like that?" He tilted his head, studying me intensely.

"Because ..." I kicked the water and it sprayed up, covering me in droplets. "You deserve to have someone like you."

"*You* are someone like me!" he exclaimed, pointing a finger at me. "Why can't you see that?" He gripped his hair. "I have never fit into this crowd, neither has my brother, and neither did my dad. I was *born* into this family, I didn't *choose* it." He jabbed his chest. "But I did choose to be normal. I chose to become a mechanic and live on my own in an apartment that *I* pay for. I chose to pull over that night in October and help a girl change her tire, and dammit if that wasn't the best fucking decision I ever made." His green eyes were fierce. "I've made a lot of mistakes in my life, Olivia, especially with Aubrey and I vowed to myself to never make those same mistakes with you."

I heard the sounds of him pulling his shoes and socks off, and a moment later, he was sitting beside me, forcing me to look at him with a finger held to my chin.

"Why do you have to be so stubborn?" he asked. "Why are you fighting this?"

"I don't want to get hurt," I whispered, biting my lip, and gazing at the ground.

"You look hurt to me." He rubbed under my eyes, where I knew they were red and puffy. "And *I'm* hurt. Do you like hurting me, Olivia?"

"No!" I exclaimed fiercely. "Of course not!"

"Then please, stop fighting what we have. I can feel you pulling away from me. I've felt it ever since you found out about my family and that's the last thing I want. I didn't tell you, because this" —he indicated the house— "isn't important. Who I am and who you are, that's what's important. Everything else is just ... details. You know the real me, Olivia. This, is me playing dress up."

I couldn't help but laugh. "I like your plaid shirts better."

"I knew it!" He grinned cockily. "It was the plaid shirts that drew you to me."

"What can I say?" I smiled. "I have a thing for lumberjacks."

Trace threw his head back with laughter. "Lumberjacks," he chuckled. Sobering, he gazed at me for a moment, and asked, "So, are we good?"

"We're good." I nodded with a smile.

"No more running away and freaking out?" His eyes sparkled with laughter.

"No more running away and freaking out," I repeated. "I promise."

"That's what I wanted to hear." He leaned toward me and pressed his soft lips to mine. I was unaccustomed to the feel of his smooth cheeks and instantly missed the stubbled ones I'd come to love.

His tongue flicked against the crease of my lips and my mouth opened underneath his skillful caress. He gripped the back of my skull and pressed me against him. The kiss went on for minutes and our temperature rose.

Trace pulled away first, his chest rising and falling heavily.

"We're already here, we might as well ..." he trailed off as he stood.

"Huh?" I asked, my brain foggy.

He began unbuttoning his dress shirt.

"Skinny-dipping, Olivia." He smiled crookedly.

"What if someone comes down here?!" I hissed as his spectacular chest came into view.

"That's part of the thrill." He let the shirt fall and started on his pants.

I took a deep breath and stood. "Fine, but you're going to have to unzip me."

His pants fell to the ground and he was left in a pair of black boxer briefs. "I'm glad you're not arguing so much this time."

"Yeah, well." I shrugged. "I'm trying to be spontaneous."

"And you're doing very well." He winked as I pointed to the zipper.

He pulled it down in one smooth motion—if only it had gone up that smoothly—and the plum colored dress fell around my feet.

"Want help with those?" He grinned, with a wicked glint in his eyes, and pointed at my bra and panties.

"No, I can manage on my own," I said with more confidence than I felt.

It was silly, Trace had seen me naked plenty of times, but I was still nervous.

"Suit yourself." He shrugged and yanked his boxers down, diving into the pool in one smooth move.

"Show off," I muttered.

He came sputtering to the surface in the middle of the large pool. He shook his head and droplets of water went flying from his hair. "Hurry up, slowpoke!" he taunted.

I'll show him slow.

Despite my nerves, I wanted to have some fun with him, and knew exactly how to do it.

I eased my panties slowly down my hips and back up.

His desire filled groan echoed around the room.

I lowered the panties again and let them fall to the ground this time.

Keeping my eyes locked securely on his, I unsnapped my bra and then caught the cups, pulling it away slowly from my body, letting my hair fall forward to hide my breasts.

Blushing, I let the bra fall from my arms.

Before I could talk myself out of it, I took a deep breath, and jumped into the pool.

With closed eyes, I swam for the surface.

I had just sucked in a lung full of air and was wiping the water from my eyes, when Trace's arm wrapped around my stomach, pulling me against his body.

"Trace!" I squealed, kicking wildly.

"You're such a little tease," he whispered huskily in my ear. "That wasn't fair." He turned me around so that we were chest to chest. His hard-on pressed against my belly and a fire began to spread through my body.

My hands wound around his neck and I watched water droplets make their way down his handsome face.

"What wasn't fair?" I gasped.

"You teasing me. I can only take so much."

"You're fun to tease," I smiled, brushing a wet strand of hair from my eyes.

"Is that so?" He raised a brow. "Maybe ... I should tease you a bit?"

I shivered at the promising tone in his voice. "Teasing could be fun."

"I'm about to show you just how much fun." His eyes narrowed in determination, a thin slit of green showing through.

With a firm grip on my waist, he dragged me through the water, and into the shallow end.

He stopped when we both could stand and licked his lips in thought.

"Come here." He grabbed my hand. I followed him over to the steps. "Sit down," he commanded.

I did, turned on by his bossiness.

He hovered above me, and his mouth descended on mine. At the same time, his fingers came into contact with my aching core.

I cried out, and he used that to his advantage, snaking his tongue inside my mouth. His finger and tongue pumped in and out of me in sync. My breathing accelerated as my body built toward my orgasm, but when he sensed that I was about to go over the edge, he backed off, slowing the speed. I mewled in protest and he chuckled.

The speed of his finger increased and his tongue plunged into my mouth at the same speed. Faster, faster, *faster*.

I was so close but he was slowing down again.

He kept the pace slower this time and after a few minutes, my orgasm was in sight, but then he stopped all together.

"Trace!" I cried out. "Please!"

"This is called, teasing, baby." He chuckled warmly.

My eyes were closed but they fluttered open to glare at him. "This is torture."

"I don't think people enjoy torture, and baby, I know you're enjoying this." He winked and ducked his head under water.

I thought he was swimming away, but instead his hands clamped down on my thighs, holding me in place, as his mouth closed around my clit ... under water.

What was he? A freakin' merman?

He came up for air and went right back down.

Something about the water swishing around me, mixed with

his tongue sliding up and down my folds, had me reaching an orgasm quicker than usual.

He came up for air again and I lost that peak.

At this point, I was on the verge of tears. I wanted my orgasm, dammit!

Trace shook the water from his hair. "No more teasing, I promise. But you're not coming until I'm buried inside you and can hear you scream my name."

I whimpered at his words.

He picked me up and my legs automatically wrapped around his waist.

He leaned his back against the side of the pool, and reached between us, guiding his cock inside me.

We both moaned at the same time as he slid in all the way.

He cupped my butt, and held me there, neither of us moving.

"God, I was right, this is perfection," he growled.

I'd agree but I couldn't open my mouth to find the words to voice it.

"I have to move, baby," he warned before he slid out a little, and back in, the water causing more friction than usual.

I clung to his shoulders and rested my head on his chest.

Our labored breaths filled the cavernous room and my hips rolled against his thrusts.

I was finally near my orgasm, one he wasn't going to steal from me, when I leaned back and opened my eyes.

Over Trace's shoulder, and through the glass on the door, my eyes connected with a deep pair of blue ones. They were narrowed in anger as they watched us shrewdly. I was too far gone in a pleasure-induced coma to care, but I knew I would be pissed later that Aubrey was watching us. *Couldn't the bitch go away?*

I tore my gaze from hers and kissed Trace, cupping his cheeks in my hands. His tongue flicked against mine and I gasped in pleasure as he nudged a sensitive spot inside me.

"Trace!" I screamed out his name and my hands dropped from his cheeks to his shoulders. My orgasm tore through me and my whole body shook. He kept a firm grip on my hips as I shook. When he was sure that I was able to stand, he set me down on my feet, and slipped out of me.

He pumped his length with his hand and growled as he came into his palm.

I watched, fascinated. When he was spent, his arms circled around me, and he kissed me deeply, leaning me back so that the ends of my hair skimmed the surface of the water. Both of our chests were rising and falling from the exertion as we clung to one another.

"I think I like pool sex," I whispered.

Trace's chuckle vibrated my body. "I like any kind of sex with you. In fact, I like everything with you, not just the really great sex."

"Good to know."

A boom sounded outside, and I turned in his arms to look out the wall of windows, where I saw fireworks going off. Red, green, blue, purple, and silver. They were beautiful the way they lit up the night sky with their colorful sparks. I had never seen fireworks in person before, only on TV, once or twice. I found myself smiling as we watched them

When they ended, we were still in the water, in each other's arms.

Trace gazed down at me, his green eyes full of an emotion I couldn't decipher.

"Happy New Year's, Olivia. Here's to a new year, and new adventures, together," he murmured and kissed me.

CHAPTER TWENTY-FOUR

School started back up which meant Avery and I were back in the dorms. The Callahans promised that my mom wasn't a bother and could stay as long as she needed. In fact, Resa and my mom had grown quite close, and Resa was helping her to find a job. Nick, thankfully, had to go back to Virginia Tech, so I didn't have to worry about him hitting on my mom anymore.

I didn't tell my mom, but I still worried that Aaron might show up. He was a bully but a wimp at the same time, so he probably wouldn't, but I also knew he wasn't the kind of person you should underestimate. He had nothing to lose, while we had everything.

I guess I was of the mentality that all good things must come to an end.

I hoped that wasn't the case, but …

"Where are we going?" I asked Trace, holding tightly to his hand, as we ran down the sidewalk of the old walking mall. I forced my worried thoughts from my mind. I *needed* to have fun.

My braid thumped against my shoulder and snow flurried around us. The late January weather in Virginia was unpredictable. Some days were warmer, with temperatures in the fifties. While other days, like today, were cold enough for snow.

"I promise, it has nothing to do with your list," he called over his shoulder, dragging me along.

I released his hand and stopped in my tracks. He turned around and jogged toward me.

"What are you looking at?" He tilted his head as he looked at me.

I pointed to the store window, where there was a red shirt displayed that said, *I Love Ketchup.* "I'm buying that for you," I declared, heading straight into the store, not caring if he followed.

Trace grumbled about us being late, but I didn't care. I grabbed the shirt and paid for it. Under normal circumstances, I would've taken the time to look around, but since Trace was on a time constraint to get wherever it was he needed to be, I didn't.

"Put it on." I handed him the bag.

"Olivia," he groaned, looking around the store at the people browsing.

"Trace." I eyed him sternly. "You're always pushing me out of my comfort zone. Put. On. The. Shirt."

A challenge ignited in his green eyes.

"Fine." He grinned cockily. He removed his jacket and long-sleeved plaid shirt. Then, with a giant smirk, he pulled his black V-neck t-shirt over his head. "Hi." He waved at the teenage girl working the cash register. The poor girl's mouth was hanging open as she stared at Trace. Someone needed to get a mop, because the amount of drool she was producing could cause someone to slip.

Trace took the bag from me and pulled out the bright red shirt. He ripped the tag off, and pulled the shirt on, tugging it down so that it covered his tightly sculpted abs.

"Happy now?" he asked, turning so I could assess the shirt.

"Ecstatic." I smiled, putting the shirts he'd been wearing before, into the bag.

He grabbed his jacket and shrugged it on. "Now that you've had your fun, we really have to go."

"Red's a good color on you." I laughed as we walked out of the store.

"Every color is a good color on me. Especially, when said shirt" —he plucked at the garment— "reflects my never-ending love of ketchup."

I shook my head, laughing under my breath at him.

"Ah, here we are." Trace held the door to a coffee shop open for me. The sign hanging above the door was in the shape of a coffee cup and declared the place as ***Griffin's***.

"Are you going to tell me what's going on?" I questioned, looking around at the crowd gathered.

"Well ..." He rocked on his heels. "Since classes started back up, you've been really busy, and I wanted us to do something fun."

"O-Okay." I hesitated as we made our way to a vacant table. People were gathered around something, but I couldn't tell what it was. "And what exactly does this 'fun' entail?"

He wet his lips and shifted in his seat. "I was *hoping* you would sing with me again."

"*What?*" I gasped loudly, causing a few heads to turn in our direction. "No way! I was scared to death the first time, and that was karaoke, where most people suck, *and* they give you the lyrics."

"Calm down," Trace pleaded. "If you really don't want to, I'll sing by myself, but I really hoped we could do it together," he pouted. "Your voice is beautiful, Olivia." His fingers brushed my chin.

My breath was shaky, my palms sweating.

I looked around at all the people, there were ten times more than had been at the restaurant when we sang karaoke, and most of those people had been drunk. These people, weren't drunk, and they were here to listen to *good* music. I knew I had a decent voice, but I wasn't confident enough to get up in front of a crowd this size.

"I don't know." I frowned, my shyness making me wish I could disappear.

"We're supposed to sing in fifteen minutes," he warned. "So, don't think too long." He paused, contemplating something. "I signed up for two songs. What if I do a solo, and then we do a duet, would that make you feel better?"

I nodded. "Yeah, that makes me feel better." *Not much better, but a little better.*

"Great," he beamed.

I wished I felt as happy as he looked. His smile seemed glued onto his face from excitement while I was trying not to throw up.

"What song are we singing?" I asked.

He contemplated, seeming to run through a list in his head. "What about 'If I Didn't Have You' by Thompson Square? Do you know that song?"

"Yeah, I know it." I nodded, my nerves kicking up several notches. At least if I made a fool of myself, I didn't know any of these people.

"Olivia! Trace!"

Dammit.

Scratch that, I did know two of these people.

"What are you guys doing here?" Avery asked, snaking her way through the crowd to our table, with Luca at her heels.

"We're going to sing," Trace announced proudly.

Avery's dark green eyes widened. "You're going to sing?" she asked me. "Like on stage? In front of people?"

"Yep." My eyes shifted nervously away from hers.

"What are you singing?" Luca asked Trace, pulling out a chair, and flipping it around backwards, before sitting.

"On my own? I haven't decided yet. I'll figure it out when I get up there."

Luca's eerie pale-blue eyes zeroed in on Trace's shirt. "What are you wearing?"

Trace sat back and pulled the shirt away from his body. "This? Olivia bought it for me."

Avery snickered. "You bought him an *'I Love Ketchup'* shirt?"

"He has a strange obsession with the stuff." I shrugged. "I thought everyone should know."

"Ketchup is delicious." Trace licked his lips.

He looked at the time on his phone and stood. "I better get up there." He pointed to the stage. "You can wait here till I finish my first song," he informed me.

I watched him bleed into the crowd.

"I can't believe you're going to get up there and sing." Avery shook her head.

"Are you good or do you suck?" Luca asked me.

Avery snorted and answered for me. "Olivia is amazing, but she's too shy to sing in front of people. I caught her singing by accident."

"Hmm," Luca hummed, adjusting his fedora to hide the scar on his forehead. I noticed, that for once, he wasn't wearing a vest. It seemed weird, seeing him without one. It was like his vests were an extension of his laidback personality. "You look more like the type to draw or something."

I snorted. "I'm the least artistic person, ever. I can't draw worth crap." I had learned that the hard way when Trace took me for painting lessons.

A finger tapping against the microphone ceased our conversation as we turned to face the stage. There were still people standing near the stage, but most people had taken a seat, so I had a clear shot of Trace sitting on a stool. Another guy sat in the corner with a guitar in his lap, he scratched his stubbled chin, and flipped his wavy dark hair out of his blue eyes.

My gaze quickly left the other guy and focused on Trace. He looked gorgeous sitting up there so casually. His dark brown hair was mused from running his fingers through it. "I'm going to sing "Only You're the One" by Lifehouse. This one's for Olivia." He smirked in my direction. He motioned over his shoulder for the guy to start playing the guitar.

I sat, riveted, as the lyrics poured over me, along with Trace's raspy singing voice.

I swallowed thickly as the words of the song registered in my brain.

His green eyes never strayed from mine, as each word left his mouth, making their meaning more powerful.

"Whoa," Avery gasped when the song ended, clapping her hands mechanically.

I clapped too, along with everyone else in the room, completely enamored with the man on stage that was mine completely.

Trace bowed his head under the crowd's praise. "Thank you everyone." He grinned. "If y'all don't mind, I'd like to sing another song, with my girlfriend." He waved me up on stage. "Get up here, Olivia."

With red cheeks, I made my way up to the stage.

An older man, who worked there, brought out another stool and microphone. "Thanks, Griff," Trace said to the man.

I sat on the stool and faced the large crowd. I took several deep breaths to calm myself but it wasn't working.

Trace's hand entwined with mine and he gave it a light squeeze. My gaze slid from the crowd and connected with his green eyes.

"You can do this, Olivia," he assured me. "Forget about everyone else. It's just me and you, baby."

I swallowed down the lump in my throat and whispered, "You and me."

He nodded, smiling reassuringly.

Trace nodded to the guy on the guitar again.

There was no turning back now.

I gripped the microphone so tightly in my hand that my knuckles turned white.

I took a deep breath and sang.

It didn't escape my attention that Trace had chosen a duet that was mostly sang by a female.

His voice mingled with mine on the chorus, and I was, once again, amazed by how well our voices blended together. My eyes never left his as we sang the chorus.

The more I sang, the more confident I became. So, before the song was over, I found myself singing less to Trace and more to the crowd. I still gripped his hand for support, but I didn't feel as scared as I did at the beginning of the song.

When the song ended, and the coffee shop erupted into applause, I found myself looking at the floor of the makeshift wood stage.

Trace stood, pulling me up beside him.

"Thank you." Trace waved to the crowd.

"Thank you," I mumbled bashfully, my earlier confidence completely drained.

Trace handed his microphone to the next performer and I handed mine to a coffee shop worker.

We hopped off the stage, hand in hand. Instead of returning straight to the table, Trace dragged me to the counter of the coffee shop.

Trace waved at the older guy working behind the counter. It was the same man who had handed me the microphone. "Hey,

Trace," the man said in a gravelly voice, rolling up the sleeves of his flannel shirt.

"Griff, this is my girlfriend, Olivia. Olivia, meet Griff, the owner," Trace introduced us.

"It's nice to meet you." I smiled shyly at the older man. His gray hair was pulled back in a low ponytail and his light brown eyes were kind.

"Nice to meet you too, doll." He chuckled. He leaned his elbows on the counter and eyed Trace. "I haven't seen you here in a while ... a *long* while."

Trace cleared his throat. "I haven't done much singing since high school. The place looks amazing," Trace looked around. "You certainly didn't have a stage when I performed here."

"Didn't need one." Griff shrugged. "But more and more people kept showing up every week, so something had to be done." Smiling at me, he pointed to the open area. "There used to be a wall there, but I took it down to make room for the stage, and give more room for eating."

"So, you have more than coffee?" I asked.

Griff nodded. "It started out with only coffee and grew from there." He shrugged his wide shoulders. "I've gotta get back to work but let me know if y'all want anything."

"Thanks, Griff." Trace waved and we melted back into the crowd.

I had hardly taken my seat beside Avery when she tackled me into a hug. I was surprised we didn't fall to the ground.

"Girl ..." She pulled away excitedly. "You were incredible!"

"Thanks." I played with the end of my braid.

"Livie! Seriously! You have to start singing more! Your voice is so beautiful!" She flapped her arms excitedly.

"Thank you," I repeated, "but as sick as that made me feel, it won't be happening again, anytime soon. It was fun, though."

"I'm waiting for Avery. We have reservations for Valentine's Day."

"Oh, of course." I shook my head. "Why else would you be here. Wait, you said it's Valentine's Day?"

"Well, yeah." Luca looked at me perplexed.

"I completely forgot," I gasped. "Crap." I smacked my forehead. You'd think the red and pink hearts decorating stores, and even peppered around campus, would've tipped me off, but no, I was that dense apparently. I had been swamped lately with coursework, and life had been passing me by faster and faster. My time had been consumed with school, Trace, my mom, and hanging out with Avery when I had the time.

"I know Trace hasn't." Luca fell into step beside me as I headed toward the dorm. He was dressed a little warmer today, with a long-sleeved navy shirt underneath a gray-buttoned vest. His fedora sat crookedly on his head and the sandy brown strands of his hair escaped from underneath.

"Shit," I cursed, something I had been doing a lot of lately. "I am the worst girlfriend on the planet. No wonder Trace was adamant that we make plans for tonight. I kept trying to blow him off. I have a paper due on Monday and I need all the time I can get to finish it."

"You still have Saturday and Sunday."

"Yeah," I agreed, "hopefully, that'll be enough time." I bit my lip. "Besides, I already gave in and told him I could go out tonight."

"It'll all work out." He clapped a hand on my shoulder.

I was surprised by how talkative he was being. I had grown used to his caveman grunts and little to no words. Maybe, like me, Luca was shy and I needed to get to know him better, for him to open up.

We reached the dorm and Avery was walking out of the double doors. She squealed when she saw Luca and ran into his

"Ugh! Olivia!" Avery exclaimed. "There's no reason for you to get sick! You're incredible!"

I stared down at the table; uncomfortable with the attention I was receiving, not just from Avery, but also from the other people in the coffee shop. I felt their stares and my skin crawled.

I glanced up and my eyes connected with Trace's. He saw that I was uncomfortable and I pleaded with him to come to my rescue.

He scooted his chair back and stood. "Sorry guys," he said to Luca and Avery. "I just realized that I've got to get to work early in the morning." Avery frowned at Trace's words. "This guy needs his car by eleven. So, um, Olivia, I'll drop you off at your dorm."

"Okay." I silently thanked him with my eyes. "See ya, Avery. Luca." I smiled at each of them and took Trace's hand.

We forced our way through the crowd and onto the cobblestone walkway.

Snow flurries were still falling from the sky and darkness had descended. String lights were wrapped around the trunks of the trees. They twinkled merrily and I smiled at the sight.

We walked, hand in hand, to his car. Trace opened the passenger door for me and I slid inside.

He started up the car, and turned on the heat, but didn't back out right away.

"Are you mad at me?" he asked.

"For what? Making me sing?" I questioned.

He nodded.

"No," I answered. "Maybe at first. But I did enjoy it, until people started staring at me." With a laugh, I added, "I've learned, though, that it's impossible for me to stay mad at you."

"It's 'cause I'm sexy." He winked.

I laughed. "Especially in that shirt."

"Don't disrespect the shirt." He chuckled with a grin. "You bought it."

"I'm already regretting that decision." I giggled as he backed out of the parking lot and headed toward campus.

"It's my new favorite shirt," he announced.

"You mean," I paused for dramatic effect, "you like it more than plaid?" I snorted.

He tapped his chin. "Okay, maybe not. *Nothing* beats plaid. If plaid was a color, it'd be my favorite."

"You're so weird." I shook my head.

"Most people find my weirdness charming."

"I guess I'm not most people." I shrugged, covering my laugh with a hand.

We came to a stoplight and he leaned over, pressing a kiss to my cheek. "And that's what I like the most about you."

CHAPTER TWENTY-FIVE

I TOOK A DEEP BREATH AS I STRODE ACROSS CAMPUS, MY books clutched to my chest, as a heavy wind breezed by, almost knocking my hat off my head.

With my free hand, I reached up to keep my hat in place, but I was too late.

The fabric flew from my head and spun in the air.

"Dammit!" I cursed, running after it, thankful I was wearing sneakers today.

"I got it! I got it!" a male voice called and I watched a tan hand reach up in the air and grasp the dark blue fabric of my beanie.

I slowed to a walk, and held my hand out for my hat, slowly looking up to meet the eyes of the guy.

"Luca," I gasped.

"Hey." He smiled, dropping the hat in my hand.

"What are you doing here?" I asked, slipping my hat back on, rather crookedly, considering I only had one hand.

arms, wrapping her legs around his lean waist, and kissing him deeply.

I turned away, feeling like I was seeing something I wasn't meant to see.

I heard him lower Avery to the ground and figured it was safe to look back.

Avery was smiling brightly at me, her cheeks flushed, and her red lipstick slightly smeared.

I pointed to a spot on my lips, indicating that she needed to wipe.

"Oh," she mumbled, and slid her thumb under her lip, to remove the smear. "Thanks."

"No problem." I smiled.

"We're going out so I won't be back, tonight." She looked at Luca significantly.

"I kinda figured that." I chuckled, shrugging my shoulders to relieve some of the pressure from the backpack straps.

I said goodbye to Avery and Luca and slowly trudged up to my dorm. I dropped my stuff on the bed, placing the various items where they needed to go, and showered.

I dried my hair and let it hang down in its natural waves.

I checked the time and knew Trace would be arriving in less than ten minutes. If I wasn't outside waiting, he'd finagle his way into the dorms. I'm sure all he had to do, was bat his eyes at some unsuspecting female, and they'd do whatever he said.

I dressed in clean clothes, but since I wasn't sure what I should wear, I tried to dress up a little bit. I wore a pair of dark wash jeans, and a white button-down shirt with a camel-colored sweater over top. I ditched my sneakers for the heels Avery had given me, and my gold star necklace, which I never took off, completed the look.

I looked at the time again, and grabbed my purse, dashing out of the dorm.

Trace was pulling up in his '69 black Camaro when I pushed the doors open. I hopped inside the car before he had the chance to get out.

"Happy to see me?" He grinned.

"I'm always happy to see you." I leaned over and placed a tender kiss on his cheek. "I'm sorry I wasn't enthusiastic about plans for tonight. I completely forgot today was Valentine's Day," I admitted reluctantly.

"I figured." He smiled, his eyes a light and playful green. "You've been so busy with school."

"Hopefully, it'll slow down soon." I took a deep breath, still ashamed that I had forgotten my first Valentine's with my boyfriend. "I don't know if my brain can absorb any more information."

Trace frowned and lightly squeezed my thigh. "I'm sorry."

"It's okay." I shrugged. "It's school, it's supposed to challenge you."

"I don't like seeing you so stressed," Trace replied, looking left and right, as he backed out of the parking space.

"Everything will slow down soon," I said, more for my benefit than his. "So ..." I rubbed my palms on my jeans. "Where are we headed?"

"Well ..." Trace winced, eyes on the road. "I know you like simple, and aren't into the whole, extravagant lifestyle, so ..." he paused. "I opted to make you dinner at my place. I thought you'd enjoy that more than going out."

I smiled, my first genuine smile in days. "You are amazing. That's perfect."

He let out a sigh of relief. "Good, I was kind of worried you'd be offended."

"Not at all." My smile widened. "This is more special than getting dressed up and going to some uppity restaurant."

He reached for my hand and entwined our fingers together. "How did I get so lucky with you?"

I snorted. "You didn't."

"I beg to differ." He grinned.

"Mmm," I moaned as Trace opened the door to his apartment, and the smell of a homecooked meal hit my nose. Garlic and rosemary were the most prominent scents and I inhaled them greedily, my stomach rumbling. "It smells delicious, Trace."

He closed and locked the door behind us. "I hope it tastes as good." He led me into the small kitchen. "I made homemade garlic mashed potatoes, rolls, and asparagus. All I have left to do is grill the steak." He pulled out marinating steaks from the refrigerator as he spoke.

Tears pricked my eyes. This was the sweetest, most romantic thing, ever. I was sure of it.

"This is great," I murmured, at a loss for anything else to say.

"Are you sure?" He seemed hesitant. "We can still go out ... if you want." He nervously scratched the back of his head.

"No." I shook my head. "This, *you*, it's perfect." I bit down on my lip to hold back the floodgate of emotions that was about to spill forth.

"Are you going to cry?" He raised a brow.

"No," I squeaked.

"You totally are." He wrapped his arms around me and cradled me against his chest. "I didn't want to make you cry, baby."

"I'm sorry, I'm being such a girl." I inhaled his masculine scent. "They're happy tears, I promise. This is the sweetest thing ever." My words were muffled by my face buried in his shirt.

"Happy tears or sad tears, I didn't mean for you to cry." He combed his fingers through my hair.

I pulled away from his embrace and wiped the dampness off my cheeks.

"I'm sorry," I repeated. "I'm not normally so emotional but with all the stress I've had this is ... this is wonderful." I pointed to the various items he had cooked.

He kissed the top of my head, his fingers grazing my hip. "Why don't you go sit down and relax while I grill these steaks?"

"Are you sure? I can help—"

He silenced me with a kiss. "No, Olivia. Relax. Let me take care of you." He rubbed his fingers lightly up my side and I shivered. The tone of his voice held the promise of being taken care of in *many* ways.

"Okay," I agreed.

Reluctantly, I sat on the couch, feeling like a useless blob.

A minute later, Trace brought me a glass of ice water. He observed my stiff posture and chuckled. "It doesn't look like you're relaxing."

"I feel like I should be doing something," I mumbled. I *hated* being unproductive.

"Nuh huh." He shook his head and sat the glass of water on the makeshift crate coffee table. "No helping, only relaxing. Unless you want to get naked?" he suggested. "I wouldn't mind that."

"I'm not getting naked." I rolled my eyes.

"Too bad." He shrugged with a grin. His eyes were a light playful green.

I squealed when he picked up my legs and lifted them onto the couch. He yanked my heels off and dropped them on the floor. He grabbed a flannel blanket off the back of the couch, and draped it over my body. A pillow was already cushioned under my head.

He gazed down at me, appraising his handy work. "*This* is

relaxing." He smiled. "Now stay, Fido," he chortled as he turned to head back into the kitchen.

"Ha, ha, ha," I faked. "You're so funny."

"I am funny." He turned back around and grinned cockily. "And smart, and handy, and insanely good looking." He winked.

"Conceited much?" I joked with a raised brow.

"No, baby, just confident." He chuckled and stepped into the kitchen. "I'll be right back," he called, opening the door. "The grill's downstairs by the garage. Sometimes, the guys grill hotdogs for lunch."

"All right," I sighed. "I'll be here" —I pointed to the couch— "relaxing."

"That's my girl." His laugh carried inside the apartment as the door closed behind him.

A few minutes later, he returned, a gust of cold air blowing into the apartment behind him.

He rubbed his hands together. "It's fucking cold out there." He shivered. "I swear, the temperature is dropping by the second."

I appraised his lightweight shirt with the sleeves rolled up to his forearms. "Maybe, like a normal person, you should wear a coat," I suggested with a smirk.

"It wasn't that cold earlier!" he defended.

"It's February, Trace." I rolled my eyes. "it's cold."

"I can't wait for spring," he grumbled, making his way to the couch. He lifted my legs and sat down, placing them in his lap. "It'll be at least thirty minutes on the steaks."

"Ah, yes, spring. Rainstorms and allergies galore, that's *so* much better than the cold." I laughed.

He picked up my right foot and began to massage the inner sole. My eyes fluttered closed, and a long, drawn out moan, escaped my lips.

"That feels so good," I murmured, "but it's going to make me sleepy."

"Then go to sleep," he replied softly. "I'll let you nap. Those dark circles under your eyes tell me you haven't been sleeping."

"Too much homework," I grumbled, "and not enough hours in the day."

"You shouldn't stay up all night to get your work done." His thumb pressed into a tender spot on my foot.

"I don't stay up *all* night," I mumbled. *Only until one or two, okay, sometimes, three, in the morning.*

Trace snorted, not buying it, but didn't say anything.

He continued to massage my feet, and somewhere along the way, I fell asleep.

I WOKE UP, blinking rapidly, to clear my vision.

Where was—

Oh, crap!

I sat straight up, looking wildly around me.

Holy crap, I fell asleep on Valentine's Day while my sweet, thoughtful, boyfriend made me a romantic dinner.

Award for worst girlfriend *ever* goes to—insert drumroll—Olivia Owens.

I pushed the blanket off of my body, and stood, looking around for Trace.

At that moment, the door to the apartment opened, and Trace strode inside, with two steaming steaks on a plate.

Oh, thank goodness. I didn't sleep *that* long.

"Hey." He smiled. "You're up."

"Yeah." I smoothed my fingers through my hair. "I can't believe I fell asleep."

He shrugged and put the plate down on the counter.

"You needed your sleep. I'm glad you were able to get a nap." He started fixing the food onto plates.

"Still," I mumbled, "it's Valentine's Day."

"It's just a day, Olivia." He smiled. "It's not a big deal, I swear." He put a hand to his chest.

I took a deep breath and decided to drop the subject.

"Can I help?" I asked.

"Yeah." He grinned and pointed to the small table behind the couch. "You can park your sexy ass in one of those chairs. That would be helpful."

"Fine," I grumbled, and pulled out one of the chairs, dropping into the seat dramatically. "Here I am, being helpful."

He bent and peered at me underneath the cabinets. He faked a gasp. "Look at you, doing as you're told, I might have to give you a sticker."

"I like stickers." I laughed.

"Then I'll make sure you have all the damn stickers in the world."

"Just the unicorn ones," I joked.

"Glitter colored unicorns?" he asked.

"Of course," I feigned annoyance, "and they have to have pink manes."

Plates clattered in the kitchen. "This is the weirdest conversation ever." He snorted.

"Regardless." I propped my head on my hands as he rounded the corner with our food. "I still want the sticker you promised."

"That can be arranged." He grinned as he set the plates down then he went back to the kitchen to grab utensils and our drinks.

"I could've helped you, you know." I gazed up at him as I cut into my steak.

"I know, but I wanted to do this by myself."

I took a bite of the melt-in-your-mouth steak. "Is that the case, or were you afraid I'd ruin something?"

"No comment. Is the steak good?"

"It's delicious," I answered honestly.

"So, I've been thinking," he mused.

"About what?" I swallowed a bite of the garlic-mashed potatoes.

"One of things on your list." He tapped his fingers against the wooden table and brought his beer to his lips with his free hand.

"Which one?" I asked and the nerves that usually accompanied the mentioning of my list were absent.

"When's your spring break?" he asked to avoid my question.

"March seventh," I answered.

"Hmmm," he hummed.

"Care to elaborate?" I persisted.

He leaned forward and our eyes connected. "On your list, you said you wanted to see the ocean," he stated.

"Yeah," I replied, even though it hadn't been a question.

"I think we, and by we, I mean you, me, Avery, and Luca, should go to the beach over your spring break. It'll be cold in March and you won't want to get in the ocean, but at least you'll get to see it."

Excitement bubbled inside me. "I don't want to get in the ocean anyway, too many fish," I shuddered, "so the temperature won't bother me. But are you sure? Can you take off work?"

"I have plenty of vacation days, besides" —he took another sip of beer— "Pete knows I work harder here than anybody, himself included. He's always telling me to take a break and this seems like the perfect opportunity."

I did a little happy dance in the chair which made Trace shake with laughter. "This is so exciting! I'm going to see the ocean! Oh, my gosh, I can finally put my toes in the sand! And collect seashells!"

"I'm glad you're excited." He took a bite of his steak.

"Excited? That's an understatement. Try, ecstatic!" I continued with my seated dance.

"It doesn't take much to make you happy, Olivia."

"No, it doesn't," I agreed.

EVEN THOUGH TRACE had been adamant that I not help with the food preparation, I managed to get him to agree, albeit reluctantly, to let me help clean the dishes.

I was one of those people who hated sitting around, feeling useless. I needed to be up, and moving, doing something productive.

I scrubbed the dishes while Trace dried them and put them away.

We worked quietly, enjoying each other's company.

I hadn't seen him much since classes started up and I missed him something fierce.

I cleaned the last dish and pulled the plug so the soapy water could drain from the sink.

Strong arms wrapped around me from behind, boxing me in.

"Happy Valentine's Day, Olivia," he crooned in my ear, burying his face into my hair.

"Happy Valentine's Day, Trace." My eyes closed as I leaned against his hard chest.

He brushed my hair over my shoulder and kissed my neck tenderly.

My body instantly responded to his tender touch.

I turned in his arms, and reached up, wrapping my arms around his neck. He lifted me onto the counter, staring at me. For once, I couldn't read what he was thinking behind his bright green eyes.

In a flash, he cupped the back of my neck and pulled me to him, kissing me long and deep.

His hand ventured down, over my breast and ribcage, and he used both to grip my thighs, pulling me against his hips.

A moan escaped me when I felt the hard length pressing against my center. I may have been tired before, but now, I was wide-awake.

I unbuttoned his shirt and pushed it off of his shoulders.

He backed a step away; gazing at me with lust filled eyes, as he removed the shirt the rest of the way, pulling the wife-beater over his head. He stepped forward again, holding me against his torso as he kissed me passionately. My hands were trapped between us and I used that to my advantage, running my fingers over the smooth planes of his abs, memorizing the dips and curves of his body.

Suddenly, he lifted me from the counter, and carried me into the bedroom.

He laid me gently on bed and covered my body with his.

I gripped his cheeks in my hands, stubble rubbing against the sensitive skin of my palms, as he kissed me.

He undressed me slowly, taking his time exploring every plane of my body.

I started begging for more, but he only chuckled in reply.

When we finally came together, my only thought was: Perfect.

CHAPTER TWENTY-SIX

"Avery, we're only going to the beach for five days. Do you really need to pack so much stuff?" I glared at my roommate as she tried to squeeze "one last thing" into her already overflowing suitcase.

"Yes!" she cried. "I never know what I might need!"

"Still, it seems like you could make do without it."

She gasped. "Olivia!"

"What?" I asked innocently.

"I swear." She shook her head, her red hair swishing around her shoulders. "Sometimes, I wonder if you're a girl."

"I'm a girl," I assured her with a smile as I sat on my bed, my packed—not-to-the-brim—suitcase, sat on the floor by the door. "I just don't need as much stuff as you seem to need."

"This" —Avery pointed to her face— "takes time, Livie. I need all my makeup, and my flat iron, and—"

"I get it, your highness."

Thirty minutes later, the guys were outside waiting for us, and Avery still wasn't ready.

"Hurry up," I begged, desperate to leave, and start the almost five-hour drive.

"I'm almost ready," she insisted, trying to close her second suitcase.

"Ugh," I groaned as I flopped back on my bed. "You said that an hour ago."

"Done!" she announced a minute later.

"Thank you, Jesus!" I cried, sitting up, climbing from my bed. I wasn't wasting any time. If Avery said she was ready, we were leaving, because I knew if we lingered a minute longer, she would think of something else she needed to bring.

I rolled my suitcase out the door and then picked it up to carry it down the steps. Thank goodness I hadn't packed much and it was light and easy to carry. Avery didn't have the same luxury.

I heard her cursing behind me as she fumbled with her two large suitcases.

"I'll tell Luca to come help you!" I yelled and my voice echoed through the empty dorm. I was sure that Avery and I were the only ones that still hadn't left for spring break. Damn her and her need to over-pack.

"That might be a good idea!" she called back.

I stepped outside and spotted Trace leaning against a gray Toyota 4Runner.

He grinned when he saw me, pecking me on the cheek, taking my suitcase to load it in the trunk.

"Luca's going to drive," he informed me, "we figured everyone would be more comfortable riding in an SUV than a car."

I nodded in agreement.

Trace held one of the back doors open, and I slid inside, tapping Luca on the shoulder.

"Hey." He smiled, showcasing a chipped tooth that I hadn't noticed before.

"Avery needs some help," I told him.

He sighed. "How much is she bringing?"

"You don't want to know," I mumbled.

"Shit," he cursed, getting out of the car, and striding into the dorm.

Trace slid into the seat next to me in the back. "Are you excited to go to the beach?"

"You know I am." I buckled my seatbelt. "I'm probably the only twenty-year-old on the planet, who's never been to the beach."

He took my hand and kissed my knuckles. "I'm sorry you missed out on so much throughout your childhood, but selfishly, I'm really happy that you're experiencing all these firsts, with *me*." He glanced at me through hooded lashes.

"I'm glad I am too," I answered honestly.

I couldn't help believing, that somehow, my list had brought me to Trace. I knew that seemed childish, like someone believing in fairies, but that's how I felt.

Luca and Avery appeared, walking around to the trunk, arguing.

The trunk opened and their voices drifted inside. "Av, I told you *one* suitcase! Not two, and a purse, and whatever the fuck that is!" He pointed to her makeup bag clutched in her hand.

"I *need* all of this," she pouted. "I wasn't leaving behind things I needed."

Luca loaded the rest of her things in and closed the trunk.

They resumed their bickering as soon as they got in the car.

"Besides," Avery defended, "the weather at the beach is unpredictable this time of year. I needed a little bit of everything. Shorts, jeans, tanks, sweaters—"

"I get it," Luca snapped to silence her jabbering, as he excited the campus parking lot, turning onto the interstate.

Avery leaned toward him, whispering, "I know I won't get to wear it outside, but I brought my bikini, so I could model it for you. I want you to take it off of me and—"

"Avery!" I interrupted. "We can hear you!"

"I don't care," she replied, and continued on with exactly what it was she wanted Luca to do with her, not embarrassed at all that Trace and I could hear every word.

I buried my face into Trace's shoulder to stifle my laugh.

"It's going to be a long ride," he mumbled.

"The longest," I agreed.

FIVE HOURS LATER, we finally made it to the hotel.

Trace hopped out and grabbed one of those rolling carts, loading our bags onto it, while Luca did the same with his and Avery's things.

Trace wheeled our stuff inside while Luca spoke with the valet.

I let Trace take care of checking in, since the room was under his name, and collapsed into one of the whicker wingback chairs in the lobby. I welcomed the silence after the long drive with Avery's endless chatter. I loved the girl, but sometimes, she didn't know when to shut up.

Trace wheeled the cart to me and held up the room key triumphantly.

Grinning, he said, "Let's drop our stuff off at the room, and then I'm taking you to see the ocean."

I jumped up, my excitement returning, and followed him to the elevators.

"We're on the top floor and I made sure we got an ocean view." He smiled, leaning against the back wall of the elevator.

"I'm so excited," I exclaimed as the elevator doors opened.

We walked down the hall, and Trace stopped in front of a door, sliding the key card in.

"Ta da," he grinned, pushing the door open.

I stepped inside first and gasped.

It wasn't like your typical hotel room. There was a small kitchen and dining table, with a full living room, and open doors leading to the bedroom.

The walls in both spaces were painted pale blue with white accents. Pictures of fish and seashells decorated the walls and the carpet was clean and plush.

But the centerpiece of the whole space was the balcony and wall of windows, extending from the living room, into the bedroom.

"Wow," I breathed, stepping up to the windows and gazing out at the blue-gray ocean. Even through the glass, I heard the roar of the ocean as it crashed against the sand.

The door clicked closed and I felt Trace step up beside me.

"Is it everything you imagined?" he questioned.

"It's better," I answered.

He opened the sliding glass door, and we stepped outside, into the cool air. A sea breeze ruffled my hair. I smelled the salty sea and I knew it would be a scent I would never forget.

I glanced around at the sand extending in both directions.

The ocean itself looked as if it went on forever.

"Can we go down there?" I asked, desperate to sink my toes in the sand, and *maybe*, let the cold ocean water wet my feet.

"That's the plan." Trace chuckled.

I raced back inside and to the door. "Hurry up, slow poke!"

Trace chased me down the hall and into the elevator. When he caught up to me, he wrapped his arms around my waist, and hugged me.

He nuzzled his face against my neck. "It's nice to get away," he murmured.

"Mhmm," I agreed, relaxing against him.

He pulled away and grinned at me. "I wish it was sunnier, because you really need a tan," he chortled.

I smacked his shoulder. "Maybe *you* need a tan." I glared.

"I was only joking."

"I *know*," I replied as the elevator doors opened into the lobby. "But I'm a *girl*, and we're sensitive," I explained, following the arrows that led us to a door straight onto the beach.

"I'm *very* aware that you're a girl." He smirked, pinching my hip.

I rolled my eyes at his banter.

As soon as my sneakers sunk into the sand, I couldn't get them off fast enough.

I picked them up, and carried them in my right hand, as I ran through the sand, squealing like a small child.

Trace's chuckle echoed through the air around me.

Since it was a colder day, we were the only ones crazy enough to be out on the beach, but I preferred it that way. It meant I could act as crazy as I wanted.

Trace caught up to me, slinging me over his shoulder, and spinning me around.

I squealed in surprise and he slapped my butt.

"Put me down."

"Never," his voice rumbled.

He ran down the beach, carrying me as if I weighed nothing.

The roar of the water got closer, and I began to panic, twisting in his arms. "Trace! No!"

"Don't worry," he murmured, "I'm not going to drop you in the ocean. I only want to get your feet wet."

He set me down, gently on the sand, and we both rolled up the pants legs of our jeans. He took my hand and we stepped forward.

The icy cold water rolled over my feet and ankles, causing me to scream shrilly.

"That's cold!" I cried as I backed away so the icy water couldn't get me again.

"It's March, of course it's cold, but I wanted you to be able to say you put your toes in the ocean."

"I can certainly say that now." I shivered and he wrapped his warm arm around me.

"Mhmm," he mumbled, kissing the top of my head.

We sat down on the sand, and Trace pulled me between his legs, wrapping his arms around my torso for warmth.

I picked up a handful of sand and watched it sift through my fingers. I loved how when you held a lot of it, or dug your toes into the sand, it felt soft, but when you touched only a few grains, you could feel the rough edges of the rocks they had once been.

"What are you thinking so deeply about?" Trace asked, rubbing his hands up and down my arms.

"Nothing," I responded. "Just enjoying this."

I smiled to myself, knowing that one more thing could now be crossed off my list. It was amazing, getting to do these things I had been longing to do, but a part of me wondered, when I had completed everything how would I feel? Would I feel satisfied or incomplete? For two years, doing these things was all I had dreamed of, but now that it was happening, what would I do next?

I PICKED up as many seashells as I could find, stuffing them into my pockets, and handing even more to Trace.

"Where are you going to put all of these?" he asked, putting a handful in his back pocket.

"In a jar," I responded, picking up another with pretty pink and white coloring. "I wish I had a bucket," I mumbled. "That would be helpful."

"Maybe Avery has one," Trace snorted, trailing behind me. "It seems like she packed everything else."

"Who knows?" I shrugged. "She might."

Trace held up two large seashells to his chest. "You could make a smokin' hot bikini top with these," he joked and did a poor imitation of a hula dancer by shaking his hips. I hated to inform him that hula dancers didn't wear seashell tops.

I rolled my eyes. "Only in your dreams."

He grabbed me around my waist, letting the seashells fall to the sand. He tickled my side and I giggled as I tried to wrestle from his grasp. "Come on, Olivia. Make my sexy mermaid fantasy come true. Don't crush a man's dreams!"

"Never!" I cried, falling to the ground, laughing as he continued his assault.

Sand covered my clothes and hair, but I didn't mind, because I was having too much fun.

"Stop!" I pleaded. "Please! Stop tickling me!"

"Only if I get a kiss." He grinned, causing my stomach to somersault. Trace's smile was lethal. "And a promise that *one* day you'll wear a seashell top for me."

"Fine!" I gasped. At this point, I'd agree to anything, if he'd stop tickling me.

He stopped tickling my stomach, and I took a moment to catch my breath, before he stole it once more with his lips.

He gazed down at me with a boyish smile. "If this was a private beach, I'd make love to you right here."

My body tightened at his words and my hips involuntarily jerked against his.

"You're not serious?" My eyes widened.

He tilted his head, studying me. "I'm *very* serious, Olivia." He pressed into me and his erection was obvious.

I swallowed thickly, at a loss of words.

He smirked and rolled off of me.

Standing, he held out a hand, and helped me up. "Like I said, *only* if it was private." He winked, wetting his lips. "I don't want anyone but me getting an eyeful of you." Pressing me flush against his body, he brushed his lips against the curve of my ear, causing me to shiver.

"Let's finish collecting these seashells you seem to love so much." He chuckled, letting our previous conversation drop.

When Trace and I had both run out of pocket space, and I was chilled to the bone, I decided it was time for us to return to our room. We emptied our pockets onto the dining table. Sand spilled out along with the shells. Maid service was going to hate us.

As the last shell fell from my pocket, I shivered and sneezed.

Trace pressed his hand to my forehead. "You're a little warm, baby. I knew we shouldn't have stayed outside for so long." Concern clouded his eyes.

I sneezed again in reply.

"Come on." He dragged me into the spacious, nicely decorated bathroom, stripping my clothes. He turned the shower on and the room quickly filled with steam. "Shower. I'm going to the lobby to see if they have any medicine and coffee. You need to warm up."

"Avery might have medicine," I joked as he slid the white shower curtain into place, "and for all we know, she brought a mini Starbucks with her."

Trace chuckled at my comment. "I won't be gone long. I'll bring some pajamas in here for you to change into. I don't want you to get sick."

"Okay," I mumbled in reply. I knew there was no point in arguing with Trace. If he thought I was getting sick, he'd play doctor, and that was that.

The shower *did* make me warmer, but I was starting to feel lousy. I had experienced enough colds in my life to know I was getting one. Hopefully, I could sleep it off.

I pulled on the pajamas Trace had left out, and climbed under the covers of the king-sized bed, turning the TV on.

A few minutes later, as my eyes were growing heavy, Trace returned.

"Feeling better?" he asked hopefully.

I shook my head no.

"I'm sorry, baby," he sat down beside me and the bed dipped down. "I got some Advil, coffee, and water." He laid the coffee and pill bottle on the table beside the bed then pulled out a water bottle from under his arm. He twisted the cap off the Advil and shook two red pills into his palm. He handed them to me along with the bottle of water.

I took the pills and drank the whole bottle of water. I hoped the medicine would work its magic and I'd feel better in the morning.

Even though it wasn't time to go to bed, sleep was calling my name.

"What can I do?" Trace asked. He looked so helpless that I felt bad for him, even though I was the sick one.

"I'm tired, I just want to sleep," I answered softly.

"Okay." He let out a breath and kissed my forehead. "I'll let you sleep."

"Thank you," I mumbled as my lids closed.

I SLEPT straight through the night and awoke the next morning feeling refreshed.

Trace had come to bed at some point last night, but I hadn't noticed.

He was on his back with his left arm thrown above his head. I ran my greedy eyes over his bare chest. Trace, shirtless, was a sight I would never get used to. His chest rose and fell in deep sleep and I looked at the clock. It was early, just after six.

I slipped from the bed, and showered, washing my hair.

I brushed the wet strands and pulled it back into a bun on top of my head. I dressed casually in jeans and a loose t-shirt.

I wrote a quick note to Trace and left it beside him on the bed so he wouldn't worry.

> Feeling better. Gone to get breakfast.
> -Olivia

I GRABBED the spare room key off the counter in the small kitchen and made my way to the lobby.

There were a few people already milling about to get breakfast, but not many.

I was surprised by the selection of food and drinks. You could even make your own waffles.

I opted to toast a bagel with cream cheese and a glass of orange juice. It was one of my favorite things to have for breakfast.

I sat down at an empty table beside the windows and basked in the quiet atmosphere as I gazed out at the dark ocean. The sun wouldn't rise for another forty minutes or so.

The seat across from me scraped across the tile floor and I looked away from the window to meet Trace's green-eyed gaze.

"So, you're feeling better?" he asked, looking me over carefully.

"Much better." I smiled. I wasn't surprised that he was awake, and down here, he was such a light sleeper.

"Good." He seemed relieved. "I was worried you were getting really sick and it would be all my fault." He drummed his fingers against the tabletop.

"If I got sick, it wouldn't be your fault." I shook my head at him and his silliness. "Go get something to eat." I nodded to the spread of food set out on the bar.

Reluctantly, he pushed back from the table, and made himself a waffle.

By the time he sat down across from me, again, I had finished my breakfast.

He kept glancing at me skeptically, waiting for a cough or a sneeze.

"I'm fine, I promise." I smiled at him. "I'm going to go get some coffee," I explained, getting up.

Trace kept looking at me like he expected me to fall over dead or something.

I poured the coffee into one of the Styrofoam cups provided, and then added a heaping amount of sugar, and creamer. I honestly didn't know why I drank the stuff since I had to doctor it up so much.

I returned to the table and Trace was almost finished with his waffle.

"Are you sure you're—"

I held up a hand to stop him. "Yes, I'm sure. You have nothing to worry about except for my nerves that you're wearing out."

"Sorry." He grinned sheepishly, adding more syrup to his last bite of waffle.

"I understand that you're concerned, but you don't need to be so overprotective," I said, taking a hesitant sip of coffee so I didn't burn my tongue.

His eyes narrowed. "When it comes to you, I'll be as overprotective as I want."

I shook my head, smiling. "I'm not a kid, Trace."

"I know." He chuckled with a small smile. "But I—" he stopped, swallowing thickly. "Never mind." He wet his lips. "I'll stop nagging you."

We ventured back up to the room, and I took my coffee with us, sitting down on the couch. As much as I wanted to go out on the beach, I was afraid to tempt fate, so for the time being, I looked out the window at the ocean.

"Are you sure you're feeling okay?" Trace asked and the worry was clear on his face. I thought it was sweet that he was so concerned, but I didn't like that he was worrying unnecessarily. Plus, it was getting *really* annoying.

"I'm sure," I answered, taking a sip of coffee. I didn't bother to say anything about his promise to stop nagging me. "I don't plan on going down to the beach today, but I don't feel sick. Please, don't worry about me," I begged.

He ran his fingers through his dark hair, rumpling it further. "I'm not normally a worrier," he admitted, "but something about you ..." He paused, glancing at me. "I don't want *anything* to happen to you, on my watch." His voice was soft and his eyes were serious.

I couldn't help but laugh. "Trace ..." I took his hand and pulled him down beside me on the couch. "I'm going to get sick and I'm going to get hurt. It's a part of life. You can't freak out because I have the sniffles."

"You're right," he groaned, dropping his face into his hands. "You'll be the end of me." He chuckled humorlessly.

I grinned mischievously, trying to distract him. "If we're not going out, there are plenty of things we can do inside."

He turned to me, a grin tugging at the corners of his lips. "And what would that be?"

I smiled slyly, and climbed onto his lap. "How about I show

you?"

"Ugh," Avery grumbled as we sunk into the sand. "It figures, the day we're supposed to go home, the sun decides to come out, and it's actually warm."

"I don't consider sixty degrees that warm." I laughed, kicking off my shoes, sinking my toes into the cold sand.

"Maybe not," she agreed, pushing her gigantic sunglasses further up her nose, "but it's better than it's been the last few days."

"That's true." I shrugged, watching the guys toss a football back and forth.

There were a few other people scattered along the beach, but not many. The temperature might have been in the lower sixties but the cool ocean breeze made it feel more like fifty-five. Trace was being overprotective and didn't want me outside, but since it was our last day here, he'd given in, and agreed to stop treating me like a small child.

I brought the pink hoodie of my sweatshirt up over my head and watched the guys through my dark sunglasses. I heard the sounds of their laughter carrying along on the wind. Since I had met Trace, I hadn't spent much time around Luca or seen how they interacted as friends, but it was clear to me now, that like Avery and me, they were inseparable. Best friends, the ones you keep for life, are hard to find, so when you do, you hold on with everything you have, and never let go.

I leaned back on my elbows and stretched my legs out, letting the sun warm me as much possible.

I let my eyes close and basked in the warmth fanning across my face.

"You're not falling asleep on me, are you?" Avery groaned,

poking my shoulder.

"No." I giggled turning to look at her.

"Good." She slid closer to me. The evil smile gracing her face told me that she was about to tell me something I wasn't going to like to hear. "We've both been so busy that I haven't had the proper time to talk to you about Luca."

"Oh no," I groaned, wishing I could teleport myself away. "Please, no."

Talking about a guy, when it came from Avery, meant I was about to hear all about Luca's prowess in bed. Whenever she did this, I was never able to look the guy she was dating, in the eye, *ever again*. Since it appeared that Luca was sticking around for the long haul, this could prove difficult.

I was surprised that I had managed to avoid this conversation with her for so long. Obviously, my luck had run out.

She continued, like I had said nothing. "Ohmigawd, Olivia, I have never been with someone that's as good as he is. Let me tell you, he knows *exactly* what he's doing." She emphasized her words with a thrust of her hips.

"Avery, I'm begging you—"

"He's so bossy and controlling when we have sex. Normally, I'm not okay with that, but strangely, it turns me on when he turns all macho and bosses me around ... I mean, I'm not okay with him bossing me around *outside* the bedroom," she rattled, waving her hands through the air dramatically. "He gets rough too." She sighed dreamily. I didn't understand what was so appealing about rough sex, but since I had never experienced it, I decided to keep my mouth shut. "And he has an apadravya."

"Am I supposed to know what that is?" I raised a brow.

She looked at me like I was a complete idiot.

"What? I don't know what it is!" I cried.

With a dramatic sigh, she explained, "It's a piercing, through the head of his penis—"

"Shut up!" I slapped my hands over my ears. "I don't want to hear this!" I shook my head back and forth. "Too much information!"

I saw Avery roll her eyes, even through her sunglasses. "Stop freaking out, Olivia. It's not necessary."

I reluctantly let my hands fall from my ears so that her voice was no longer muffled.

"I hate you so much right now!" I exclaimed. "Now, every time I see him" —I pointed to Luca out on the beach— "all I'm going to be able to think of is that, that, that, *thing*," I stuttered.

"It's *wonderful*," she sing-songed. "It hits my g-spot *every single time*."

I covered my ears once more.

She pushed my shoulders and I fell over into the sand.

"For someone that's having regular sex, with their smokin' hot boyfriend, you can be such a prude," she grumbled.

"I'm not a prude!" I defended. *Okay, maybe I was, but who wanted to hear about their best friend's, boyfriend's, penis piercing? It was far too much for anyone to handle.* "There's a fine line between talking about girl stuff ... or even the rough sex you're enjoying, and telling me all about his man parts."

"Oh, Olivia," Avery sighed, lying back on her propped elbows. "You are such a preacher's daughter."

I shook my head. I could never get anywhere with Avery. She was never able to see when she crossed a line.

I decided to try a different tactic.

"How would you feel, if Luca was over there, telling Trace all about your vagina?" I reasoned.

She shrugged. "I wouldn't care."

The girl had no shame.

"I don't understand you."

She pushed her sunglasses into her hair and looked over at me with a wink. "The joys of being one of a kind."

CHAPTER TWENTY-SEVEN

A KISS WAS PRESSED AGAINST MY NOSE AND I STIRRED IN my sleep. I slowly opened my eyes and found Trace hovering above me, a grin plastered on his handsome face. How was he always so peppy in the mornings? It took me forever to wake up.

"What?" I yawned, slapping a hand over my mouth, to cover my morning breath.

"Get dressed, we have places to go, and people to see." He tossed my clothes at me. "And hurry."

"Ugh," I groaned, rolling out of bed, and dressing. I pulled my hair back in a sloppy ponytail and grabbed one of Trace's baseball caps to hide how bad my hair looked.

I laced up my Converse and wiped my sleepy eyes as I stepped into the kitchen area. Trace had cooked eggs and bacon for breakfast. I shoveled some onto a plate and ate it mechanically.

"Where are we going?" I asked, stifling another yawn, "and what time is it, anyway?"

"It's seven," he answered, striding into the kitchen. He was dressed in typical Trace fashion. If he didn't make those plaid shirts look so darn good, I would be so sick of them by now. "And we're going to see Gramps and Trent. I need their help with something."

"Oh. Why do I need to come?" I finished my breakfast and rinsed the plate.

"It involves you." He grinned, grabbing two bottles of water from the refrigerator.

He tossed one at me, and even in my sleepy state, I managed to catch it.

"Of course." I rolled my eyes.

He grabbed his car keys and started for the door. I followed slowly behind him, blinking my eyes rapidly as I tried to wake up.

I had been having so many late nights studying that I had been looking forward to sleeping in on this Saturday morning. Leave it to Trace to ruin my plans. I was excited to see Warren and Trent, though. I had grown fond of both of them.

THE TREES OPENED up and the mansion came into view. I gazed at it in awe. I was sure I would never get used to the sight of it. The lawn was massive and had been recently mowed. Purple, white, and blue flowers dotted the landscape.

Trace parked, and instead of going inside, we headed around back, past the outdoor swimming pool, and tennis court.

I saw Trent and Warren in the distance but couldn't see what they were doing.

When we got close enough, my eyes zeroed in on the targets set up. My eyes widened.

"Think you can handle a gun?" Trace smirked.

"I can handle you," I countered, "so I can definitely handle a gun."

His laugh rumbled through his body. "That's funny."

"Hey." Trent smiled. He was dressed casually in a pair of shorts and t-shirt. The tattoo that covered his upper arm looked like some sort of waterscape. His dark hair was tousled in the front, making him look even more like his brother. "Ready to learn to shoot?" he asked me, pointing at one of the targets. "Trace said you wanted to know how to shoot a gun."

"Uh, yeah," I muttered.

"You don't need to look so scared." Trent chuckled and bumped my shoulder with his. "Us Wentworth boys have excellent aim. Right, Gramps?"

Warren shook his head, hobbling toward us. "You have nothing to be afraid of, Olivia," he assured me.

"This will be fun." Trace smirked cockily, and strode over to a golf cart I was sure Warren and Trent had used to get here from the house. Poor Warren obviously had trouble getting around.

Trace opened a lock box that was on the back of the golf cart. I walked over and peered over his shoulder at the weapon that could kill someone with a simple pull of a trigger.

Trace clucked his tongue, looking at the different guns in the box. "Let's try a revolver and a semi-automatic pistol for you. Those should be easier for you to handle since you're a beginner, but they still have some firepower to them," he murmured, tapping a finger against his lips.

"You're taking forever," Trent groaned from behind us. "Just pick one and show her how to shoot."

"Why do you have to be so impatient?" Trace snapped at his brother.

"Why do you have to be so annoying?" Trent raised a brow.

Trace shook his head and grabbed two guns. I followed him over to one of the targets Trent and Warren set up.

"This is a revolver." He held the gun in his right hand aloft. It was of medium size with a silver cylinder that held chambers for the bullets. "And this one" —he held the other where I could see it— "is a semi-automatic." This one was sleeker looking. "Which one do you want to try?"

I pointed to the semi-automatic.

He grinned. "Why am I not surprised?"

He returned the other gun and jogged back to my side. Warren and Trent were already shooting at their targets while Trace explained what I needed to do.

"Semi-automatics are slimmer and lighter than a revolver." His eyes were serious as he spoke. "They can fire more bullets, quicker, and the trigger is easier."

He loaded the magazine with bullets, and directed me with how to stand and hold it, before he finally handed it to me.

I held it in my hands, surprised that I wasn't shaking.

"Take a deep breath," Trace coached. "Look at the target, and when you think you're ready, aim and fire."

I swallowed, eyeing the paper target.

I pulled the trigger and resisted the urge to close my eyes. The bullet missed by a few feet, not even connecting with the paper, but I had done it. I had actually shot a gun.

"That was close," Trace chuckled.

"You're such a liar. That was nowhere close." I shook my head at him.

"I was trying to make you feel better," he defended.

"I want to try again," I told him.

He helped me back into position, but he kept distracting me with a brush of his fingers over my shoulders ... down my back ... playing with my ponytail.

"Trace," I warned, "you're distracting me."

"Sorry." His chuckle vibrated my body with his close proximity.

"You don't sound sorry." I rolled my eyes. "You sound mighty pleased with yourself."

"Maybe." His fingers skimmed up my bare neck and his lips grazed my ear. "I like distracting you."

"You're very good at it." My eyes fluttered closed and my teeth sank into my lip.

"I'm good at lots of things." His voice was husky.

"Boy!" Warren yelled. "Stop bothering that poor girl!"

"Sorry, Gramps!" Trace laughed and stepped away from me. "It was too fun to resist," he added to me with a lick of his lips.

God, that man could talk me into doing anything, with a few simple words, and a lick of his pouty lips.

I eyed the target again and let loose another bullet.

I whooped in joy when it connected with the paper. It may have been in the bottom right corner, but I had *hit* it.

"Try again." Trace smiled. "Aim a bit higher and to the left, though."

I did as he said and hit the target again, closer to the center this time.

"This is fun!" I exclaimed.

Warren, Trent, and Trace all chuckled at my enthusiasm.

"You're a Wentworth now," Warren cackled and shot his target, hitting it in the center. "One of you boys do me a favor and change my target."

I saw that his paper target was completely hollowed out in the middle from his accurate shots. Trent's looked similar but with a few that had missed the mark slightly.

Trent put his gun down and changed the targets.

"You're doing really good," Trent assessed my progress.

I smiled at him. "Thanks."

Trace continued to work with me until I finally hit the center of the target. He changed my target and set up his own. We shot side by side. He had to stop and help me a few more times, but for the most part, I had gotten the hang of it nicely. I was definitely better at shooting a gun than painting a picture.

I found myself getting distracted by watching Trace shoot his own gun. He was obviously at ease with the firearm and it was a huge turn on seeing him look so masculine.

He twitched under my scrutiny and missed the target.

Trent and Warren burst into laughter.

"That was your fault." Trace mock-glared at me.

"Mine?" I batted my eyelashes. "What did I do?"

"If you keep looking at me like that then we're going to have a problem."

"I didn't know I was looking at you in any particular way?" I played dumb.

He stepped forward and gripped my elbow in one of his warm hands. He whispered in my ear, "You know exactly how you're looking at me, Olivia. If you keep it up, I'm marching you straight to my bedroom and spanking you." His intense green gaze had me shivering, despite the warm temperature.

I looked over my shoulder at Trent, who was watching us with a smirk, and Warren was staring at us with a raised brow.

I blushed, clearing my throat, and took a step away from Trace.

"That won't be necessary," I mumbled, turning back to my target.

Trace chuckled. "Too bad."

Around noontime, we headed inside for lunch.

Cecilia had made sandwiches and we ate them in the dining room.

"You did extremely well today." Warren smiled at me, wiping crumbs from his mouth with a flick of his napkin.

"Thanks." My head bowed at his praise.

"Yeah, you were good ... for a beginner," Trent said with a smirk.

Trace glared at his brother. "She was better than a beginner."

"You're only saying that because you're getting some action,"

Trent eyed Trace.

Trace stiffened beside me. "Little brother, you never did know when you were crossing the line."

"Little brother? Did you seriously just say that? You couldn't think of anything more insulting?" Trent tilted his head.

I reached for Trace's hand under the table to calm him.

"Boys" —Warren banged a fist against the table— "that's enough. Trenton, apologize to Olivia for that crass remark."

"*Gramps*," Trent groaned.

"Do it." Warren narrowed his eyes at the youngest Wentworth brother.

Trent looked me in the eye with a small, embarrassed, smile. "Sorry, Olivia. I didn't mean it to insult you. I was only messing with Trace."

"I know." I took a sip of water. Trent's comment hadn't upset me. In fact, the whole conversation had fascinated me, since I didn't have siblings to bicker with.

"Happy?" Trent turned to Warren.

"For now." Warren chuckled, lifting a glass of water to his lips.

I finished my sandwich, and asked Trace, "Where's your mom and grandma?"

"Spa day. They always go once a month."

"Oh." I nodded.

Trace ate a second sandwich and we excused ourselves from the table.

We were strolling along the main hallway when Trace suggested we go swimming.

"But I don't have my swimsuit!" I whined.

"Then get naked." He winked, leading me out the backdoor. We stepped onto the patio and into the pool area. The water was a crisp blue.

Trace stripped down to his boxers and dove into the water.

"Why is everything so much easier for guys?" I grumbled to

myself.

He surfaced in the middle of the pool, shaking his dark hair, sending water flying.

"Get in." He grinned, splashing the water.

I shook my head. "I don't have anything dry to change into."

"You can wear some of my old clothes," he reasoned.

I shook my head at him and stretched across the diving board on my stomach. It swayed under my weight but quickly steadied. Trace swam over, underneath the board, and gazed up at me. I removed the baseball cap I was wearing and tossed it onto the patio. I pulled the ponytail holder out of my hair, and it fell forward, the ends skimming the water. I had already taken my shoes off in the house.

Trace grabbed ahold of the diving board and I squealed as it dipped down.

"Get in," he pleaded.

"No." I smiled.

Still holding onto the diving board, he leaned forward, and kissed me. His lips tasted like chlorine.

"How about now?" he asked.

"I might need a little more convincing." I giggled.

He kissed me again and his lips lingered against mine.

"All right, you've convinced me."

He smirked, letting go of the diving board. It shook me roughly up and down and I found myself toppling over the side, plunging into the water.

Like the indoor pool, this one was heated, so I didn't have to worry about icy water shocking my system. My clothes were soaked, and since I was wearing a white shirt over a hot pink bra, Trace got an eyeful.

"That was *not* nice." I wiped water from my eyes.

"I was afraid you'd chicken out on me." He swam toward me.

"I think I got water up my nose," I complained.

He pressed a kiss to the end of my nose. "There, now it's all better."

I wrapped my arms around his shoulders. "Definitely not. But if you want to believe you made it feel better, then that's fine with me."

"I can make anything better with a little kiss." He pressed his lips against my neck where my pulse raced.

He most certainly could, but I wasn't telling him that.

"I had fun today with your brother and grandpa," I said instead.

"Gramps loves you." Trace chuckled. "Even more now that you can shoot." He winked. "Gramps always tried to get Grammy to learn, but she never wanted to."

"I'm glad I put that on my list. Now I feel … unstoppable." My fingers tangled in his hair.

He chuckled. "Unstoppable, huh?"

"Yeah, you better watch out," I laughed.

"Should I be afraid?" He grinned, his eyes a light green.

"Very." I smiled. "My boyfriend taught me and I have excellent aim now."

"Remind me not to make you mad," he murmured huskily, sucking a spot on my neck.

"If you keep doing that, I don't think I'll ever get mad," I whispered. My eyes closed and I bit down on my lip to prevent a moan from escaping.

"Cannonball!" Trent yelled, a moment before he catapulted into the pool, and splashed our faces with water.

And just like that, Trace's little brother had effectively ruined the moment.

Swimming over to us, Trent pushed his hair out of his eyes. "Wanna play a game of water volleyball?"

I looked at Trace and shrugged. "Sounds fun." I smiled at Trent.

"That's fine with me." Trace ruffled his brother's wet hair.

"Don't do that," Trent complained, swimming away while fixing his hair. He unrolled the net that stretched across the pool and hopped out to grab the ball.

I swam to the shallow end so I could stand and Trace followed me.

"I'll be on your team." He winked at me as he stood. The water slid down his chest and I prayed I didn't drool.

Trent returned, jumping into the pool with the ball. He surfaced and sputtered, "I would say two against one isn't fair but since I know I can beat you two easily, I'm not going to complain."

"Keep on thinking that, little brother!" Trace chimed as Trent spiked the ball.

Trace hit it back over the net and so it went.

"TOLD YOU I'D WIN." Trent smirked as we dried off with the blue and white striped fluffy towels.

"How long are you going to brag about this?" Trace grumbled, pulling his jeans on, over his wet boxers.

"Till the end of time sounds about right," Trent chortled.

Trace shook his head, sending water droplets flying. "Come on, Olivia. Let's grab you some dry clothes and then we'll get out of here."

"Okay." I smiled. I turned to Trent and hugged him. He seemed surprised by the gesture but quickly wrapped his arms around me. "Thanks for hanging out with us today. I had fun."

"I did too." He smiled and his adorable dimples popped out.

I scurried after Trace and up the staircase. I was surprised there wasn't an elevator. Then again, maybe there was, and I had never seen it.

I followed Trace into his closet, stripping out of my wet t-shirt and shorts, changing into one of his oversized t-shirts and a pair of mesh shorts that I had to tighten all the way with the white drawstring.

"You make my clothes look so much better than I do," he murmured in my ear, wrapping an arm around my waist, pulling me against him. I inhaled his natural scent mixed with chlorine from the pool.

"Is that so?" I beamed.

"Uh-huh." He pulled one of my earlobes between his teeth and nibbled. "Wanna go back to my place? Or do you want me to drop you off at your dorm?"

"What do you think?" I smiled as my arms went around his shoulders.

"I think, option number one sounds like a mighty fine idea to me."

"Same here." I kissed his lips. I meant for it to be a quick kiss but Trace had other ideas. His tongue flicked against my lips, seeking entrance. "Mmm," I hummed as his tongue flicked against mine.

"We better get out of here," he breathed as he took a step back, away from me, "but first, you have something to cross off."

I took the piece of paper from him as he produced a pen from his pocket. The items I had crossed off myself had a straight line drawn through them, while Trace's lines were squigglier.

~~Get drunk~~
Fly in a hot air balloon
Go to the carnival
Go to a concert (even if it's someone I've never heard of)
~~Go to a party~~
~~Lose my virginity~~
Dance in the rain
~~Go roller skating~~
~~See the ocean~~

~~Learn to paint~~
Get a dog…or a cat…or a rabbit. Any pet will do.
~~Sing in front of real people. Avery doesn't count.~~
Make more friends
~~Shoot a gun~~
~~Smoke~~
~~Get a tattoo~~
Learn to pole dance
~~Go skinny dipping~~
~~Pierce my belly button~~
Fall in love

I couldn't believe that so many things had been completed. I handed the paper and pen back to Trace and he stuck it back in his pocket for safe keeping.

"Ready?" he asked.

I nodded.

Ellie and Lily had returned from their spa day, and everyone was gathered in the family room where we said our goodbyes. I may have been nervous to meet them, and overwhelmed by the big house, but the Wentworth's truly were some of the nicest people I had ever met. I hugged Warren for an exceptionally long time. When classes ended, I hoped I'd have time to visit him some.

"Be a good girl now and keep that grandson of mine in line."

"I will."

"Stop trying to steal my girlfriend, Gramps." Trace laughed.

"I can't help it that the ladies can't resist me." Warren chuckled warmly. "It's the cane." He winked as he hobbled over to Ellie, kissing his wife.

It was clear, that even after all these years, he loved his wife and she loved him. I wanted that and I believed I'd found it in Trace.

CHAPTER TWENTY-EIGHT

I closed the lid of my laptop and took a deep breath.

One paper down and a thousand more to go.

I stood, about to grab my stuff for the shower, when there was a knock on the door.

I glanced at Avery, relaxing on her bed, listening to music on her iPhone. She pulled out her ear buds and raised a brow. "Need something?" she asked.

"Are you expecting someone?" I pointed my thumb over my shoulder at the door.

"No. Must be for you." She shrugged, replacing the ear buds.

With a sigh, I yanked the door open.

Trace stood there, casually, as if this was an everyday occurrence.

"Busy?" he asked.

"I just finished a paper." I rubbed at my tired eyes.

"So, you're not busy." He grinned, shoving his hands in his jeans pockets.

"I'm going to shower and go to bed. I'm tired." I leaned against the doorway.

"No, you're not." He shook his head. "You're coming with me."

I sighed, dropping my head forward. "Trace, I can't." He could be so impossible to deal with sometimes.

"I promise I won't keep you out late. I know you're busy with finals, but there's something we *have* to do."

"This involves my list, doesn't it?" I whispered, in case Avery was eavesdropping.

He nodded, still smiling. "There's only a short window of time for us to complete this one."

I didn't bother to ask him what it was. I knew he wouldn't tell me.

"Fine, I'll go." I gave in with a dramatic sigh. "But I'm showering first."

There was no way in hell I was going anywhere with dirty hair and in the sweatpants I was wearing.

"Deal." He grinned. "Avery's welcome to come too. Luca will be there."

"I'll tell her." I covered a yawn. Hopefully, I wouldn't fall asleep standing up.

"I'll be in the parking lot." He grinned and disappeared down the hall.

I closed the door, and Avery eyed me, pulling her ear buds out once more.

"What did Tracey-poo want? He really should stop sneaking into the dorms like that. *Someone* will babble to the R.A.." She rolled her eyes. "Someone always tells on me when I have guys over," she mumbled under her breath.

I bit down on my lip to hide my laughter. *I* was the one who tipped off the R.A. to Avery's habits. After one too many times of walking in on her and some random dude, having sex in our dorm, I decided something had to be done about it. Best friend or not. Thankfully, she and Luca seemed to be sticking to his place for their—uh—needs.

"Trace and I are going out. He said you're welcome to come along. Luca will be there," I informed her.

With a squeal, she hopped from the bed, and scurried to her closet. "Where are we going?"

"I have no clue," I muttered, grabbing my shower bag. "Trace wouldn't tell me."

Avery pouted. "How am I going to know what to wear?"

"Just wing it," I told her as I closed and locked the bathroom door.

A SMILE SPREAD across my face as I spotted the Ferris Wheel up ahead.

Trace parked in the gravel beside a shady, run-down strip mall, and I slid from the car, my eyes wide with excitement. I couldn't believe I was actually at a carnival.

I took a moment to soak in the bells, dings, and cheers from the people playing games. The smell of popcorn, hotdogs, and cotton candy invaded my senses, along with the scent of pot. Lovely.

I felt Trace's calloused hand slide into mine and we started toward the entrance. We stopped and paid for the bracelets that allowed us on the rides.

I stuck the purple paper bracelet on, sure that with my luck, it would fall off.

"I'm going to meet Luca." Avery waved as she backed away,

her phone held in front of her, the glow of the screen illuminating her face.

"So …" Trace's hands wrapped around my waist. "What do you want to do first?"

I looked around at all the booths with all the different games. Different colored lights flashed all around on the rides. Pinks, purples, silvers—you name it, the color was flashing somewhere.

"What do you think we should do?" I asked. "I've never been to a carnival before, so this isn't exactly my forte." I laughed as we passed a stand selling corndogs.

"Hmm." He tapped his chin. "Since it's not as crowded as it will be soon, I think we should do the Ferris Wheel first. There will be a wait now, but it shouldn't be too long, not like it will be later."

"Okay." I smiled up at him.

We made our way to the large round circle in the distance. Lights winked all along the structure and excitement bubbled inside me.

While we waited in line, I looked around at the other various rides. There was a swinging ship, cars that spun in circles, and a ride that lifted straight up into the air, on a metal pole, before it came flying back down to the ground.

Music pumped through the massive speakers throughout the area.

I grinned like a small child when it was our turn to get in one of the swinging chairs that would lift us high up into the sky.

For some reason, I had never been afraid of heights. When I was little, I used to watch the birds, longingly, wishing I could take flight with them.

The Ferris Wheel started its ascent into the sky and I giggled giddily. Trace was going to hate me by the end of the night. I planned on riding everything, even the carousel.

When we reached the top, I gasped aloud as I gazed below us.

The carnival looked beautiful. The rides were cheap and silly, but with all the sparkling lights, music, and the cheers from people, it seemed ... magical.

"Wow," I breathed. It seemed like the only word to describe what I was feeling. It was incredible, how different the world seemed, when you got a different perspective of it.

Trace's warm hand covered mine, where it gripped the metal bar.

"This is amazing." I gazed at him with wide eyes. "The world looks so big from up here. Infinite."

He smiled. "The world is big, we're the ones that pretend it's small."

His words were so true. It was so easy to forget everything that was happening outside your own circle and not directly to you.

He leaned toward me and the chair we were in shook slightly. His lips pressed gently against my cheek, his stubble rasping against my skin. My eyes closed involuntarily at the small touch and my heart lurched.

"I think you're a more beautiful sight than this," he waved his hand to encompass the carnival below us and the surrounding town.

I eyed him. "Are you trying to get laid?"

He threw his head back with laughter. "Olivia, you should know by now that I have smoother moves than that."

My pulse accelerated at his touch and he grinned when he felt the increase. His hand fell away and he gripped the bar as the Ferris Wheel began to descend.

We hopped off the Ferris Wheel and he took my hand. "Do you get motion sickness?" Trace asked, stopping at the end of the line for the spinning car ride.

"No." I shook my head.

"Good." He grinned. "This is one of my favorites."

He helped me climb into one of the cars, and I gripped the

metal bar that held us in place, tightly in my hands, since I wasn't sure how fast we'd actually be spinning.

It turned out to be really fun, and under normal circumstances, I would've been embarrassed by the amount of screaming and laughing I was doing.

Still dizzy from the spinning cars, we walked around for a little bit.

Trace stopped in front of one of the games where you could win prizes. A guy currently stood there with his girlfriend, throwing baseballs at plastic pins. "I'm going to win you one of those." He grinned cockily, pointing to the large stuffed animals hanging from the booth. "But not until later. Neither one of us is going to want to lug that around for the rest of the night."

He took my hand and before I had the chance to respond, we were climbing onto the swinging ship.

I screamed as it rocked higher and higher into the air, holding on tightly to Trace's hand.

From there, he dragged me to the ride that went straight up in the air and dropped to the ground *really* fast. I screamed at the top of my lungs on that one, but thankfully, there were a few other girls that screamed louder than me. I was surprised one of the girls didn't squeeze her boyfriend's hand right off by the way she was gripping it.

After that, we took a break, stopping at one of the food stands.

We both ordered a corndog and sat down at a wooden picnic table to eat. I was amazed by how good it tasted, but since I hadn't eaten much today, *anything* would taste good.

"Ooh! Ooh!" I squealed, pointing at a stand selling cotton candy. I had never tried it before, but I felt like I had to, in order to complete my carnival experience.

Trace turned to look over his shoulder to see what I was pointing at.

He turned back to me, finishing his corn dog. "Cotton candy?"

"I've never had it! I have to at least *try* it, even if it sucks!" I exclaimed, staring dreamily at the pale pink and blue swirls.

Trace shook his head, unable to hide his smile. "I'll be right back."

I shrieked in delight, like a small child, as he made his way to the cotton candy stand. He swaggered along slowly, to infuriate me.

"Hurry up, Trace!" I yelled, earning a glare from a passing mother carrying her toddler.

Somebody slid onto the picnic bench seat, beside me, and I turned to see Avery and Luca.

"Why are you yelling at Trace?" Avery asked, pulling her long hair into a ponytail.

"Because, he's taking forever to get my cotton candy!" I cried, pointing at him as he stood in line.

Avery laughed. "I think this carnival has turned you into a five-year-old."

"Probably." I shrugged, calming down. "I've never been to one."

Luca's eyes widened as he sat across from Avery and me. "Never?"

"Never," I replied. "I wasn't allowed."

"Who were you raised by?" he asked, stunned. "Nuns?"

I laughed. He was pretty darn close to the truth. "Something like that." I took a sip of my Snapple sweet tea.

Luca removed his fedora and ran his fingers through his hair before replacing it. "That's nuts."

Avery nodded in agreement.

"Here ya go." Trace grinned as he handed me a plastic bag filled with cotton candy. He sat beside Luca, across from me, with blue cotton candy.

"How do I eat it?" I eyed the fluffy candy.

Three sets of eyes looked at me like I was crazy.

"Seriously, I don't know," I added.

Avery giggled. "You grab it, Livie." She shook her head. "Like this." She demonstrated, reaching into the bag, and tearing a chunk of the candy fibers. She promptly stuck it in her mouth.

"Oh," I mumbled, embarrassed, and mimicked her action.

The three of them watched me take a bite.

I winced at how sugary it tasted.

"It's ... okay. Too sweet, though." I tentatively took another bite, licking the threads of candy off that had stuck to my fingers.

After a few more bites, I had had my fill, and handed the rest to Avery.

"You can have it." I shoved the mostly uneaten cotton candy in her hands.

"You didn't like it, did you?" Trace chuckled, grabbing a handful of the blue fluff, and shoving it in his mouth. "Tell the truth, Olivia."

"Not really," I admitted.

"It's not for everyone." He grinned mischievously. "*I*, however, have quite the sweet tooth." He winked. "And you have such a sweet p—"

I jumped from the table before anything humiliating could come out of his mouth. "We better get going." I grabbed his hand and dragged him away from the table. "I don't want to miss out any of the rides," I told Luca and Avery.

Avery snickered. "Uh-huh. That's exactly why you're running off, Livie!" she called after us.

"I hate you." I glared at Trace, but I couldn't stay mad for more than a few seconds, because a piece of blue cotton candy was stuck to the corner of his lips, and I wanted nothing more than to kiss it away. So, I did.

"You say you hate me, and then you kiss me. Woman, I can't read these mixed messages." He chuckled, finishing the last bite of cotton candy, and tossing the plastic bag in the nearest trashcan.

"It makes me mad when you start spouting about that kind of ..." I crossed my arms over my chest, floundering for the right word. "*Stuff*, in public."

"And what stuff would that be?" He grinned.

"You know ..." I paused. "You were about to say the 'P' word," I hissed under my breath.

"What 'P' word? Popsicle? Potato? Pistachio?" He raised a brow.

"You know exactly which word I'm talking about," I hissed.

"You mean," he enunciated each word carefully, and leaned down to my ear, "pussy?"

"Yes! That one!" I cried, pushing him away with a gentle shove.

"Hmm," he hummed, "but you like it when I lick your pussy and it's so sweet."

"Oh, my God!" I covered my face, wishing I could disappear.

"Don't hide your face." He grabbed my hands and pried them away.

"Why do you say this stuff to me? You know it embarrasses me?" I glared at him.

"But you're so cute when you're embarrassed." He winked. "And it makes your spitfire side come out. I like it when you get all *feisty* with me."

"You are so weird." I shook my head, staring at the ground.

He lifted my chin. "I'm not weird, *but* if you like weirdness, I'm sure I can think of a few interesting things for us to try out."

I shook my head rapidly back and forth. "I can assure you, I won't be trying anything weird."

"Too bad ..." he paused. "We got really excited."

"We?" I questioned.

"Yes." He smiled. "We." He pulled me against him so that our hips were flush and there was no mistaking the bulge in his jeans.

My cheeks flamed red. "Trace! We're at a carnival!"

"I know," he sighed, "and since there's no way to fix my ..." He glanced down. "... problem, we better find something to do. What would you like to do next?" he asked, flicking his dark hair off his forehead.

I pointed behind him and he turned to look.

"The carousel? Really?" He raised a brow. "That's for like ... toddlers."

"I've never been on one." I frowned. "Please?" I begged, making puppy dog eyes.

He sighed. "Fine," he agreed. "But this is gonna hurt." He glanced down at his pants.

"Yay!" I cheered, not at all concerned about Trace's *problem*. I was at a carnival, for the first time *ever*, and I planned on taking full advantage.

I ran up to the carousel, giddier than the small children, and hopped on.

Trace grumbled under his breath and climbed onto the empty horse beside mine, adjusting himself in his jeans.

The ride started up and I squealed in delight as it spun, and the horses slid up and down the gold metal bar impaling their bodies.

People were looking at me weird but I shut them out.

I had never been to a carnival before and I wanted to experience all the things I had missed out on as a child.

After the carousel, we rode a few more rides, and I insisted on doing the Ferris Wheel again.

"We better head back soon," Trace announced, checking the time on his phone.

"Crap!" I exclaimed, seeing how late it was.

Trace stopped walking and faced me. "I'm going to win you a

prize, because you deserve the whole carnival package, and then I'll take you home."

I nodded. "Okay, that sounds good." I *really* wanted him to win me a prize. I knew it was stupid, but that's what all the guys in the movies did, and I knew I would cherish that prize forever.

Trace assessed the different games and picked one where you threw darts to pop balloons.

"Are you sure you can do this?" I asked skeptically.

"I got this." He winked. "I have excellent aim, remember. It's in my blood. I *am* a Wentworth after all."

I stood back as he spoke with the man running the game. He handed Trace the darts and Trace looked over his shoulder, grinning at me.

"Watch this, baby."

I stepped forward so I stood beside him.

He drew his arm back and let the first dart fly. It connected with the yellow balloon and the pop echoed around us.

He successfully popped the remaining balloons. "Told ya."

"Pick your prize," the man working the booth intoned dryly. He looked bored and half asleep.

"Which one do you want?" Trace asked, pointing to the various stuffed animals hanging above.

There weren't many options. A giant teddy bear, a blue gorilla, and for some reason there was a stuffed banana.

"That one." I pointed to the gorilla. It was the cutest, with its pale blue wrinkly face, and fluffy body.

The guy removed the stuffed animal from the hook and handed it to me.

"There ya go." He waved his hand for us to leave.

With a hand on my lower back, Trace guided me to the exit, and then to his car.

I sat my giant blue gorilla on my lap. It smelled like popcorn.

"Did you have fun?" Trace asked, exiting the parking lot. We passed by the Dairy Queen we had eaten at a few months ago.

I nodded my head eagerly. "It was great. I had way more fun than I thought I would. It was nice to have a night out, not worrying about school." I leaned my head against the headrest and let out a heavy sigh. "I can't believe the school year is over in only nine days."

Trace swallowed thickly. "There's something I've been wanting to talk to you about."

"Really? What?" I asked, forcing my sleepy eyes to stay open.

He cleared his throat and his hands flexed against the steering wheel. "You can't stay on campus for the summer, and your mom is still living at the Callahans' ..." His fingers tapped restlessly against the steering wheel. "So ..." he paused nervously, "where are you planning to live?" He glanced at me anxiously.

"I figured, I'd stay at the Callahans' as well," I shrugged. "You know I got that job at the jewelry store in old town that starts in two weeks, and Resa was able to get my mom a job at the hospital. My mom and I are hoping that by the end of the summer, with our combined incomes, we'll be able to rent a place."

"What if *you* didn't have to rent a place?" His green eyes flicked my way for a moment.

"I don't understand." I shook my head. "What are you saying?" I was pretty positive I knew where he was going with this, but I needed to hear him say it. I had to know for sure.

"Move in with me," he stated, like it was that easy.

"Trace," I gasped, "I can't do that."

"Why not?" His brow furrowed together when he looked at me. "You spend most of your free time at my place, anyway. Move in."

"I-I—" I stammered. I didn't know what to say to him. Moving in together was a *huge* step. It was a step in our relationship I wasn't sure either of us was ready for. I mean, he'd never told me that he loved me. True, I hadn't told him either, and I did love him. I wanted to tell him, *badly*. I had come close to spilling out those three little words, several times, but always held back. I needed to hear him say them first. I knew it would break me if I confessed my feelings, and he didn't return them.

He parked in front of the dorm, forcing a smile. His green eyes were sad. "Just think about it, Olivia. Please?"

"I can do that." I nodded.

"Thank you," he murmured, leaning over to kiss me chastely.

With my blue gorilla in tow, I made a slow procession up to my room.

I was so confused about what to do. Trace had thrown a wrench in my plans, and I only had nine days to decide what I was going to do.

CHAPTER TWENTY-NINE

I sat down at a table in Starbucks and unwrapped the paper from the green straw, sticking it into my Frappuccino. I took a sip of the caramel goodness.

Avery stirred the whipped cream into her drink, eyeing me. "Spill, girl, I know you're worried about something."

Avery hadn't come back to the dorm last night from the carnival, so I hadn't had a chance to tell her about Trace wanting me to move in.

For a distraction, I wiped the condensation forming on the clear plastic cup. I decided to bite the bullet and tell her. There was no point in putting this off. She was my best friend, and right now, she was the only person I could confide in. "Trace wants me to move in."

"*What?*" she shrieked, earning us glares from the staff and patrons.

I nodded. "He told me last night."

"What did you say?" she asked, wiping a dribble of Frappuccino from her lip.

"I said I would think about it," I mumbled, removing the straw from my cup, and licking off the whipped cream.

"How do you feel about this? Living together is a big deal," she remarked, pulling her red hair back into a ponytail.

"I don't know," I answered honestly. "I don't want to rush our relationship, you know?"

"I totally understand." She leaned forward and bit down on the green straw. "If Luca asked me to move in with him, I'd give him the middle finger and tell him to fuck himself."

"That's because you're a commitment-phobe." I pointed an accusing finger at her.

"Damn straight." She winked, slurping her Frapp. "But *you* are not."

"Ugh," I groaned, burying my face in my hands, and shaking my head. "I don't know what to do!"

"Go with your gut. My gut's never steered me wrong."

The espresso machine whistled beside us.

I took a deep breath. "I think it might be a good idea but my mom—"

"No buts," Avery interjected. "*You* have to do what's right for *you*. Your mom will be fine. She can get her own place. Although, I'm sure my brother would be willing to get an apartment with her."

"That's not funny!" I exclaimed.

She laughed. "I wasn't trying to be."

That only made it worse.

I shook my head back and forth. "I'm so confused."

"Why are you confused?" she asked, tilting her head. "You said you thought it would be a good idea to live with lover boy. If that's how you feel, then that's what you should do," she reasoned.

"I know I shouldn't talk, because I haven't been in many long-term relationships, but you can't judge everything by a timeline." She shrugged, taking a sip of her Frappuccino. "Love doesn't work that way. When it's right, it's right, and when it's not, it's not."

I was taken aback. *When did Avery become so wise?*

I began to look under the table and over my shoulder.

"What the hell are you doing?" Avery questioned with a short laugh.

"I'm looking for my best friend. Her name is Avery. She's about this tall" —I raised my hand up to Avery's height— "has red hair, and never says anything wise."

She scoffed. "I can be wise!"

I gave her a look that said, 'Oh, really?'

"Joke all you want, but what I said is true."

"I know, that's why I couldn't believe you said it."

She tossed the wadded-up paper from her straw at me and it got caught in the waves of my hair.

I pulled it out and dropped it onto the lacquered wood top.

"So, you're going to move in with him, right?" She picked a chocolate chip off the rim of her cup and licked it off her finger.

I fiddled with my hands. "Yeah, I am."

MY LAST CLASS of the year came to an end and I grinned to myself as I walked out of the classroom.

Only two more years to go and I would have my degree.

I walked along the sidewalk with a skip in my step, humming a song under my breath.

Trace was supposed to meet me at the dorm so I wasn't surprised when I caught sight of his lean form lounged against the brick building. I took a moment to take in the sight of him.

His dark hair had been recently cut so it no longer fell into his eyes. Stubble dotted his jaw and cheeks. His elegant nose was rounded on the end and his lips were a perfect cupid's bow. Long thick eyelashes emphasized his green eyes.

He wore his red plaid shirt unbuttoned over a wife-beater, with the sleeves rolled up, showing off his toned forearms. His hands were large and always swallowed mine. Today, he was wearing a pair of khaki shorts, and instead of his usual combat boots, he wore Nike tennis shoes.

My eyes ventured back up and connected with his. I blushed at being caught.

"Like what you see?" he asked, fighting a smile.

"Just ... enjoying the view," I mumbled.

"Uh-huh." He chuckled, striding forward the few feet that separated us. "There's some drool there, on your lip." He pointed.

I swatted his hand away. "Trace!" I groaned in embarrassment.

He chuckled. "We better hurry, we don't have much time."

"To go where?" I questioned. Trace had told me we were celebrating my last day of classes but that was all he had said.

"Olivia," he whispered my name huskily, guiding me to his car. "I can't tell you that."

"Oh," I drew out the word. "We're doing something on my list," I stated.

"Mhmm," he murmured, opening the passenger door for me.

I leaned back, ticking through what was left on my list, but it didn't help me figure out what we'd be doing.

Trace parked in an open field and my eyes zeroed in on a group of people standing around.

"What's going on?" I asked.

"Just wait."

I followed him toward the people, looking around for anything that would tip me off.

My eyes lit on a large basket and rainbow-colored fabric spread out in the grass.

"Oh, my God!" I stopped in my tracks. "We're going in a hot air balloon!"

Trace laughed at my reaction. The people turned to look at me, chuckling as well.

"You're the best boyfriend ever!" I squealed, jumping into Trace's arms, kissing him.

"Whoa there." Trace chuckled, pulling away from my monkey-like embrace. "I didn't know the hot air balloon would make you this excited."

"I'm sorry." I blushed, steepling my hands in front of my face. "When I made the list, this was one of the things I was most excited to do, but figured I'd never have the chance."

"Well, here's your chance."

I squealed again and the men gathered around the hot air balloon laughed.

"Normally, the girl is scared to death to get in one of these," one of the men remarked.

"Not my Olivia." Trace grinned, throwing his arm over my shoulders as we stepped toward the guys. "She's one of a kind." He kissed my nose.

"Ya wanna help?" another man asked. He was older with graying hair and a heavy beard. His brown eyes were warm and caring.

"We can help?" I gushed.

"Of course," he replied in his gruff voice, waving his hand for me to join him, "it's all a part of the experience."

"Eeeek!" I squeaked and went to help him. I think my behavior was embarrassing Trace but I was too excited to care.

This was going to be *way* better than the Ferris Wheel and I had thought that was awesome.

The older man introduced himself as Richard and the other three men were his sons, Kasey, Jackson, and Matt. Richard owned the business and was in charge of flying the balloon while his sons were the chasers.

Since when you went up in a balloon you never knew exactly where you were going to land, it was the chaser's job to follow the balloon to give us a lift back here to our starting point.

"Ya always have to land in an open field," Richard explained. "Any open land will do as long as ya have permission from the owner to land there. But that's the beauty of these things" —he tapped the basket— "ya never know which way the wind will blow ya. Kinda like life."

I smiled at his words. I had instantly taken a liking to the older man. He was kind and funny.

"All right, y'all get on in here. We're 'bout ready to go up."

I ran by Trace and hopped into the basket, not very lady-like, but I didn't care.

The fire that lifted the balloon roared to life and the heat warmed my face.

The ginormous rainbow balloon rose above us, its stripes running up and down. I gazed above me at the inside of the balloon, blown away by the sheer size of it. They looked small when you saw them up in the sky, but in person ... they were breathtaking due to their massive size.

"I'm beginning to regret this decision," Trace muttered as the basket lifted off the ground.

Richard chuckled and clapped him on the back. "Don't be a sissy, boy, it's only a few feet."

I laughed at Trace, and gripped the edge of the basket, peering below us as the people on the ground grew smaller and smaller.

I saw the cars zoom by on the highways that intersected neighborhoods and farmlands. The straight lines of the farm plots were beautiful to see from above. Little black dots were scattered around the grassy area and I marveled at how small the cows looked from this high.

"Special occasion?" Richard asked us.

"Nah," Trace explained, "we wanted to do something different."

"We don't get a lot of young folks comin' to us, unless there's a proposal," Richard chortled.

Trace choked on his saliva. "Nope, no proposal, sir."

Richard's chuckle echoed through the air around us. "Ya don't need to get all worked up, boy. Ya look like ya can't breathe."

"Sorry," Trace mumbled and I looked over my shoulder at his red face.

I laughed at his expression of terror and went back to sightseeing.

"Isn't she a beauty?" Richard voiced. "The Shenandoah Valley."

"It's beautiful," I agreed.

The fire that propelled the balloon quickly beaded sweat on my neck.

"Oh, my gosh!" I gasped, peering below us. "Trace! Look at the deer!" I pointed to a cluster of five deer running through a field. They were hard to see but their elegant gait gave them away.

"Totally awesome," Trace replied.

I turned around, and he was still in the same spot, near the middle of the basket. "Trace! You didn't even look!"

"I'm perfectly fine over here. There's no reason for me to stand so close to the edge where I could possibly fall to my death," he mumbled.

"Oh, so it's okay for me to fall to my death?" I raised a brow.

"No, I'd prefer that you were over here with me. But seeing as I doubt you'd come over here willingly, and I'm sure as hell not moving, we have a conundrum."

"Fine." I turned back around so that I wasn't missing any of the view. "But you're really missing out."

I looked down at the tips of the green trees and the birds flying nearby.

We had been in the air for about an hour and the sun was beginning to set. On the ground, sunsets were beautiful, but in the air, they were breathtaking. We were swathed in hues of orange, pink, red, and even purple. It felt like we had become a part of the sunset.

"We gotta land now," Richard announced.

I frowned. I didn't want it to end. This was one of the greatest days of my life.

We came to an open field and Richard lowered the balloon.

It touched down shakily and Trace immediately hopped out, walking back and forth.

Richard began the process of dismantling the balloon while we waited for the chasers.

"Are you okay?" I asked, climbing out after Trace. I put a hand on his back, between his shoulder blades, trying to soothe him.

"I am never doing anything like that again," he declared, shaking his head rapidly back and forth. "I'm not scared of much," he paused, taking a deep breath, "but that was terrifying."

I instantly felt bad that he had been so uncomfortable while I was enjoying myself.

"I'm sorry—"

"Don't apologize," he cut me off and ceased his pacing. "I'm glad you were able to experience that and I would have never wanted to stay on the ground and miss out on the smile on your face. Planes, I can do. Open baskets that teeter back and forth? Not so much." He grinned, cupping my cheek.

"I'm glad you were with me but—"

He pressed his index finger over my lips. "No buts. We're not going there."

I sighed. Trace's stubborn side was rearing its head.

"Fine," I grumbled and pushed his hand away from my mouth.

The chasers arrived and they hopped out of the truck to help Richard with the balloon. We rode back, joking and laughing. I really liked all four of the men. They were funny and easy to get along with. They kept picking on Trace for being scared, much to his chagrin.

It was late when we made it back to the starting point and got into his Charger.

I yawned as the calming roar of the engine threatened to make me fall asleep.

"Wanna stay at my place tonight?" he asked, flipping his headlights on, and merging onto the road.

"Sure," I replied, leaning my head against the glass window.

"I have another thing we can cross off your list, tonight." He grinned smugly.

"Oh, no," I groaned, as dread settled in my stomach. "I'm afraid."

"It's going to be so much better than the hot air balloon ... At least, for me it is." He winked.

"YOU HAVE GOT to be kidding me?" I stared at the DVD in my hand.

A scantily-clad girl posed on the front, leaning against a tall metal pole. In large pink font across the top, it said: *Learn How to Pole Dance in 5 Easy Steps.*

"I'm not kidding." Trace grinned, nodding his head eagerly. "Pole dancing is on your list, Olivia," he reminded me.

Why the hell had I ever wanted to do that?

"I'm tired," I whined, in the hopes of a reprieve.

"Nope, no way. That isn't going to work. You're doing this," he declared, taking the DVD from me, popping the disk out, and into the DVD player. Some cheesy music began to play as the main menu popped up.

"There's not even a pole!" I cried.

"Ah!" He held a finger triumphantly in the air. Obviously, he had been prepared for me to say that. "This" —he grabbed the slim metal support column— "is your pole."

"I'm going to bruise my butt!" I glared at him with arms crossed over my chest.

"Then I'll ice your cute ass for you." He lightly smacked the rounded curves.

He wasn't going to let me talk my way out of this.

"Fine," I grumbled, "hit play and watch me break my butt."

I listened to the girl's instructions and tried to mimic her moves on my makeshift pole.

"Take your shirt off!" Trace cat-called as he leaned against the wall, watching me.

"You take your shirt off," I snapped, embarrassed that this pole-dancing thing was harder than it looked. You had to have some major up body strength to pull off those moves, and I was a weakling.

"I will if you will." He smiled cockily.

"Then do it." I glared at him, trying to twirl around the pole.

He removed both of his shirts and I immediately regretted telling him to take them off. His chest was too big of a distraction. No man should be that lean and muscled. The trail of hair leading from his naval to below his jeans was calling my name. I wanted to run my fingers down his chest and explore further.

"Your turn." He smirked, biting on his lip.

I let go of the pole, and yanked my shirt off, throwing the garment at his head.

"Happy now?" I asked, as he pulled the fabric away from his face.

"Very." He licked his lips, looking me up and down.

I thanked the lingerie gods that I wasn't wearing a frumpy jog bra like I did on most days I had classes. I wasn't wearing anything lacy or super sexy but at least I didn't look like a grandma or something.

I tried to shimmy my way up the pole but it wasn't working. I let out an exaggerated groan.

"You know, in my mind, this was a whole lot hotter."

"I'm sure it was," I retorted, "so keep on imagining it."

Finally, I gave up on following the crappy instructions the girl in the video was spewing, and did my own thing. I tried my hardest to make myself look sexy but I wasn't sure I was succeeding. When I caught sight of Trace's erection tenting his shorts, I figured I was doing something right.

I shimmied around the metal column that served as my pole, and a hand snaked out, grabbing me around the waist.

Trace pulled me against his bare chest, and plastered his mouth against mine, before I had the chance to shriek. My body automatically responded, curving into his. One of his hands tangled in my long hair while the other rested against my back.

His hands slid to my waist and he walked backward toward the couch, collapsing onto the cushions with me straddling him.

I cupped his cheeks in my palms, my fingers delving into his hair. He pulled my bottom lip between his teeth and let it go with an audible pop. I moaned, rotating my hips against his.

With skillful fingers, he undid the clasp holding my bra in place, and pulled the fabric from my body. He palmed my breasts in his hands before taking one in his mouth. I arched my back, biting down painfully on my lip to contain the mewling sounds that wanted to escape.

I buried my face into his neck, inhaling the scent that was uniquely Trace. The fresh woodsy scent of his soap clung to his skin, along with the scent of motor oil, and leather.

He released my breast and I found myself flat on my back on the couch with him hovering above me. His eyes were a dark lust-filled green. His chest rose and fell heavily with every shaky breath he took. I wrapped my arms around his neck and tried to pull him to me but he was too heavy.

"Please," I begged.

He closed his eyes, and wet his lips, his jaw tightening. His right hand fisted my jean shorts and he flicked the button open. The zipper slid down and I lifted my hips so he could pull them off.

He suckled my neck, whispering, "I can't resist you."

I felt exactly the same.

From the moment I met Trace, he was my undoing.

He sat up and grabbed his wallet from his back pocket, pulling out a condom.

The rest of our clothes disappeared and he sunk inside me. "God, you feel so fucking good," he moaned into my ear.

I kissed his chest and my body arched against his. I felt like I was an instrument and Trace knew how to pluck all the right strings to make my body sing.

He licked a wet trail between my breasts and circled his tongue around one of my nipples, drawing it into his mouth, and suckling. The sensation shot waves of pleasure straight to my core and my muscles tightened around him.

"Oh, God, Olivia," he panted, releasing the taught peak from his lips, and quickening his pace as he rubbed his thumb over my clit.

My fingernails dug into his arms and my toes curled.

He sealed my mouth with his and his tongue flicked lightly against mine.

My hands skimmed up his smooth back and settled in his hair. My eyes closed and my body tightened.

Trace drew back from my lips, and even though my eyes were closed, I felt his burning into me.

My neck arched and I whimpered as my body shook underneath him.

"Beautiful," he murmured, "you're so incredibly beautiful."

I opened my eyes, in time to watch the expression of bliss tear across his face.

He peppered small kisses all over my face and slipped from body.

I closed my eyes again, too drained to move. I heard him pad across the floor to the kitchen to throw away the condom. A moment later, he was back, picking me up, and carrying me to bed. He curled his naked body around mine and I smiled contently.

CHAPTER THIRTY

I AWOKE IN BED ALONE BUT THE SOUNDS AND SMELLS OF breakfast being made could be heard outside Trace's bedroom. I sat up, inhaling the scent of freshly-cooked bacon. My stomach immediately began to rumble, reminding me that with the excitement of yesterday, I hadn't eaten dinner.

I rolled out of bed, dressed in a tank top, and a pair of Trace's old boxers.

I padded out into the open kitchen and living area, taking a seat on one the stools. I rested my elbows on the raised bar, watching the drool-worthy sight of Trace making breakfast in only his boxers.

"Hungry?" he asked.

"Starving," I replied, watching the way his hands and arm muscles flexed as he flipped an egg in the skillet.

It still amazed me that Trace was such a skilled cook.

He slid a plate with a fried egg, biscuit, and two pieces of bacon my way, along with a fork and glass of orange juice. He fixed a plate for himself and sat on the stool beside me.

"Thank you." I smiled at him. "For yesterday. The balloon ride was amazing."

"I'm glad you enjoyed it," he said genuinely. "I like seeing you happy like that …" he paused. "When you're carefree and don't care what anyone thinks," he elaborated.

"It's nice sometimes to be … free," I replied.

"So," he cleared his throat and sipped at his juice to stall, "have you—uh—thought any about what I asked you?"

"About moving in?" I questioned.

He nodded.

"I have," I answered simply.

"Annnnnnnd?" he drew out the word.

"As long as you're truly okay with me living here, then yes, I'll move—"

His arms wrapped around me and he kissed me soundly.

"I'm so happy that you're gonna move in." He brushed strands of my hair away from my face. "My space is your space. My stuff is your stuff. Anything that's mine, baby, it's yours."

I thought that was quite the declaration for someone that hadn't said, "I love you", yet, but I chose not to comment.

"So, you're really okay with this?" I asked. I didn't want to pack all of my things and move in here, only to have him change his mind a week later and ask me to leave.

"Of course I am. I wouldn't have asked you if I wasn't sure." He took his seat once more.

"Okay." I smiled widely. "We have to be out of the dorms by Friday." That was only two days away and I hadn't done a lot of packing. My procrastinator side had decided to rear its ugly head.

"I'll make room for all of your things," he promised.

"Thanks." I watched him from the corner of my eye, looking for any sign that he was unsure of us living together, but it was obvious that he was pleased about this. His lips kept turning up in a smile.

I was happy too ... but scared at the same time.

Our relationship was going so well, but despite my gut and what Avery had said, I wasn't sure if almost seven months of dating was long enough to know someone was your forever.

But damn, if I didn't believe that anyway.

TRACE DROPPED me off at the dorms after breakfast since I had plans to have lunch with my mom. I showered and dressed for the day and spent some time packing before I had to meet her. Since my mom was now living nearby we tried to get together at least once a week. With her new job, and classes winding down, it had been two weeks since I had seen her.

I glanced at the clock on our dorm wall and jumped up. I should've picked my mom up twenty minutes ago, since she didn't have a car yet.

I grabbed my keys and bag, dashing outside, and drove to Avery's house. I called my mom on the way, apologizing for letting the time get away from me.

When I pulled into the Callahans' driveway, she was already waiting outside.

"I'm so sorry," I told her as she climbed into my old blue Ford Focus.

"It's okay, sweetie. I know you have a lot of packing to do."

I nodded, nervous about having to tell her that our plan to live together wasn't going to work anymore.

"Where do you want to eat?" I asked her.

"How about T.G.I. Fridays? Don't they have an area to eat outside? It's so nice today that I'd like to be outdoors," she suggested.

"That works for me." I shrugged. I loved being outside, rain or shine, hot or cold.

The restaurant was fairly busy but we only had to wait five minutes so it wasn't too bad.

The red umbrella shaded us from the brunt of the sun. The humidity in Virginia could kill you, I swear. Some days, it felt like you were walking through a thick wall of steam.

A waiter came and took our orders, and when he disappeared, I slipped my sunglasses into my hair and eyed my mom.

"You look like you have something to say?" She sipped her ice water, eyeing me over the glass.

"Um, yeah." I looked down, fiddling with the strands of my hair, searching for split-ends.

"So, what is it?" she questioned.

"Um …" I wet my lips, "You see … Trace … he … um … he asked me to move in with him, and I said yes." I cringed.

"Oh, honey, that's great!" She reached for my hand, giving it a small squeeze.

"Really? You're not mad?" I brightened, the anxiety draining from my body. I had been worrying unnecessarily since I had made my decision.

"Of course not." She scooted the metal patio chair back so she could see me better. "I understand completely. He's your boyfriend, and you need to further your life with him, not worry about me."

"Still, I feel bad," I admitted, adding sugar to my tea and using my straw to mix in the granules. After what happened with Aaron, I felt responsible for my mom.

"Don't," she demanded. "I'm fine. I'm doing great at the hospital. They've already been hinting that if I keep up the good work, I could possibly be considered for a promotion," she explained, excitedly.

"That's great, Mom!" I exclaimed. It was so nice to see her

starting a life of her own, where she was able to do what *she* wanted.

"And ..." She took a deep breath. "With Resa's help, I'm seeing a lawyer next week to discuss my options for leaving Aaron. I was scared to do it earlier, but I'm ready for a divorce. It's been five months since I left. I need to completely cut my ties with him and that life." She swished her hands through the air in a cutting motion. "I'm ready to move on and I can't do that if I'm still tied to Aaron."

"I understand completely." I grinned, so incredibly proud of her. She had come a long way in only five months. There had been a change in her almost immediately, but the differences now were drastic. Sometimes, it was hard to recognize her as my mom. She seemed so much younger and vibrant now. Her skin glowed and her hair shined. But the biggest change, in my mind, at least, was the fact that she smiled and laughed all the time, which were two things she never did while she was with Aaron.

She smiled gratefully at me. "I'm so lucky I have you, Olivia. You're the greatest gift I've ever been given."

"Mom," I groaned, "you're just saying that."

"No, I'm not." She shook her head forcefully. "I always wanted a daughter and I never imagined that I would have one as strong as you." She reached for my hand, giving it a squeeze. "You're a fighter, Liv. I know you don't see yourself that way, but you are. Most kids that grow up with someone like Aaron as a 'father' don't turn out well. It usually pushes them over the edge and they let it affect everything about them. But not you, Liv."

Her words pleased me. That had always been one of my biggest fears. That the way I had been treated by my so-called father had caused me to lose my grip on who I really was. But it hadn't. I was ... me. I was shy and quiet, but passionate, and as Trace liked to say, I had my spitfire side.

"Thanks, Mom." I smiled at her, sliding my sunglasses back down to hide my eyes from the bright sun.

Our food was brought out and we continued to talk.

"Is there—uh—anything going on with you and Nick?" I asked. The words tumbled from my mouth of their own accord, but I *was* curious.

The pink staining my mom's cheeks told me all I needed to know. "He's just a friend." She picked at a fry.

"Uh-huh." I smirked, not buying her statement.

"Honestly," she added.

It may have only been five months since she left New Hampshire and Aaron behind, but I felt that if she was ready to move on, then she should ... even if she was moving on with someone who could be my brother. It was gross, but my mom had been through so much that she deserved to find love, in whoever she wanted.

"Mom, don't lie to me." I smiled at her to ease my words. I wanted her to understand that I wasn't judging.

Heck, I was moving in with my boyfriend and neither of us had said those three very important words.

"If there's something going on with you two, you can tell me. I'm not here to judge you. I want you to be happy," I added.

She sighed, staring across the road at the rows of shops and eateries.

"I have no idea what's going on with Nick," she answered honestly. "While he was home, we spent a lot of time together. He's nice and wonderful to talk to." She smiled wistfully and I wondered if she was thinking of Derek, my real father. "He doesn't seem as young as his age suggests. He's insanely smart and I love talking with him about whatever. Since he went back to school, we've been talking on the phone ... a lot," she added reluctantly. "I really like him, but he's young and has his whole life ahead of him.

There's nothing that I can offer him." She shrugged, motioning the waiter over for a refill of water. "He deserves someone young and vibrant. Not someone like me who's been hardened by life."

"Everyone deserves happiness," I told her. "We're only here once."

She smiled. "I'll see where things go with Nick, but I doubt it will go far. There's no need to pick out bridesmaid's dresses if that's what you're afraid of."

"Okay." I laughed. "No bridesmaid's dresses."

We spent the rest of the afternoon together before I dropped her off. I returned to my dorm to finish packing. I didn't have much stuff so I spent most of the time packing my clothes.

Avery returned around six in the evening and cursed. "Shit! I haven't packed anything yet!"

I looked over at the clutter covering every surface of her side of the room. If I wasn't in such a good mood, I would've never offered, but I found myself opening my mouth, and saying, "I can help you."

I taped my last box shut.

"You can?" Her eyes widened. "You're a life saver, Livie!"

I packed her things neatly into boxes while Avery dumped things in them.

"You know, you're only making things harder on yourself, in the long run, tossing things in like that."

"Whatever." She shook her head, grabbing a pencil cup, and dropping it into a box.

Since I wouldn't have to help her unpack, I shut my mouth.

"Did you tell lover boy you decided to move in?" she asked.

"Mhmm." I nodded. "I told him yesterday after the hot air balloon ride."

"Hot air balloon ride!" she screamed. "You went in one those! I would've shit my pants!"

"I've always wanted to do it." I shrugged, folding a pair of her jeans, and added it to the box in front of me.

"You're nuts!" she exclaimed, abandoning the box she was packing, to look at me. I could never get in one of those!" She shuddered. "I *hate* flying. I'd have a heart attack if I had to get in one of those tiny baskets." She shook her head and started packing again.

"It was amazing." I smiled fondly at the memory. "Everything looked so beautiful," I gushed.

"You are a freak of nature, Livie."

"Heights don't bother me," I replied. "Trace didn't like it too much." I giggled, closing the box, and taping it shut.

"I'm Team Trace all the way." She fist pumped the air. "Not Team Crazy Livie." She tossed the box she had filled onto the floor. I was surprised it didn't split open from the force.

"I'm not crazy," I defended.

"You are. No sane person would willingly get in one of those things. But I'm happy you had fun."

"Thanks." I smiled, filling another box.

I looked around, hoping we had made a sizable dent in packing her stuff, but it looked like we had done nothing.

I groaned. "We're going to be up all night packing."

She winked. "I'll get the coffee."

Since residence halls closed today, I loaded my car up with boxes and drove to Trace's apartment. I couldn't fit everything in my small car so I knew I would have to make at least one more trip.

Trace was leaning against the outside wall of the garage, chatting with Luca, who was puffing on a cigarette.

Trace was shirtless since it was such a hot day and his perfect body was drenched in a light coating of sweat. My eyes perused over his tattoos. I loved his tattoos and how they revealed little bits of information about him. I especially loved the one over his heart that expressed how much he loved his dad.

I parked and Trace left Luca to greet me.

"I see boxes." He grinned, nodding at the interior of my car. "I was afraid you might change your mind."

"No." I shook my head, standing on my tiptoes to kiss him tenderly.

"Let me help you with those." He gently pushed me aside and lowered my driver's seat so he could reach the boxes.

"Don't you have to work?" I nodded toward the garage.

"Nah." He shook his head, lifting one of the boxes out, "I asked Pete for the afternoon off."

"Oh," I mouthed, and reached for a box, following him up the staircase to his apartment.

He opened the door and gently placed my box on the floor. I positioned the one I held on top.

"You have to have all your stuff out of your dorm room tonight, right?" Trace asked.

"Yep." I nodded.

"I have something we need to do, so how about I shower, and we'll go do it, then pick up the rest of your stuff. Is that okay with you?" he questioned.

"Sounds great." I smiled and turned to head back for another box.

Trace carried the last box in and went to take his shower. While he was doing that, I decided to get a head start on unpacking. I placed my items in neat stacks on the floor, figuring Trace would tell me where to put my stuff later.

The bathroom door squeaked open and I looked over my shoulder, watching him step out of the bathroom with a simple gray towel wrapped around his waist. Water droplets clung to his hair and skin, causing me to lick my lips. I thought Trace was drool-worthy all the time, it didn't matter what he was doing—working, making breakfast, you name it—he looked like sex on a stick while doing it. But nothing beat a naked and wet, Trace, fresh out of the shower.

He chuckled, smiling cockily at me. "If you keep looking at me like that," he warned, "we're not going anywhere."

I turned away hastily.

"Suit yourself," he crooned as he made his way to the bedroom, the scent of his woodsy soap lingering behind him.

I crushed the empty boxes and leaned them against the wall, beside the door, so that I could drop them in the dumpster later.

I turned around, and Trace was coming out of the bedroom, shrugging into one of his trusty plaid shirts.

"Ready?" he asked, flattening the collar.

"Yeah." I picked up the crushed boxes.

We walked down the steps to his car, and I dropped the boxes into the large blue dumpster.

"Hey there, little lady," a raspy voice said from behind the dumpster.

I squealed, jumping back, and fell over a small rock. My butt hit the ground and the air whizzed out of my throat.

"Sorry, I didn't mean to scare ya." A person appeared, accompanying the voice. He was a small man, about my height, with a hooked back that made him appear even shorter. His white hair was wispy and a white goatee adorned his chin. The blue jumper he wore hung loose on his small frame. When I met his eyes, I found that they were a unique shade of gray. He smiled, showing off yellowed crooked teeth. He dropped the cigarette he was smoking to the ground and stomped it out with the toe of his boot. Wiping a greasy hand on his jumper, he held it out to me, to help me up. "I'm Pete."

So, this was Pete. I had never seen him around here. In fact, I hadn't met most of the employees. They had usually left by the time I met Trace at the garage.

"Olivia." I took his dirty hand to be polite, hoping I hid my cringe.

Despite his age and obvious frailty, he lifted me easily from the ground with little help on my part.

"You're Trace's girl," he stated.

I nodded, wiping the back of my jeans free of dirt and gravel.

"He talks about you all the time." Pete tapped out another cigarette. "Nice to finally meet you."

"Nice to meet you too," I replied, smiling at the older man. I waved goodbye as I backed away and headed toward the car.

Trace was adjusting the volume on the stereo when I slid inside the Charger.

"What took you so long? I thought you were throwing away boxes?" he questioned, pulling onto the road.

"I ran into Pete." I shrugged.

"Ah, I see." Trace chuckled, changing gears in the car. "And what did you think of good ole' Pete?"

"He's nice." I shrugged. "I'm surprised I haven't seen him before now, though."

"Pete doesn't get around as well as he used to," Trace explained, navigating through traffic. "He usually only comes in to make sure we're getting our work done. He misses working on cars, it's been hard on him, but his arthritis really affects his mobility."

"Aww." I frowned. "Poor Pete."

"He's a great guy," Trace added. "I'll always be indebted to him, for giving me a chance. My—uh—last name, made people reluctant to hire me." He scratched the back of his head nervously. "They all thought I was some hotshot playboy who wasn't serious about a job, but Pete didn't look at me that way. He took a chance on me when no one else would and even let me rent the apartment above the garage." I saw in the fierceness of his words how much Trace cared for Pete, and I found it endearing.

Most people looked at Trace and thought "Cocky bad boy" at first glance. But there were so many other layers to Trace underneath his smug exterior. He cared so deeply for the ones he loved and I admired that about him. I knew Trace would go to the ends of the Earth and back to help someone he loved. I realized that I knew the *real* Trace. He could be cocky and arrogant, but at the end of the day, he was always sweet and attentive.

He turned onto a narrow road that led back to a brick building. Unfortunately, I had missed the sign.

"We have to hurry, they'll be closing for the evening soon," Trace explained, hurrying out of the car.

I followed after him and up to the blue door. When we stepped inside, we were greeted to the musty smell of the old building, mixed with the sounds of cats meowing and dogs barking.

"Since, you agreed to live with me, I thought now would be the perfect time for us to add to our little family."

Tears stung my eyes at his words.

He pushed open the swinging door. The dogs immediately jumped up and started clawing at their cages, desperate for attention. I made sure to talk lovingly to each one. I didn't want any of the 'puppies' to be left out from my affections.

The last cage we came to appeared to be empty at first glance.

Slowly, a small form crept forward and a small black lab puppy peered up at us with gray eyes. He looked so sad and I noticed that he held his front left paw up slightly.

A woman came in from another door, her hair frazzled. She looked exhausted.

"That one there likes you." She pointed to the black puppy. "He came in two days ago and we've had quite the struggle with him. He was found alongside the road with injuries that are obviously from being beat."

"Aw." My heart broke for the puppy peering up at me.

"He's been sittin' in that corner, wouldn't come out. Normally the puppies go really fast around here, but nobody's taken to him."

I frowned, looking at the sweet black dog. His eyes peered up at me and I felt like he was begging me to take him home and love him forever, which I would.

"I want him," I stated, not caring if Trace agreed.

"I'll get the paperwork ready." She smiled, pleased. "Y'all can get him out and play."

I eagerly opened the cage and sat on the floor.

The puppy didn't want to play though. He immediately climbed onto my lap, struggling with his long gangly legs, and collapsed with his eyes closed.

"He likes you." Trace chuckled. "I think I have some competition now." He squatted beside me and petted the puppy's head. The puppy relaxed against Trace's touch, lovingly rolling over to get his belly rubbed.

I giggled. "I think he likes *you*."

"What's not to like?" Trace scoffed. "I'm wonderful." He petted the dog for a few more minutes and asked, "What should we name him?"

I bit my lip. "I was thinking Ace."

"Ace," Trace repeated, rolling the name around his tongue like someone sampling wine. "It's perfect."

Ten minutes later, the lady came to tell us everything was ready. We filled out the paperwork and Trace handed them cash for the adoption fee.

"Good luck, y'all," she called as we left.

From there, we headed straight to the local PetSmart. I carried Ace inside, clutched to my chest.

Trace grabbed a shopping cart and we made our way to the dog section. He grabbed two bags of dog food; the same one Ace had been eating at the SPCA, and added them to the cart. We picked out a heaping pile of toys, a cushion, bowls, and leash. Lastly, I picked up a braided light blue and gray collar.

We checked out and Trace got tokens for the machine that made nametags. We agreed on the silver dog bone shaped tag and Trace entered all the information in. Within a minute, the nametag was made.

"Well, Ace," I cooed to the dog as we strolled outside, "I certainly hope we're not forgetting anything."

Trace laughed, pointing to the overflowing cart. "We better not be."

Ace slept in my lap as we stopped by the dorm to pick up the last of my boxes. All of Avery's things were gone already. Trace grabbed the two remaining boxes while I glanced around the room in nostalgia. I looked back one last time as I closed the dorm room door, feeling as if I was closing a door on a chapter of my life.

CHAPTER THIRTY-ONE

I brought Ace inside after doing his business and smoothed my hands over my dress clothes. I was starting my first day at the local jewelry store. It wasn't too far from Trace's—*our*—apartment. I still wasn't quite used to the fact that *his* place, was now *our* place.

"You look nice, babe." Trace grinned, stepping out of the bedroom, in jeans and a wife-beater.

"Thanks." I smiled, and my stomach rolled nervously.

"You'll do great," he assured me when my smile turned into a grimace. "You have nothing to worry about."

"I don't want to do something wrong," I passed Trace and stepped into the bedroom, grabbing a pair of black flats from the bottom of the closet. I padded into the living room, slipping on my flats, and found Trace drinking a bottle of water. He screwed the cap back on and eyed me.

"What could you possibly do wrong?" He raised a brow. "You're selling jewelry."

"I could enter the price in the register wrong or—"

"You are *really* overthinking this." He tossed the empty water bottle into the recycling bin and wrapped a hand around my waist. "Just relax," he murmured soothingly, running his lips over the curve of my ear. My eyes fluttered closed as his stubble tickled my skin deliciously.

He pulled away slightly and his green eyes bore into me. "If it makes you feel better, I'll bring you lunch," he suggested.

"I don't know." My hands tangled in his shirt.

"I make a delicious ham sandwich, you know you want one," he crooned, skimming his nose along my jaw.

"I think, knowing you were going to show up, would only make me more nervous," I admitted.

"All right, fine." He smiled, his eyes sparkling. "No ham sandwich for you. I'll eat lunch with Ace." He pointed to the black puppy sleeping peacefully on the couch. He had grown surprisingly larger in the week that we had had him. Ace seemed to love his new home and I was happy that Trace and I were able to give him that.

"I'm sure he'll be a much more enthusiastic date than I would be," I joked.

"He's not as cute, that's for sure." Trace winked, kissing me soundly. "I've got to get to work."

"Me too," I sighed. I needed to stop stalling.

I kissed Trace one last time and hugged Ace goodbye. "You'll check on Ace, right?" I questioned Trace as he walked me to my car. I was nervous. Since we'd adopted Ace, he hadn't been left at home alone. We'd bought a crate for when we were gone, but he hated the thing, so I refused to put him in it.

"Of course I will," Trace promised, kissing the end of my nose. "When the others leave, I'll bring him down with me."

"Okay," I nodded, still worried about my hairy baby.

"He'll be fine," Trace assured me, "and so will you."

My breath came out ragged from nerves. I hoped I didn't make a fool of myself on my first day.

I waved goodbye to Trace as he watched me leave the parking lot. The drive was a little more than five minutes and I spent the whole time freaking out.

I parked behind the building, in one of the spots, Marcy, the owner, had said was reserved for employees.

"You can do this, Olivia," I pepped myself before forcing my unwilling body from the car.

I walked up to the back door and paused before entering. The door was painted a bright lime green, and I wondered why I was surprised. Marcy was on the eccentric side.

I forced my hand to turn the knob and stepped inside, "Hello?" I called. Marcy had told me she'd leave the door unlocked, and to come inside when I arrived, but it still seemed weird to walk in.

"Oh, thank God, you're here!" Marcy cried, scurrying from the front of the store, to the backroom I had entered. Her blonde hair was dyed every shade of the rainbow on the ends and her clothes were very bohemian. "I've been so busy this morning, I haven't had any time to design. My daughter, Alba, should be here within the hour to help you. I'll start your training in the meantime," she smiled.

"Great," I replied, for lack of anything else to say.

Marcy handmade all her jewelry and even offered custom designs. It was quite funny actually; she had taken one look at my star necklace, and knew it was one of hers. She had even remembered Trace, oohing and ahhing over him.

She had hired me to help work the front of the store so she could spend more time making jewelry. When I had applied and immediately been hired, her daughter hadn't been around. But Marcy mentioned that Alba helped her out, although she couldn't cover many hours.

"You can put your purse here." Marcy pointed to a cubby painted bright neon purple. I did as she told me, sliding my purse into one of the cubbies.

The walls in the backroom were a lime green that matched the door I had come through. I knew that the front room, where she sold her designs and had them displayed, was painted bright yellow.

"I want you to feel comfortable here, Olivia. There's no need to be so shy." She smiled kindly and waved her hand for me to follow her.

Thankfully, there were no customers at the moment. Marcy showed me where the key was to open the glass cases so people could try on the necklaces, bracelets, and rings. After that, she showed me how to use the iPad that she used instead of a regular cash register. Everything seemed very straightforward and simple. I immediately started to feel more at ease. Marcy hung around to help me with the first few customers that trickled in. After being successful with all the customers, Marcy felt comfortable enough to leave me on my own.

I handled two more customers on my own before Alba showed up. There was no mistaking her as Marcy's daughter. They both had the same pointed features. Her hair was dyed black with streaks of crimson and purple. Thick black bangs curtained her forehead and she had a nose ring. Her eyes were a light blue that I was sure was the product of contacts. No one's eyes were naturally that shade of sky blue.

She held out a hand to me. "I'm Alba." She smiled, showing off straight white teeth.

"Olivia," I replied.

"I'm glad my mom was able to get some help. I can't help her as often as I'd like. I recently started my own tattoo business," she explained.

"Oh." I nodded. "So you're an artist like your mom, just in a different way."

"Yep, we're very artsy people." She nodded, looking around. "You appear to be doing very well for your first day," she appraised me, hands on her studded belt.

"Thanks," I breathed, relieved that she thought so.

"If you think you can handle yourself out here, I'll go back there, and help my mom out." She pointed to the beaded curtain that separated the backroom from the front.

"I think I'm good." I smiled.

"Awesome." She clapped her hands together. Her nails were painted black with red skulls drawn on top. "If you need one of us, give a holler."

Alba disappeared behind the curtain and I was left alone once more.

At lunchtime, my phone vibrated in my pocket. I pulled it out, wiping my Cheeto stained fingers on a napkin, and smiled at the picture Trace had text. He held Ace in one hand while the other held the phone out. A ham sandwich was clasped between his teeth. I giggled.

TRACE:*MISS u. I no ur doing gr8.*

I REPLIED BACK to tell him that he had been right and my first day was going well.

Marcy breezed by me with new products to display. "Based on the smile on your face, I'd say you're talking to your beau."

I paled at being caught. "Sorry," I mumbled, putting my phone away.

"Sweetie, you're on your lunch break. I don't mind if you're texting that fine specimen of man. If you know any more like him, maybe you can send them Alba's way?"

"Mom!" We heard the groan from the back. "I am a smart independent woman, I don't need a man!"

Marcy rolled her eyes and shook her head. "That may be so," she whispered to me, "but I want some grandchildren before I'm dead."

"Mom! I can still hear you!" Alba called.

Marcy and I snickered.

"I may know of some guys for Alba." I shrugged, thinking of Justin and Brian from the tattoo shop.

"Really?" Marcy asked, brightening.

"Mhmm." I nodded.

"I don't need a man!" Alba yelled and a moment later appeared from behind the beaded curtain.

"Well, someone has to clear out the cobwebs in your vagina." Marcy pointed at her daughter.

"Mom!" Alba shrieked, her face coloring an unhealthy shade of red. "Don't say things like that! It's disgusting coming from you!"

"Oh, please, Alba. Don't be so dramatic. Everyone has sex." Alba cringed at her mother's words. "Sex, sex, sex," Marcy chanted.

"I think I'm going to be sick." Alba frowned, shaking her head back and forth.

"You young people can be so ridiculous, acting like us older people have never had sex," Marcy defended with her hands on her narrow hips. "How do you think you came into this world? A stork?"

"Ugh," Alba groaned, "if you keep this up, I'm leaving."

"Fine, I'll shut my mouth" —Marcy rearranged some necklaces— "but only because I need your help today."

"Way to make me feel used, Mom." Alba laughed, the beads swishing closed as she returned to the back.

"Say hello to that handsome man of yours for me." Marcy squeezed my arm lightly as she breezed around me. "Oh, and sweetheart, you look nice and all, but there's no need to be so dressed up. You're making the owner look bad." She chuckled.

I glanced down at my slacks and dress shirt. "What would you prefer me to wear?" I asked with a smile, amused at my boss.

"Jeans, shorts, whatever you want, really. I mean, look at me," she pointed to her own long skirt and breezy shirt. "Some people might say it's unprofessional but it's my business and I'll run it how I want to," she said firmly. "Besides, my fashion sense doesn't seem to keep the buyers away," she chortled.

THE REST of the day went by quickly and Marcy closed the store at five.

"I hope your first day wasn't too bad." She smiled as she flipped the sign from Open to Closed and lowered the blinds over the glass door.

"It was great," I answered honestly.

"So, you're not sick of us yet?" Marcy asked, pointing to herself and Alba.

"Of course not." I laughed. "You guys are great."

"Phew." Marcy pretended to wipe sweat from her brow. "I was worried we'd be too much for you to handle and you'd quit."

"Not at all," I replied, straightening the displays in the glass case.

"If you don't have to get back to that love muffin of yours, would you like to have dinner with us?" Marcy asked.

I giggled at her term for Trace. "I don't have plans, but I don't want to intrude." I bit my lip nervously. "I would hate to feel like I'm imposing."

"Nonsense," Marcy scoffed. "I'm inviting you, how could you be imposing?"

"If you're sure," I agreed reluctantly, looking between the mother and daughter.

"It'll be fun." Alba smiled genuinely.

"All right, I'll go," I finally agreed.

Between the three of us, we finished cleaning and straightening the store in no time. I grabbed my purse and followed them outside.

"We had planned to go to Olive Garden, is that fine with you? If not, we can go somewhere else," Marcy informed me, her rainbow-colored hair blowing in the wind.

"That'll be great."

"Excellent." She clapped her hands together and headed toward her car, a bright yellow Fiat.

I got in my car and texted Trace to let him know what I was doing so he wouldn't worry.

I met Alba and Marcy at the restaurant that looked like it belonged in the Tuscan countryside with its stone walls and terracotta roof tiles.

We had to wait fifteen minutes before being seated but spent the time chatting casually. Somehow, much to my dismay, Marcy always managed to bring the conversation back to Trace. I was beginning to think she was the grown up, hippie version, of Avery.

We finished dinner and parted ways. I felt completely at ease and excited for my next day at work.

I UNLOCKED the door to the apartment and giggled at the sight that met me.

A song by 3OH!3 was pumping from the iPod dock in the kitchen, and Trace was dancing around the apartment in only his jeans, a bowl of ice cream in one hand. He sang along with the lyrics, trying to coax Ace into dancing with him. The puppy simply cracked his eyes open and promptly went back to sleep.

The door closed behind me and he turned around quickly.

"Hey, you're home." He grinned, spooning a mouthful of chocolate ice cream, his thick-framed black glasses were perched on his nose.

"I'm home," I repeated, smiling as I dropped my purse on the floor. "I'm going to shower."

"All right, how was dinner?" He licked a smear of ice cream from his lip.

"It was great." I started unbuttoning my blouse as I made my way to the bathroom. "Marcy is awesome, and her daughter, Alba, is great too."

"Looks like we can cross, *make more friends* off your list." He chuckled, making his way across the room to me. "I'm so happy your first day went so well." He planted a sticky kiss on my cheek. "Although, I never doubted that it would be anything but fantastic."

"We can't all be as optimistic as you," I joked.

"Need me to wash your back?" he quipped as I moved to close the bathroom door.

"I think I've got it covered." I shook my head at him.

"Are you sure? I'm an excellent back washer."

"I know." I rolled my eyes, remembering the morning after the first time we'd had sex, when we showered together.

I finished my shower, alone, and dressed in my PJs, taking my spot on the couch beside Trace. Ace curled into the curve of my legs to be close to me. I loved that little dog.

I laid my head on Trace's shoulder, not paying attention to whatever was playing on TV.

I smiled to myself, thinking about how at ease Trace and I were with living together. True, it had only been a week, but I felt so at peace ... and loved, even if he hadn't said it yet. I didn't think it was possible for anything to burst my bubble.

CHAPTER THIRTY-TWO

I said goodbye to Marcy and made my way home so I could shower and get ready. Trace and I had plans to meet Avery and Luca at a restaurant nearby.

"You look nice," Trace commented when I stepped out of the bedroom in a new sundress I had bought.

"I wanted to dress up." I shrugged. Lately, all I had been wearing was shorts and t-shirts, so I wanted to look nice. "How long before we're to meet them?" I asked, sitting on the couch to put on the heels Avery had given me.

"We should be heading out now." He smiled at me from where he lounged on the couch with Ace curled against his body.

"I swear, all that puppy does is sleep." I laughed. "Aren't most puppies into mischief?"

"Probably, but not Ace." Trace rubbed the puppy's back, and at Trace's touch, Ace rolled over to get his tummy rubbed. We had quickly learned that Ace loved belly rubs. "He's special."

"Let me fix my hair and I'll be ready to go," I informed him as

I strolled into the bathroom. I quickly side-braided my damp hair and added some gloss to my lips.

Trace was already grabbing his car keys when I walked out.

"Bye, Ace," I crooned to the dog, kissing his soft head, and handing him a treat.

Trace shook his head at me. "That is the most spoiled dog ever."

"He deserves to be spoiled." I laughed, passing by Trace, and making my way down the staircase to the parking lot.

"How was work?" he asked, starting the old Camaro.

"It was great. Marcy is so awesome," I gushed. After three weeks of working at Marcy's store, I had yet to run into a hiccup. The customers were great and Marcy was the best boss ever.

"See, you had nothing to worry about." He grinned, his eyes a light shade of green today, which meant he was in a happy care-free mood.

"Do you want me to admit that you were right?" I laughed.

"Just one teeny tiny 'Trace you were right' would be awesome." He held up his fingers a centimeter apart.

"Fine." I rolled my eyes. "Trace, you were right."

"Those words warm my heart." He grinned with a hand over his heart.

"Look at the road," I warned.

"You worry too much," he mumbled, but his eyes strayed back to the road ahead.

He hadn't driven far when he turned into a parking garage. We got out of the car and I followed him around the side of a painted stone building to a gate. He pushed the gate open and I spotted Avery and Luca seated at one of tables with a yellow umbrella.

I saw a band setting up on a stage in the far corner of the outdoor patio.

"Another thing you can cross off," Trace whispered in my ear with a steady hand on my back as he guided me to the table.

I shook my head in amazement.

Trace and I, met by chance, and something made me show him my list, but somewhere along the way, my list stopped mattering to me. It became, not so much about accomplishing these things, but about living in the moment and just ... being happy. As simple as that may sound, it's true. Happiness is everything.

Trace pulled out a chair for me to sit down and then scooted me into the table.

"Have y'all already ordered?" Trace asked the other two.

"Nah, we were waiting for you guys to get here," Luca replied, slouching in his chair with an arm thrown casually across the back of Avery's. He was in one of his vests, again, with no shirt underneath. Quite a few girls kept eyeing his impressive arms, trying to get a peek at what the vest was hiding.

"I already know what I want." Trace pushed his menu aside. "Luca and I come here all the time," he explained.

The restaurant's name, Piccadilly's, was scrawled across the top of the menu in a swirly font. I perused the different items, settling on the club sandwich. It was a hot evening so I wasn't in the mood for warm food.

A waitress appeared with her pen already poised against her notepad. She appeared frazzled with all the tables and I felt bad for her. I knew I could never be a waitress. I'd never be able to carry those heavy trays of food and walk at the same time. She was dressed casually for the summer heat, in a pink polo shirt, and khaki shorts.

"Have y'all decided?" she asked.

We all nodded and rattled off our orders.

"Great." She smiled as she took the menus. "I'll get that in and I'll get your drinks right out to you."

We had only been outside for maybe five minutes, and I already felt sweat beading on my skin. My dress began to stick to my body from perspiration.

The umbrella, although it provided shade, did little to squelch the heat. I prayed for a breeze as I fanned myself with a hand.

The waitress returned with our drinks as the band started to play. They were only a local band but they were pretty good. I recognized the first song as an old beach song.

I slurped greedily at my sweet tea, and soon the glass was empty, but I was still thirsty. I should have been smart and ordered water. In this heat, sweet tea did little to quench my thirst.

"I know it may not be the concert you were hoping for, in a big stadium, but I thought this would suffice." Trace leaned over to whisper in my ear so that Avery and Luca didn't hear.

"It's perfect," I beamed at him.

He smiled in response and sat back to enjoy the show.

Our food was brought out and the band took a short break.

"This is really good," I mumbled around a mouthful of sandwich.

"Yeah, this place is great." Avery smiled, dipping her fry into ketchup. I *really* hoped Trace didn't start up an argument with me about ketchup again. "My family comes here a lot."

"And now, I feel like the odd man out," I grumbled, chewing on a non-ketchup-covered fry.

"That's because" —Avery pointed at me— "up until Tracey-poo, over here" —she pointed a finger at Trace and he smirked in response— "came into your life, you rarely left the dorm, unless it was to do your homework or read a book outside."

"I can't help it that I have a really strong work ethic and you don't," I joked, pointing a finger at her.

Avery's eyes zeroed in on a spot over my shoulder, just before I heard the words, "Well, well, well," from a voice I never wanted to hear from again.

The hairs on my neck stood on end as I cringed.

"Can I ever catch a fucking break?" Trace grumbled under his breath, turning around to face our visitor. "What do you want, Aubrey?"

I recoiled at the sound of her name coming off of Trace's lips.

"I was hoping my *date*," she emphasized the word, "and I could join you?"

"Hell to the mother-fucking no," Trace seethed.

I turned to watch Aubrey's reaction. Her blue eyes widened briefly. I was sure she had expected Trace to remain cordial since we were in public. "Trace," she scoffed, "you shouldn't use language like that, with small children nearby."

"And maybe *you* shouldn't walk up to people that obviously don't like you. You're not welcome here." Trace waved his hand like he was shooing her away. "When things ended between us, they ended." His words were harsh and Aubrey crossed her arms protectively over her chest. "Stop trying to revive something that died a long time ago." Trace looked up at Aubrey's date. "If you were smart, you'd drop this one, she's nothing but trouble."

Aubrey's mouth opened and closed in shock. "Trace!"

"What? It's true." He shrugged. "You're like a fucking plague, sucking the life out of everything you touch, just like you did with me. And yet, somehow, you wonder why no one likes you?"

My stomach clenched, not because I felt bad for Aubrey necessarily, but if, for some reason things between Trace and I ended, I didn't think I could stand it if he spoke to me that way. Why? Because I was hopelessly in love with the man sitting beside me. I loved his cocky attitude and smiles. I loved that he could be arrogant. I loved that when he was with me, he was sweet and attentive. I loved that he was caring and passionate. Hell, I even loved those stupid plaid shirts he always wore. But most importantly, I loved *him*. Down to his very core, the good and the bad, I loved it all.

And despite being upset that Aubrey was once again, causing a scene, I decided in that moment that I was going to tell him that I loved him. Not now. But soon. It didn't matter anymore that he hadn't told me. I had to get these words off my chest.

Aubrey's face turned an unhealthy shade of red, like those kids who held their breath when they got mad. It made her already light blonde hair appear even lighter.

"I am a very likable person," she hissed, causing Luca to snort.

"Yeah, and a great white shark doesn't have sharp teeth," Luca said sarcastically.

Her dark blue eyes narrowed.

"Who are you, bitch?" Avery snapped, standing slowly.

Oh, God. Avery is about to lose it.

"*I* am Aubrey Montgomery, who are you?" Aubrey looked Avery up and down with a sneer marring her pale pink lips.

"*I* am Avery Callahan," Avery mimicked Aubrey's snarky tone, "and *you*, Malibu Bimbo Barbie, have overstayed your welcome," she scowled. "Stop harassing my best friend's boyfriend. Understand?" Avery smiled but it was anything but friendly.

Aubrey's eyes narrowed further as her gaze slid to me. "You are nothing but a piece of ass to him. You can't love him the way I can." She glared at me. "You watch and see, it won't be long until he's over you, and comes crawling back to me. Let's go, Zach." She tugged on the guy's arm to leave.

"Listen here," Avery's voice had turned icy cold and I knew trouble was coming.

"Avery," I warned but she ignored me. I pleaded with my eyes for Luca to do something but he was rooting her on. Some help he was.

"*You* are nothing, because if *you* were *something*, Trace would still be with *you*," Avery spat. "Obviously, you're nothing but a cold-hearted bitch, while my friend here" —Avery pointed to me — "is the kindest, most giving person, I've ever met. So no, Trace won't be *crawling* back to you. It's you that'll be doing the crawling, *honey*," Avery glowered, "and it won't be to a man. You'll be crawling on your precious hands and knees, scrubbing floors because I'm gonna make sure your world crumbles around you."

Aubrey rolled her eyes. "I don't know who you think you are, but that'll never happen."

"I'm not someone to mess with," Avery warned in a deadly tone.

"You're really hanging out with some low-class people," Aubrey scoffed at Trace. "When you decide to climb back up the social ladder, don't expect me to answer the phone."

"That's it!" Avery tried to lunge across the table to grab Aubrey but Luca, thankfully, sprang into action and caught her around the waist, forcing her back into her seat.

"She's not worth it," Luca told her.

"I'll be right back," Trace muttered, pushing away from the table, his jaw rigid. He strode quickly after Aubrey and disappeared around the side of the building.

My stomach sank.

Had he realized she was right and was going after her to beg forgiveness?

I bit down on my lip to hold back tears.

I had finally admitted my feelings for Trace to myself, and watching him run after his ex-girlfriend was breaking my heart.

"I'm not very hungry." I pushed my chair back and stood slowly. "I have to go," I mumbled, not meeting Luca or Avery's eyes.

I didn't have any money on me so I hoped Trace returned to pay for the bill. If he didn't, I'd owe Avery later.

I left a stunned Luca and Avery behind and fled through the gate.

My perfect evening was ruined.

The sounds of the band starting back up rumbled behind me.

I put a fist to my mouth to stifle my sobs.

My pace was quick as I tried to make my escape. But apparently, not quick enough, as footsteps rapidly sounded behind me, and a body forced me against the wall of the restaurant.

I went to scream but Trace's hand covered my mouth before a single sound could escape.

"Where are you going?" he asked fiercely, removing his hand so I could speak.

"I'm leaving," I sobbed, "so go back and enjoy your evening with Aubrey. You don't owe me an explanation. I get it, I do. She's like—"

"She's nothing like me, dammit! You promised me this wouldn't happen again! You promised, Olivia! But here you are, running from me!" he seethed, his eyes manic as they roamed over my face. "I can't help what and who my past is, but it's no more. *She's* no more," he spoke furiously. "How could you ever think I was going back to that?" His tone softened.

"I don't know," I choked as the sky darkened above us with an impending summer rain shower.

"You don't know?" he repeated. "Do you not know me at all, Olivia? I know I'm not the most open guy in the world, it's not in my nature to confess everything about myself, but I've opened up to you, more than I have for almost anybody." His eyes searched my face. "Why can't you see that? When I'm with you, I'm *me*," he growled angrily. "For *years*, I played the part of this happy rich party boy, but the truth is, that's never been me. The real me" — he pointed a thumb at his chest, holding me securely against the wall with his other hand— "is the guy you've known from the beginning, Olivia. I'm Trace Alexander Wentworth. I'm a mechanic and I live above the garage I work at." He wet his lips with a quick flick of his tongue. "I like plaid shirts, not tuxes. My favorite color is red ... sometimes green, depending on my mood. And there's this girl that I care about more than anything. She's beautiful and she's stubborn but she captured my heart from the moment she opened her mouth and started rattling about Prince Charming coming along to save her. That's *you* Olivia and no one else." His eyes and words were fierce.

My chest rose and fell with heavy breaths and the stone wall was hot against my back.

"I'm sorry," my lower lip trembled.

"You should be sorry," his brow furrowed together as he gazed down at me with intense green eyes. "You're *everything* to me."

Before I could reply, he crushed his lips against mine. Our tongues tangled together as he lifted me effortlessly, my legs wrapping around his waist. "Everything," he whispered between our lips. "You are *everything*," he growled the last word.

I gripped his face in my hands, leaning forward to deepen the kiss.

He gripped my thighs, pressing into me.

"Let's get out of here," he growled, pulling away.

I nodded, my body and brain having turned into Jell-O.

"You're lucky you're hard to stay mad at." He grinned as he took my hand, and led me to the parking garage. "It's impossible, actually, for me to stay mad at you."

"Why?" I asked.

He stopped walking, as we reached the car, and stared down at me.

"Because, I see the hurt in your eyes, and I know you believe whatever crazy thing it is you're thinking in your head, and I can't stay mad at that," he said firmly, opening the passenger door for me.

I slid inside and no words were spoken between us. Glances were exchanged and small touches, but nothing more.

As we pulled into Pete's Garage, it began to rain. The water slid down the windshield in thick torrents.

I prepared myself to make a run for it, but Trace grabbed my arm.

"What?" I asked with wide eyes.

He grinned crookedly. "Dance with me, Olivia," he pleaded huskily.

A smile touched my face. "That sounds wonderful."

I slipped from the car and the rain immediately drenched my dress and body. My wet hair clung to my forehead and when I met Trace in the middle of the parking lot, he pulled the elastic band loose that held my braid in place. He shook my hair out around me and murmured, "Beautiful."

Rain slicked off his skin, dripping from his nose and chin.

He placed a hand on my waist and pulled me to him. "And now, we dance."

He dipped me low and the rain pelted my exposed neck and chest. The rain felt amazing against my warm skin and the asphalt fogged around us as the rain cooled its heated temperature.

Trace spun me around and we kicked at the puddles that formed in the potholes.

I laughed and smiled and danced and lived.

Trace grabbed me around the waist and spun us in circles.

"Trace!" I squealed, holding onto his shoulders. His plaid shirt and white wife-beater clung to his skin.

He lowered me to the ground and dipped me again, placing a kiss on my neck.

The feel of the rain, mixed with his lips, caused me to shake.

Raising me up, he took my right hand, and used it to twirl me.

We both completely forgot about our fight and enjoyed the moment.

I licked rain off my lips as I danced around. The cool liquid tickled my tongue. I pushed my clingy wet hair off my forehead.

"This is amazing!" I cried, spreading my arms out wide.

"It's only rain." Trace chuckled, watching me.

"It's beautiful," I chimed, twirling so my wet hair fanned around me.

He grabbed me again, planting a kiss on my wet lips, and we danced together.

I'm sure we looked crazy and awkward to anyone passing by, but from my perspective, it was perfect.

Trace lifted me up and my legs wrapped around his waist. I gripped the short, wet strands of his hair between my fingers and leaned my head back to look up at the sky. I let out a cry of joy.

I looked down at Trace and the warmth in his eyes melted me.

I moved my hands from his hair, to his cheeks, and lowered my head to kiss him.

The rain clung to our kiss, making it that much sweeter.

Those three little words desperately wanted to escape my throat but I pushed them down. Now, wasn't the time. Not when I had acted the way I did at the restaurant.

When I finally told Trace I loved him, I wanted it to be special, and I didn't want the confrontation with his ex to cloud the moment. I wanted it to only be about the two of us.

"Have you had enough dancing?" he asked, meeting my stare with an intensity that caused my whole body to quake.

I nodded.

"Thank God." He crushed his lips against mine as he slowly lowered me down his rain-slicked body. We were both soaked to the bone, but I had never felt better in all my life.

Like clumsy teenagers, we made our way up to the apartment.

I found my back pressed against the door as his lips explored mine and his hands fumbled to get the key in.

Finally, he managed, and we went slipping into the apartment.

He kicked the door closed behind us and grabbed my cheeks in his large hands.

We stumbled into the bedroom and crashed onto the bed in a tangle of limbs.

We were both in a hurry and awkward in our effort to rid one another of the wet garments stuck to our bodies. His combat boots fell to floor with a clatter and he lifted my dress over the top of my head. It hit the floor with a wet thump.

He sat up and pulled his drenched shirts over his head and they joined the pile of clothes on the floor.

I reached out and undid the belt on his jeans, popping the button, and lowering the zipper. He kicked them off and covered my body with his.

His hard length pressed against me and I hesitantly ran my finger over the curve. He shuddered above me.

"God, you have no idea how good that feels," he moaned.

I pushed the fabric of his boxers down so there was nothing separating my touch.

He pressed his face into my neck, kissing a tender spot just below my ear.

"I need you, now," he panted.

"Then take what you need," I breathed, meeting his smoldering gaze.

Kissing me deeply, he removed my bra and panties.

Standing up, and stepping out of his boxers, he grabbed a condom and rolled it on.

"Those" —he pointed to my heels— "stay on."

"You really like these, don't you?" I smirked, lifting a foot in his direction.

"You have no idea," he growled, sliding me up the bed so that my head rested on the pillows.

He slid into me in one hard thrust and gripped my hips.

"Oh, my God," I cried.

A long drawn out moan escaped between Trace's perfect pouty lips. "You always feel so good, Olivia. It's like you were made for me, and only *me*," he reaffirmed his words with a hard thrust.

I grabbed his forearms. "Only you," I panted, staring into his eyes as he pounded into me. "I'm yours."

"You're mine," he growled, lowering to seal my lips with a kiss. His tongue flicked against my lips and my mouth opened to allow him entrance.

The hard, rapid, pace had me coming sooner than normal.

My fingernails raked his back as I screamed.

"Yes," he said as he bit his lip, "scream for me baby. Let me hear you."

"Harder," I panted, and he obliged, quickening his thrusts.

Sweat and rain mingled together as our bodies met.

He continued his relentless pace and my core tightened around him. We had never had sex like this before. It was hard, it was fast, it was intense, and it was passionate.

Just like us.

Trace's eyes closed and when they opened they were full of an emotion I couldn't describe. "I love this. I love being inside you. I love watching your face and seeing the pleasure I can give you."

I wet my lips and ran my hands over his chest, then lower, to where we connected.

My core was tightening again and my back bowed off the bed as my orgasm ripped through me. Trace shuddered and quaked inside me, growling as his own orgasm took hold.

Spent, he gently lowered his weight on top of me, placing kisses along my face, down my neck, and over my collarbone and breasts.

He slipped from me and disposed of the condom.

Then, he climbed back in bed, and pulled my naked body against his.

Night was far away, but for now, we needed to hold each other.

A chuckle escaped his lips and his breath stirred the wet hairs plastered against my neck.

"What's so funny?" I asked.

"We dented the wall," he chortled.

"What?" I sat up and turned to look at the wall the bed was against.

"Oh, my God," I stifled a laugh with a hand over my mouth. "We did."

Sure enough, there was a long dent in the wall where the headboard had banged relentlessly against it.

"It's a good thing I don't have neighbors." Trace smirked, kissing my shoulder. "Wanna see if we can make it bigger?"

CHAPTER THIRTY-THREE

"Hey, Mom." I smiled as she slid into the backseat of Trace's car.

"Hi, sweetie." She patted my shoulder. "Trace." She smiled in his direction.

"Nora." Trace nodded and backed out of the Callahan's driveway.

"There's so much I need to tell you," my mom said, buckling her seatbelt. "I feel like I haven't had the chance to see you in so long, and talk about things, what with both of us working and everything."

"So, what do you want to talk about?" I peered over my shoulder at her as Trace drove to the restaurant to meet his family for lunch.

"For starters, I got a promotion, and found an apartment I'll be able to afford, with my new salary. It's small ... but clean. It will be nice to have something of my own."

"That's great, Mom!" I exclaimed. "I'm so happy for you!"

"That's awesome, Nora," Trace piped in.

"But that's not at all." She smiled giddily.

"What is it?" I asked curiously.

"I went into the lawyer's office last week and filed for divorce. He sent the papers to Aaron, all he has to do is sign." The relief on her face was obvious.

"Mom! That's fantastic!" I grinned.

Finally, after more than twenty years, she would be completely free of Aaron Owens.

"I wanted to call and tell you, but I felt it was better to tell you in person." She smiled.

"I'm so happy for you, Mom." I reached back for her hand and gave it a light squeeze.

When we arrived at the restaurant, Trace's family was already there.

"If it isn't my favorite future grand-daughter-in-law." Warren chuckled, standing shakily on his cane, hugging me tightly despite his frail state. "I've missed you. You need to come visit me."

"I'll try, I've been really busy." I took the seat in-between my mom and Trace. "I got a job." I really had been meaning to visit Warren. I missed him.

"That's right." Warren nodded. "I remember Trace mentioning that. How's the job working out for you?"

"I love it." I smiled, picking up the menu.

The restaurant was attached to a hotel and it was surprisingly upscale with dark wood accents and tile floors. Part of the kitchen was open to the space so you could watch them cook.

"I'm glad to hear that," Warren coughed.

"Gramps, are you okay?" Trace asked, his brow wrinkling in concern.

"Just a little cold, nothing to be worried about, these old lungs don't work quite as well as they used to." He shrugged, taking a sip of water.

Trace didn't seem to be buying what Warren had said.

A waiter appeared and I ordered a chopped salad.

When everyone's order had been taken, I looked across the table at Trent. "How've you been?" I asked.

"Eh. I haven't been doing much."

"He's been sulking," Lily piped in.

"About what?" I asked Trent. "You certainly don't have to tell me, but you can."

"Just a girl," he mumbled, reluctantly, squirming under everyone's gaze. He scratched his chin, staring at the table.

Trace chortled. "Is she resisting your infamous charm?"

"Yes," Trent groaned, rolling his eyes. "She completely ignores me and not even my dimples affect her! Girls can't resist the dimples!" He pointed dramatically to his cheeks.

"Guess you're going to have to try harder, little brother. Maybe, the whole 'flirt' thing doesn't work for her." Trace shrugged.

"Ya think?" Trent snapped.

"Why don't you just be yourself around her?" I suggested. "A lot of girls aren't attracted to the showy type."

"Whatever," Trent grumbled, as he unfolded his napkin, and spread it across his lap. "I don't want to talk about this, anyway."

The waiter brought our food out and we settled into easy conversation.

"Oh, I keep forgetting to mention that the lake house renovations are finished," Lily explained to Trace. "You and Olivia should come up this summer. We'll be leaving in two weeks, to spend the rest of the summer there, but you're welcome to go beforehand by yourselves, or join us. You too, Nora," she added.

This was the first time my mom and Lily had met. I was extremely pleased by how well they were getting along.

"That sounds nice." I nodded at Trace. "I've never been to a lake house."

"Great!" Lily clapped her hands together. "And seriously, Nora, please join us."

"I would love to," my mom replied, "but since I was recently promoted, I don't think it would be best to go on a vacation so soon."

"Oh, of course. I completely understand. Just know that the invitation is open and I mean that sincerely." She smiled pleasantly. Raising her water glass in the air, Lily said, "Here's to new beginnings."

"To new beginnings," we all echoed.

"IT'S A BIT BARE, isn't it?" I assessed my mom's new apartment.

It was smaller than Trace's apartment and not as nice, but at least, like she had said, it was clean. The carpet was brand new and the walls were freshly painted. The appliances weren't stainless steel, but they were new as well.

A single couch decorated the designated living area, and when I poked my head inside the only bedroom, it contained a simple bed and mattress.

"It's not like I have much." My mom sighed. "All I brought with me was clothes. I'll add some decorations later." She pulled her hair off her shoulders and tied it in a ponytail. "But for now, it's my own place, and that's what matters."

"Let me know when you want to go shopping," I replied, looking over the couch to make sure it was clean. "I'd love to help you."

"I will." She placed her hands on her hips over her stretchy yoga pants. "It'll probably be a while, though. I really don't have the money right now. I had to pay the first three months' rent up front and it has all but wiped out my bank account."

"I'm sorry, Mom." I bit my lip. "I should have moved in with you."

"No, no, that's silly." She shook her head. "You're happy where you're at and you don't need to worry about me. I'm fine on my own. I even made sure this place has a security system." She pointed to the wall beside the door where a white panel was inserted.

"What are you going to do about a ride to work?" I asked. Since Resa didn't work, she had been lending my mom her car or driving her to work if she had errands to run.

"Don't be mad." Her cheeks flushed. "But Nick will be taking me. He has a job for the summer near the hospital and he said it wouldn't be any trouble."

"I'm sure he did say that," I grumbled. Apparently, I was going to have to have a talk with Nick and let him know my mom was *off-limits*.

"He's a nice guy, Liv. Don't crinkle your nose like that. He's sweet and he helps me out." She rolled her suitcase into the bedroom.

"He's also a twenty-two-year-old man who wants to get in my mother's pants," I grumbled.

"Olivia!" my mom exclaimed, glaring at me with wide copper eyes, the same eyes she had given me.

"It's true!" I countered.

She shook her head rapidly back and forth, staring at the ground. "I can't help how old he is-"

"Oh, my God," I turned around so that she was to my back. I *couldn't* look at her right now. "You've slept with him, haven't you?"

Her silence was answer enough.

"Mom!" I turned to face her.

Her face was beet red and she looked like she was choking on her own saliva. "Olivia, that's none of your business."

"Ew, no!" I squealed, shaking my head. "I can't. I *can't*." I covered my eyes.

"Then you shouldn't have said anything," she defended.

"Oh, my God. I think Avery's rubbing off on me. This is bad. I wouldn't have normally asked that. I'm sorry. It's none of my business," I apologized.

"It *is* your business, Liv. You're my daughter. But I shouldn't have to tell you something until *I'm* ready," she said softly.

"I know. I'm sorry," I repeated. "I shouldn't have asked."

"Let's move on and pretend this conversation never happened," she pleaded.

"Sure," I agreed, not meeting her eyes, because I was positive that I wouldn't be able to pretend it never happened.

Since there was nothing left to bring in, I mumbled, "I'm going to get out of here. I have to stop by the grocery store." I really did have to go to the grocery store, but at this point, I would've made any excuse to leave. The awkwardness from the Nick situation had yet to leave.

"All right." She seemed relieved at my imminent departure. I figured either Nick was expected to show up any minute, *or* she felt as awkward as I did. "Let's do lunch next weekend, if you're not working?"

"Sounds good." I smiled, striding toward the door, and *Nick* would *not* be a topic that I was ever bringing up again.

I started my small cobalt blue Ford Focus and drove to the grocery store closest to Trace's apartment. I still had trouble thinking of it as "ours".

Trace was working late tonight and I wanted to make him dinner, because despite what he believed, I *could* cook. My mom had taught me most of her recipes, and while I wasn't the best cook, I wasn't horrible. I wanted to surprise him with a meal and *finally* get those three important words off my chest. Several times in the past few days, they had come close to rolling off my tongue, but I kept my mouth shut.

I pushed the cart around the store, adding the ingredients I needed, and headed to the checkout.

I planned to make homemade Fettuccine Alfredo from one of my mom's recipes.

I loaded the plastic bags into my car and drove home.

I noticed a car in my rearview mirror that appeared to be following me, and my heart rate spiked when it pulled into Pete's parking lot. I reasoned that maybe they were having car trouble, and it was by coincidence that they followed me home.

But ... my gut didn't believe that.

Not looking at the person, because I didn't want to get involved in a conversation, I lifted the trunk and picked up the two bags, the keys to the apartment clutched in one hand.

Gravel crunched behind me and fear slid like a sheet of ice down my back. Swallowing thickly, I started up the steps that led to the apartment.

A hand pushed into my back and I fell on the wood steps. Splinters imbedded in my hands and knees.

"What the—" I exclaimed.

Someone rolled me over, pinning my wrists to my sides.

I gasped when my eyes connected with dark ones, outlined by wire-framed glasses.

"Aaron," I gasped.

"My name is not Aaron, to you. It's Dad." He shook me. "I'm your dad."

His hold on me was tight and I was surprised my bones didn't snap.

"Let me go," I begged, hysterics arising.

I kicked him hard in the stomach and he was forced to let me go as he stumbled down a few steps.

Thankfully, the key was still clutched firmly in my hand, and I ran for the door. I managed to get it open, but by the time I tried to close it, Aaron had recovered and was barging his way inside.

He slapped my face so hard that I fell to my knees. Tears clouded my vision as I clutched my stinging cheek. He towered above me, the look in his eyes anything but human. They were dead eyes. They were the eyes of someone who had lost everything and no longer cared.

"I came for your mom," he growled, "she's an idiot to think I'm going to give her a divorce. I'm prepared to drag her ass back home. I was driving around looking for her, when I saw you walking out of the grocery store." He kicked my ribs.

I grunted from the impact and clutched feebly at my side.

Oh, God. It *hurt*.

"Hurting *you*," he sneered the word like it was dirty, "will hurt your mom more than anything else. *This*" —he kicked my face and I tasted blood— "will break her. She needs to be broken. She needs to know she can't run." He punctuated each sentence with a kick to a different part of my body. My side. My chest. My arms. He didn't care where he hit me; he just wanted to hurt me. "I told her there would be consequences if she ever left me. But she didn't *listen!*"

His anger was rising from deadly calm to unchained fury.

I whimpered as he beat me, trying to crawl away from him.

Ace barked and growled but there was little he could do.

Aaron reached down and gripped me by my hair, slamming my head into the wood floor.

I screamed, scratching at his bare arm. "Get off of me! Let me go!"

There wasn't much I could do to fight back. My whole body was sore and I felt like I was choking on the blood pooling in my mouth.

He beat my skull repeatedly into the floor yelling and screaming nonsensical things.

My vision began to blur and go spotty.

"Stop, please stop," I begged, crying.

"Trouble! Nothing but trouble!" he yelled.

I tried to swallow but blood clogged my throat. I began to choke and gasp for air.

He punched my face and blood went flying out of my mouth. I rolled over, trying to spit the blood out, and suck in oxygen at the same time. My eyes zeroed in on the spot where my head had been. There was a sizeable pool of blood there and I reached up, feeling a gash on the back of my head. My fingers came away red and I began to sob, which did nothing to help my breathing.

The air left my lungs with a sickening wet sound.

"You'll pay for everything you've done to me!" Aaron screamed and kicked my other side.

My whole body felt like it had been run over by an eighteen-wheeler.

"You-goin-ta-kill-me," I choked, not able to get the words out as I gasped for air, trying to crawl away again. I was so weak and there was so much blood. I felt it dampening my hair.

I rolled back over, onto my back. I was too tired to move and too weak to fight back.

I begged silently for an easy end. I didn't want to suffer any more than I already was. I needed the pain to end.

Footsteps echoed around the doorway and I watched Aaron turn. A moment later, Aaron was crashing to the ground beside me as Trace wrestled him to the ground.

Trace.

Trace.

Trace.

Trace was going to watch me die. I didn't want that for him.

There was no hope for me. Air wasn't reaching my lungs and I knew I had little time left.

Punches were thrown and grunts echoed around the space.

Ace came to my side, licking my sore face, and curling up beside me. It was as if the puppy thought that his presence alone could heal me.

My eyes started to drift closed but someone was shaking me.

Why is Aaron prolonging this? Can't he get it over with already?

But when I opened my eyes, it was Trace's worried green ones staring down at me. "Olivia?" He sounded like he was talking to me through a tunnel. "Can you hear me, baby? Olivia, please, focus on me. Just look at me, baby. Can you do that?"

I tried so hard to keep my eyes focused on him but they kept drifting to the side and closed.

"Olivia, keep your eyes open. I know you want to go to sleep, but you can't. Just listen to my voice, okay?" He tried to sound calm but I knew he wasn't. "Paramedics are on their way. Hang on, baby. Don't leave me, please don't leave me." Tears fell from his chin onto my face. "I can't lose you. Stay with me, Olivia."

"S-s-s-o t-t-t-i-i-r-r-r-e-e-d," I stuttered.

"I know, baby. I know you're tired but you can't go to sleep. You have to stay awake. I'm so sorry, Olivia," he sobbed. "I couldn't protect you. I'm sorry. Please, baby, stay with me," he pleaded desperately. "I can't lose another person I love. Don't do that to me. We stick together, Olivia. You and me, baby, till the end of time." His hands fluttered above my body, seeking a place to hold me, but my whole body was battered. Taking the end of my chin, gently between his thumb and index finger, he stared down at me fiercely. "You're going to be okay, Olivia, but I want you to know I love you. I love you more than anything in this world. I'm sorry I didn't tell you sooner. I wanted to tell you so many times but the time was never right." He swallowed thickly. "I wanted it to be perfect when I told you, because even though perfection doesn't exist, I'm never going to stop searching for it when it comes to you." He gently brushed my hair away from my forehead. "Please, forgive me baby. Please," he begged, crying hard now. I had never seen a man cry like this before. Like his whole world was crumbling beneath him.

"I-I—" I tried to speak but everything was fading around me. I was sinking into a deep well of water and I couldn't see the surface.

"I know you do," he silenced me. "Don't talk. Conserve your energy. I'm going to try to stop the bleeding from your head," he ripped his wife-beater off his body and lifted me slightly so that he could press the fabric to my scalp.

I whimpered in pain.

Trace continued to speak but I only heard faint rumblings as everything faded around me.

My eyes fluttered closed. I couldn't keep them open any longer.

Blackness cloaked me and peace settled in my soul as all my pain faded away.

CHAPTER THIRTY-FOUR

I WAS FLOATING, BUT I WAS SUSPENDED AT THE SAME time, like a balloon whose string was held by a small child. I was trying to escape the grasp that was holding me, but it was too strong.

Someone was speaking, no, pleading, with me.

I tried to make out their words, but it was like I was underwater, while they were above.

There were so many noises, but I blocked them out, focusing on what the voice was saying. I knew it was important, and that I needed to hear what they had to say, before I floated away forever.

I finally managed to distinguish what the voice was saying, more like screaming, at me.

"Olivia. *No*. Breathe, baby. *Breathe*. Come on. You can't leave me. Let me go!" The last part was addressed to someone else. "Listen to me, Olivia, you can't leave me like this. I love you. Do you hear me? *I love you*. We have our whole lives ahead of us, Olivia. Please, don't leave me," the voice pleaded desperately.

"We're going to get married one day and have lots of pretty babies that will look just like you, Olivia! You're going to write that book. But most importantly, you're going to *live*, Olivia."

"We have a heartbeat," another voice said, just as the blackness swallowed me once more.

"WAKE UP, PLEASE, WAKE UP," a voice begged.

I swam for the surface, my arm outstretched, trying to reach it.

"Wake up, Olivia," it pleaded, "open those pretty brown eyes."

I kicked my arms and my legs, my lungs about to burst with the need to inhale oxygen, but I was still too deep in the water.

I kicked faster.

"Come on, Olivia. Open your eyes. You can do it."

My eyes came open and air rushed out of my lungs in a mighty exhale.

The pain was excruciating, and if I had the energy, I'd yell at the person who had woken me from my peaceful depths where there was no pain.

"Oh, God, Olivia," the voice cried and gently took one of my hands in their own.

I slowly turned my head and found Trace bowed over my bed, sobbing.

"I thought I had lost you," he cried. "I've never been so scared in all my life."

I wanted to comfort him, somehow, but I couldn't get my body to work. Tubes and wires seemed to run from every part of my body into various machines.

I tried to say his name but no sounds came out of my mouth. Finally, he looked up at me with red-rimmed eyes. "You've been asleep for a week, Olivia. I thought you were never going to wake up," his voice cracked. "They told me to keep talking to you, so I did. I've talked about anything and everything, trying to get you to wake up." He took a deep shaky breath. "I thought I was never going to see those pretty brown eyes ever again." He gently brushed my hair away from my eyes, carful of my injuries. "I watched you *die*, Olivia. I watched your heart stop beating." He swallowed thickly and I knew this was hard for him. But there was nothing I could do but listen. "I vowed, after watching my dad die, that I would never witness anyone I loved dying, ever again." His voice was fierce and carefully contained tears shimmered in his green eyes. "I felt so helpless, Olivia. I couldn't do anything but watch you drift away from me. When I thought you died," he choked, "I wanted nothing more than to die too. I know that sounds dramatic, but when you find the person that completes you in every way, when something happens to them ... it happens to you too. I can't live without you, Olivia." He placed his hand gently in my open, bandaged, palm.

I squeezed my hand around his slightly, offering him as much comfort as I could muster at the moment.

"I-I-I'm s-s-sorry," the words were forced between my lips and the effort of forming them left my throat dry.

"God, baby." He kissed my fingers. "Don't apologize. You did nothing wrong."

A single tear leaked from my left eye and skated down my cheek. Trace gently swiped it away.

"Please, don't cry. I didn't mean to make you cry. I was upset. I thought I lost you." His eyes were full of remorse.

"E-e-every-t-t-thing hurts," I confessed.

"I know." He hung his head. "I didn't get there in time. The back of your skull was fractured and you have three broken ribs, one of which punctured your lung." He looked at me sadly, a frown marring his face. "Not to mention the beating your whole body took." He looked me over and I knew he was wishing he could take away my pain.

"I m-m-must l-l-look a-a-awful," I said tiredly. The effort of speaking was beginning to take its toll.

"You're always beautiful, Olivia. Even battered and broken, you're the most beautiful creature I've ever set my eyes on. And most importantly, you're alive." He licked his dry lips.

He looked so tired and thin. This past week had obviously drained him. His hair was a mess and his red-rimmed eyes had gray circles from lack of sleep, beneath them. His clothes were rumpled and I was sure he'd been wearing them for days, heck, maybe even the whole week.

The door to my hospital room opened and the nurse jumped in surprise when my eyes met hers.

"You're awake!" she exclaimed, striding over to me, and quickly checking the machines I was hooked up to. "*You*" —she glared icily at Trace— "were supposed to let me know if she woke up."

"I'm sorry," he apologized to the nurse but the quirk of his lips told me he didn't mean it. "I got distracted." He rubbed his thumb softly against the spot where my thumb and index finger connected.

"Mhmm, I'm sure you did," she hummed. Looking at me, her face softened. "You're a lucky girl, Olivia. You nearly lost your life. It's nice to see you awake, and maybe this one will eat something now." She pointed to Trace. "He hasn't left your side since you came out of surgery."

"S-s-surgery?" I croaked.

Changing my IV, she explained, "You had to have surgery to repair your lung." I watched as she shot medicine into the IV tube. "Sweetie, you're going to start to feel very sleepy. Just let your body relax. We need to keep you sedated for as long as possible to speed up the healing process."

I nodded, already feeling drowsy as the medicine hit my veins.

I glanced over at Trace, and stuttered, "I l-l-love y-y-ou."

A calm stole through my body as I finally confessed my feelings to him. He smiled, bringing my hand to his lips, where he pressed a small kiss. "I love you too, Olivia. Sweet dreams. I'll be right here when you wake up."

My lips couldn't help but turn up in a smile at his words.

"Hey, sleepyhead," Trace crooned when I opened my eyes.

"Hi." My voice was stronger and steadier this time, but dry and crackly like sandpaper. "Was I asleep for long?"

He nodded sadly. "Two days."

How was it possible to sleep for that long and not be aware of it?

"Your mom's here," he nodded his head toward the door. I could see the nurses' station through a rectangular pane of glass. "She went to get a bite to eat in the cafeteria so she'll be back soon. Avery and Luca have been by too. Even Marcy and Alba came to see you."

"Like this?" I asked incredulously. "I look horrible."

I hated the thought of anyone seeing me, beaten and bruised like this, and smelling like old meat ... because I was pretty sure that nasty smell was me. Then again, it could be Trace, because he was *still* in the same clothes he was wearing two days ago.

Trace's laughter shook his body, and although I was serious, it was nice to see him laugh.

"Yeah, *like that*, silly girl." He shook his head.

"I hope they all still want to be my friends after this," I grumbled.

"You don't look that bad, Olivia." Trace rolled his eyes at me.

"I know I won't be going near any mirrors for a *long* time," I snapped. "I probably look like my skin has been tie dyed with all these bruises."

Trace opened his mouth to say something but the door to my hospital room swung open and stopped him.

"Olivia!" my mom cried upon seeing me awake, dropping her coffee on the floor, in her haste to reach me. The brown liquid seeped across the white tile floor; reminding me of the pool of blood I had seen in Trace's apartment.

I closed my eyes in remembrance, trying to block out thoughts of that day. I didn't want to relive it. I wanted to put it behind me, but I knew that would be impossible.

When I opened my eyes again, my mom was peering down at me, with tears streaming down her face. She was desperately seeking a place to touch me but my whole body was battered. Finally, she hooked her index finger with mine and sighed in relief.

"You have no idea how worried I've been, Liv. I thought I was going to lose my baby girl." She bit her lip. With her free hand, she clutched at her chest. Trace stood and grabbed a tissue. She took it from him and wiped her face free of tears. "Thank God you're going to be okay. I would've never forgiven myself. I didn't think the divorce papers would have that much effect on him, since so much time had passed. I'm still in disbelief that he showed up here, and went after you, Liv. This whole thing doesn't seem real," she sobbed and Trace reached for more tissues.

"Mom, please don't cry," I begged. "This isn't your fault. Aaron's a nutcase."

"Only you, Liv, would be bruised and battered in a hospital bed, and comforting *me*." She wiped her nose.

"Seriously, Mom." I curled my finger tighter around hers. "This is *not* your fault. This is no one's fault but Aaron's. What—uh—what happened with him?" I asked reluctantly. I really didn't want to keep talking about Aaron. Just thinking his name was causing flashbacks of my beating to come back to me. Did it make me weak, since I didn't want to remember?

Trace cleared his throat. "I knocked him unconscious, but since he wasn't seriously harmed, he's in the local jail right now. Thank God he doesn't have anybody willing to bail his sorry ass out of jail, because if he was free and walking around, I would go after that fucker and ..." he paused. "You don't want to know what I would do to the bastard that hurt you. And—uh—sorry for the cussing," he muttered the last part at my mom.

"What's going to happen to him?" I asked. I needed to know if the man who had tried to kill me was going to walk free.

"He's going to go to jail for the rest of his life," Trace promised me. "My family and I are doing everything we can to make sure there's no chance of him walking free. You have nothing to worry about, Olivia. He won't hurt you ever again."

"Will there be a trial? Will I have to testify?" I questioned, swallowing thickly. The thought of getting up in front of a jury and describing what Aaron did to me—God, I couldn't even think about it.

"We're trying to avoid that," he explained. "Everything is pretty cut and dry. The evidence of what went down was obvious."

Relief flooded my body and surged through my veins. I took a deep breath, which hurt my chest, and let it out.

"That's good," I breathed. "How long am I going to be in here?" I asked. Now that I knew what was going to happen to Aaron, there was no point in talking about him ... ever again.

"There's no way to tell," my mom said, pulling up a chair beside my bed, so that her and Trace were on each side of me. "It all depends on how well you do. A physical therapist has been coming in every day, to work with moving your legs and arms so that it will be easier for you to walk."

"I don't like that guy," Trace seethed.

"The physical therapist?" I croaked.

Trace nodded. "His smile is creepy."

I started to laugh, which turned to a cough, and I ended up

clutching my ribs in pain. "Ow," I cried, fighting tears. My chest felt like a bull had stepped on it.

"Don't laugh, baby, it'll hurt your ribs."

"You think?" I glared at him.

"Sorry," he mumbled and sat back in the chair.

"I'm sorry for snapping at you, but it really hurts," I whined, "and I'm thirsty."

"I'll get you some water." He hopped up from the chair and ran for the door. I think he was relieved to be able to do something to help me.

My mom was still sniffling, and I really wished she'd stop, because it made me feel bad. I didn't like seeing her or *anyone,* this upset over me. I didn't want anyone to suffer, because I was suffering. That didn't seem right. The sadness that lingered in her eyes, as they fluttered over my body, upset me. Trace had that same look in his eyes when he looked at me. It was a look that said they wished they could heal me by glance alone.

The door opened and Trace stepped inside with a Styrofoam cup of water with a straw. Since I was so weak, he held the cup for me while I wrapped my lips around the straw, sucking slowly. My throat was still raw from the screaming I did … and for all I knew, I might have had a breathing tube, at one point.

When I nodded that I was finished, Trace placed the cup on the tray over my bed.

"I talked to a nurse. They'll be in to check on you and take your temperature. They're concerned about you getting a fever," he explained, with his arms crossed over his lean chest.

"Why would they be worried about a fever?" I questioned.

Trace swallowed. "Your body has sustained a lot of damage and your system is weak. You're going to be more susceptible to getting ill and if you get a fever … it could escalate fast." The worry on his face tore me apart.

"I feel fine," I assured him, desperate to make the line between his brows disappear. I wiggled my fingers and he placed his hand lightly in mine.

Looking over his gaunt appearance, I reluctantly muttered, "You should go home and eat, Trace. Take a shower and get some sleep. You look exhausted."

"I'm not leaving." He shook his head vehemently.

"What about Ace?" I hoped the mention of the puppy would spurn him into action.

"Trent's staying at the apartment with Ace, so he's fine," Trace assured me.

"Still, you should get some rest. I feel guilty."

He placed a tender kiss on the tip of my nose. "Don't pull the guilt card, Olivia. I'm not going anywhere."

I swallowed thickly. How did I get so lucky with Trace?

Continuing, he added, "I'm *not* leaving this hospital until you do."

"What about work?" I inquired.

"Pete knows what happened, hell, all the guys do. My apartment was a crime scene for a few days until the police got everything they needed. So, he understands why I need to be here," Trace explained, running his fingers through his hair.

"Okay," I finally agreed, "but can you at least shower?"

His chuckle rumbled through his chest. "Are you saying I stink?"

"I'm saying I'm pretty sure that smell isn't me." I sniffed my arm for emphasis. I smelled like plain hospital soap, slightly citrusy.

"Fine, but *only* because there's a bathroom with a shower attached to your room." His eyes twinkled with laughter.

"Call Trent and tell him to bring you clothes," I added.

"Is there anything else I should ask Trent to bring?" Trace shook his head at me.

"Um ..." I smiled. "Think he can sneak in Ace?"

I wanted to see my sweet Lab and give him kisses. I hated that Trace and I had been away from him this long.

"I'm sure if I asked him, he'd try," Trace chortled. "But they don't allow dogs in the hospital."

"They should," I pouted. "Ace wouldn't hurt anybody. He would lay right here, beside me" —I pointed to the empty spot in the hospital bed that was big enough for the puppy— "and wouldn't bother anyone." I smiled at Trace.

"I know he would, but I don't want them to kick me out for letting my little brother bring a dog into a sterile hospital."

"Fine," I grumbled. "I'll just suffer."

"I'm so happy you're feeling well enough to argue with me," he snorted.

"Someone's awake and talkative." The same nurse from the other day breezed into my room. Her short auburn hair was straight and her pink scrubs were the only sign of color in the plain white room, aside from the clothes Trace and my mom were wearing.

She looked over my vital signs. "Everything seems to be looking good, sweetie. I'm going to take your temperature." She promptly stuck a thermometer under my tongue. Ten seconds or so later, it beeped, and she checked it. "Temp is normal, so that's excellent news. I'm going to check your blood pressure now," she explained.

My mom scooted out of the way, and let go of my finger, so I could lift my arm for the nurse.

The cuff tightened against my arm and I winced as it dug into my tender skin.

"I'm sorry," the nurse apologized as she removed the cuff. "Your blood pressure is excellent though. The doctor will be making his rounds in the next thirty minutes." She smiled at each of us and ducked out of the room. The heavy door clicked closed behind her.

I relaxed against the fluffy pillows, fighting against the exhaustion that was threatening to pull me under. I didn't know how it was possible for a person that had slept for two days straight, and a week before that, to still be sleepy. But I was.

Trace noticed my eyelids fluttering open and closed. "Olivia, if you need to sleep, go to sleep. Your body needs the rest."

"No." I shook my head slightly. "I need to stay awake. I've been sleeping so much—"

"Don't fight what your body needs." His green eyes were fierce.

My stubborn side kicked in and I looked away from him.

"Olivia," he groaned warningly.

"I want some more water," I requested, to sidetrack him.

He sighed and held the Styrofoam cup to my lips. "Don't think I don't know what you're doing."

I finished the water and fanned my eyes at him. "More please."

"I'll be back." He sighed.

My mom slid her chair closer to the bed and hooked our fingers back together. "I'll stay until the doctor checks on you and then I really have to go." Apology was clear in her brown eyes.

"It's okay, Mom," I assured her. "I know you can't stay here with me. Heck, I don't expect Trace to stay with me, but he's so stubborn."

"He loves you." She smiled. "And he wants and *can* be with you. I don't have that luxury. I have to be at work early in the morning. I work on the lower level of the hospital but I'll try to stop by if I get the chance. If I don't, I'll come by after my shift ends."

"You don't need to do that, Mom." My eyes started to close again but I forced them open.

"I'll find a way to see you tomorrow," she promised.

"Okay." I swallowed, because, selfishly, I wanted to see her. I was hurt, and I wanted my mom to comfort me, like a small child sick with the flu.

Trace came back with my water and a doctor followed behind him.

"I'm Dr. Richards," the gray-haired man said, grabbing a clipboard attached to the end of my bed, and looking over it thoroughly. "I've been following your progress closely and you're doing extremely well. You sustained quite a beating." He looked at me with kind blue eyes. "You're lucky to be alive, Olivia. Count your blessings." He skimmed over my chart again and placed it back in its slot at the end of the bed. He looked me over and said, "I want to keep you, for at least four more days, to make sure you're breathing okay and everything's fine with your lung and ribs. If that checks out, you'll be free to go home."

"That sounds great," I breathed.

"I want you to try walking, today. I can see that you're tired, but before you go to sleep, I'd like for your mom or husband to walk the halls with you." He smiled kindly.

"Sure," I agreed. "Wait, wha—"

Trace silenced me with a hard glare.

What's going on? Did we get married while I was sleeping or something?

"Walking's fine." I tried to cover myself.

"I'll check in on you tonight." He smiled and strode from the room.

"Husband?" I snapped, eyeing Trace.

He grinned sheepishly. "If I said I was your boyfriend they wouldn't let me stay around the clock. So, be a good girl, and pretend to be Mrs. Wentworth." His smile turned cheeky.

"You're ridiculous." I shook my head.

My mom stood and moved the chair back to its original spot. "I have to go. I love you, Liv." She kissed an uninjured spot on my forehead. "I'll see you tomorrow."

"Love you too, Mom," I smiled.

Trace waved goodbye to my mom. "I'm going to go get a nurse to unplug you from all of this junk" —he pointed at the various monitors I was hooked up to— "so you can get some walking done."

"Okay, I'll—uh—be here," I joked.

He shook his head at me and left.

I forced my arm to move, reaching for the cup of water. Being helpless, was getting old really fast.

I managed to get my hand to grip the cup and slowly brought it to my lips. My body was so sore and weak that I knew walking was going to suck the last of my energy right out of my body.

"I hear you want to walk." The nurse smiled, breezing into the room. The scent of her floral perfume permeated the air around her.

"More like, I'm being forced," I pouted.

"Walking will be good for you. Just do ten minutes and come back. You don't have to walk for long. If you're tired after five minutes, that's fine too. Don't overexert yourself, but you do need to move some."

Great, no one is on my side.

In no time at all, she had me unhooked from most of the machines except for the IV and oxygen tank that had those weird pointy things stuck in my nose, because both of those wheeled along beside me.

"I can take it from here," Trace assured the nurse as he draped a blanket over my shoulders.

I leaned heavily against him as we strode down the carpeted hall. The oxygen tank's wheels kept making this annoying shrieking sound.

"Can we go look at the babies?" I asked. "At least, I'll get to look at something cute."

Trace feigned that I had hurt his feelings by frowning and

placing a hand over his heart. "And I'm not cute to look at?" he questioned.

"I look at you all the time. I'm sick of your face," I snorted, shuffling along like a ninety-year-old lady.

"That's a new one." He chuckled. "Most people never get sick of this face." He rubbed a hand over his chin. For the first time, I noticed that he hadn't shaved in quite a while, and almost had a light beard.

"You really need to clean yourself up," I joked. "You're looking like a—"

"Don't even finish that sentence." He narrowed his eyes playfully. "I always look fabulous, even when my girlfriend has nearly worried me to death."

"Oh, that's right. I forgot. How silly of me." I shook my head as a cough raked my body.

Trace stopped and looked me over. "Are you okay? Do we need to go back? Can you breathe?" The questions tumbled from his lips without a breath in-between.

"It's just a cough, Trace. Calm down." I proceeded to shuffle forward on the carpeted floor.

"Sorry." He smiled bashfully. "It's been a rough ten days." He bit his lip. "I'm still a little jumpy."

"I feel ... not fine ... but not like I'm on my deathbed. Chill, okay?" I pleaded.

"I'll try to tone down my concern a notch." He cleared his throat.

"Or three." I eyed him.

He shook his head at me. "No promises on that one. Let's get this over so I can get you back in bed where you're safe."

"What are you going to do when I go home? Bubble wrap me to the bed?" I scuffed along in the hospital issued socks.

His lips quirked up in a small smile. "That sounds like a good idea."

"You're ridiculous," I muttered scathingly.

"No, Olivia. I'm concerned. I *never* want to have to watch you almost die, again," he spoke seriously.

"I'm sorry," I apologized. "I know you're worried about me, and here I am, acting like a bitch." I frowned.

"You're sore and tired, it's expected for you to be a little snappy." He chuckled. "I'd be more worried if you were acting like nothing was wrong." He read a sign and pointed to our left. "Babies this way."

We, or *I*, shuffled forward the last few feet and stopped in front of the glass window separating us from the newborn babies.

They were so small and helpless. Most of them were sleeping but one was crying, her small arms forcing their way out of the blanket, swaddling her small form. Another, a boy based on his blue knit hat, eyed Trace and me with wide blue eyes. His small pink lips formed an O as he looked at us. Dark hair peeked out from the edge of his hat. He was so adorable with his plump cheeks.

"I think he likes us." Trace pointed at the baby.

"What's not to like." I poked Trace's side lightly. "We're *ah-mazing*."

"Ah, how could I forget." He winked at me. Growing serious, he gazed down at me, with dark green eyes. "One day, I'm going to put babies in your tummy and watch my love grow inside you."

I laughed. "You're full of it."

"I'm serious, woman," he scoffed.

"I know you are." I wet my parched lips with my tongue. I really needed some more water. With one last glance at the sweet babies, I turned around. "I'm going back to my room. I'm tired."

Trace helped me back to the room and into bed. I finished the cup of water and asked for more before I finally let myself fall asleep.

"You're doing extremely well, Olivia." Dr. Richards smiled kindly at me. "We're going to re-tape your ribs and you'll be free to go. I want you to follow up with your regular doctor next week, to check on your ribs. Melissa will get your prescriptions ready, then you can get out of here."

"Great." I grinned. I couldn't wait to get out of this bed and back home. I'd had enough of hospitals to last me a lifetime.

The whole process of signing release forms, and getting everything together, took at least an hour. I had to change, with Trace's help, into my own clothes, and then be wheeled down to the lobby. The nurse waited with me while Trace brought his car around.

With the nurse and Trace's help, I hobbled into the car. The rest of my body was healing well, but my chest still felt like an elephant had sat on me.

"Don't be mad." Trace winced as we pulled away from the hospital.

"Nothing good ever comes after those words," I grumbled, slipping my sunglasses on. "Just tell me what it is and don't sugar coat it."

"Avery and Luca are meeting us at the apartment. I've managed to keep her away the last few days, but she wants to see you. She's your best friend, Olivia. She's been really worried about you and she hasn't seen you since you woke up."

"Ugh," I groaned. "I don't want her to see me like this." I ran my fingers through my hair, trying to make it look semi presentable. "Besides, I'm tired and cranky. I want to go to bed."

"I know." He took my hand tenderly in his. "But she needs to see you, to know you're okay."

"I've talked to her on the phone!" I cried.

"Yes, you have. But that's not the same as seeing a person in the flesh," he reasoned.

I sighed. "I want to see her but—"

"I get it, Olivia. I do," he interrupted. "You've been through a lot and you're not up to seeing people. I tried to talk her out of coming over but ... you know Avery."

"I do and that girl is not easily deterred," I shook my head.

When we pulled into the garage's parking lot, Avery and Luca were there in her red beetle, and there was another car, a black Dodge Challenger, which I assumed was Trent's.

Avery slipped out of her car, as Trace parked and I took a deep breath, silently pep talking myself.

"Stay put," Trace warned. "I'll tell them to head on up and then I'll help you out."

I nodded in agreement, because I knew there was no way I'd be able to make it up those steps by myself.

I watched Trace greet Avery and Luca and point at the door to his apartment. Avery shook her head adamantly and pointed at me. Trace waved his hands forcefully and I saw his jaw working as he spoke rapidly. Finally, Luca took Avery by the hand and towed her up to the apartment. They knocked on the door, and I watched Trent open it, Ace ran through his feet and sniffed at Luca and Avery.

Trace opened the car door and unbuckled my seatbelt. He lightly wrapped his arm around my body and helped me from the car. He kept a steady hand on my waist as I shuffled toward the steps. I bit my lip at all the stairs I was going to have to climb and dreading the pain I knew they were going to cause me. I hated being so helpless.

Noticing my look of distress, Trace smiled. "Just try, Olivia. If you get tired after one or two, I'll carry you."

I took a deep breath and fought back tears. "I can do this," I whispered, for my benefit, not his.

"I know you can." He helped me slowly make my way up. By the time we reached the door I was exhausted and leaning my body heavily against his. My body had taken quite a beating, and I still wasn't completely healed everywhere, meaning the simplest tasks exhausted me.

"I want to go to bed," I begged as he opened the door and Avery rushed toward me.

"Back off," Trace warned her with a steely gaze in his eyes. I had never heard him use that tone of voice with anyone before.

Avery immediately took a step back, and kept her mouth shut, which surprised me. Avery wasn't the kind of person who was too keen on being bossed around.

"She's tired, and I told you she wouldn't be up for company, but you insisted on being here. I know you're her best friend and you're worried. But please, let me get her in pajamas, and in bed. *Then*, if she's feeling up to it, you can see her," Trace explained.

Avery muttered, "Okay." Looking over me, she added, "I've been so worried about you, Olivia."

"I know," I whispered since I didn't have the energy to speak any louder.

Trace helped me into the bedroom and closed the door. I shuffled over to the dresser and pulled out short pajama bottoms and a long sleeve shirt of Trace's that would hide my fading bruises. *I didn't like to see my bruises, and being reminded of what happened, so I knew no one else did, either. It was hard enough, knowing something bad has happened to someone, but seeing the evidence all over their bodies tears you up inside.*

"I can do it myself!" I yelled at Trace when he tried to help me out of my clothes.

He flinched like I had slapped him. "Are you sure?"

"No!" I croaked and collapsed onto the bed, sobbing. "I *hate* this, Trace. I feel so helpless. I can't walk up stairs or change my own clothes! It isn't fair! Why did this happen to me?" I buried my tear-streaked face in my hands.

I heard Trace kneel in front of me and then he was prying my hands away so he could see my face.

"I don't know why this happened to you, baby, and I know it isn't fair. But you're *alive* and that's something to be grateful for." His eyes bore into me, straight to my very soul. "I watched you *die*, Olivia, and that's something I'm never going to forget." He swallowed thickly. "But you came back to me, because you're a fighter, and you'll fight through this and you'll get through the pain. In no time, all of this will be nothing but a distant nightmare." His eyes were clouded with tears and his voice was thick with emotion. "It's okay to question why this happened to you, Olivia. That's normal. But don't let it eat you up inside. You have to move on and put it behind you, so you can live your life to the fullest, because that's all anyone can ever do."

I took a shaky breath and hiccupped. "How do you always know exactly the right thing to say to me?"

He chuckled but it was weak. "It's a talent. Now please, let me help you. There's nothing wrong with letting me help you."

Slowly, I lifted my arms above my head and he removed my shirt, careful to keep space between his hands and my healing ribs. He lifted the shirt I had grabbed, over my head, and it fell to my thighs. He removed the sweat pants I was wearing and replaced them with my blue flower pajama shorts. He helped me up and then pulled the covers back. I lay down in the bed and he pulled the blankets up to my chin.

"Do you want me to send Avery away? Or do you want to see her?" he asked.

"I want to see her, but tell her I'm really tired," I pleaded, gazing up at him. I hoped the concern in his eyes would fade soon. I didn't like it.

"I'll tell her." He bent, kissing my nose, and strode out of the room.

He'd barely walked out when Avery came barging in. She sunk to the floor beside the bed.

"Oh, Olivia," she cried. "It's so good to see you awake. I came to see you at the hospital but you were sleeping and then once you woke up, Trace wouldn't let me come in and—"

I didn't want her blaming Trace, for not being allowed to see me, so I quickly interrupted, "He kept you away because I didn't want to see you."

"But ... why?" She was confused.

I reached for hand. "You're my best friend, Avery. I didn't want you to see me like that. So hurt and tired. I was a mess. I slept most of the time anyway, and my medicine made me a little loopy." I added a smile to hopefully relieve some of the tension from her body.

"Olivia, none of that matters. I'm your best friend and I wanted to be there for you." She squeezed my hand.

"I know," I whispered, my eyes growing heavy. I fought against the sleepiness that was clawing through me. "But after everything that happened ... I needed some space."

"Well, you're home now and I'm not letting you withdraw from me ... or anyone. What happened to you was *horrible*, Olivia. But *please*, don't let it change you."

"How can it not change me?" I questioned. "I was almost murdered, Avery, by a man that for twenty years of my life, I believed was my father."

She climbed into the bed beside me. "I know you're going to be ... affected by this," she paused, running her fingers lightly through my hair to relax me. "But I don't want to see it make you a different person. This wasn't your fault, Olivia."

"It was," I sobbed. "And if he had found my mom first, he would've killed her, and I would've had to live with the fact that I got my mom killed, for the rest of my life. I thought I was doing the right thing, getting her away from him."

"You did the right thing," Avery held me as I cried. "I know it may not seem like it right now, but you did. You saved her, Olivia, and Trace saved you. Not everyone gets a second chance at life, but you've been given one. So, live it."

EPILOGUE

A FEW MONTHS LATER...

MOVING ON, after going through something like I did is difficult, to say the least. There were many days that I didn't want to get out of bed and face the world, but I knew I had to, and Trace helped to push me. He didn't let me dwell on what happened. He helped me move on. I didn't know what I would do without him.

Before I knew it, summer was over, and I was starting my junior year of college. It didn't seem possible that so much had happened to me in such a short period of time.

But it did.
I lived.
I died.
I came back.
I moved on.

I wasn't letting my past define me. Instead, I was choosing to embrace my future, and whatever it had in store for me.

"What are you thinking about?" Trace asked as the air rushed through the open windows of the Camaro.

"Just thinking," I murmured, staring out at the orange, yellow, red, and brown leaves. Fall was in full swing.

"About what?" he asked again.

I sighed dramatically at his stubbornness. "Life."

"That's vague," he muttered.

"It was supposed to be." I giggled. "You still haven't told me where we're going."

"And I don't plan on telling you." He smirked. "Be patient. Good things come to those who wait."

"Sometimes, I wonder why I love you so much." I shook my head, my long wavy hair falling forward.

"It's because I'm a beast in the sack." He glanced at me, waggling his eyebrows, before returning his attention to the road.

"You're so full of yourself." I snorted.

"When you've got it, *you've got it*." He enforced his words with a thrust of his hips. "Ah, here we are." He pulled off onto the side of the road.

I looked around, my brow furrowing in confusion. "Where are we?"

Trace grinned crookedly at me. "Look around, Olivia."

I did and a smile spread across my face.

"It's where we first met." He took my hand and placed a tender kiss on my knuckles. "A year ago today, I pulled over to help this beautiful girl change her tire. She made me laugh with her incessant use of the word, uh, and her mention of Prince Charming." He winked. "She woke up something inside me and I knew I had to get to know this girl. You changed my life, from the moment I met you, Olivia." He feathered the lightest touch of his fingers over my cheek. "Your smile stirred something inside me that I had never felt before." His eyes were a fierce dark green. He pulled his bottom lip between his teeth. "This last year has been a rollercoaster. But I wouldn't change a thing. Every moment with you, is a moment I treasure."

My heart skipped a beat at his sweet words and tears of happiness pricked my eyes. That stupid flat tire, that I had been so mad about, had changed my life. One moment, that's all it took, for my life to change completely, and veer onto a different path.

I was reminded of one of my favorite quotes: "Life is not measured by the amount of breaths you take, but by the moments that take your breath away." From the moment I met Trace, he'd been taking my breath away, and showing me what life was really about.

"Come on." He grinned and opened his car door. I did the same.

We climbed onto the hood of his car and watched the sunset. The color of the sun reflecting off the leaves made them seem as if they were on fire.

"I think there's one last thing to cross off," he beamed, pulling the folded piece of paper from his pants pocket.

He kissed my cheek before placing the paper in my hand. He grabbed a pen and handed that to me as well.

He skimmed his nose along my cheek, and pushed my hair back, so he could whisper in my ear, "I love you, Olivia."

I smiled at him and leaned my head against his shoulder. "I love you, too."

The metal hood of the car wasn't the most comfortable place, but I didn't mind. I was here, with my love, and nothing else mattered.

I looked down at the list in my hand, reading through all the things that just a year ago, had merely been dreams of mine, and now I had accomplished all of them.

Everything was crossed off except for the very last thing.

With a smile aimed at Trace, I drew a line through the last item on the list, the most important one.

~~Get drunk~~
~~Fly in a hot air balloon~~
~~Go to the carnival~~
~~Go to a concert (even if it's someone I've never heard of)~~
~~Go to a party~~
~~Lose my virginity~~
~~Dance in the rain~~
~~Go roller skating~~
~~See the ocean~~
~~Learn to paint~~
~~Get a dog... or a cat... or a rabbit. Any pet will do.~~
~~Sing in front of real people. Avery doesn't count.~~
~~Make more friends~~
~~Shoot a gun~~
~~Smoke~~
~~Get a tattoo~~
~~Learn to pole dance~~
~~Go skinny dipping~~
~~Pierce my belly button~~
~~Fall in love~~

I never meant to fall in love with Trace, but I did, and by some miracle, he fell in love with me too. We had some crazy adventures along the way, and I wouldn't change any of it for the world, because all of those crazy things defined us. All the laughs, all the tears, all the kisses—it was all us, and it would always be that way, because I had found someone worth loving through the good and the bad.

I handed the piece of crinkled up paper to Trace and he smiled as he read it over.

"Well, what are we going to do now?" he asked with his signature cocky grin that I had learned to love. He threw his arm around my shoulders and pulled me fully against him. Both our legs were stretched out, my left flush against his right.

His lips pressed tenderly against the top of my head.

I stared out at the setting sun, squinting against the brightness, as it disappeared over the line of trees.

"I'm sure we'll think of something."

ACKNOWLEDGMENTS

Writing and finishing a book is always a labor of love. It can be very difficult and very emotional at times. For me, this book has affected me more than any other I have ever written. Trace and Olivia hold a special place in my heart...all my characters do, but there's something about these two that's even more special.

Every time I write my acknowledgements, I'm always afraid I'm leaving someone out (and I probably am) but hopefully I remember everybody.

Thank you to my grandma, for being supportive of my crazy ideas from the beginning, and being my biggest support system and best friend.

Thank you to my dad, for planting the seed of self-publishing. Without you, I wouldn't be where I'm at, and this has been the greatest journey of my life.

Thank you to my mom, for being so supportive of my dream.

A big HUGE gigantic, thank you, to my bestie for life, Shelby. I seriously don't know what I would do without you. Thank you for reading and replying to my long-winded ranting emails, reading Finding Olivia early and giving me advice, and for being so supportive. There are a thousand and one other things I should thank you for, but my brain is dead, so I can't remember.

I also want to thank Emily, my "personal cheerleader" "tyrant" and whatever other nicknames you have now. I love talking with you and you always motivate me. I know we've never met in person but you've become a really good friend and one day we will meet in person, I promise!

Thank you, Regina Wamba, for creating another FABULOUS cover, and for doing the photo-shoot! Thank you for bringing my characters to life. I wish I could give you a hug, for all your hard work, you're amazing.

Thank you to the cover models for bringing Trace and Olivia to life for me! Y'all are awesome and rocked the photo-shoot!

I have to thank Mari Arden, for being my author support system. You're always so encouraging and I love talking with you.

A big thank you to Stephanie, for reading and reviewing Finding Olivia, plus putting together the blog tour. YOU are a rock star.

Thank you to, Michelle, Bianca, and Three Chicks and their Books, for reading advanced copies of Finding Olivia. Seriously, I can't thank you enough for taking the time to read my book; it means the word to me. And thank you to all the bloggers who participated in the Finding Olivia blog tour.

Last, but certainly not least, I want to thank my fans. Y'all are AH-FREAKIN-MAZING! I swear, when I started this crazy journey in November 2011, I never expected one fan, let alone all that I have now. Without y'all I couldn't do this as a job full-time. You've made my dreams come true. I wish I could hug and thank each of you individually, but since I can't, I'm writing this.

Honestly, though, I don't say it enough, but I love you guys. It warms my heart when I get an email, message, or even a short comment from one of you telling me how much you enjoyed my book(s). It means the world to me.

www.ingramcontent.com/pod-product-compliance
Lightning Source LLC
LaVergne TN
LVHW031608060526
838201LV00065B/4773